places
to look
for a
mother

places
to look
for a
mother

nicole stansbury

CARROLL & GRAF PUBLISHERS
NEW YORK

for my parents

James Hilman Stansbury and Sabrina

and for Damien Echols, on death row

PLACES TO LOOK FOR A MOTHER

Carroll & Graf Publishers
A Division of Avalon Publishing Group Incorporated
161 William St., 16th Floor
New York, NY 10038

First Carroll & Graf cloth edition 2002
First Carroll & Graf trade paperback edition 2003
Book design: Paul Paddock

Library of Congress Cataloging-in-Publication Data is available.

ISBN: 0-7867-1177-9

Printed in the United States of America
Distributed by Publishers Group West

Acknowledgments

I'd like to thank my much-adored agent and friend, Ren Soeiro of the Peter Lampack Agency. Ren, you're amazing. Thank you!

Kudos, too, to my most excellent editor, Tina Pohlman, whose enthusiasm and wisdom and painstaking readings helped shape this book.

To the Utah Arts Council, for their generous support.

Thank you, thank you, to Grant Sperry, most hilarious and good person, as well as my very finest reader; Dawn Houghton, who endured endless revisions; and my sisters, Janine, Annie, Mia, and Wendy. Finally, I want to thank Roni Wilcox, who helped so much with Otis and Jack, during the writing of this book.

One

SOFT SAD SHAPES IN THE DARKNESS

Just outside of Las Vegas the trailer fishtailed, flew out across the desert, rolled twice, and smashed into a Joshua tree. It started as a little noise, my dad said, a sort of *jiggling*—and when he looked in the rearview mirror he saw the trailer go, lurching uncertainly in the direction of the desert but going fast, almost like it was trying to keep up with the car for a ways before it rolled, bouncing, like a little orange toy that weighed no more than a box of animal crackers. He had a minute, he said, with the car pulled over and everybody still asleep, to think about what he'd done, or what he hadn't done, which was make sure the trailer hitch was secure when we'd left Los Angeles. He'd had time to turn the car around and take us back to our old life in the House on the Hill, if he'd been so inclined. He was a man with options. But my dad had been taught to move ahead in life. So he did what anyone would: he put on his shoes, got out of the car, walked a short distance to relieve himself, and stood chewing his mint toothpick, thinking it all over.

Jen and I woke up when we felt the car stop. It was early morning but already the air was thickly hot, and dust floated on either side of the car. My dad had slammed on the brakes when he saw the trailer go and our car was parked now at a crazy angle, the tires creaked hard to one side, we saw when we got out, and the back end of the car jutting up toward the road. Someone in a passing car might've thought we'd stopped so one of us could throw up, or because of a quarrel that got too big for the interior of the car, or for some other urgency: which now our mom was running toward, full out across yellow gray dirt, my dad catching up and then overtaking her like he might be able to fix it all before she got there.

No one had given us any instructions and so for a minute Jen and I just sat. No one had said, *stay here girls,* or *hurry, hurry, get your shoes on.* We could see colorful billboards all the way up the highway: the closest one advertised a ninety-nine-cent steak dinner, with a baked potato alongside a pulverized-looking piece of meat and a sprig of freakishly green parsley at the edge of the plate. Farther on was a woman lounging poolside, her legs open as if she'd fallen from a treetop and landed with perfect aim on the chaise longue made of stripey plastic straws: CIRCUS CIRCUS, SINGLE AS LOW AS $10.95 PER PERSON DOUBLE OCCUPANCY.

Jen took the lead and got out. We could hear my mom from the car, her wailing insane and heartbreaking. That made us both run, out across the dirt with our plastic thongs flapping and catching in the brush. There were snakes everywhere, that much I was sure of, and my ankles tingled at the thought. Somewhere along the way my mom's wails got to me and something caught in my own throat, a hard ball of salt and fear, and I let the sound out. My dad saw us and came toward us with his arms open. "It's okay, kids. Everything's okay. We lost the trailer but we're fine, everyone's fine, your mom's just upset—"

"It's not fine!" our mom cried. "Not fine!" She was kneeling in the dirt, her fingers wrapped in her hair while she rocked. "All of our things, all of our things—!"

"We're okay. We're okay. We're all in one piece." My dad felt warm and solid. His arms were thick with black hair and up close each hair sprouted from a large pore, as though the hair had been stitched on. The trailer had landed upright and it looked friendly enough, the way it had looked in our driveway when my dad slid the bolt and said, *there. And we're off.* But the back of it was smashed upward and the door and bolt were both twisted so that our dad spent some time kicking and heaving at the bolt. Every now and again a semi sped by on the highway and it was the only sound beside our mom's crying and my dad's grunts as he worked at the lock. Then it sprung open and my dad gently pried the door back. "Things are fine," he said. "See, Miriam? Things look okay, I don't think much is broken. See?"

Jen took my hand. Inside the trailer boxes lay on their sides, straining at the clear strapping tape with their smashed contents. Leaving the House on the Hill the night before, I'd imagined the inside of the trailer as a miniature replica of the rooms we'd left behind, with beds made and the couch in front of the window and books lined neatly in the bookcase. But now we were somewhere on the outskirts of Las Vegas with snakes all around, and my mom rushed forward to one of the boxes marked FRAGILE! DINNER DISHES. She ripped through the tape and newspaper and we heard the tinkle of broken china even before we could see it. The whole box was like that, and then another. My dad tried to take her arm. "Go! Go away!" my mom cried.

"I'm sorry," my dad said. "I'm sorry, I'm sorry, I'm sorry. Look, the chairs are fine. The table even. I'll hitch a ride into town. Why don't you come back to the car? We can't stand here all day." It was warming up and my dad's glasses were reflective cubes beneath his shaggy eyebrows. "Come on. We can't stand here."

"You go. You just go. We never should've left, we never should've left."

"Don't talk like that, Miriam. Come on, let's just take care of this."

"If you hadn't wanted to move us. Because you were suspicious. Everything is wrong!"

"Please don't be sad, Mom." Even in the dry air my mom was strangely moist. She was a center, a focal point in the jaundiced landscape, and I moved toward her.

"You think everything's okay, you think everything's okay," she looked at my face but her eyes were somewhere else. They looked odd and flat, like my real mother had seeped out. She touched Jen's hair, moving her palm over it in an absent circle. I felt something touch my foot and yanked back. "Here," my dad said. "Come on," and lifted me. A beetle was moving crookedly around my mom's thong, trying to get around it. When it got to the other side it sped under a rock.

"You go, you just go," my mom said. She sat in the dirt and more tears came. She couldn't get over it. "We never should've left. It's your fault. Your fault."

"The car's fine. *We're* fine. Now come on, we're all gonna get a sunburn."

"I don't care. I don't care. Why did we? Have to leave? Because you thought I was *cheating*, is why, I know why you want so bad to get us to Provo, so you can keep me locked up like Rapunzel, if it weren't for the kids I'd just *go*, oh, I can't *believe* it, we've lost everything, *everything*." She went to another box and when she heard the sound of broken dishes inside of that one she just let it drop, then collapsed over it.

"Come on, Mom," Jen said. "We have sandwiches and ice in the car."

"You go, you all just go. Really. I'll be fine, I'll just stay till you get back. Go fix yourself some sandwiches and get a cold drink and I'll just wait. Okay?"

"Goddamnit, Miriam, you're being selfish." My dad picked up the boxes and put them back in the trailer, slammed the bolt. "I need to call a tow truck. You need to pull yourself together."

"Me! Me! Me pull myself together!" My mom went at my dad. She cracked him on the cheek and his glasses flew off his face. "You've ruined everything! Everything!" I started to cry. Without his glasses my dad looked lizardlike, his eyes slits.

"Stop it!" Jen yelled. "Everybody stop it!"

"What do you want me to do?" my dad said. His voice broke. "What do you want me to do?" He retrieved his glasses and moved around to the front of the trailer, tried to lift it. "Is this what you want me to do? Haul it on my back all the way to Utah? I will if that's what you want. I will."

"Don't, Dad," I said. It was awful to watch him. He'd get one knee under the hitch and strain and then pause to shove his glasses up his nose and then try again.

My mom laughed. "You look like an imbecile," she said.

My dad kept at it, pausing and kneeling to breathe hard and then getting himself back up under it. The trailer stayed right where it was, shipwrecked. I saw the beetle scuttle out, freeze, and take off in another direction. It was as if suddenly all the things I knew were behind me, useless and small. In front of me were snakes and broken dishes and wet spots that had appeared under my dad's armpits as he heaved. And behind me was our old life, so far away that not even squinting could bring it into focus; when I looked back all I saw was dirt and highway, tiny cars and trucks speeding off into nowhere. Until today, I thought, I'd known a lot of things: that *opera* was when people sang loudly on a stage, for example, and knelt and clutched at their hearts. That markets sold heaps of apples and grapes hissed on with hoses that left the fruit dripping and glistening, and that outside the market was a large gold horse with a western saddle that for a dime would hump in a slow motion gallop, and if I waited patiently I would get to ride him.

I knew that my nana liked to kiss us on the mouth when we came to visit, so that we lingered with dread on the front steps after ringing the doorbell, waiting for the sight of her bloody-looking mouth and its medicinal smell. And that once she'd strung a bulldog from a clothesline for biting my dad when he was only five and that now, because of the dog bite, my dad's eyeball wandered around when he was tired, drifting to the corner of his eye like it was off duty.

When a picture got taken, what we did was smile. When dried beans were poured into a pie pan, we glued them onto a paper plate in the shape of a rooster. Popsicle sticks were chewed, and sleeping bags could be rolled into neat stools and tied with strings, then unrolled in front of the TV for watching cartoons. Always, the mom gave the baths. Always, the dad drove the car.

I t was 1966, and we were *The Taylors.* That was something else I knew because it was written on our mailbox, in a sturdy black bank-like font that anyone would trust; and the day we left the House on the Hill, the day we drove away and everything started to change, I stood near my dad's leg, watching the plaque under the mailbox flap in the wind. It sounded chinking and lonely, an empty swing on the playground. We were waiting for our mother. She drifted past the upstairs windows, weeping and taking her time. We were leaving behind a leaning white clapboard house with ancient pyracantha bushes that had stinging branches, bushes my dad went at hatefully, dressed like a bee-keeper. And we were going to a better house, one that was practically brand-new, with pea-colored, wall-to-wall shag carpeting. In the new house our mom would use a lawn rake to bring the carpeting back to life, or for a dime one of us kids would do it, dragging and scraping until it looked again like the carpet we'd been promised in the early days, not yet flattened and muddied. And then it was like we had a chance again, like everything could still start over.

My dad leaned against the car with his arms folded, patient, still the authority figure. It was the 1960s and he was the dad, with nothing to lose. So he waited.

My mom passed before the window. She seemed always onstage and now she paused, threw us a heartbreaking look and then pressed on, leaving the window, her shoulders full of grieving, looking for something she could never get back. Jen and I were still little; we didn't know about leaving things. We thought that as long as our parents were together in the front seat of the car, with the windows rolled tight against whatever might harm us, that we could go pretty much anywhere. So we waited, too, coloring pictures in the back seat. I was doing a kitten book, and Jen colored trees and puppies. Our coloring books were generic, with large hollow shapes for things: *cloud, dog, car, bus.*

My dad had seat-belted us in and after a while he unbuckled us and peeled open a pack of gum. He passed us each a stick and huffed on his glasses and rubbed the lenses with his shirttail. "You girls can get out and play for a while, if you want," he said. "Your mom just needs some time." He inspected the trailer hitch, jiggled it and then kicked it hard a few times. "I hope this is going to be okay."

My dad had very brown, strong hands, and though he was short, and though his hair was already combed in threads over the top, he had a virility that women responded to. His place was behind the wheel of the car with all the windows rolled up. He drove with his seat reclined and talked often, fully, with a lot of pauses; we were a captive audience and whenever our car was finally on the highway and he'd started talking, things seemed right with the world. Then he was expansive, then he had the floor. At the time he seemed to say whatever came into his head, as though things were just occurring to him; but I can see now that his conversation was saved up and carefully designed to teach us rules and virtues, what kinds of people and situations to avoid, for example, and what was expected of us as Young Ladies. Talking like this, my dad made sense of our lives: he was the one who explained what the world outside of the car was like, the one who locked all the doors when we passed through scary neighborhoods. He was the one at the wheel. If outside of the car my dad had times where he felt his masculinity was threatened, or times when he wasn't sure he could provide for us, it only took his getting behind the wheel and arranging us—three lovely females, full of love, listening and clucking sympathetically and nodding along—to restore his sense of himself. We needed this too, I think,

9

even my mom. Imagine what we must've looked like, behind the enormous curved windows of our station wagon: my mom with her cat-eye sunglasses, my dad's arm strong and brown resting at the window. Two daughters in the backseat with matching pink hair ribbons, white knit sweaters, our faces like the faces of little lambs, dull puffs of cotton, foolish.

When our mom drove it was a whole different ballgame. Then Jen and I yanked the radio dial back and forth, and climbed from the front to the backseat and talked too loud and too much and swung at each other. My mom was terrified of driving and at these times it was all she could do to keep the car on the road: she kept her eyes fixed and if we offered her anything, a graham cracker or a swig from a thermos, her hand clawed frantically at the air, waving us off. *I'm driving! I'm driving!* she'd say, and the car would shiver and veer. Then we fell silent and watched the road, quiet with fear, until we got to wherever we were going.

"Maybe one of you should go see if she's okay," my dad said finally. "She's pretty unhappy about leaving. One of you want to go check?"

Without our furniture in it, the house already felt like someone else's. My mom was in the bedroom at the top of the stairs, curled in the window seat. Her face was red and wrenched up and when she saw me she dropped from the seat to her knees, reaching and reaching. "Honey, Honey, Baby," she said. "I can't stand this, I can't stand this. I never thought we'd leave. I thought I'd grow old and die here, do you know that? That this is where we'd raise you kids." The pineapples and orchids on the curtains sprouted above her head in columns of pink and white and yellow; she looked like she was sitting at the base of a fountain and I pushed my hand into one of the curtains, making the pineapples sway in treetops far above. "I just never, never thought."

"Dad gave me some gum."

"Oh, that's good. That's nice. I didn't want you girls to see me so upset. Come with me, let's walk through the house one last time, okay? Say good-bye, we'll never ever see this house again, oh I can't believe it, Lucy. I really can't. No matter what we'll never live in this house ever again." She was sobbing, and stumbled a little trying to get me on one hip. I was nearly seven and getting bigger all the time. She carried me into the bathroom and tore off a piece of toilet paper, then blotted her eyes. On the walls, in silvery wallpaper, crafty-looking French waiters in berets and striped shirts twirled trays of bubbling champagne flutes, and the waiters commented to pink dancing poodles: *Excusez-moi!* they said. *Merci beaucoup!*

"There's one last thing," she said. "Now I don't want you to breathe a word of this, this is just our secret, okay? So don't blab it to your dad, he'd be just furious. Don't blab it to your sis." She carried me into their old bedroom, glanced out the window to wave at my dad. Then she moved nervously to the closet and set me down long enough to bring a wadded brown paper bag from the shelf. Inside was a Maxwell House coffee can and my mom shook it, peeled back the lid to show me the crumpled ones and fives and loose change. "Our Nest Egg," she said. "For if and when we have to make our getaway."

"To Utah?"

"No, Silly. I shouldn't have showed you. You have to promise. It's our special secret. Do you promise? Your dad will kill me, if you tell. I really mean that, Luce. He'll hit me, he hates when I keep things from him. He'll give me a black eye, okay? So you can't tell." She dumped the money out and stuffed it in her bra, then faced me. "Can you see anything?"

"No."

"How's your sister doing? Is she okay? Is she out in the car?"

"Dad said we could get out for a minute."

"Well, Utah's a long haul. Good-bye, house. Good-bye stairs. Do you want to try going tinkle again?"

"No."

"It's a long haul," my mom carried me downstairs and we paused in

11

the kitchen. "Good-bye, noisy old refrigerator." She started to cry again, and I started to cry with her, more out of sympathy than sorrow. There was an unopened box of circus animal cookies in the car, pink and white and waxy. We were going on a long car trip and on the way we might stop and swim in a motel pool, maybe at the Travelodge, with the sleepwalking bear in his white nightcap, and Jen and I would squabble over who got to tear the white paper strip off the toilet and also unwrap the motel glasses from their crinkly twisted white tissue paper, and there would be a rollaway bed and TV channels to flip through and outside by the pool would be a white rescue donut, chaise longues we could adjust—upright, reclining, flat, upright again—until my dad would say *stop, would ya?*

"Good-bye, mud room," she said, and held a tissue to my nose and said *Blow*. "Good-bye sweet little doorway." She moved her fingers fussily over the high, sticky whorl of her hair, stalling. Then my dad whistled, clapped his hands and called, *bus is leaving,* and we stepped out into white sunshine.

My mom cried most of that afternoon; then a sort of dark calm set in and she rode slumped against the window, ignoring us.

"Can we get another goat in Utah?" Jen said. She was two years older than me, with thick white legs. She had a scab on one knee and was picking off little flakes and eating them. Jen was a redhead with skin that looked puffy, like it could easily puncture. My own skin was different, close-fitting and grubby-looking around the ankles and elbows and ears, and my feet were bony and the toenails looked like they sat on the surface of my toes. Whereas Jen's toenails looked embedded, clear tiddlywinks pressed into cookie dough and baked. Her eyes were green with little flecks and her front teeth collided, which somehow made her look eager, ready to contribute to the conversation. She pulled off a flake and put it in her mouth and showed it to me. "See food."

"I miss Amy," I said. "There could never be another goat like Amy."

"Well, our new yard is smaller," my dad said. "It's in the city this time, I don't think it's exactly zoned for a goat. But maybe something else, maybe a kitty or a rabbit. We'll have to see."

"Can we make a snowman?" I said.

"We'll make a snowman, then we can make snow angels," my dad said. "There are all kinds of things to do when you live somewhere with snow. And there are mountains, and we can go camping and hiking."

"Can I get a horse?" I said.

"It is the wide open west," my dad said. "You never know."

"That would be really nice for you, wouldn't it?" My mom roused herself to pass a box of Saltines over the back seat. "Not many horses in Los Angeles. So maybe that part will be nice. And I sure like the idea of a deck. We can have big terra-cotta planters with strawberry plants spilling out, and we can sit out on it in the mornings and look out over the valley and sip our coffee. How big is the deck? Bigger than our old patio at least, I hope?"

"I don't know, maybe ten feet across," my dad said.

"And the bedrooms are all on the main?"

"Right," my dad said. He'd made the trip to Utah a few weeks before and put a down payment on a house. Jen and I were each going to have our own room and my dad said that from the deck, you could see the sun come up over the mountains. "The layout's a lot like the old house, is the thing. But it also has some things that I like, too, like a disposal. No more stinky sink, right girls?"

"Right," I said. The old house was far behind us now, birds calling in the orchard. If I thought about it too much I would start to cry so I turned instead to my sewing card cut in the shape of a girl with a bonnet. I poked a red lace in the precut holes, moving all around the card. Then I passed it over the front seat so my mom could break the yarn with her teeth and tie a knot. *Very nice,* she said. Our old house had a driveway that made a circle around the avocado tree, so that from the kitchen window we could watch visitors arrive and circle and finally come to a stop. My parents called it the *House on the Hill* after the Peggy Lee song, and some nights my dad played it over and over on the record player, coaxing my mom into a dance while Peggy Lee sang, husky and intimate. The house in the song had something called a verandah, and it was a new house, one I imagined with gleaming yellow floors and a grand piano. But our house wasn't new; it was ramshackle and drafty, which was exactly what my mom liked about it, and exactly what my dad hated. Years later, in photographs, I saw what my parents must have seen: the peeling paint on the wall behind our small heads, the doubtful construction of the staircase, doors leaning in their jambs. But it was the house of my babyhood and the only one I knew. My mom smoked Newports on the verandah, and at night they played cards and Scrabble together in the family room. Before marrying my dad, she'd had two years of college and used words like *rhetoric* and *dissipate* with us kids. As in: *Don't give me any of your rhetoric, young lady.* And: *Please close the curtains, heat dissipates through glass, you kids don't know it but our family is poor right now, very poor, we need to save money, we need to hold on to every last penny.*

"Anybody want juice?" my mom passed us the thermos, and Jen chugged it.

"Jen's hogging," I said. "When are we going to get there?" We'd been on the road most of the day. It was twilight, a time of day that always made me sad. Other families were in their houses now behind yellow windows, the kids doing their homework and waiting to be called to dinner.

"Do you girls need a blanket? There's one on the floor if you get cold, okay? We're going to stop soon, and then you can watch TV in the motel."

"Is there a Knott's Berry Farm in Utah?" Jen opened the blanket over us. It was plaid, with fat wool worms along either edge. When I was sick I braided the worms over and over, listening to my mom move around the house. The vacuum went on and off, and she made phone calls. My mom was beautiful, with olive skin and large white teeth and a telephone voice that was professional and sexy. She cleared her throat before she picked up, getting ready, then said *hullloooo*, low and with a little thrill, ready to win a prize. I loved watching how she crossed her ankles and sat up very straight, then looked up numbers in a black metal phone directory that sprang open at the base and clipped hard and shut with the same nasty efficiency. It whanged open extra hard if you slid the button to *Z*, where there were never any numbers written in but where the weight of the whole contraption was in the front so that it practically back flipped out of your hands when you hit the button. *Whang.*

"No, but probably something like it. We'll miss Knott's Berry Farm, won't we? We went there a lot with you kids." Sometimes my mom talked like this, like everything was behind us, moony and distant. Whereas my dad talked about what was in front of us, the things we were going to do next. I liked my mom's way better. "Maybe someday we'll be back, you never know. We could buy back our old house."

"Miriam," my dad said.

"I can say whatever I want," my mom said.

"Let's think about how nice Utah will be, instead, why don't we?"

"Remember when we were at Knott's Berry Farm and that goat ate the flower off my purse?" I held my Bozo the clown doll up to my chest, remembering. Jen had colored blue circles all over his head with a Magic Marker so that he would have hair. Now she reached for Bozo, pulling his arm gently, insistently, until I screamed. Then she released him and went at the back of my dad's seat with her feet, humming *Chopsticks* and doing a little dance. Jen, my mom said, was fragile and high-strung. She tantrumed a lot, on the floor with her toes hammering, and if I got too close she went for my shins. She looked most like my dad, with his short thick limbs and ski-slope nose, and I looked more like my mom, bony and yellowish, like I was looking for trouble.

"No kicking the back of my seat," my dad said. "I'm trying to drive up here."

"And no screaming." My mom took out her mirror and checked her lipstick. "Remember? We had to buy you another purse from the gift shop that very same day, you cried so hard. Is it only me that's homesick already? Aren't you going to miss things?"

"I won't miss commuting to El Segundo every day, that's for sure," my dad said. "I won't miss all the hippies and Mexicans. LA doesn't feel safe anymore, it's not a good environment for the girls. But I think it's a good change. I think we need a fresh start."

"What about the Mormons?" Jen said. My mom had a single story which for her represented the Mormon religion and everything she hated about it: at Fullerton Junior College, she told us, she'd actually almost *turned into one*, because she'd fallen in love with a campus security guard who was Mormon, who'd promised to marry her, who as it turned out was *already married*. But in the meantime my mom had nearly joined up, a fact that still grated. My mom wasn't used to being tricked, especially by men. With our dad she won almost every single argument. When she was losing she resorted to tears, blotting her face with a pink hanky and looking punished. Then my dad would give in, speaking gently and guiding her with one hand on her lower back. She was the patient and he was Florence Nightingale.

"Oh, I don't know," my mom said. "I've always liked Mormons well enough, I mean all except for that lousy Bill. But not all of them are like that. They're real family-oriented. And they keep a food storage, for emergencies. I really like that idea. Ask your dad, *he's* the one who hates them."

"I don't hate anybody," my dad said. "I don't have anything against that religion, in fact I think they have some good lessons. The main thing is I think it will be a good place to raise you girls. Provo's clean and it's small and it's right up close to the mountains. LA's a hole. An armpit."

"Mormons bake a lot, too," my mom said. "I've never been much of a cook but I wouldn't mind learning. Things like pie crust. And they can fruit. Doesn't that sound wonderful? On a cold winter day, in front of all those wonderful warm sweet-smelling pots. I can picture myself doing something like that, I really can. In an apron, with my hair up off my neck. And then your dad will come up from behind and kiss me. I can see myself, I really can, just perfectly. And finally we're going to *fit in* somewhere, gosh the last few years have just been so hard on us."

"Well, like I said, the neighborhood's not a wealthy one. But it's solid, family-oriented." My dad opened a mint-flavored toothpick, then passed extras back to us girls. "I'll have my own business finally. That's what this is all about. That's how we need to think, okay?"

"Okay."

"That's my girl." He patted her leg. "I'm thinking of driving a little bit longer." It was dark inside the car now and he turned the heater on. "Come give me some sugar," he said, and extended his arm across the seat. My mom scooted closer. He liked when she was agreeing with him, being sweet and nodding and not putting up a fight. Then it was like we could drive forever, my dad telling long stories and jokes and us girls curled warm together in back and looking out at everything that couldn't hurt us. I pushed at Jen until she gave me more room, and then I lay down and turned my face to the crack, which was comforting and private and made my nose itch like crazy. But scratching it felt delicious, like scratching a mosquito bite.

"And if you don't like the house, well, maybe in a few years," my dad said. "Things'll be easier, with me making more money." He glanced in the rearview mirror. "I hope the trailer's okay."

"Did you check the hitch?" my mom moved the mirror. "It looks weird. It's moving around an awful lot."

"Of course I checked it," my dad said. "It just does that if I go over fifty miles an hour. I have to drive slower is all."

"I think we just need a new start," my mom said. "A change of scenery. But I'll always miss that place, I really will, I just can't stand the thought of someone else living in it." Her voice caught. "I know it was too much of a fixer-upper for you, but still."

"Well, and El Segundo. I think the lawn thing will be better, I mean hey, I can set my own hours. I can come and go as I please and be around a lot more for you and the kids. I don't like working for someone else, making some other guy rich while I punch the clock. This way I'll be making my own money."

"What's punching the clock?" I dangled an old gum wrapper in front of Jen's nostrils to make sure she was still breathing. It fluttered gently.

"It means day in, day out, never getting ahead," my dad said.

"I wish it weren't *lawns*," my mom slipped off her clip-on earrings. They pinched her earlobes and made them look pink, infected.

"You don't have to be snobby. Everybody needs their lawn mowed, including us. And it's not just lawn mowing, I'll be doing sprinkler systems and landscape design. It's hard work, Miriam."

"I know. I don't mean that. I know how hard you work, Hon. I just wish sometimes you got more credit for it, more respect from the world instead of getting treated like a hired hand or something. And I'm sure you'll do just fine but with these kids, well with so many mouths to feed of course I worry about the money. I just think we should think of this as a trial period. And hope that there'll be enough. Money."

"I can take care of my own family."

"Well gee Hon, I know you can. I'm not saying that. I'm saying, if it doesn't work out, we should have other options is all. I can always take the kids and go stay with my mom, if we're having trouble."

"You're not going *anywhere*. Of course we'll have enough. If I don't make enough with the lawn thing I'll take another job. It's that simple."

"Or you know I could take a job, help out."

"No wife of mine is going to work."

"I'm freezing," I said. Jen was asleep against my arm and I put Bozo between us so I wouldn't get drooled on.

"Do you want your sweater?" my mom dug it out of a suitcase and I tried to pull it on without waking up Jen. The sweater was hand knit from Norway; we all had one. The sweaters were sixty dollars each and our mom had saved up for months, sending for the sweaters one by one, until at last, complete, we stood in a row to have our picture snapped. It was as though our family were meant to stay together forever, if only for these sweaters; so densely knitted that they weighed as much as blankets, and when I pulled mine over my head hardly any light showed through.

"Are we going to stop soon?"

"Why?" My mom turned; her stare affixed me. "Tinkle or BM?"

"Tinkle," I said, though I wasn't sure; sometimes I answered wrong. But it seemed important to try to tell the truth, to gauge whether there was more pressure in my stomach or my bottom; so that at last when we pulled into a filling station, my dad exasperated, surrounded by females and their bladders, glancing from his watch to the odometer—when at last my mom had me settled on the toilet, it was important to do whatever I'd said—*tinkle* or *BM*—and it shamed me when a BM slid out after all, rabbity small and sorry, or when—worse—nothing happened at all. I had to do something, because my dad had pulled off just on account of me, and it made my mom impatient, too. She tinkled speedily, efficiently, the gas bubbling out at the end in an unladylike way, *puht puht puuhht.* My dad called it Breaking Wind, and when his own bathroom visits were productive he came out cheerily for a book of matches, returned to wave one blackened stem in slow circles above the water. Then he stepped back out saying *whew!* And folded the newspaper carefully, patting his waistband: *whew! That was something else, boy, that one.* Which antagonized my mom, every time. *Okay, okay, we all get the point,* she'd say. *Boy,* he'd say. *That one, that one, let me tell you.*

PLACES TO LOOK FOR A MOTHER:

BETWEEN HER LEGS,

the best place to look for my mom, during hide-and-seek when my sister counted to ten, always too fast, then said *here I come, here I come.* My mom read the newspaper in bed and when I appeared in the doorway, panicked at the thought of all the familiar places—closet, under bed, pantry—she saw me and silently flicked back the covers, offered the cubbyhole beneath her knees. She was wearing a pink nightgown, pink rayon panties; when I crawled in I tried not to look at or breathe in the direction of her crotch. Jen never found me. She ditched me and wound up across the street at the neighbor kid's house playing Freeze Tag and tetherball, so fuck her.

But I think my mom liked for us to see. At least it seemed that way. And she loved our bodies. It was like she couldn't stay away, like she hadn't finished shaping us before we slid, gummy and bloody, into the world. She'd hug us and then, coming out of it, let her fingers drag across our chests, cupping in the briefest instant what she never got to see, never, not if we could help it, though she walked in on us—in the shower, on the toilet—no matter how often we shrieked at her, pushing her out and slamming the door while her eyes, greedy, took it all in. Later she was interested in our bleeding, our boyfriends, our butts, our hair and nipples: her hands dragging, dragging, over our hips and thighs. Every chance she got. *What?* She'd say, widening her eyes. *What? What did I do this time?* She was always hungry like this, and her hunger was like an electrical current. Men went crazy for her. When I was fourteen, our landlord offered to put both us girls through college at the college of our choice if only my mom would sleep with him in exchange for rent. I remember how proud she sounded, announcing this to us. What did we think, she wanted to know. Was he really all that gruesome? Did we think he was ugly? She refused the offer, though it seemed to make her despondent. *Any college,* she said, drifting from couch to chair, restless, still incredulous. *You could've both gone to Yale.*

In California mornings felt like beginnings, with the low three-noted call of doves in the avocado orchard and the tangy smell of eucalyptus and an occasional breeze from the coast, though my dad said by the time the breeze got to our house it had so much grime and soot in it that it was a wonder it made it to our house at all. Still we could sense it, its salty heave and romance, and my mom always tipped her nose to take it in. It took all morning for the haze to burn off and that was the time of people rising and getting ready, sliding behind steering wheels and crunching over curved gravel driveways. Yellow school buses moved down hills, and in our house my mom would pad around with her third cup of coffee, her hair springy in the humidity, and any one of us could feel it: the day green and damp and gathering energy as it moved toward noon, the time when at last the beginning of the day felt complete. By then the day had sorted itself out, the sky blue or rainy or still hazy, and we could make decisions about whether to spend the rest of the day indoors or out.

But mornings in Utah were different; they happened quickly, in the hours just after the sun came up, so that by the time we'd slurped bowls of Cheerios in front of cartoons and gotten our shoes on, the day was already hard and hot and flat. Then it was as if the air had never been cool, and in the morning instead of hearing birds we heard crickets chirping pointlessly in dry grass.

• • •

Our new house was a split-level on a sloped lot a few blocks from Brigham Young University. From the front yard we could see practically the whole campus, and at our backs was the enormous white letter Y on the hillside. The BYU campus itself looked like a factory, with long yellow brick buildings and an incinerator stack at the very center of our view, also in pale brick, with the giant letter Y painted on the side. Some days, after we'd been living in Provo for a while, the incinerator stack gave me the creeps. Other days it just looked friendly, like you could climb to the top and take pictures. It was like everything else that I didn't quite understand: the way the Mormon temple spires reminded me of the dentist's office; and how I imagined that the green water tanks on the edge of town, on the freeway between Provo and Orem, held women doing the backstroke and wearing flowered rubber bathing caps. But for now everything looked plain and literal. It was our new life, our fresh start, and the corners of things still seemed sharp. The air, so high and thin, made my lungs feel like they'd been scrubbed with lemon.

When we drove up to the house for the first time, my mom refused to get out of the car. The house had a petrified wood facade and she sat looking at it miserably. Each slab of wood had been sliced laterally and then opened like a bagel and cemented on the front, so that the overall effect was of lots of circles and triangles and zigzags back to back.

"What a nightmare," my mom said. Jen and I explored the house, staking out bedrooms. "Well," she said, when we came back. "It's not the House on the Hill, is it."

"It's nice inside," I said. "The fridge has two doors in the front." That made my mom laugh hollowly. Then she did a spiraling thing with one finger and said in a small voice, *big whoop*. She wore a scarf over her head and cat-eye sunglasses; when we'd bought them at Gibson's, back in California, they'd looked daring and hilarious, but here they just seemed silly, her whole glamorous look out of place among the squat brick houses and carefully sculpted shrubs. "Do you think people actually live in this neighborhood?" she studied the street over the top of her sunglasses. "I've been sitting here fifteen minutes at least and I haven't seen a single car go by. Maybe they're all dead. Or maybe just peeping at us through the blinds. I figured out what the front of the house reminds me of. A *migraine*. Very optically disturbing, I must say."

"You'll like the master bedroom," my dad said. "Come on, Miriam. Just come look around. Our bedroom has a sliding glass door that goes right into the backyard."

"I liked our *old* master bedroom," she said. "I liked our whole old life, and everything in it. Do you actually think we're going to fit in here, do you?"

"We can try. That's all I'm asking. For the girls' sake. You haven't even seen the inside."

"You'll like the downstairs," Jen said. "Come on, Mom." She took my mom's hand and we sat there for a while. My mom seemed to sense that she'd been tricked: that the house in Provo was part of the life my dad wanted, and that it looked in every way like a house she'd have to change her own shape to get comfortable in. It wasn't like that with the House on the Hill, and that's why she was so mad, that's why she sat now in the driveway playing with her glasses and the radio, postponing her future. With the House on the Hill it was the other way around. The floors creaked, and there were cobwebs and ghosts in every single room. It was old and creepy and crumbling, filled with antique furniture. The rooms didn't have closets and the windows had single panes that rattled. There was ornate molding that had been painted over so many times you could see drips and brush strokes, and all the colors it had been—white, green, pink, blue, then white again. But my mom had looked right at home in the house, with her hair long and her toenail polish chipped, slouching around in thongs she'd gotten at Skaggs. She wore capris and whatever old shirt of my dad's she could find and her calves always needed lotion. It wasn't going to be like that here. Here she would have to be someone else. In the winter she'd have to wear close-toed shoes and pants that went to her ankles and sleeves that went to her wrist, though much of her charm had to do with her exposed flesh—profuse, pale, like rising bread dough, with the same frightening lively smell and heat. And so she sat looking at the house, trying to imagine a new look for herself. And my dad knew all this. He stood in the carport, ten years older than my mom, wearing a white T-shirt and a crew cut and plaid madras trousers. He looked trustworthy, like he'd always lived there. He looked ready to mow the lawn.

After a while my mom sighed and got out of the car. She put on her shoes and stretched. "What do you think, Lucy Loo?"

"I like it," I said. And I did. There was a cherry tree in the front yard and a slope of lawn that ran down to the street. The house across the street had kids' bikes in the carport, and there were wells in front of the basement windows, which would be good for hide-and-seek. My bedroom had wood paneling and shelves at the back of the closet, where I'd be able to hide my journal from Jen. All in all it looked pretty good to me.

"Come on, come inside," my dad said. "Let's not keep standing out here."

"It's okay," my mom said, after she'd wandered through. "It'll do, for what we need. We don't have to live here forever, do we? It's just temporary, until we can find something else."

"Not that temporary." My dad dumped our suitcases on the floor of the kitchen. "I signed the papers, so don't get too antsy. But maybe in a couple of years. It's a good house. And I won't have to do much work on it, it's got new wiring and plumbing. That's what I like. That's what I *really* like." He winked at me. "Right? I won't have to be the handyman, fixing up some ramshackle old dump. Everything here is *done*."

"I'm glad about that," my mom said vaguely. "And maybe our next house can be old again, have some history. How old do you think this place is? Twenty years maybe? Fifteen?"

"About twenty," my dad said. "The realtor said he thought it was built in about nineteen fifty."

25

"I've never liked Ramblers," my mom pulled out an empty kitchen drawer and perched on the edge. "They're so *dull*, not aesthetic, at all."

"What's aesthetic?" I said.

"Pretty," my mom said. "Charming, like the House on the Hill. Well, it'll do. I should do some unpacking, shouldn't I? Get something together for dinner I guess." She pulled me against one knee. "Anyway, I'm glad you like it here. That's all that matters, isn't it? I just hope the neighbors will accept us, don't you?"

My dad called his new lawn care business All American Landscaping Services Inc., and within a month he was ready to go. He designed his own logo, a man in profile on a riding lawn mower with an American flag fluttering from the bumper. Then he went to Sears and bought everything he needed on credit: two mowers with mulchers and a riding John Deere for big jobs, and hoes and rakes and bags of grass seed and fertilizer. He printed up flyers and Jen and I stapled them to telephone poles all over Provo, and he placed an ad in the *Big Nickel*. My parents firmly believed in the power of the printed media to get the message out. We were forever placing ads or answering them, having yard sales or going to swap meets. It seemed like pretty much anything we wanted—a puppy, patio furniture, a car, pea gravel—could be got through the paper, and the *Big Nickel* was best of all. It only cost a dollar a week to run an ad and the paper was fat, bright yellow, free, and always available on a metal stand just inside the automatic door at Safeway.

Business for All American was slow at first, which my parents blamed on the Mormons: they were too industrious, too ready to save a buck, and they kept things all in the family. In our neighborhood it was the teenaged boys who did all the mowing. They kept their shirts on and their hair was neatly clipped and they worked fast. In our old life, in Whittier, skinny Hispanic boys had done most of the yard work. They worked fast, too, but with a different sort of energy, and their eyes always blazed at Jen and I when we drove past. Their backs were sinewy and deep brown and they rode in the backs of open pickup trucks, seven or eight to a load, and looked famished and hard. My dad called them Wetbacks and explained how they were taking all the jobs from people like us, the real citizens. He said they were stealing from our economy. He said the cotton-picking sons of bitches had crawled over some barbed wire fence in the middle of the night near the border of San Diego and then migrated up here like a string of black ants to take all the jobs so they could send money home to Mexico, where they had too many kids and wives and no clean water. He was glad to be living in Provo, where there were only a few Mexicans who knew their place. These Mexicans either opened taco shops or laid sod, sometimes for my dad, who hired them from Sunshine Temporary Services. Practically any day you could drive around Provo and see them, high in the limbs of box elder trees, going at the limbs with a chain saw while on the ground, men like my dad stood next to shiny trucks and waited. They were the ones who dug ditches, dug trenches for sprinkler systems, dug graves and wells. They toiled mechanically in the sun and never spoke. They drank from the hose, worked long hours, and stared into space over their lunches, which lasted no more than the time it took to eat. Then they started up again. And at the end of the day they disappeared into neighborhoods we'd never even driven through. In Whittier our family had lived more or less in the middle of it all, so that there were rich and poor people pretty much in any direction. But in Provo the lines were drawn more clearly: in Provo you were either black or white, Mexican or non-Mexican, Mormon or non-Mormon. It was a distinction that my dad seemed to appreciate.

One Mexican family in Provo owned Diego's Taco Shop, a tiny stucco building across the street from the limestone courthouse. The food was cheap and good and after a while it became our Friday night thing to eat at Diego's and then cross the street to the city park, which had a water slide. Afterward, our hair greening in the sun from the chlorine, we went to Emigration Market for banana Popsicles.

It was at Diego's where my mom first got the idea for a job. She was bored out of her mind staying home all day, she told our dad. Bored to tears. And it wasn't like we couldn't use the money. Jen and I played with the bottle of hot sauce, trying to see who could eat more hot sauce without changing our expression. I usually won because Jen's fair skin gave her away; when she ate something spicy, or got nervous or stayed too long in the sun, pink blotches crept up her neck and on her cheeks, like was happening now. I squirted more sauce onto a chip and put it carefully in my mouth, staring her down. The one who lost was the one who reached first for her glass of water.

"I *know* how to run a cash register," my mom said.

"No wife of mine is going to work in a *taco* joint," my dad said. "Forget about it."

"I think it sounds pleasant," my mom leaned back in the orange vinyl booth and stretched her arms across the back, making herself at home. "I'll bet they'd hire me. I already know how to make guacamole." She pronounced it *wak-a-mole*.

"Wakka whatta?" my dad said. "Whack a mole?"

"Just a few hours a week. Maybe at lunchtime. The girls are in school, I'm sitting home, it would be fun to get out and meet people and it would help with our finances, I mean gee."

"Our finances are just fine. Why don't you make friends with some of the other girls on the block? Jeff's mother. Then there's that German gal, what's her name?"

"All the Mormon girls on the block, you mean? I don't have anything in common with them, Bob. You know I don't. They want to recruit us. I don't hate the idea of being Mormon, but talk about the women not *working*. I get lonely at home all day." They'd had this conversation before in Whittier, right before we moved. My mom wanted to work in a stationery shop one day a week and my dad had put his foot down then, too. There was no way he was going to let her work at Diego's, and I thought she might be using it as a decoy to get something else she really wanted. Jen and I used the same strategy and it almost always worked.

"If you want to help out with our finances, how about helping me? You could keep the books. You're good at math."

Jen popped another chip in her mouth and made a choking noise and guzzled her water. "I win." I said. "I get to watch 'H.R. Puffinstuff.' "

"It's such a mature show," Jen said. "That's what I like." Her whole face was hot pink and she kept refilling her water glass. She was such a wimp, I felt sorry for her.

"But I want to *meet* people," my mom said. "That's the whole point."

"I thought the whole point was to help out with our finances," my dad said. "I wish you wouldn't sit like that."

"Like what?"

"Stretched out like that. I can see your underarms, it's unladylike. You look like a *trucker*."

My mom picked up the bottle of hot sauce. "I'd be a good employee. This bottle of hot sauce, for example, badly needs refilling. *Somebody* has been playing with it."

"I think it would be cool," Jen said. "We could walk here during lunch hour and you could serve us."

"Might as well forget about it," my dad stared off, working his way through the basket of chips. "Ain't gonna happen."

"Maybe you could work in a department store," I said. I didn't like the idea of her working at Diego's, either. It had a jukebox and seemed cheap. But I thought a department store sounded okay. She could wear high heels and work behind the perfume counter and bring us home free samples.

"You're not working *anywhere*," my dad stood up. "You don't *need* to work." He wadded up the white paper from the bottom of the chip basket and stood up. My mom helped him clear, but you could see she was still planning.

"Gracias," she told the woman at the cash register. "See you soon, I hope."

• • •

Like most kids, Jen and I seemed to live a secret life apart from our parents: we all shared a house but they had their lives and we had ours. My dad's life involved leaving in the morning with a thermos of sugared coffee and the newspaper tucked under one arm; he read it maybe in some donut shop, or in the front seat of the car between jobs, or sitting under a tree before he went onto the next job. My mom's life was cleaning and moving nervously through the house half-dressed, looking for things she'd misplaced, and she drank black coffee all day long and instead of sitting down for meals she nourished herself on crackers and slices of sharp Cheddar cheese, or peeled carrots or handfuls of Cheerios from the box. Meanwhile Jen and I had the run of the house. We went off to school dutifully, but by three o'clock we were home making messes and racing through the house again in our socks, our lunchboxes and books and papers dumped by the front door and the TV going loud, until finally our mom got fed up and made us take our school crap to our bedrooms. We both had signs on the door: KINGDOM OF JENNIFER JUNE TAYLOR. KNOCK BEFORE ENTERING! Mine said: NO SISTERS BEYOND THIS POINT! NO TRESPASSING! Jen's bedroom was connected to the bathroom but my room was bigger, and had two windows. We were ferocious guardians of our own turf. If Jen caught me in her room it was understood that she'd shove me backward onto the bed and, keeping me pinned with her bony knees, crawl up and fart on my face, which didn't always work because sometimes she had one saved up and sometimes she didn't. If she couldn't I'd say *oooh, I'm so scared I'm shaking,* which was risky; then she was likely to grip my wrist and flap my own hand against my face again and again: *why you hitting yourself, Stupid, why you hitting yourself?* and all of this went on with a lot of yelling that must have driven our mom crazy, and sometimes in the middle of it all my dad would show up and yell that we were hooligans, couldn't we for once act like ladies, and then we were told to go clean up our rooms and not come out until we did. Then I lay on the bed in a bar of sunlight, drawing horses. It was the only thing I could draw and I was good at it, the outline done carefully in a single line, the mane whipping wildly in the wind though the horse stood still. My room was all my own, a nest that smelled like me, a Snoopy pillowcase with my own private drool stains and my hamster cage stinking up the corner. My hamsters were Lady and Ted.

It was my mom who seemed without a place of her own, my mom who seemed the most unhappy and transient. She wandered in the house in Provo, bored and restless, unable to land anywhere for very long. It was worst of all when she got her migraine headaches. She'd always had them, and in our new house they came once or twice a month so that at night we could hear her move out into the hallway and then the sound of things falling from the medicine cabinet while she rifled blindly for painkillers. Then she went to Jen's room, speaking low, seeking comfort, and in the morning she and Jen would be curled together under her Scooby Doo comforter. My mom disliked that we had signs on our doors, disliked that we could ever shut them against her. She took it personally. It was easier sometimes to just let her in, let her flood her helpless self all over us until she was sure we still loved her.

I kept badgering my dad about getting a horse, and finally he relented and said I could at least take lessons. Jen was already taking swimming; she was a regular guppy, my dad said, and could turn around underwater and push off with her foot against the side of the pool when she did laps. I hated everything about swimming except doing the back-float, staring up at the green dome with my ears underwater so that the other kids' shrieks and splashes sounded very far away, echoing and hollow. I liked moving my feet in little spastic swishes now and again to propel myself and then drifting to a stop again. But Jen was energetic and competitive, a green nylon streak underwater, and I was glad when the pool became her thing and horseback riding mine, because otherwise everything we did had to be *shared*: our clothes, sandwiches, packs of gum, the television.

I took horseback riding lessons on Saturday from nine to ten in the morning. My horse, Liddy, only had one eye, which moved me; she'd had it kicked out by another horse and when I rode her, her head listed sideways a little, trying to compensate. I loved everything about horses, their creepy huge nostrils and their sharp manurey smell and their yellow overbites. I loved Liddy because she was pathetic but also fast, and because she loved to run. Our lesson usually only lasted a half hour; then the teacher, Kevin, who was getting ready to leave on an LDS mission and liked to spend time talking to his girlfriend on the telephone, would swat Liddy out into the pasture and let me run her as long as she didn't come back with foam on her chest. When my dad came to pick me up he always looked afraid, and he always waited over by the car and then hugged me hard. He didn't trust horses and he didn't like their smell. But Liddy's smell by then was in my palm, and if I rubbed it with a saliva-moistened finger in the car on the way home the dirt came off in salty boogers. And always my dad stopped for an ice cream. The place we went to served root beer floats with translucent, red plastic monkeys that hung from the side of the mug, and turquoise-blue licorice ice cream. My dad was worried about my mom, worried about how she wanted a job and wanted out of the house and never seemed happy.

"Does anyone ever come around?" he asked me once. I was trying to make the monkey hang by the tail on the side of the glass. The monkey was a brittle ruby-colored jewel and I had a dozen saved up at home, hidden in a roll of socks.

"Does she ever have company?"

"Sometimes Mrs. Jeffries comes over."

"But I mean, *company*," my dad said. "Other men. Does anyone ever come around?"

"No."

"It's hard for both of us," my dad said. "You're too young to understand. I shouldn't even be talking to you about this. How was your lesson?"

"Did you see me trotting on Libby?" I tried again with the monkey one last time, then gave up. "I got to trot. I'm learning to post."

"That's great, Honey. I'm glad you're having such a good time. I myself have never admired the equestrian arts. They *smell*, for one thing. Then you have to walk all around their twitchy behinds. They always look mad."

"You can tell, though, if they're going to kick. Because their ears go flat back."

"Is that so?" my dad looked impressed.

"But you shouldn't ever really walk behind them anyway. It makes them nervous."

"I just think your mom's been acting kind of *weird* lately, that's the only reason I'm asking, I don't mean to talk about her behind her back but it's like she wants to be someone else. And now this whole Diego's thing. I mean maybe, *maybe* I could understand if she wanted to work in a bakery or something for a few hours a week, but *Diego*'s. I just don't get it. Do you ever go there with her when I'm not around? Do you ever see her talking to anybody?"

"No."

"Well that's good. You'd tell me, wouldn't you, if your mom ever had any male guests? Because I'm off working all day, I can't keep her under surveillance. Would you tell me?"

"Yes."

"It's our secret, okay? I don't want you to say anything."

"Okay."

My dad stood up. "You ready to go help me mow some lawns?"

"Next week we're going to try cantering," I said. "That's just right below galloping, kind of between a trot and a run."

"That's great," my dad said. He rolled out a toothpick from the dispenser next to the cash register. "Kevin seems like a pretty good teacher. Kevin, I trust. Some day I hope you'll meet a nice young man like him."

"If I ever get married I'm going to marry a horse."

"*Wow*," he handed me a dime for the gum machine and we strolled out to the car. "That's going to be some wedding. Just don't make me walk behind the groom, okay?"

• • •

My dad had always been a hard sell, and the thing with my mom wanting to work at Diego's was no exception. She kept at him a few more weeks and when he wouldn't budge she laid low for a few days and planned her next strategy. The whole thing made me nervous. My dad was stubborn, but my mom was stubborn and shrewd.

One morning she came to breakfast wearing a long cotton dress with colorful embroidery at the neck. She put everything on the table without looking at us, Frosted Flakes and milk and the bowl of sugar, then went into the living room. My dad went after her. They quarreled, my mom coming back into the kitchen and walking a circle around the kitchen table, trying to keep us girls between them. I dumped the Frosted Flakes out into a huge mixing bowl, taking advantage of their fight to look for the prize. Jen saw it first and we both dove into the cereal at the same time and struggled with it at the bottom of the bowl until my dad saw and said, "Put that cereal back in the box *now*," and held out his hand. Jen forked the prize over. It was a tiny Tony the Tiger sticker book.

"I think it's a good idea. They're not going to hire some *white* girl, I need to at least look the part. Anyway I think frankly, Bob, that I probably have some Mexican blood. I mean look at my mom. Doesn't she look sort of ethnic to you? And Lucy, Luce has my same dark skin. Something's going on."

"I'm not a Mexican," I said. If anything, I thought, my skin was *yellow*, the color Jen's turned when she snuck QT tanning lotion from the medicine cabinet. But my mom and I did have the same hair, wiry and dark, that knotted easily and always needed hair conditioner. Whereas Jen's was sleek, the color of goldfish.

"You can't walk around looking like that, honestly Miriam. It looks like a nightgown. Do you even know if they have any openings? But just for your information, they're not going to hire you looking like *that*. You look like someone *pretending* to be Mexican."

"I do not," my mom said. "I look authentic and you know it. It's a traditional Mexican wedding dress and I like it. I look beautiful in it, you know I do, my nice long jet-black hair. It just *scares* you when I look sexy. And I *do*."

"That has nothing to do with it. This is Provo. You're my wife. You're supposed to act normal."

"I think you look pretty, Mom," Jen said.

"Lovely," my dad said. "Great. That's just what she needs, encouragement."

"I think you look slutty," I said. "Dad's right. You don't look like any of the other mothers around here and I don't even want you to drive me to school."

"Well isn't *that* a good one," my mom said. "Go ahead then. *Walk*."

"Nobody's walking anywhere. And I want you to get rid of that getup and act like a decent mother and wife for a change."

"I hate to break it to you, Charlie Brown, but the times they're a-changin'. Guess what, some women hold jobs now, it's called Women's Lib. You can't just crunch me under your thumb like a bug because I'll crawl right back out. You're not the boss of me."

"You don't *need* to work. What you *need* to do is watch the girls." My dad dumped cereal in a bowl and drew the box close to read it, which meant, End of Discussion.

"You don't even know what Women's Lib is, do you?"

"Is that where all the lesbians burn their bras and wave picket signs on TV?"

"I know what it is," Jen said primly. "The suffragettes. Women who just wanted the right to vote, like men."

"Well, did the suffragettes wear bras?" my dad looked at me for encouragement and I snickered.

"You're *obsessed* with the thought of women's breasts." My mom got the whisk broom from the pantry and swept up sugar from the floor. "And will you all *please, please, please* try to make an effort not to get sugar on the floor? It's not that hard, just keep the sugar bowl close to your cereal bowl, is that so much to ask? It makes the floor crunchy otherwise and *I can't stand it*. The point is women should be allowed to work, men aren't the only ones, look at Rosie the Riveter. And I thought this outfit could help, I'm not going to get a job at Diego's if I don't stand out and at least make some sort of impression. And here's something else, I can't just go in there and announce that I'm *Miriam*, I have to fit in. I'm going to call myself 'Juanita' and if you want to support me and help me out you'll help."

"You're going to call yourself *what*?"

"You heard me."

" *'Juanita'?*" My dad's spoon stopped above the bowl and his face was truly wondering. "Are you *insane?* I know what I'll call you, '*Sybil*,' that's what."

"Get used to it," my mom said.

As Juanita, my mom squeaked through the house in cheap leather sandals, and spoke in a slight accent that hinted of a life south of the border. The sandals hurt her feet, cramming her baby toe cruelly upward. *Shit*, we heard now and again, as she paused to adjust. *Goddamnit, goddamnit—*. The shoes disappeared one day, abruptly; I thought Juanita had gone with her, and that maybe my real mom was back. But she was padding around the house in bare feet instead. *Mexico is a tropical country, after all*, she said. *They probably don't even wear shoes most of the time there, is what I finally figured out. They move around in the sunshine on warm tiled patios. I'll bet.* And: *It sounds like I would have a big family, doesn't it? Like we would be a big laughing family gathered around the dinner table every night, with lemon trees growing right there in our very own backyard.*

A couple of days after their fight, my mom wrote notes to excuse us from school and drove us to Salt Lake to shop. We hit Mexican import shops that sold terra-cotta planters and bright woven blankets; skinny candles with images of Jesus and weeping saints on the label, and piñatas and ristras. My mom bought all of it, then took us to Diego's for lunch. We sat at the counter this time so my mom could jaw it up with the cashier and the cook. Then she asked for a job application. The cashier looked puzzled, but she gave her one, and my mom filled it out excitedly. We noticed she put her name down as Juanita Taylor, and when we got out to the car I said, "Dad's going to kill you. You know he doesn't want you to work there."

"Blah blah blah," my mom said to me. "That's what I have to say to the both of you, *blah blah blah*. Women should be allowed to work if they want. I know your dad doesn't agree but he's not the boss of me, he's not my *master*, I'm not just his little *sex slave*."

"Are they going to call you?" Jen was finishing her churro in the front seat.

"She said they were looking for somebody," my mom said. "I'm sure I'm qualified to do something, I mean I have lots of kitchen skills and I know how to do the cash register. But what I like is how *exotic* it would be, just listening to the Spanish tongue all day and seeing people use *hot sauce*, for a change. Now listen I'm making tacos tonight and I might bring it up with your dad, if I get the nerve, and I just want you girls to stay quiet. I'll handle it. Don't go blabbing about what we did today *Lucy*, I'm the mother and I know what's best for us and I don't want you kids to grow up without a good, strong female role model. Got it?"

When we got home my mom laid out her treasures and looked unhappily at everything. "I know what's wrong," she said finally. "The *context*, I don't have the right backdrop, what would be perfect is if we lived in a little whitewashed adobe with bright blue flowers out front. But I'll bet, I'll just bet if I start working at Diego's I can get some good decorating ideas." She went to the kitchen and started dinner, ground beef tacos on flour tortillas with cheddar cheese and iceberg lettuce grated in.

"Did you go to Diego's today?" My dad hunched over eating his taco, pretending to read the hot sauce label though it was all in Spanish.

"They said maybe they'd be doing interviews next week." My mom peeled the lid from the sour cream and set it on the table.

"Doing interviews for what? Fake senoritas?"

"I filled out an app," my mom said. "I could make forty dollars a week. It would help us out a lot."

"You're not working at Diego's, Miriam."

"I *will*, if they want to hire me."

My dad put down his taco. He looked at me and I shrugged.

"There are worse things," Jen said.

"You keep your little nose out of this." My dad opened his taco and spread sour cream thickly up one side. *Ha ha*, I mouthed to Jen. "If you want a job, if you really really just have to work somewhere, well then, maybe we can negotiate that. But not Diego's, there's no way. That dress makes you look like a slut and I don't want you buddying up with a bunch of Mexicans."

"You always think it's about sex, which it's not. You think I have a crush on some suntanned Mexican cook, which I don't. You know just from looking I'm probably at least part Mexican, I don't know why you won't just admit it."

"Can we go to the waterslide later?" Jen stirred the sour cream and my dad took the spoon away from her.

"Quit playing with your food."

"They're probably going to call me next week," my mom said. "Probably by Monday."

"Let 'em call."

"You'd better let me do this. If you don't I swear I'll make your life a living hell. There's no reason I shouldn't be allowed to work."

"Look, if that's what this is all about, maybe, *maybe* we can negotiate the job thing. You could do some of the paperwork for All American, or if you just really want to get out of the house maybe we could find you a nice bakery job or something. A few hours a morning, after the girls go to school."

"I told you, I have Mexican blood. I don't know why that's so hard for you to understand."

"Is there someone in particular at Diego's that you want to spend time with, is that it?" My mom met his gaze, and for a minute they had a staring contest. "Because you're pretty interested in hanging around there, if you ask me. Your mom likes dark-haired men," he told us. "Especially if they have furry hair on their knuckles. That's even better. An added bonus."

"Can Jen and I go play?" The kids across the street, Lisa and her twin sister Louise, were going to have a Kool-Aid stand.

"Take one more bite," my dad said. We left them at the table, my mom absently pinching fingerfuls of Cheddar cheese up to her mouth.

One night they left us at home so they could go to a movie. At first Jen and I did all the things we weren't supposed to, searched their drawers and threw the sofa cushions on the floor so we could jump on them, and made chocolate chip cookies with blue food coloring. After a couple of hours we crashed on the couch. It was close to eleven. We turned on the TV and when I woke up I saw them in the doorway, my dad singing, my mom stumbling into him for a slow dance. They stayed like this a minute, moving in a circle, my dad's face in my mom's hair. They both had their eyes closed and their expressions were deeply serious. My dad paused to set a white styrofoam to-go container on the table by the front door.

"What would I ever do without you?" He pulled my mom against him, then lifted her and hugged her tightly. My mom's legs dangled and I heard her giggle.

"That's what I like to hear," she said.

"Are you about ready?" my dad said. "We don't want to be late to this thing."

"Somebody can get the guacamole out of the fridge, if they want to. Which dress looks best on me? I need a professional opinion." The neighbors had invited us to a barbecue and my mom was taking forever. She stood in front of the mirror in her underwear, trying on different dresses. She wore high-waisted white underwear and a white cotton bra, with lacy white cups so immense that the cones seemed to jut out into the air over her stomach.

My dad went to the window and yanked the curtain shut. "Put on a robe or something, would you please?"

"Why?"

"In front of the girls," my dad said. "And we don't want the neighbors looking in, seeing you parading around naked. We've only lived here a few months. We don't want to make any enemies."

"Enemies," my mom said. "Are you kidding? This body would stop traffic. We might make *friends*, is what you mean."

"Don't talk like that in front of the girls."

"It's okay," Jen said. "We can handle it." She was sitting on the floor of the closet, eating croutons from the box. I lay on the bed, watching our mom. When she was half-clothed like this, her presence took over a room. Her nipples were the size of pencil erasers and I always waited, hoping to catch a glimpse. When she took off her bra she lifted down first one cup, then the other, then slid the itchy lacy contraption all the way around until the clasp was in the front and she could unfasten it. Then she scratched herself under both boobs, saying *ahhh*.

"You're not even nine, Jen," my dad said. "And anyway, that's not the point. Just put something on, Miriam. This whole thing is making me nervous."

"Alright, alright," my mom said. She pulled on a pair of black boots that zipped to mid-calf, and struck a pose. "How about this? Maybe I could just go to the barbecue like this."

"This isn't funny. It really isn't." My dad picked her dress up off the bed and threw it hard at her. "Put this on. I mean it." He combed the thin hairs across the top of his head, then sniffed his fingers. "This thing's important. Don't you want to fit in?"

"Oh, I don't know. I guess."

"Do you have to wear that dress? Is that who I'm taking to a barbecue? Juanita? I didn't marry *Juanita*, you know. I married *Miriam*."

"Whatever dress you want," my mom sat down on the bed. "Just pick it out. I'll wear it. Whatever you want me to do. However you want me to act."

"Oh stop," my dad said. "Wear it, then. But if you could at least please try to act normal for the girls." He went to the closet and came back with one of my mom's non-Mexican looking dresses. "You look great in this one."

"That reminds me," Jen said. "Janelle's mom said to tell you that there's a Relief Society meeting. She's going to call you. You're invited."

"Relief from what?" My mom said. "Janelle, Janelle. Is that the family on the corner? What kind of a name is *Janelle*, anyway? I don't know why Mormons have to give their kids names like that. Janelle, Loreen, Doraleen. Is that the family with all the kids?"

"Yes." Jen was making angels on the floor. "She said she'll let you know what time when she calls you."

"Is this dress too short?" my mom turned around. "I could let the hem out."

"You look great," my dad said. "Ladylike. Not trying to draw too much attention to yourself."

"I just have to do my hair, then I'm ready."

"Oh boy," my dad said. "Look out, everybody. Get the gas masks."

My mom went into the bathroom, and I slipped in behind her before she shut the door. She wore her hair like other women in those days, high at the crown and made shiny and crispy with multiple and thick mistings of Aqua Net hairspray. She kept the bathroom door shut because the hairspray made my dad sneeze and complain. And if you were trapped inside when the door shut, which I always schemed to do, *look out*: then my mom opened fire, the hairspray can moving in circles over her head, her switching it from one hand to the other, around, around, around yet again, an *impossible* quantity of hairspray—the air thickening to a fog, her still in the middle, still spraying. She was so brave. When she was done, it took several minutes for the air to clear. She was at the center of it all, her fingers plucking with increasing urgency at the hardening loops, moving quickly to get her hair *just so* before it dried. When my mom checked out her reflection, her eyes widened and stayed that way until she stepped away from the mirror. It was spooky-looking. Then came the moment after spraying where she paused, and then shook her head, unhappy, saying everything was wrong, her hair and teeth, her clothes, everything, just everything.

"I don't even want to go to some silly barbecue, anymore," she said. "Look at this hair, I look like a floozy. I don't know a soul there, and they're not going to accept us. We don't have a single friend in Provo. We left everybody behind in Whittier." She went to the closet, undressed, and started over with a new outfit. "They're all going to be *rich*, and they're going to take one look at us. They're going to see us coming. I don't even want to go anymore, why don't you just go, Bob, you and the kids, I'm still not over my migraine, you'll have a better time without me anyway. Just go. Nothing's right, I don't even have any nice clothes to wear, everybody will be looking and looking, judging us, seeing how we're dressed so poor." She made small circles in the closet, trying to choose something.

"It'll be fine. Wear your red pants, you look great in those," my dad said. "Sexy. You'll be the prettiest gal there."

"I'm not *supposed* to look sexy. Isn't that what you just said? I'm not supposed to wear what I *want* to. I'm supposed to look *respectable*. I need a purse to go with these shoes, is what I need. If I had the right purse this whole outfit would come together."

"You look terrific, Miriam."

"I do *not*." My mom pulled a face, and went for the red pants and a white sleeveless shirt. She looked at herself in the mirror and pulled everything off again. "Everything's so wrong," she said. "Just everything. My Juanita look makes me look so much more exotic and interesting and you don't even care."

"You look pretty." Jen dumped the rest of the croutons onto the floor, then made a pile and loaded them back in the box. I went to the mirror and checked out my own reflection. We were going to the Poulsons', and I had a wicked crush on my friend Margaret's older brother Jake. His teeth always looked clean and his hair was a chocolate-colored triangular point that stuck out over his forehead.

"It's not going to help," Jen said. "You're too young for him."

"Shut up." I borrowed my dad's comb and parted my hair on the other side, which made me look forlorn, with a low monkey forehead. My mom had orange frosty lipstick and when I put it on Jen har harred, slapping one knee.

"Come on now, put those away." My dad took the box from her. "And Luce, take off that lipstick, it looks just awful. We don't want to be late."

"I just wish I had more nice clothes," my mom said. "That's all."

"We're not that bad off," my dad said. "We have enough to go around. Not a lot of extra. But as soon as All American gets off the ground we'll be doing better."

"I guess," my mom said.

"Come on, Miriam," my dad said. "Let's just go to this thing, could we please? I'm sorry I don't make enough. I'm sorry that makes you unhappy. I'm doing the best I can."

"Oh, I wasn't saying that, Bob. Really I wasn't. I look *fat*, don't I? Why don't you all go without me? You'll have more fun, anyway. I'm kind of in the doldrums right now."

"We want all of us to go," Jen said.

"Fine," my dad said. "Come on kids, get in the car. Jen, get the dip. I wish you'd come, Miriam. We really want you to. You look beautiful. If you change your mind."

We dawdled going out to the car. It always happened like this. After our dad had revved the engine for a few minutes my mom rushed out, carrying a pink lipstick and a wad of Kleenex for blotting. "*Well,*" she said, climbing in. "You never know, it might be fun. How do I look, do I look okay?"

"You look great," my dad said.

He was right. We all did. The house had been double checked for locked doors, and the front porch light was a white dot. Everything was in its place. My mom was bringing guacamole to the barbecue and she had the bowl on her lap, double wrapped with aluminum foil. Nothing *could* go wrong, it seemed, not with us all like this.

43

"Anyway, let's not stay long at this thing," my mom said. "I hope the food isn't *all* going to be bland and gringo. I can't just eat guacamole."

My dad sang for a minute: *La Cucaracha, La Cucaracha, running up and down the block.* He slapped my mom's leg, being playful, and she moved away.

"Maybe you can find someone there to flirt with," my dad said. "I live with a whole household full of flirts, don't I? A whole bunch of beautiful girls. I'm lucky, is what I am."

"Ha ha about the flirting thing," my mom said. "Now that I look like a white girl again you're happy, I see."

In Bay Windows, Where She Looked Especially Tragic:

My mom was staring out at the patio, one hand anchored to the curtain, her gaze unblinking and full of sorrow. Was I six? Seven? The house empty.

Well, she said. *You wanted it, so it's what we got. It doesn't look right, it'll never look right.* She collapsed into the window seat, shoved a gingham cushion irritably behind herself. *I should've gone with the other pattern, I shouldn't have listened to you, oh it looks horrible, doesn't it?*

I like it, I said. It was a small brick patio at the back of the yard and we stared at it together while I tried to think what to say. My mom had set up the wrought iron chairs in a semi-circle and a bird flicked from one chair to another, pecking at something we couldn't see. My mom pounded the window furiously. *Get off,* she said, *get off. I hate birds,* she said. *Birds, and secondhand shoes. You never know whose foot has been.*

Herringbone, she said. *That's what I asked, would a herringbone pattern look better. And you said, you said no, and now look at it, just look at it, redoing that thing would cost hundreds of dollars, hundreds, and well now we're just stuck with it. Aren't we.* She gave me a little smile, trying to be brave, trying to rise above. Then her face caved in again and she was sobbing, her hand a claw at the curtain. I knew I should go to her but I stayed in the chair, my feet twined at the rungs. *I'm sorry,* I said finally, and then my own mouth started to wrench up. It was my fault. Together we'd laid the bricks in different patterns across the ground and it was true, I had helped pick. But now I couldn't remember any of the patterns, and now outside the patio was permanent. Because the men had used cement. And cement could never come off. The men had mixed it up and then when it dried between the bricks was what we had now. Gray lines between the bricks which could not be removed, no matter what.

No, I'm sorry, I really am. I don't mean to cry. My mom shook her head at herself. *I mean honestly, honestly Hon, it's just fine. A patio's a patio, isn't it. We can have parties on it. We can have people over.* She looked out again. *It's just, it's just that a herringbone pattern would've looked so nice, so* elegant, *and now it just looks like a regular old patio, doesn't it? Why did you think* this *would look better?*

I don't know.

It just looks so regular, is all. Like we're not anybody. She saw me crying. *Oh, it's okay, Honey. It's no biggie. I can have it done over again. Someday.*

I can't really remember what herringbone looks like, I said finally. The words came out small, something you could swat with a newspaper.

Oh but you do, you do, you absolutely do, remember we looked at it and you said, you said, it looked a little too busy. Like the overall effect was too much.

I still think it looks good. The bird was hopping around, riffling its feathers, happy. Taking a bath.

Oh it doesn't, it doesn't Luce, truly, it looks horrible. I know you didn't mean anything by it but just, just for future reference. Next time we'll try harder, won't we? Her voice caught. *And I can have it redone, I can redo it, maybe in a couple of years. We can wait to have parties, can't we? No biggie. Maybe even in two years, is what I'm thinking. And then we can do a birthday.*

The Poulsons had seven kids and a trampoline in the backyard. When I went to their house after school we watched TV and worked through boxes of Fruit Loops and Frosted Flakes. Their family felt like a real family to me, with noisy teenagers coming and going, giving me high-fives and challenging me to arm wrestle. The TV stayed on right up until dinner time, when Mrs. Poulson called everyone to the table and Mr. Poulson blessed the food. When I stayed for dinner I lowered my head to pray faster than anyone else, and squeezed shut my eyes so hard that it made my forehead hurt; I didn't want to be a Mormon, not if my dad didn't, but I wanted the Poulsons to know I was sympathetic to their cause. They had to be doing something right, I thought, because their family was rich and ours wasn't.

Mrs. Poulson met us at the door, and my mom reached for me automatically. When she was nervous, like when she drove, her hand shot out across the front seat to keep me from flying through the windshield, and then she was my protector. But at other times, like now and like when she had to use the bathroom in a public place, I was the human shield. She dragged me into her, forcing us to hump awkwardly up the stairs into the Poulsons' living room like we were in a two-legged race.

"You can just chuck your stuff on the counter," Mrs. Poulson said. She was wearing a pink baseball cap that tied at the back and a necklace that looked like it was made out of blue Jolly Ranchers. "We're all out back."

"Oh your kitchen, your *kitchen*," my mom said. "Oh you have French doors, I'd *love* to have French doors." She wandered in and tapped at the glass. "Are these beveled?"

"I don't know," Mrs. Poulson said. "I guess."

"Beveled windows." My mom leaned close. "Are they oak? Gee, they look so expensive, they almost look like *gumwood* or something, some tropical wood. I'll bet they are. I'll bet they are." My mom set the guacamole on the counter but her eyes kept jumping around at everything, greedily taking it in. "Oh your house is *great*, it's just great." Her voice sounded pained, like it did whenever she noticed the stuff other people had. Sometimes she even bit her lip and shook her head a little, like it was all just too much. She pulled the foil off the guacamole and cast it off and Mrs. Poulson drifted in noiselessly and plucked up the gooey piece of foil, folding it neatly into a small square before putting it in the trash. My mom didn't even notice.

"Can I go outside?"

"I'll show you the way," Mrs. Poulson said. "Let me just get a serving spoon, this avocado dip looks wonderful, by the way. You really didn't need to bring a thing. Just yourselves."

"You're so sweet," my mom said. "But I always have to bring something, you know, even if it's just little."

"Let me just run a spatula around the rim here," Mrs. Poulson said. She winked at me, but I saw suddenly what was wrong: my mom was serving up the guacamole in the bowl she'd mixed it in, and there was green-brown goo hardening up the sides of the bowl. Plus it looked like she'd yanked the spoon right out before she'd finished even stirring; the guacamole was heaped here and shallow there, like she'd gone to the door in the middle of making it and had forgotten to come back. It looked nothing like the other side dishes Mrs. Poulson had laid out, the glossy untouched rounds of green Jell-O salad and coleslaw garnished with parsley. Mrs. Poulson worked fast and winked at me again, and my mom took the opportunity to wander to the door of the formal dining room.

"What the *hell*," she hissed. One whole wall was covered with china plates and framed photos of Queen Margaret, and a glass curio cabinet held silver commemorative spoons, coronation cups, souvenir tins and wedding plates and medallions. "Oh my God, this is *appalling*."

"Mom, be quiet."

"She can't hear, she's *busy*. Cleaning up my *dip*."

"Are you looking at my collection?" Mrs. Poulson called. "I have to keep everything, *everything*, hung up high or behind glass. John says if we ever win the Publisher's Clearinghouse he'll build me a little studio so I can keep everything out there. But in the meantime I have to make do."

"So you like the Royal Family, then?"

Mrs. Poulson came in, drying her hands on a dish towel. "Now you've got me started," she said. "This is my most treasured piece. It was handed down from my parents." She lifted the plate out carefully. It was a soft focus photo of King George and Queen Elizabeth, and written above their head in a wreath were the words, COMMEMORATING THE VISIT OF THEIR MAJESTIES TO THE UNITED STATES OF AMERICA, 1939.

"Are they dead?" I said.

"He is," Mrs. Poulson said. "Isn't she elegant?"

"Why the Royal Family?" my mom said. "I mean but gee the things are all just beautiful, they really are."

"Our family goes back," Mrs. Poulson said. "We're related to Richard, the Duke of York. And I have the same birthday as Princess Margaret."

"Wow," my mom said.

"I'd better get back out there and be the hostess."

We went back to the kitchen, where Mrs. Poulson offered me a can of 7-Up. That was another thing I liked about their family. Each kid got a whole can of soda every time they wanted, instead of sharing a can between two paper cups poured over ice cubes. My mom started to follow me outside, but at the last second she dashed over to peer into the formal living room. Then she scurried to catch up, dragging at my arm. There was a glassed-in breezeway that led to the backyard, hung with tropical plants, and an ornate wrought-iron chair with an antique doll propped in the seat. "I hate dolls," my mom hissed. "Seriously, they really give me the creeps. I'll bet it's fake anyway, who'd have a real antique doll with kids around?" She paused to peer closely at the chair, and I kept going. Margaret was in the backyard, at the very back of the lot, jumping on the trampoline. I could see her every now and then as she jumped, her knees drawn up to her chest and her hair flying all over. Margaret could do a forward cannonball on the trampoline and off their diving board, and she'd promised to teach me.

"Wait, *wait up*. What does Mr. Poulson do for a living, anyway?"

"How would I know?"

"Don't get smart with me. I'm just trying to help, maybe he could give your dad a job if All American doesn't work out. I'll just bet Mr. Poulson does something with taxes, that's how all these Mormons make their money. Or something with pawnshops, that's what I read, all these straight-laced Mormon men selling guns and tacky gold jewelry on the side. You just know it's true. Where's your dad?"

"He was out front talking to Mr. Poulson. They were looking at his lawn mower."

"Well, I wish your dad wouldn't do that. That's all we need, to be giving away free *lawn care* advice. Look at their yard, look at this *yard*. I'll bet they have a private gardener. I'll bet they have a private Asian gardener, the Asians know so much about aesthetics. I'll bet they do."

"Can I go play with the other kids?"

"Well sure, I mean I guess. Go ahead."

Margaret and I jumped on the trampoline for a while and then went off to snoop in Jake's room. He always wore a red sweater with the lapels of his shirt folded neatly out, and said that when he grew up he was going to be President of the United States. "Boring, boring, boring," Margaret said, after we'd ransacked his drawers, full of neatly folded shirts and rolled socks. "He's going on his mission next year and then my mom said maybe I could have his bedroom." Margaret said. "Oh! My mom said I could take English riding lessons, so you have to ask too."

"What's a mission?"

"That's where a young man goes out into the world and serves the lord by teaching people about the true church."

It sounded mystical to me; I liked the way Margaret said "world," too, like it was a huge crowd of painted people her brother would move through, or like the boat that floated through the "It's a small world" ride at Disneyland. There, the dolls of Many Different Lands sang in chimy, mechanical voices and waved at our boat as it passed, and the harmony of all their voices, the melody as it rose and swelled and our boat was thrust through a wall of canvas flaps, signaling the end of the ride, always made me want to cry and burst out, rush back and climb again into the boat and be carried, back, back to the sweet phony music, the pink plastic hands and creepy pink faces, all smiling, smiling, the Swiss girls and Eskimo boys and then finally—near the end of the ride—the children of America, all different colors and all holding hands this time, the song achingly perfect to me, the little world of the boat and the dolls and everything in color.

We went back outside, where our parents were sitting in a semicircle on the patio. The patio furniture had vinyl flowered cushions and I knew exactly how the chaise cushion could feel under my own bare legs, how it could heat to an odor of dust and plastic and sweat, and how, if I stood up too fast, the vinyl would make a slurpy ripping sound at the back of each thigh. The rest of the kids were racing wild circles on the lawn, the once-white edges of their sneakers stained to green from skidding across wet grass. Mrs. Poulson had laid out the packages of hot dogs and Mr. Poulson was lording over the barbecue grill in a chef's hat. The hot dogs were Oscar Mayer brand, pale and thin and understated, different in every way from the hot dogs our family bought—ones bloated and rubbery and deep pink, twelve to a pack, swimming in juice and a buck less than these.

All around were voices, families. It was twilight and we were safe, everyone was happy, my dad was stroking my mom's ankle, and my mom laughed and kissed him on the cheek. I could hear an airplane, and a lawn mower from somewhere else, and a dog barking far away.

The mountains were a purple gray backdrop and the air was cool with fall, and when I'd stepped through the sliding glass doors and onto the red brick patio it was like stepping into my future, what was promised me, what was promised our whole family if we could just stay together, not fight or move around, not change houses and jobs and schools and cars and names but just act normal and stay put. It was chilly now and the parents had blurred, contented faces; they held clear drinks with paper napkins wrapped pointlessly around the cups.

I stepped off the patio, away from the adults, remote chaperones that seemed all background, while us kids, clear-eyed and quick in bright shirts, were what mattered. When I turned to look back—my dad still leaning forward, my mom's hand still in his lap—they seemed not to have moved, frozen like children in a game of Freeze Tag, their poses exaggerated and creepy, though I imagined I felt movement at my back, felt them race and shuffle and settle themselves before I turned again to look. And still they seemed to move closer, as though the patio were really a parade float: authoritarian and insisting, as it bore toward me, that our family was *just like everyone else's,* that these intact families, ours included, could ride along wearing fixed smiles, waving to the crowd. And if our family stayed together I might someday be one of the homecoming queens who waved and waved, clearing a tiny swathe from a fogged-up windshield, I might someday look like Natalie Wood. And if I didn't want to be Homecoming Queen, maybe that was something Jen might want to be, and I could ride a horse behind the float, instead, kissing it into a trot, the horse's tail braided with silver ribbons.

I knew all about horses: pintos, which were the spotted horses Indian maidens rode, and *appaloosas*, which sounded like *applesauce*.

"You just look so *California,*" Mrs. Poulson was saying to my mom. "So fresh, like you've been getting a lot of sunshine. What's Los Angeles like? We drove through a few years ago, when we took the kids to Disneyland. But how was it to live there?"

"Pretty crazy," my mom said. "There's a lot of political stuff going on right now, lots of young people protesting, you know. I'm not sure what about, but there's lots of activity, we didn't think it was very good for the girls to be exposed to that sort of thing. We liked the idea of being somewhere family-oriented. Or anyway, *I* liked the idea. I'm not sure how Bob feels about it, but," my mom smiled at Mrs. Poulson, and gave a small shrug. "Husbands," she said. "What are you going to do?"

"Well, we're certainly glad to have you in the community." Mrs. Poulson said. "Are you finding your way around okay?"

"Oh yeah, Provo's really beautiful. I wouldn't mind being a little closer to the border, but this is closer to Bob's mom, so."

"Close to what border?" Mrs. Poulson pretended to listen to my mom, but her eyes were going everywhere else, making sure things were set. "Could you put some more napkins out, Margaret?"

"Close to Mexico," my mom said. "That's where I'd really like to be. That's where my family's from, way back."

"Really?" Mrs. Poulson said. "Wow. That sounds so *exotic*. What part of Mexico?"

"I'm still doing research," my mom said. She stared down into her cup of punch and ran her finger around and around the rim, thinking. "I'm not really sure, to be honest, because you know there aren't very good records. My dad was kind of a bigot and he didn't really want to admit to it. But it's so obvious, just from looking at all of us." She touched my hair. "I mean look at her skin color, look at mine."

"She likes to think she's Mexican, anyway," my dad said. "If you ask me we're just plain boring American. Or like you, Julia, from Britain. Anyway, John, I do it all. Not just lawn-mowing, even though that's probably what it looks like. But landscape design, that sort of thing."

Mr. Poulson pointed at my dad with the spatula. "You having a dog? Can I grill you a bun?"

"Can I take English horseback-riding lessons with Margaret?"

"Whoseywhadda?" my dad said. "Whoseyhorseywhadda? You're already taking lessons."

"She's starting *English*." Mrs. Poulson was eating her hot dog with a knife and fork, the plate balanced carefully on her lap. It made me want to push it off, just like seeing all her little glass things in the dining room made me want to break them, though not out of any meanness. "It's a lot more refined, more ladylike, really, than western. They'll even teach her to ride sidesaddle."

"I always thought English riding was kind of, I don't know, *cheesy*," my mom said. "No offense. But just, you know, it was the native Indians who really knew how to ride. The women rode bareback across the plains in freezing temperatures, without a saddle or stirrups. Just wrapped in a bearskin. Can you imagine?" She picked up her hot dog and took a huge bite. She had ketchup on her face and my dad silently motioned her to wipe. But my mom let it stay there for a minute, just long enough to show she wasn't intimidated.

Mr. Poulson was looking at my mom, directly and frankly. He smiled. "Let me know when you're ready for another."

"Oh, she will," my dad said. "She can really tuck it away. She eats more than I do. I think she's got a hole in the bottom of her foot, doesn't she, Luce?"

"I like that about a person," Mr. Poulson said. "It's especially refreshing in a lady."

"You say that now," Mrs. Poulson sipped at her paper cup of Hi-C, then wiped the edge of the cup to catch a drip. She seemed to wipe everything. "But you wouldn't really like it, would you, if I were a big eater. If I polished off a stack of hotcakes with butter, gave myself a big behind."

My mom was fooling around with the chaise longue. "Does this thing adjust?"

"You bet," Mr. Poulson stepped forward and fixed it while my mom stood with her head tipped to the side, gnawing the cuticle of one pinky.

"Could you turn the hot dogs, Hon?" Mrs. Poulson said. "I don't think people want them charred."

"Hey, who's the cook here?" Mr. Poulson said, but he turned them. I liked when my hot dogs blackened and split up the side and got blisters, but Jen said then they were carcinogenic.

"We got the chairs at Leisure Living last year," Mrs. Poulson said.

"Can I ask a personal question? What kind of perfume are you wearing?" My dad leaned towards Mrs. Poulson and held his hand out. She hesitated, then placed her wrist in it and he lifted tenderly, inhaled. "That's really nice," he said. "Thank you. That's smells real feminine. Real European."

"*Smells* European." My mom was lying almost flat on her back and she took off her sweater. "What does that mean, you mean like a Parisien subway or something? In that case give me good old Mexico, any day." A string of pink paper lanterns ran the length of the patio, and in their soft pink light my mom looked unbearably romantic to me. "Those lights look like something your mom would have, don't they, Bob?" I knew that that was a mean secret joke against Mrs. Poulson, since my mom hated the way my nana's house was decorated, with paper fans and bonsai tree landscapes with miniature trickling waterfalls, the sound of which always made me need to pee. Plus, the first time my mom had defined the word "orientalia" for Jen and I, she'd said *sounds like genitalia*, and then she'd had to define *that* word, and she and my dad had quarreled the whole rest of the way home.

"Put this back on," my dad said shortly, and tossed my mom's cardigan over her.

"I'm *hot*," my mom said. "Jen. Where have you been? Off chasing boys already? I thought we had a few more years at least, before you reached puberty. *Please* don't start all *that* yet, I really don't think I can handle the stress."

Mr. Poulson laughed, but he was looking at my mom's chest. Her nipples were hard and showing right through the fabric and Mr. Poulson was staring straight at them. He looked down when he saw that I saw.

"Janelle was showing me her record player," Jen said. "And guess what record she has, The Monkees."

"Davy Jones is kind of sexy," my mom said. She stretched her arms up over her head, getting comfortable. My dad said *I mean it*, and tossed the sweater again. This time my mom just let it slip to the ground. "But too short, I mean obviously Bob's not some strapping macho man but I heard somewhere how Davy Jones is a whole *five-foot-two* or something, I mean you have to wonder about the size of *other* things."

Mrs. Poulson picked up a stack of napkins and fanned them out, the same way she'd done with the magazines on her coffee table. "Has everyone eaten?" She kept her eyes down, fussing with the napkins, her mouth turned down.

My dad stood up. "Well, gotta get these girls home," he said, and shook Mr. Poulson's hand. "It's way past their bedtime."

"We usually stay up until *nine*," I said, but my dad was already heading inside, holding my mom's arm hard at the elbow like he'd just arrested her for shoplifting. "I'll call you tomorrow," I told Margaret.

When we got home my dad sent us straight in to brush our teeth. "Why did you do that?" he was asking my mom in the kitchen. "You had one on when we left, I saw you, we all did, then we go over there to make a good impression, trying to fit in, they were nice enough to invite us and you go and pull that stunt."

"You *told* me to look sexy," my mom said. "You said it would *help*." I heard her yank open the dishwasher. "It was your whole idea."

"You looked like a cheap slut, is what you looked like. My wife, gee, I sure was proud of her tonight. I'm sure your daughters were too, you set a very nice example for them." Jen and I kept brushing, not looking at each other. When they fought we kept on doing whatever we were doing, partly because it scared us and partly because it bought us more time, like tonight. I squirted a fresh blob of toothpaste on my brush and started all over.

"All you do is criticize me," my mom said. "Just pick pick pick. Nothing I do is good enough for you, is it. I'll bet you'd like me to be like *Julia*. All that Royal Family crap. And I loved how you were *courting* her practically, I thought you were practically going to start *serenading* her."

"Do I ask so much, do I? For you to wear a bra so your boobs aren't shivering around all over the place? For you to not lie about being Mexican, which by the way your family sure as hell isn't from Mexico, I don't even know where you got *that* one. Jesus, Miriam."

"Dad should lay off," Jen said, and spit in the sink. "Do you want to sleep in my room?" Her room was at the back of the house, farthest from their voices. "It's okay if you want to."

"Okay." I missed the old days, when Jen and I shared a room and fell asleep every night talking. Then our beds were like little, safe boats, side by side. Her voice always came like one in a dream, fogged over and warm, and practically everything made us giggle.

"Just tell me then," my mom was saying now. "Tell me exactly what you want me to be and how you want me to act, I'll do it. I'll just be your little robot. You won't let me do anything, you don't want me to work, you don't want me to go to college, you don't want me to have any fun." We could hear her in the hallway.

"That's not what I mean, Miriam. That's not what I want. I don't like to boss. I just want you to act *normal*. You scare me. I don't even know what you do all day and then I come home and you're dressed like some senorita. What am I supposed to do?"

"I'm bored," my mom said. "I'm bored!" She pounded something. "I hate Provo! And I hate you!"

"Well, hate me then," my dad said. "And wear a bra next time, for Chrissake. They have bras in Mexico, too, you know."

My dad's side of the bed was firm and smelled like his T-shirts; while my mom's mattress was soft, the pillows flat and sad, smelling of used Kleenex and the space up under her hair. She slept lightly and uneasily, so that by morning her side of the bed was tangled, the covers roped and twisted, her small pillow wadded against the headboard. With my mom it was all hiding, all knots. She slept on her belly with one knee up and kept wads of cotton in her ears and a black eye-mask over her eyes. But what you could see of my dad was right out there. He slept flat on his back, the top sheet tucked under his armpits. He looked like a person sleeping on TV, and when we crept in at night, sick or scared, and said their names—*Mom, Dad*—his breathing stayed even; while my mom—blind, her ears packed shut—murmured to us instantly, inviting us into the warm snarl of her nightgown. When I was sick she was who I wanted. But by morning, after she'd held my head through the vomiting and doled out baby aspirin and sips of water and crackers, I was already turning from her, gravitating to my dad's side of the bed, its cool professionalism and lack of memory.

Nights, I snuck into their room to sleep between them. One night the door was locked, though I could hear them on the other side of it, their voices low, considering me. I fell asleep there, pounding and crying, and in the morning, my mother opened the door, humming, and looked down at me as though I were a bottle of milk. I'd cried so hard that the blood vessels in one eye had popped. It was my dad I was mad at: I knew he'd heard me in the night and reached instead for my mother. Her hands, for as long as I could remember, were musky and warm, as though she'd been touching herself in private places and then had forgotten to wash. Now she touched a hand to my forehead. "You are a little bit warm."

"I know you guys could hear me," I said.

"Luce, I promise. We didn't hear a thing. I wouldn't lie to you. We were so tired, darn it, we both just sacked out."

"I was *pounding*. I was *yelling*."

"Well, I'm sorry. Next time you'll know to just go back to your own bed, won't you? You can't sleep between us forever, Luce. You're almost eight years old. Now look, I have stuff I need to do. Let's not spend all day talking about this. If you want to stay home today that's fine. Is that what you want to do?"

"Can I watch TV?"

"You can watch TV. Boy, your eye looks plain awful. But I have a lot to do today, so you'll have to occupy yourself, okay?"

In the middle of the day in our house was when I liked it best. Then the house felt like some other family's, clean and unoccupied. My mom sat at the table working her way through a second biscuit of Shredded

Wheat. The kitchen floors were freshly mopped and she kept her legs tucked under herself, her white feet cracking at the edges, the sight of which always moved my dad. He bought her lotions that smelled like gardenia and green apple but still her feet hardened and yellowed, around the edges especially, like they had freezer burn. My mom and I had the same feet, with baby toes lying helplessly alongside the other toes, too high on the foot, useless. The phone rang and I watched her talk on the phone, one foot bobbing in her sandal. "We have the same baby toes," I said when she hung up.

"Guess who *that* was," my mom said. "The manager at Diego's! I got the job!"

"Wow," I said. "Congratulations I guess, even if dad is going to kill you."

"Listen, young lady, we can always use money. You never know when circumstances are going to change, you just never know when we might need a nest egg, need to take care of ourselves. You can't just always depend on men, men, men."

"What about Dad's job?"

"What about your dad's job?"

"He makes enough money." I thought about the coffee can she'd shown me when we were leaving the House on the Hill. "You can give him the money from the can."

"What can?" She looked at me sharply.

"From the House on the Hill."

"Listen, Lucy. I'm not kidding at all about this. I'm too happy to get mad at you right now, I don't want to dampen my mood, but trust me, if you ever let on to your dad about our secret you will be one sorry girl. Just one sorry girl. If you want to see me with my jaw broken, if you want to see your dad do horrible things to me, to *us*, well you just go on ahead then and blab it. That money's a secret, it's for if we ever want to go away. Do you understand that?"

"Go away from Dad?"

"You know exactly what I'm saying. Don't act all innocent. So anyway I'm supposed to start tomorrow, oh I can't believe it Luce I'm *so* excited,

I haven't worked since way way before you kids were born, it's just going to be great. But I can't wear sandals, I don't know what I'll do about that, I guess I could wear tennis shoes but now that won't look very authentic, would it, especially with my dress. I'll have to see what the other women wear. Move your leg, okay? I have to check on the meatballs. At least that will make your dad happy, some gringo meal. But I'm going to start eating at Diego's. I'll bet all the employees eat together anyway, sitting around some big round wooden table and laughing. I don't care *what* your dad says, I didn't bring you girls into this world so you could grow up and turn into *housewives*, you need a role model and anyway, the money's really going to help. That's what I'm hoping will change your dad's mind, once he sees that big fat paycheck. Move your leg."

She went to the kitchen. Meatballs were one of her specialties: she mixed ground beef with ketchup and crushed saltines, then cooked the balls in a pan with a can of Campbell's Cream of Mushroom soup, plopped in a slimy beige cylinder from the can. The trick was to *not add water*. It was salty and gloopy, its flavor aggressively bland. Spices were from faraway lands, and burned the tongue and had probably been carried on the back of a camel somewhere, if you thought about it, borne by the hands of men with black pointed beards. Men who wore *sandals*. We kept salt and pepper on the table, and paprika in the pantry for deviled eggs at Easter and Thanksgiving, but that was it. My favorite meal was creamed tuna on toast:

> *Creamed Tuna on Toast*
> *1/2 stick margarine*
> *2 T. flour*
> *2 T. milk*
> *1 can tuna*
> *Melt marg. In saucepan. Whisk in flour and milk. Add tuna, and heat through. Serve over toast.*

It was served over toasted white bread and sometimes, for variety, my dad squirted on a little ketchup.

After lunch my mom and I went shoe shopping. "Our lives are going to change soon," she told me on the way to the mall. "I love your dad, I mean of course I love him, but love isn't everything. People change."

"I don't want to leave Dad," I said. My voice caught. He was somewhere in Provo mowing a lawn, the sweat soaking into the white perma-press handkerchief he wore as a bandana, and I wanted badly to find him, to tell him she had something up her sleeve, even though I wasn't quite sure what. None of us ever knew. She had schemes and plans.

"Well I don't mean *permanently*. I mean, I just mean, after so many years of marriage, you know, it might be time for a break."

"I don't want a break."

"Are you always such a stick-in-the-mud?" She looked over at me. "We could have a good time, you know. You wouldn't have to go to school. We could drive until we got someplace where there were *a lot* of horses. Wyoming. Montana."

"What about Dad?"

" 'What about Dad, what about Dad,' " she mimicked. "What about your old *mother*, how about worrying about her for a change? Anyway, I'm just saying. Not right now, I mean gee I'm supposed to start work, hey I have a job, I know how attached you are to your dad and I'm not saying anytime soon. Just something to think about."

"You aren't working at goddamn Diego's," my dad lunged at my mom and got her dress at the neck. He twisted, trying to tear it off. My mom screamed and tried to get away and then my dad let go suddenly and she fell backwards. Her hand caught on one edge of the tablecloth and then everything went down with her, the plates of meatballs and spaghetti, all fake-blood and cartoon. Jen had her hands clamped over her ears and was shouting *stop just stop*. "You happy now?" my dad said. "You happy?" My mom struggled to get up. "I'm sorry, kids," my dad said, and his voice broke. "Your mom and I, your mom and I—" but he couldn't seem to think what else to say.

. . .

It was the middle of the night and my mom was carrying me to the car. Jen was already strapped in, awake and watching the house alertly, a sentry, as my mom got me settled. "He just needs to know," my mom said. "He needs to know that he can't treat me that way."

I started to cry. "I want to stay with Dad."

"After the way he treated me?" She coasted to the end of the driveway, starting the engine just as we went over the bump.

"Clean," Jen said to my mom, looking back at the dark house. She leaned in and whispered to me, "Just play along."

"Where are we going?" I asked.

"I don't know yet," my mom said. "Any requests?" Her hair was loose and she checked herself out in the rearview mirror. "See, I already look happier. This is how I *should* look. Your dad, your dad just needs to learn that he can't push me around that way. I don't know, maybe we'll just drive for a while. Maybe we'll find a hotel, one with a pool. Maybe we'll drive all night and wake up tomorrow in the House on the Hill." It was cold in the car, and the streets were empty and blue-black and desolate. "Oh, stop it, Luce. Stop *crying*, we're having an *adventure*." I'd started to shake, and Jen drew me in, crooning something tuneless. "It's just really lucky anyway if you ask me that I *had* saved up a little money. Do you want a donut? Would that make you feel better, should we hit a Winchell's?"

"I don't want a donut! I want my dad."

"Luce, it's just to teach him a lesson. Can you understand that?"

"Dad's going to need the car in the morning. First thing. He has to leave at six."

"*I* know what time he leaves. But you know this is our car too, it's not like he has first dibs on it."

"Where are we going?" Jen asked. "What's the plan?"

"Like I said, I'm open to suggestions. I mean we could go all the way to California, why not? It would be nice to at least *try* to have a pleasant visit with my mother, ha ha."

"But then you'd miss your first day," Jen said. "You put so much work into getting hired, is the thing."

"Oh, I know what you're doing. I know what you're doing." She wagged a finger at Jen. "You little imp. Now I'm having fun here, don't rain on my parade, we're on an adventure. We could go to the mountains, maybe we should go to the mountains. And then wake up with birds singing and maybe we could sleep right by a waterfall."

"If we had sleeping bags," Jen pointed out.

"That's true, that's true," my mom produced a duffel bag from under the front seat. "I grabbed a few things. Toothbrushes and panties and pajamas for you both. Oh, Luce, get a hold of yourself. It's not like you're never going to see him again."

"This is crazy. Other moms don't do this. I want to go home."

"You know what other moms do? They obsess over the Royal Family. You'll go home when I'm good and ready. After he's suffered awhile. How come *I'm* suddenly the bad guy, he's the one who hit *me*. Just for having the gall to want a *job,* for wanting to help with the precious *finances.*"

I was trying to figure out how to sneak and call my dad. I crawled onto the floor of the car and ran my hands around, looking for change.

"Anyway, if you're going to be so sour about it, we can stay in a hotel tonight. Instead of camp or drive to California. To tell you the truth I only have forty-four bucks, which sounds like a lot but, plus I have to be at work tomorrow. So we'll go get a bite, maybe get waffles if that'll make you happy, Luce, then find somewhere with a pool. Okay?"

"We should at least call Dad," I said. "He'll be worried." But her plan was working on me. Hotels had cool large beds, and lots of TV channels and tiny paper soaps. Ice buckets, candy machines. Room service.

"Your dad sleeps like a log. You know that. He probably doesn't even know we're gone. This is just a run-through. It's no biggie. We can get waffles *and* donuts *and* stay somewhere with a pool."

"Okay. But I want to be home before Dad wakes up."

"Me too," Jen said. "We really shouldn't worry him, even if you do need a break."

"See, your *sister* at least understands," my mom said. "Well, fine. So it's something. Waffles."

After Village Inn, and then Winchell's, my mom cruised Main Street looking for a hotel. I'd had in mind the Lamplighter Inn, with its logo depicting a horse and bowlered coachman, next door to a miniature golf course. But the Lamplighter was closed, and by two A.M. we were on the outskirts of town. The motels here not only weren't *hotels*—hotels, as my dad always argued, being two stories with room service—but low squalid buildings, past their day and almost all closed anyway, for the season or altogether.

"A pool, huh?" my mom said. "That might be a tall order. What if we stayed somewhere with a TV? How would that be?"

"You said a pool," I gripped the Winchell's bag with its gnawed-on chocolate bar. I wanted to prove things, that a person couldn't just say one thing and then do another. "You promised."

"Well, shit. How should I have known? There aren't any places with pools, Luce. What do I know? I'm a California girl. Be reasonable."

"Maybe we should just go home."

"No way. He's going to pay," my mom said. "Now I know you don't like the looks of it, but I'm out of options, practically, let's at least *try* here, okay?" She pulled into The Aquarius. It was a pink ramshackle place advertising HOT TUBS/X-RATED, TWENTY-TWO-NINETY-NINE A NIGHT, and through a screen of anemic shrubs I could just make out the swimming pool. My mom checked us in. "I just told him," she said, coming back. "I told him, my husband had knocked me around, I'm sure he's no stranger to the ways of the world, well, he shook my hand and then he even *kissed* it, Lucy, kissed my hand like I was a perfect lady." She looked lit-up, ecstatic. There were cigarette burns on the bedspread and I sat down carefully. My mom carried a sleeping Jen in, who woke up halfway, looked at us both blankly and fell back asleep. My mom set her on the double bed and cruised the TV channels. She hooted when a naked woman appeared, then tore the paper from a water glass. "Our new casa," she said. "Damn it, though, I wish they at least had room service. For morning. Oh well."

I sat on one of the beds and took off my shoes. "What are you doing?" my mom said. "What about that midnight dip?"

"Go swimming *now?*"

"Now or never. We have to be out of here by eight if I'm going to make it to Diego's on time. Come on. I even packed your suit."

"It's *dark.*"

"Well that will make it more *fun.* Come on." She tried to take off my sweater.

"I don't want to. I'll go in the morning. When it's light out."

"Luce, I told you. There won't be time. Now you said, it had to have a pool. Well I drove and drove all over looking and now you don't even want to. I can't believe this. *I'm* going, this is my only chance for an adventure, I already promised we could go back to our regular boring life in the morning so why don't you just do this one thing. For me."

"Ask Jen. She'll do it." I could feel my eyes tearing up again.

"Come on. Five minutes." My mom held out her hand and I took it. We went out to the pool, which was dark and black and kidney-shaped, a relic. The chaise longues were all flipped upside down but my mom pressed on. "You first," she said.

"I don't want to, Mom."

"*Fine.*" She took off her clothes, all of them, and executed a glamorous pointy-toed dive. I looked back at the motel lobby. It was dark and still. And then I started to cry again for no reason except that it was the middle of the night and she was scaring me, her bold, naked white body and the way she popped up to the surface, saying *ahhh*, her legs doing an immodest butterfly. The next morning our dad would go to his knees and cling to us, Jen and I together and then my mom, and I would feel his trembling, his fear and dampness, through his thin yellow shirt. "Come in," she called. "Are you coming in?" I shook my head no. She paused at the edge of the pool, gasping, her hair slick, like a model in a mouthwash commercial. "Are you *crying* again? Because you know what, Lucy, there's a whole world out there. I don't mean to lecture. But this is preparation for Life. Preparation one-oh-one." She started back across the pool, doing laps. "Fine, so fine. Just give me *five more minutes,* okay? That's all I ask."

My mom worked at Diego's three days. At the end of the third shift she came home exhausted, her feet blistered and her white embroidered dress stained with enchilada sauce. She'd been hired as a *cashier*, she told us, but instead they wanted her to do *everything*: shred lettuce and wipe down tables and even clean the *bathrooms,* the *Men's Room*, if we could believe it, and it was just rush rush rush all day long and they practically never let her sit down for a break.

"If I just spoke Spanish," she told us sadly, peeling open Band-Aids for her blisters. "But I didn't really fit in, I mean even though we have some Spanish blood they still just think I'm white, that's what's so crazy."

"Well anyway, we're glad you're back," my dad stood in the bathroom doorway. "Wait," he said, and put antiseptic ointment on her blister before she applied the Band-Aid. Then he got down on one knee and kissed her foot. "And if you really want to work. Diego's wasn't good enough for you, was the thing. We'll find you a nice job in someplace air-conditioned." When she stood up he held her hand while she hobbled down the hallway and that was sweetest of all because then they looked like an old couple, leaning and tottering their way to the TV set.

"You did a good job, mom," Jen said. "It was just too much work."

"Well, I hope you kids aren't ashamed of me. I really did try." Jen and I tagged along behind. Even though she'd only been gone three afternoons in a row it felt like she'd just come home from the hospital after a long illness.

"We're proud of you," I said, and meant it. "I'm sorry I didn't want you to work there before. Do you want a pillow behind your back?"

"That would be nice," she settled onto the couch. "Let's do something fun later, shall we? Go to the drive-in or go get ice creams. How's that sound?"

Once, on the way home from school, Jen and I took a shortcut through the vacant lot near our house. I hopped up onto a piece of plywood, ran the length of it before it tipped to reveal a litter of puppies in a torn Hefty bag underneath. Four of the puppies were dead, their muzzles hard and cold, their tiny triangle ears unbelievably soft. But two were still alive, and Jen and I took one into each sweater and made them a bed in the basement. We kept one of the puppies, the one with a peanut butter–colored face and a head that looked too large for her body, and called her Peanut Brittle, Brittle for short. I couldn't get over it: someone knotting shut a garbage bag full of puppies and tossing it in an empty field. I couldn't get over that the other puppies had died while every day Jen and I had passed the lot on our way to school, and then passed it coming back again, and that each time the puppies had been a little weaker and still I'd just walked on without knowing, a spelling test dangling from my hand, my thermos rattling in my lunchbox. Margaret believed in God, but not me; and I was glad neither of my parents did, glad I didn't have to. If there was a God, He was cruel at worst and sloppy at best, leaving the puppies to die like they were no more important than a bag of shoes. I wanted nothing to do with Him.

Jen and I were watching *The Courtship of Eddie's Father* when the phone rang. Eddie and his dad had the kind of relationship that I sometimes fantasized about having with my dad, one without siblings or mothers and where I'd ride on my dad's shoulders as he strolled the beach, and then I'd ask a wise question and he'd give me a wise answer while the theme music kicked in. If there were a mother figure, she'd be there by proxy, like Mrs. Livingston, the Asian housekeeper who never picked at my dad or forgot to wear a bra or caused trouble.

"You get it," Jen said.

It was Mr. Poulson. "Is your mom around?"

"Who's calling?"

"This is John. Margaret's dad. Is this Lucy? How are you?"

"Good."

"Well, that's good. So listen, is your mom there?"

"She went to get hamburger buns."

"I'll just try to catch her another time."

"Okay." I hung up and wrote his name next to the phone. My dad especially hated when we forgot to take down messages, since it might be a customer for All American. Then he called back.

"Never mind," he said, and laughed a little. "I mean you don't need to leave a message for her. I'll probably talk to her soon and anyway, it's not important."

"You don't want me to tell her?" I could hear the theme music starting: *People let me tell you about my best friend—*

"Nah. Forget it."

"Okay." I hung up, and wrote his name in large letters next to the phone and drew a dark box around it: JOHN POULSON CALLED FOR MIRIAM, 3:20 P.M. Then I went back to the TV.

"Who was it?"

"Mr. Poulson called for Mom."

"Mr. Poulson? What for?"

"I don't know."

"Well, you'd better not have written it down. If Dad sees it he'll kill her." Jen went to the kitchen and tore the message off the notepad, then came back. "Are you stupid? Do you want to see her get a black eye?"

"Why?"

"What do you mean, 'why'?"

"Why would she get a black eye?"

"In case you hadn't noticed, Dad's *afraid*. He gets *jealous*. Am I the only person who notices anything around here?"

"Well, it's her fault, if she's not even going to wear a bra."

"Typical," Jen said. "I'm sure you're going to defend him. Daddy's little favorite."

"Well, you're Mom's," I said. Then we both subsided, because there was nowhere else to go. It was like there was an invisible line sometimes dividing our family, with me and my dad on one side and Jen and my mom on the other.

When winter came, my dad decided to run a Christmas tree lot. He had to do something to make money, he argued. It was that or shoveling sidewalks. He already had the trailer, which would help with transporting trees. My mom hated the idea.

"It's *worse*," she said. "*Worse* than mowing lawns, it really is, Bob, we're going straight downhill."

"I knew you'd say that." My dad had his *Reader's Digest* open, but he was jiggling one leg, getting mad. "I'm doing it. It's already a plan, and I thought you might even be able to help. It'll have to be a family enterprise, I can't do it all myself, the hours will be pretty much round-the-clock. But I was thinking maybe you could help with the books, practice your math skills before you start at the Y. Plus we need to save up for your tuition." He was trying to compromise now, trying to meet my mom halfway.

"Really?" my mom said. "Don't tease me about this, because I really want to go. Can we afford it?"

"I think so. But I have to do the Christmas tree lot. What do you girls think?"

"We could make signs," Jen said. She was the artist in the family, the one who lettered signs for lemonade stands and our yard sale. She'd spread the paper out on the floor and work with her tongue at one corner of her mouth.

"I think it sounds cool," I said. "We could work the cash register."

"A college girl," my dad said. "Who'd have thought I'd be married to a college girl?" My mom kissed him, giving him the tongue. She reached down to tip back his recliner and crawled on top of him. "How's about you two go outside and scout for trees?" my dad said.

We sold trees right up until Christmas Eve, trying to get everything done in time to go to my nana's for Christmas dinner. My dad rented a parking lot a block away from the elementary school and most days Jen and I walked there, cramming into the trailer to warm our hands at the space heater. Then my mom would show up, still nervous from having had to drive in snow, and she always brought soup and rolls and oatmeal cookies. My dad didn't really need the help; the customers were happy to tie their own trees to the top of the car, and he could ring them up. But he said it was good for public relations. All his life he'd wanted us to have a family business. He wanted us to be a singing group like the Von Trapps or the Jackson Five and travel the country in an RV.

My dad called the lot "Olde English Trees," and had the sign made up in an antiquated font that was hard to read until you got up close. His idea was to set the lot apart from all the others by making it seem classy and British, and it seemed to be working: we were selling five or ten trees a day in the weeks before Christmas. He had Jen and me tie green-and-gold plaid ribbons to some of the display trees and he set up a cassette player that played "O Tannenbaum" over and over. His last idea, the one he said would really blast the trees out the door, was to dress up like characters from *A Christmas Carol*.

"I'm telling you," my dad said. "Look at all the other lots, you have the trailer and chain-link fence and then some guy smoking a Marlboro and wearing his hat backwards. Those guys don't care about atmosphere. They're just there to make a buck. Our place will be different. People will come here to buy their trees and then come back every year afterwards, right girls?"

My mom kept shaking her head no. "I'm not dressing up like I work at Disneyland."

"You'll dress up like *Juanita*," I said. I was always on my dad's side. I didn't think it would kill any of us to dress up, not if it meant our family would make more money. It would be fun.

"Juanita is my heritage, young lady. Yours too. You keep up like that and I'll wash your mouth out with soap."

"What do you think, Jen?" my dad said. Jen was peeling the plastic from a tin of shortbread. "Put that next to the cash register, would you, Honey? Oops, customers." He pulled his jacket from the hook and stepped outside. My mom set up one of the folding chairs and plopped down. She passed out shortbread.

"It wouldn't be too bad, Mom," Jen said. "You could wear a long dress and your hair in a bun. What else is there for me to do?" Jen was always organizing something. The shoes in her closet were lined up in rows and she folded her underwear before she put it away, and her hair was never in her face and she chewed with her mouth shut. She was the lady of the family, and I was the tomboy.

"You could put change in the cash register. Break open a roll of pennies, why don't you?" We watched my dad stroll the lot, trying to help the couple choose a tree. He always started with the most expensive trees and then worked his way to the back. The man had a dog on a leash and when they paused too long, the dog lifted its leg. Jen and I rapped at the window, trying to get my dad's attention.

"Let him do his thing. Don't bug him. Can you believe your old mother's going to start college? You'll probably graduate before I do." She took off her shoes and held her feet in front of the orange coils of the space heater. My dad came back with three dollars and waved at the couple as they dragged their small tree past the window.

"They're newlyweds," he said. "They just wanted a little one for their first Christmas. Have you thought any more about the costumes?"

"If you want to do some fake Limey thing, well fine," my mom said. "But I'm not dressing up. You three do it. I'll even help make the costumes, how does that sound? That'll be my contribution."

"You'll stand out like a sore thumb," my dad said. "We're supposed to be a family. Come on, Miriam. It's not gonna kill you. We sure could use the money. Tuition's three-hundred dollars a semester."

"No," my mom said. "No no no no no. I have to say, though, I like this cookie idea. I haven't had shortbread since we left Whittier."

"That was actually Julia's idea," my dad helped himself to a short-bread. "Didn't I tell you? She thought we might want to do hot wassail, too, to pass out while customers looked around."

"What's wassail?" Jen had dumped open too many packets of pennies and now she couldn't get the cash register shut.

"Like cider."

"Oh *Julia's* idea," my mom said. "Well, that figures. Why does everybody always think they're related to *royalty*, anyway? Why isn't anyone ever related to an eighteenth-century garbage man?" She reached for another piece of shortbread, shaking it free of the pleated paper wrapper. "The British are just a bunch of *imperialists.*"

"Then stop eating all those," my dad said.

The trees were my favorite thing. They were like people. Most of them were Blue Spruce, a soft purpley blue and bushy and thick, but my dad stocked a certain number of Austrian pines for the families who needed a cheaper tree, and he took the time to try to make them look nice. The other lots in town that sold cheap trees left them lying in a depressing pile with twine still hanging from the trunks like the trees were prisoners. Then when you stood them up the trees looked skinny and crushed and that's what you got for your three dollars, like the poor people had already done something wrong. But my dad was sensitive to this. He stood the cheap trees right alongside the spruce and spritzed them all with Tree Seal so they'd stay fresh-looking. He gave away boughs for free instead of charging fifty cents a bunch like the other lots did, and made the lot a sort of fairyland by putting lights on some of the trees and arranging others in clumps so that customers could walk into piney cold groves and not be able to see the trailer at all, like they were in a forest.

For our costumes, my mom bought Jen and me long, dark-blue dresses from the Salvation Army. Mine had a strip of bandana print fabric along the hem, but other than that I thought it looked authentic. We wore bonnets with white lace sewn at the edge and velvet capes with a drawstring at the neck, and Jen wore her hair in a bun. But my dad looked best of all: he'd rented a Ben Franklin costume from the costume shop, with knee-length velvet britches and a white-shirt with lace at the cuffs, and black chunky-heeled shoes with enormous silver buckles. He had a cravat and his coat had long dark tails. "You look like a cross between Ben Franklin and Jiminy Cricket," my mom said, but my dad was right: after we started wearing the costumes, business more than doubled. He hired two boys from the high school to help and by Christmas Eve there were only seven trees left.

"We should pack it in pretty soon," my dad said. "When is the turkey supposed to be ready?"

"I tried to time it so it'd be done around six," my mom said.

"That means nine, right girls?" my dad winked at us, because she could never time it right. She tried, sometimes setting the alarm for five in the morning so she could get up before all of us and stuff it and have it ready at the same time all the neighbors were eating. But invariably she'd sleep in or forget to preheat the oven or have to send my dad to 7-Eleven at the last minute for a roasting pan or aluminum foil. She could never seem to remember the equation: twenty minutes per pound of meat? Or was it fifteen or thirty? So that one of us girls would have to fetch her copy of *The Joy of Cooking*, my mom's only cookbook, and get lost in the crisp yellow pages, the talk of dishes we didn't recognize: chitterlings ("just after slaughtering, empty the large intestines of a young pig while still warm . . .") tomato aspic, Eggs-in-a-Nest, things only my nana would know about. And my mom hated dealing with the turkey itself. It was goosebumped and slippery in the sink, the pelvis yawning lewdly. She'd dig out the neck and gizzard and give the gizzard to my dad to fry up in a pan with butter, because my dad was Old School and Iowa and ate such things and also pronounced two-by-four, *tuba four*.

"Should we close up?" my mom said. "Do you think we'll have any more customers?"

"Here comes somebody," Jen said.

It was Mr. Poulson. "Ho ho ho!" he called. "Season's Greetings."

"We were just about to close up shop," my dad said. "Where's your family?"

"Oh, Julia's doing something with cookies and melted Lifesavers. Don't ask me." He looked at my mom and then his eyes went to us, my dad, nervously back to my mom. "She's always got some project."

"Merry Christmas," my mom said. She looked too long at him and my dad stepped between the two of them, just enough to block her view.

"You girls should go inside before you freeze," my dad said. "You too, Miriam. I'll take John around the lot."

"I'm okay. I like the crisp air," my mom said. She drew it in, then wrapped her arms tightly around herself and stamped her feet in the snow. "Brrr! It makes me want to go for a nice, snowy moonlit walk."

"Get in the trailer," my dad said again. "You'll freeze. You don't want to catch cold, have to miss out on school next semester." He stepped away, and Mr. Poulson followed reluctantly. "Over here are where we put the spotlights," my dad said.

"Did you see how he looked at me?" my mom asked. We went into the trailer and she turned the heater to the highest setting, then peered out at them. "See how it is, even though he's Mormon he can't help it. That's what's really so sad. Oh, just how his eyes went all over me." She looked bright and strange. She kept touching herself, her neck and hair, her throat. "You girls will see, when you're older. How much power you have."

"That makes me sick," I said. "How you're acting. You're married, in case you hadn't noticed."

"Lay off," Jen said.

"You both make me sick."

"You'll see what I mean, when you get closer to puberty. Your sis understands, don't you Jen Jen? Oh, I feel all *tingly*. Just the way his *eyes*."

"I'm going back out," I said.

"I'll come, too," my mom said.

"Mom, don't," Jen said. "Just stay here."

"Great. He's leaving already," my mom said. "Your dad probably

made him feel threatened, is what happened. Probably scared him off."
We watched Mr. Poulson get in the car. He beeped as he pulled out.

"It's a wrap," my dad said, coming back. "Let's get out of here."

"What did he want?" My mom fiddled with my dad's collar and he
fixed it himself, impatiently.

"He just wanted a few business tips," my dad said. "He's thinking
about doing his own lot next year."

"No kidding, his own Christmas tree lot? Gee. I didn't know they
needed the money."

"Contrary to what you think, this has been quite the money maker,"
my dad said. "We've made enough to pay for your college tuition, don't
forget. How many husbands would do that? Let their wives go to
school? Probably not John, for example."

"True. True," my mom said. "Oh, Hon, I'm so excited. Gee, that
really is terrific of you."

"Let's hit the road," my dad said. We helped him line up the
remaining trees at the curb and Jen lettered a FREE TO GOOD HOME sign.
And when finally the lot was empty, when finally it was spring and it was
a regular parking lot again, it seemed like our family was still sometimes
there, still at the beginning of things. I'd think about how maybe we'd
rent it every year after that and how the same families would come back
for their trees, just like my dad said, standing like secrets out of the sight
of the trailer. Taking in the cold air and then leaning to a branch, like Jen
and I did, and breathing in for the deep cold pleasure. It was like
smelling the wrist of a beautiful lady, to do that. And it was a private joy.

But the next winter was different. The next winter someone else would
have to rent the lot because by then, our family was somewhere else.

IN LUNCHBOXES,

where very often we found her loving and attentive, in boxed lunches packed neatly; the stinky thermoses full of milk, the sandwiches on white bread and cut into animal shapes. Alongside the sandwich, affectionately tucked, two cookies and an apple. Now and again, pink frosted cupcakes. But my mother had never been much for protocol, and later all this changed; by then she was working two jobs and our lunches were last-minute, tossed into brown paper bags reused so often that they were like soft fabric around the top. The sandwiches themselves were spread with gritty health-food store peanut butter, and, in the interest of reducing our sugar consumption, nothing else. Also, to save time my mom had started to break, rather than cut, the sandwiches in half; leaving jagged edges exposed to the inside of the Baggie, where the peanut butter left smears. When pressed my mom would laugh, as though this whole mothering business, this whole silly housewife thing, was ludicrous, bewildering. I think that she was right about this. But we were children; we longed for potato chips, for whole sandwiches cut in half with a knife. The lunches continued to get thrown together and we compelled her to make them, though we knew it made her late for work. We continued in cafeterias to peer into bags that held unwashed and unshaven carrots, or very brown bananas, or sugar-free sesame cookies. The cookies were homemade, and missing, as always, certain essential ingredients; since when it came to baking my mom believed in leaving out every dry ingredient, spices included, beyond salt and flour. *You don't need baking powder,* she'd say, *forget about cream of tartar, I never put it in. Pepper? I don't think we have any.*

Later, in college, I baked the way she'd taught us: everything for forty-five minutes at 375 degrees, which as it happened pretty much did work for everything: baked potatoes, chicken breasts, casseroles. She cooked her way through the nineteen sixties that way, which you had to love.

Y ou girls okay?" My dad checked us in the rearview mirror and my mom turned her head to give us a small, sad smile. I loved her so much; we all did. Without her our family was nothing. For Christmas I'd gotten a stuffed poodle, white with a single bristly pink curler on the very top of the dog's head. A tiny pink brush dangled from its paw. Also, I'd gotten a red cowboy hat with a string under the chin, for my Saturday riding lessons. Jen had slippers with rabbit faces on the toes.

In the front seat my dad was trying to be jovial. He kept moving the mirror around and making faces.

"She hates me," my mom said. "She always has, she's never liked me. And now we have to spend the whole day. Our *whole Christmas.*"

"I thought we decided, Miriam," my dad said. "Thanksgiving with your mom and Christmas here."

"I know," my mom said. "I know. We did decide. And I don't want to quarrel, not on Christmas."

"We don't have to stay overnight." My dad unwrapped a stick of Juicy Fruit and kept his hand to his face, smelling it. "Sap," he said. "We made a lot. I'm glad we decided to do it. I know that having a tree lot isn't the most glamorous job but let me tell you, Miriam, that's going to cover your tuition for at least one quarter. We did great." He passed the rest of the gum back to us. Our grandpa worked selling Wrigley's gum and he liked to see us chewing and enjoying it when we showed up at the house. "It's just for dinner, just for a couple of hours. We can check into a motel, if you want. She's got too many people at the house, anyway."

"Why does she hate me?" My mom accepted a stick of gum from Jen, and pushed it slowly onto her tongue. "That's what I wonder. Because I'm not good enough for her son, is what she thinks. Because I'm not pretty enough or smart enough."

"She's old," my dad said. "Things make her cranky, is all. It's not personal." He winked at me in the mirror. "Did Santa treat you okay this morning?" I gave him the thumbs up. Sometimes it felt like it was just me and him in the Real World, acting normal while Jen played games in the basement and my mom sat upstairs being sad. None of us ever seemed to know how to bring her back.

"Well it's personal when she takes it out on me, isn't it. When she won't even look me in the eye. Won't even have a conversation with me. Never wants me to help in the kitchen."

"She's old and set in her ways, that's for sure." My dad flipped on the radio.

"But why *Christmas* with her. And why *Thanksgiving* with my mom? Why did we decide it that way? Spending the more important holiday with your family. It's always like that, isn't it? Because you still have both parents but I don't. So yours come first."

"Can we finish this conversation later? It's Christmas. Let's not fight."

"Anyway, the girls get bored. Don't you?" my mom looked back at us. "No toys, nothing. I don't know why she can't at least have toys, with all the grandkids coming over. Doesn't that seem weird to you, Luce?"

"I brought my poodle and hat," I said.

"That's right. That's good. I'm glad you'll have something to play with, something to do. At least my mom makes an effort, I mean she doesn't have a lot of money but at least she tries."

I took the curler out of the poodle's hair and brushed out the tuft with the tiny hairbrush. Next to me, Jen made the rabbits sniff up and down the back of my mom's seat, and I swung an invisible lasso and dropped it over my dad's head. I thought about my nana's house, enormous and shadowy with thick burgundy carpeting and back-lit curio cabinets crammed full of statues. My nana liked things from the Orient and most of the statues were of kneeling Asian women wearing satin kimonos, their tiny white hands making a bed for one dainty painted cheek. After she kissed us girls, enthusiastically and on the mouth and with a satisfied *mwah* sound, she would say, *now don't touch anything without asking*. Her dishes were an apple pattern, heavy and off-white, and she used saucers under the coffee cups and real silver forks and her toaster cover was a black mammy grinning and holding open her skirt to make way for the yawning, bulbous chrome toaster. The bedrooms were dimly lit and smelled like lilac talc, and in one back bedroom—the one where we were instructed to play, if we felt like being rambunctious—was a daybed thick with slick round pillows, the pillows deep purple with narrow, elaborate pleats. Sometimes we drew the curtains in this room and when the light flooded in, it always surprised us. There was a whole world out there, with people bicycling and cars honking.

"Well let's just not stay all weekend, okay?" my mom said. "I know she's your mom. I know it's Christmas. But honestly, honestly, I just can't believe we're doing this. It's just not the way I imagine my Christmas. Provo's one thing, but *St. George*. It's just tacky and full of old people. When I think of Christmas I think of sledding and hot toddies and singing carols by the fire. This isn't exactly what I had in mind for my life. Listen, can we please stop? I really do need to use the restroom."

"What did you have in mind for your life?"

"Oh, I don't know," my mom said. "Lots of dancing, far into the night, under tropical skies." She flipped on the radio. *So don't play with me, 'cause you're playing with fire*, Mick Jagger sang.

"Please turn that off," my dad said. "He's a fairy."

"I think he's kind of cute," my mom said.

" 'Playing with fire,' " my dad said. "Yeah sure, Mr. Puny. What are you gonna do about it? You and who else's army?"

"He's not that bad," my mom said. "I think he has a great voice. We hope you girls are having a good Christmas." My mom draped her arm across the top of the backseat, turning to see us better. "I need kisses. I need some sugar. I'm lonely. Are you going to find a gas station?"

We swarmed her, kissing, until my dad said that's enough, we're gonna go off the road already. Sit back, that's my girls. He pulled into a Chevron station.

"You girls stay here," my mom said. "I'll be right back." She took her purse, and for a minute my dad thought about it. He drummed his fingers, watched her cross the parking lot and turn the corner of the building. But then it got too much for him. He started the car, swearing when the engine wouldn't turn over, and drove around and lurched to a stop directly outside the grimy white door of the Ladies' Room. When my mom came out she looked incredulous and slammed the door too hard when she got back in. "You don't have to *watch* me every second, now do you. Gee I mean I might want to do something crazy like go buy myself a pack of *gum. Jesus.*" She stared out the window for a few minutes, replaying the scene in her head, shaking her head slightly with disbelief. "So we're not gonna stay all weekend, right?"

"Well, we can't be rude, we can't just go and leave. But we can eat and then open presents and make an early getaway."

"I mean your mother's nice, she's been great to the kids, I'm not saying that. But I'm too liberal for her, I know that's what she thinks."

"Just don't bring up the college thing." My dad said.

"I can go to college if I want. I can even get a full-time job afterwards, if I feel like it." My mom pulled out a fingernail file, and worked over her fingernails one by one.

"Don't talk like that," my dad said. "The Christmas tree lot was one thing."

"Oh *please.* There are worse things than my offering to help." My mom pointed the tip of the file in his direction and I made an invisible lasso and dropped it over my mom's head, yanking her back against the seat.

"No fighting," Jen said. "Merry Christmas, everybody."

"Gee whiz, Honey, we're not fighting. Your dad and I just don't see eye to eye on some things, and that means we have to have a discussion. That's all. Let's talk about something else, shall we? Anybody see any interesting license plates?"

Nana met us at the door. The door of their house was wide and opened slowly and it always took a minute to decipher my nana in the dusk of the foyer, bent and exotic looking. She looked that way right up until the time, thirty years later, when she died: her hair coppery and elaborately rolled, her lipstick hot red. Nana had been a figure skater and she was strong and long-legged, with a smoker's voice and painstakingly penciled eyebrows.

"Merry merry!" my nana said. Grandpa Lee loomed behind. *Hey hey!* he said when he saw us kids, and snuck us each a trial-size pack of Freedent, the newest gum from his company. It was for people with dentures, he said, but we girls should try it out, chew it and see if it didn't feel less sticky than traditional gums. *And then let me know,* he said. *I can expect a report. But take your time, chew slowly, really get all the flavor.* His eyes, magnified by ancient lenses, trembled and bobbed like goldfish. Lee wasn't particularly smart, my mom told us, but he meant well. He took us girls through the living room and out the sliding glass doors to the patio. At some point Grandpa Lee had learned to pour concrete and now the whole backyard was one giant patio, with a thick ring of lush tropical plants at the perimeter and concrete rabbits and squirrels crouching in the leaves. Over the years, as my grandparents waned, the plants on the patio did, too; slowly the Bird of Paradise and gardenias died off and the ring grew wider and thinner so that you could see beyond the plants, to the concrete-block fence. But for now it was scented and dense. We worked at the gum and waited to open presents, waited to be called to the table where my nana served olives and pickles and cocktail onions from a cut crystal saucer. Nothing in my nana's house ever seemed to change, which we liked, though it gave my mom the creeps. *New carpeting at least*, she'd say. The Freedent was oily and chlorine blue, probably perfect for people with dentures. We tried to blow bubbles but our tongues kept breaking through, and then there was Grandpa Lee dressed as Santa, ho-ho-hoing and waving us back inside.

"You want some of these?" The spoon hovered over my plate, and I nodded. Nana deposited a glob of yams onto my plate, and I swirled them with the back of my spoon. When my nana cooked yams she cut them up in a casserole dish, alternating layers of yam with brown sugar, butter, marshmallows, and maple syrup. It appalled my mom, who couldn't even eat them. Jen was already on her third helping, and my mom shook her head no.

"Eat some ham first," she said.

"Bob tells me you're going to start college," my nana said.

"Well, just a couple of classes." My mom laughed nervously and toyed with her neckline. My nana's gaze was piercing, her eyebrows frightful. She watched my mom pick at her salad.

"Who's going to take care of the girls?"

"We can stay home alone. We're old enough." Jen helped herself to several olives and slid one on each finger.

"Oh no, you certainly can't, young lady. And take those off, we don't play with food in this house."

"May I please be excused for a minute?" Dinners at my nana's always took too long, so I tried to break them up with trips like this one to the guest bathroom, where I took off my shoes and stood on the bathroom scale or spritzed a piece of toilet paper with my nana's perfume, which came in a dispenser with a stiff pink rubber bulb. Then I flushed the piece of toilet paper and slid open the window above the toilet to see if any of the neighbor's cats had appeared in the backyard. Nana's bathroom was carpeted and the lid of the toilet had a fuzzy maroon slip-on to match. I stalled as long as I could and when I finally got back to the table everyone was right where I'd left them, around the table drinking cup after cup of weak coffee, and the conversation seemed to be in the exact same place.

Jen was taking care with her posture but her gaze had glazed over. "Ask if we can go watch TV," she hissed.

"Why do you need to take classes?" Lee said. "You're a smart lady, as it is."

"Let's change the subject," my dad said.

"It's only for fun. Just so I can keep my mind stimulated. That's all." My mom was playing with the relish dish, using the tiny fork to stab at a pickle, a radish. My dad took the fork away from her and she gave him a look. He handed it back, shrugged at us kids.

"How can you afford tuition?" Nana said. "That's money you should spend on other things. Are you thinking about getting some kind of job, later? Is that what you're thinking? I don't like that idea one bit. I just have to let you know my two-cents-worth."

"Lay off, Mom. She doesn't *have* to work, I've told her that."

"Didn't your own mother work in a bank?" Nana said, and ladled a creamed onion onto my plate. "Just one," she said. "One onion never killed anybody."

"She worked part-time," my mom said.

"Let's talk about something else," my dad said. "Everybody doing all right? Everybody getting enough to eat?" He looked at Jen and me. "You're excused."

"Well, you worked, as a young woman," my mom said dangerously. "I mean, gee, you taught ice-skating, didn't you?"

"That was different," Nana said. "A whole different thing, I didn't have little girls at home. Just Bobbie, and he was no trouble. He used to come to the rink with me and eat a sandwich and do his homework. And I did it because I had to."

"Well really, *really* it's nobody's business but ours, is it," my mom said. "I mean, gee."

My nana made a face, to show she wasn't impressed. But she shut up about it, and after a few minutes my mom excused herself. My dad went after her and Jen and I slipped away. *None of her goddamn business,* my mom hissed, and then the sound of a door closing hard.

"Hey," Jen poked me. "Would you rather die from freezing to death, or from heat?" I let my mouth fall open a little to make my sleep look more convincing. Then she pinched my nostrils shut until I gave up and said, "Heat."

"Not me. I'd rather freeze. Because if you *froze,* you'd just gradually go to sleep. If you were in the heat you'd start to see mirages and crawl along the sand, going, *water, water.*"

The waistband of my lacy tights was cutting a mean line across my stomach. I pulled off my shoes and wriggled out of my tights, threw them on the floor of the car, where they snapped back into a punishing little ball.

"I miss being closer to my own mother," my mom was saying. I watched her talk, her mouth making soft sad shapes in the darkness. She brought a Kleenex to her nose and her shoulders started to shake. "I miss her!" she said. "Couldn't we move farther west, couldn't we, just so the girls could have her close?"

"We'll see," my dad burrowed in the glove compartment and found a cigarette.

I thought about what Jen had said about the heat. But on the other hand freezing to death would be a slow hardening, ears and toes and nose first. "I'd still rather die of heat," I said. I pictured myself naked on a rock, stretched and burnt out and sinking. In a few months what was left on the rock would just be an outline, like someone had traced me with chalk.

"What kind of a conversation is that?" my dad said.

"Maybe Lake Tahoe."

"You don't even *like* your mother," my dad said. "She drives you crazy. Can you imagine it, really Honey, if we all lived in the same town?

She drives *me* crazy. All that artsy stuff she does, when really it just means she can't hold down a job. All that unicorn crap."

"She's an artist," my mom said, but I heard her giggle. My dad was encouraged. "All those drawings of castles and fairy princesses."

"Well, she is talented. She definitely is."

"I'm not saying that. But do you really think it's a good idea? Imagine having her next door. You two don't even get along."

"Just because she'll never own up to anything." My dad passed her the cigarette, and she took a long drag. "Every time we ever had a fight, well, you know. I don't think we've ever been able to talk about one bad thing that's happened between us. 'Life's too short,' that's what she always says. That's the way she shuts people up." She touched my dad's neck and moved closer to him. Sitting close that way, they looked like lovers. It was one of my favorite views of my parents. My dad's neck sprouted salt-and-pepper hairs and sometimes my mom's dress tag stuck out. But from my angle it looked like they were leading us, riding into the sunrise at the front of our lives, facing the future so that us girls, in the backseat, could trust and sleep.

"I don't know," my mom said finally. "Maybe it's just time for another change of scenery."

"Don't even think about it. We haven't even been in Utah a year."

"You could do your business pretty much anywhere, though, couldn't you? Because there are plenty of colleges. I really could go anywhere."

"I *like* Provo," I said. "I don't want to move again."

"Me too," Jen said.

"Nobody's moving. Go back to sleep." My dad passed his glasses to my mom. "Could you clean these, please? Nobody's going anywhere, girls. I promise."

"Do you want to read?" my mom passed a flashlight over the backseat. I chose *Dr. Doolittle* and settled in. The Pushmepullyou was my favorite, destined to move endlessly in a tug-of-war, each delicate, flared foot leaving a print in sand as it pulled back and forth, back and forth.

Each head was alert and beautiful, with almond-shaped eyes and wooly white ears. And the Pushmepullyou could never decide what to do. One half pulled one way, and then the other half pulled the other way. My mom had read it from *Dr. Doolittle,* the night before we left the House on the Hill.

Silly, isn't it, she'd said, and moistened her finger to help turn the page. Our room was very small and pink and empty now, the cardboard boxes stacked and labeled with a black permanent marker: GIRLS' BED-ROOM. My clown lamp was packed, and the utility light my dad had hauled in from the garage made the room look the orange of baby aspirin. Still, there were comforts; my mom's breath smelled the same as it always did, milky and damp, and her finger left a tiny wet imprint. In every way, my mom was moister than I was. In the morning her eyes, like my dad's, leaked a little when they sat up in bed to read the paper. And both parents blew their noses a lot, my dad in a loud, sharp snort that sounded painful, my mom in little huffs, rubbing like her nostrils itched. Both of their toes cracked when they padded each morning to the bathroom, and their farts sounded wetter than mine. I woke up like most other kids I knew, with crusties in my eyes and at the edges of my mouth. The crotch of my underpants was yellow and stiff and salty-smelling at the end of a day, and my mom's panties—I'd *seen*, because she mostly left the door open to pee—had little coin-sized wet spots. I was small and dry and salty, and my parents were large and damp and spreading. And all together we made one thing, a family, that moved all in the same direction and not like the Pushmepullyou and not like men in a horse suit, loose and flapping, without light, who kept colliding.

What's tomorrow, my mom had said. *Do you know what day it is tomorrow?*

Moving Day.

That's right, that's right. We're at the start of our new life.

Partway through *Dr. Doolittle,* she'd asked my dad to take over reading. By nature she was impatient and easily bored, and though she read to us diligently every night you could see that she had things on her mind: she moved all over the room, folding clothes and returning crayons to their tin, and her eyes would go again and again to the window. At night you could see out over the whole city and my mom would stare, or lean and look out, letting my dad finish the book. Or she would leave early, looking grateful and blowing a kiss from the doorway, and slip off downstairs and return with a drink that looked like one they'd serve on a spaceship, in a fluted glass with a large green olive that bobbed in the bottom. The olive had a red bellybutton and my dad would say, *where's mine?* Then my mom would smile in a distracted way, and push at the olive with her finger; and sometimes eat the pimento, going at it delicately with her front teeth, and slide the olive onto one finger and say, moving the finger-puppet olive, *hello Little Ones, hello, hello.*

The night before my mom started at BYU, I went with my dad to the car wash. He cleaned it more thoroughly than usual, vacuuming intently under the seats and floormats and pocketing whatever spare change he found. He opened and closed the trunk pointlessly and his face was shut, cautious. My mom was home trying on outfits and getting fashion advice from Jen.

"Just give me a buck's worth," my dad told the gas station attendant. Then he looked over at me and slapped my knee like always, having a good time. "That ought to keep her around, right? She wouldn't make it any further than Orem. A buck's worth. You have to give your old dad points for that one."

My mom loved going to college. During the day she acted like a regular mother but in the evenings, after my dad stomped the lawn clippings from the heels of his boots and changed into a clean white T-shirt, my mom daubed blush on her cheeks and backed the station wagon out of the driveway, honked twice, and sped away. Her class ended at seven-twenty and if she wasn't home by seven-thirty my dad got our coats and we all walked the block to the main intersection, where she'd pull over when she saw us. *"Five whole minutes,"* she'd say. "Gee whiz, forgive me for having to ask the professor a *question."* All the same when she got home she talked fast and laughed a lot and then played checkers with Jen and me before putting us to bed. She practiced making pie crusts and most days when we got home from school there'd be a pie waiting, the crust stingy and mealy and tough. My mom kept her apron on long after she'd stopped baking, and threw open the front door when she saw us coming, and kissed each of us on the head as we filed in. Then she went to the kitchen and pulled off the apron and yanked the venetian blinds shut so she could smoke a cigarette.

Our dad seemed happy, too. He was making good money with All American and for months we went on this way, with regular bed times and homework and chores. Saturday was the best day. On Saturdays our family went to Sears and charged all the things that an intact-looking family needed, a tent and coolers and a lantern for camping, and Craftsmen tools and dollhouses and a crock pot and a vacuum cleaner, and new school clothes. Also painting supplies, shoes, wall coverings, floor coverings, towels, candlesticks, a necklace with an emerald heart-shaped pendant for my mom, neckties for my dad. And *toys:* wagons and chalkboards and an Easy Bake oven and stuffed animals. Bicycles with banana seats and tassels on the handles, toy nail polish and lipstick and a miniature makeup mirror and whole swing sets, and hot salted cashews from the revolving tray at the back of the store; and finally, a studio portrait of our family, my dad on top, my mom's shoulder under his hand, us kids making a pyramid at the bottom, kneeling in front of a cardboard fireplace. We looked like everyone else, that was the important thing. At school the teachers knew our names, and we still seemed to have so much *time.* We had a garage where you could go if you needed stuff like spray paint or rope, and neighbors who waved to us when they took walks. We could eat as much as we wanted and weasel extra TV time at night and take money to school for the Book Drive and order paperbacks, posters of lions with the song "Born Free" printed in cursive over the picture of the lion. We could have hot lunches at school. My dad washed the station wagon every Saturday and eventually traded it in for a sleeker, darker model, a car that none of us were ashamed to be seen in, and most of all we had *both*—a mom *and* a dad—and a basement with Barbies in it, and a backyard for sleepovers, and a cherry tree heavy with bird-pocked fruit, and we each had a bike and a sled, and once a month we went out to brunch where we waited for pancakes that the cook, Jacques, made in the shape of Mickey Mouse's head. To a restaurant in the mountains owned by *Robert Redford,* a short man who now and again strolled through in cowboy boots, his face creased and waxy-looking, and my dad would say, *There he is, girls. Which one of you is going to marry him?* So that we'd giggle, and rush nervously onto the deck laid with heavy red planks, where *four* St. Bernard dogs slept—beautiful, strewn, golden, drooling. Four, with white paws the size of teacup saucers. We had time for all this, to fool around while our pancakes cooled, and then take the slow drive home on the winding mountain road, curving back, curving forth, so that Jen and I fell a little against each other, in the back seat, then righted ourselves before the next curve, then tipped again; it all felt so dreamy and heady, and our ears filled up with the sound of the car's engine so that at home, spilling out of the car finally, we could barely hear each other, our ears still filled with noise, with that cotton of white roar.

"Quick, quick." My mom switched off the TV and carried me to the basement. "I have something to show you, now we have to be quick, they'll be back any minute but it's our secret, I have to show you, now you have to promise you won't tell." She set me on a box that held Christmas decorations and unzipped a hanging wardrobe bag. "He'd never look here, for sure he wouldn't, it's the wife isn't it, who always has to take care of the old clothes, make sure everything is stored and put away." She tugged out a brand new Samsonite suitcase and opened it. Inside there were provisions, three unopened packages of flannel pajamas and three brand new toothbrushes and three pairs of white sneakers, the kind we bought for two dollars a pair at Skaggs. A bottle of Coppertone sunscreen, three bright beach towels.

"Where's Dad's stuff?"

"Ha ha, very funny. Now I just had to show you, I probably shouldn't because I know how it is between you and your dad, loyal loyal loyal, like your sister and I don't even exist." When she was excited like this, everything she said came out in threes. "Now, I *mean* it, you can't say anything, I'm not saying we'll ever need to use this but it can't hurt, can it, no no no it can't, for a girl to be prepared."

"Where are we going?"

"Well we're not going anywhere now, are we, silly, just for the future in case we need it. And you know it's taken me forever to get all this together and frankly I would've rather showed your sister, she's so much better at keeping a secret, I'll try to show her tomorrow when your dad's at work. Why are you sniveling?"

"I don't want to leave Dad."

"Well, I mean, gee, like I'm chopped liver, I'm not *saying* we're going to leave. Did I say that? This is just for *emergency,* a Nest Egg, because, I mean, you just never know. Is all. Aren't you even going to say anything about your special towel?" She held it up. Josie and the Pussycats.

"I'm telling Dad."

"You are *not* telling him, oh no, you are *not.*"

"I *will.*"

"How can you say that, after seeing how he treats me? You know what you are is ungrateful, forget it I'll just give this towel to your sis, she's at least halfway loyal, you and your dad are just buddy buddy buddy. *Please* stop crying, Jesus. I meant this all as a surprise and now look how you're acting." She held and rocked me a little. "I wouldn't ever really leave your dad, you know that, Luce, I mean, hey, I love your dad, too. It's just that there are things you don't know about a marriage, ways you have to be prepared for the worst case scenario. Is all." She smoothed my hair. "It's just for surprise. For if we ever go to California."

"But with Dad?"

"Oh, fine, if it's so important. Sure. With your dad. You're going to blab it to him, aren't you? I can see it in your face. And then he'll hit me, is probably what he'll do. If you tell. You have to promise."

"I don't want to be a liar."

"Am I asking you to lie, is anyone asking you to tell a lie? Lies are wrong, we all know that."

"Then why can't I tell him?"

"Because it's for *emergencies.* I *told* you. It's a surprise, is what it is. I don't know why you always have to think the worst of me. Now swear."

"I swear."

"On Brittle. Swear on Brittle's life."

"I won't tell. I want to go upstairs."

"Swear. He'll hit me."

"I swear on Brittle's life!"

"Was that so hard? Do you want a piggyback?"

"No."

"You're just like your dad," my mom sighed. "You like everything to stay the same. Not like me, I'm more spontaneous. Here I was so excited to show you and look what it got me. Now *remember*," she turned to face me, then zipped up her mouth and threw away the key.

"I'm trying to fit in, darn it," my mom said. She was sitting with my dad at the kitchen table, shelling walnuts and eating them absently instead of putting them in the bowl. "It's just that whole coffee thing that I don't understand, I mean, gee, Sanka is decaffeinated. I don't know why I shouldn't be allowed to drink *that*."

"Well, just don't make an issue of it," my dad said. "We can do whatever we want in our own house. I don't love sneaking around with my cigarettes, but that's a small enough thing." In the House on the Hill he'd sat on the front porch to smoke, rocking and humming in the porch swing; now, whenever he wanted a cigarette, he stood in the carport behind the big metal garbage can, keeping the lit cigarette close to his side and waving at passing neighbors with the other hand. It was cold in the carport and I knew he wanted to be out in the sunshine, smoking and sweeping the driveway or inspecting the lawn for dandelions. Instead he stood in the dim light near the paint cans, wearing a hat with earflaps.

"I guess because they still consider it coffee. I guess it's just the whole idea. We should quit altogether, Bob, we really should. It gives you heartburn. And I really am thinking about the Church. I think it would be good for the kids."

"I'm not joining," my dad said. "No way. Take the girls, if you want, but I like my beer and cigarettes."

"That's not all there is to the Mormon church," my mom said. "They really do teach lots of good messages. I don't fit in at the Y, and it's because we're not church members. I look around at how they're all so young and have nice skin and they all look so *sure* of themselves. And tuition's cheaper, a *whole lot* cheaper, for members. I mean there must be *something* to the church. It can't be all bad."

"Like what?" My dad stomped open a walnut with his foot. "Want one, Luce?"

"You're supposed to be getting enough so we can make brownies," I said. "You keep eating them all."

"Well, come on up and help then." My dad got me a nutcracker and a sharp silver pick. "Pitch in. Have at it. Pull your weight." He elbowed me and winked. I still hadn't told him about the suitcase and it was making me feel bad, because I was his favorite and never kept secrets. On the other hand I knew things, like that my dad kept the car low on gas and we only had one car key anyway, the one my dad kept snapped in a worn yellow billfold. I didn't really think my mom would try to leave, but one thing I knew was that if she did, she was on her own. Jen could go with her if she wanted but I was staying, and I'd already taped a row of dimes in my diary as preparation for an emergency phone call if it ever came to that.

"Like to always take care of your own," my mom said. "I really like that idea, just of belonging. If a family is low on money, if you're really tight, the Church will give you free food. Cheese and rice and cereal."

"Aha," my dad said. "Now we're getting somewhere."

"That's not the only thing. But I think it sounds, nice, don't you? Just calling a perfect stranger for help. What's your sister doing, Luce?"

"Playing Operation."

"Would you go tell her dinner's almost ready? We're having creamed tuna on toast." My mom finished off the bowl of walnuts. "I guess I'll have to shell more, after dinner. But you know, I'm thinking about it. Of at least going to church a few more times. It wouldn't kill us. We're a family. Luce, you really need to change that shirt. What is that, chocolate syrup? Go change, please. Go on."

I went to my room and sprawled out on my bed to write in my diary. I kept it under a stack of towels in the bottom of a purple backpack, the backpack hung at the back of the closet on a nail. But when I pulled it out this time I saw that the tiny gold key, which usually dangled from a silky cord attached to the book, was gone. The lock had been left hanging open and I stormed to the basement. Jen was reaching in for the bone on the Operation game and I swatted her hand away. "You read my diary."

"Hey! I almost got that. No I didn't."

"Look." I showed it to her. "This is *my diary*."

"I didn't read it, Lucy! I swear."

"You're a liar." I pushed her backwards and she came up and got me by the hair.

"Stop it! I didn't touch it. Why would I even care whatever stupid thing you write?"

"Hey cut it out!" my dad came to the top of the stairs. I went for a handful of Jen's hair. She'd *promised*: never to read it, never to go in my room without permission. And because she was bigger and smarter she had, and now the lock was broken and there was nothing I could do about it and she'd probably read every word. Her hair was so slippery and shiny; it felt good to dig in and pull. Jen really screamed then, and kicked me hard in the stomach. Then my mom had Jen and my dad had me, trying to keep us off each other. "You little maniacs," my dad said. "If you could see yourselves."

"Jen read my diary."

"*I* read it," my mom said. "It was mighty interesting, let me tell you, I guess when I was little I had a wild imagination too, full of lies about castles and mermaids and imaginary suitcases and *lies*."

"You did?" That one caught me off guard.

"Look at that, a whole wad of hair." My mom pointed to the floor, where penny-colored strands lay across the carpet. I was surprised, too. I looked at Jen and saw that she had a pale spot the size of an egg above one ear. She hadn't cried when I pulled it out but now she started, twisting free of my mom so she could look in the mirror over the utility sink.

"I'm gonna kill you," she said. "You are dead, dead, dead."

"You did what?" my dad asked my mom. "Why?"

"Look, it's not a big deal. Luce, I'm sorry, I was just in there one day, I felt something in the bag, I was curious. It's no big deal. If I kept a journal I'd let you read it. You're not keeping any secrets from me. Are you? *Are* you?" She put her hands on her hips, accusing.

"It's *private*," I said. I tried to think if I'd written anything else she couldn't see, but that wasn't it: it was the image of her on the edge of my bed in the middle of the day, turning the pages and probably laughing. And the way she'd broken the lock. Now it was ruined. It was ruined and she wasn't sorry, she was my mom, there was nothing I could do. "You're always like that," I said. "You always walk in the bathroom. We can never have locks. You never knock. You *broke* it." I showed her, and then she did look apologetic, like she hadn't realized she'd been so rough.

"Well, I'm sorry about that. I'll buy you a new one if you're so upset," she said. "I'm not going to stand here talking about this all day, it's not like I committed some big *crime*, Jesus." She shook her head. "No wonder I'm on pins and needles all day, no wonder my nerves are shot. I can't do anything, can't make a single move without being accused. I don't know what you're so afraid of my seeing, what the big secret is. You don't even have *pubic* hair yet. But okay, fine, you want me to knock first I will."

"Miriam, you're getting out of hand."

"*Me* out of hand. *Me.*"

"Come on. You owe her an apology."

"What did I do that was so terrible? *What did I do?*" my mom yanked the diary away from me. She shook it in the air and then it felt like everything I'd written, all my secrets, might rattle out onto the floor. It flapped out in the open, the white pages with their lines of gray cursive. "Didn't I say I'd replace it? I said I'd buy you a whole brand new one, just because I was bored one afternoon, there's never a single thing going on, just because I committed some big crime, boy what an evil mother you have, well maybe you should just go find another one. If you hate me so much. Just go find someone else who'll be a better mother, *good luck*, the way you kids just fight and fight and fight and I have to listen to it. I have to listen to it." She waggled her head, thinking about how awful we were. Her face was incredulous. She really couldn't believe it, how rotten we were, tearing out wads of hair every day and screaming so the neighbors could hear.

"It was private," I said stubbornly.

"Fine! Fine!" my mom's arms went everywhere, a hysterical rendition of her throwing up her hands. "I can never do anything right, can I! I'm just the bad, bad, bad, bad mother!" She ran upstairs, her knees high and her feet slapping hard. She paused before slamming the door, giving herself time to make it a good one. I'd done the same thing plenty of times and with this slam the whole house rattled magnificently, a Popsicle-stick house held together with rubber bands.

My dad looked at us. "No more hair-pulling," he told me. "Your sister has a hole in her head the size of a silver dollar."

Sometimes Jen and I walked to the corner market. Hershey Bars were a dime, and Popsicles were seven cents, and usually my dad gave us each a dime and watched us from the front door. Beehive Market was three blocks from our house and at the intersection across the street from the store was a canal. The water rushed deeply and there was a single metal railing around it and the thought of us even passing it made my mom crazy, which it should have, since while we waited for the light to change Jen and I usually found twigs and trash to throw in, watching the water catch the wrappers and whip them into a tight circle before swallowing them up. I don't know how deep the water was, but it was brown and ran fast, and just standing over it tempted me. Then the light would change and I was back to thinking about how I'd use my dime.

Once my mom sent Brittle along, thinking that would keep us safe; but Brittle was heavy-headed and clumsy, her brown, long nose tipped to the ground, and that time she'd slipped at the edge and then one of us really had almost fallen in, catching her collar at the last minute. Her collar was too tight because Jen and I had been preoccupied with other things while Brittle got fat and it was a good thing, because the collar was what saved her. Her troll legs scrabbled crazily at the lip of the canal and we could see her eyes rolling crazily down at the water before Jen heaved her up. Brittle usually passed most of the day sleeping on the cool concrete floor of the basement, so this view of things must've come as quite a shock. She shivered when we tied her up at the bike rack across the street, and was still shivering when we came back out, and shot to the far end of her leash when we passed the canal going home. Brittle was a good dog, but not the kind of dog you were proud of. When we threw food to her she never caught it in her mouth. She just looked puzzled and let the noodles or bites of cookies land in her fur, on her head. She'd walk around like that all day if we let her, a single cheesy macaroni hardening between her ears.

Provo felt so safe: maybe that's why my memory of the canal stands out. It yawned open and putty-colored and cold; and a few years later, when we drove back through, we saw that a fence had been erected around it, and the cashier at the Beehive Market told us how some kid finally had fallen in. Her sister had run alongside but the girl had drowned and only then had the city decided to fence it, and I think now about my mom's expression when she finally saw us walking back, or the way my dad came looking for us once in the car when we'd stayed gone too long. Jen and I had no clue. We were just dragging home, already over our sugar high and ready for something else to do. But our parents had been changed into old people. Their eyes were tired, their jaws slack. In their imaginations they'd already lost us, so that our actual return left them unmoved; they seemed to look at us without seeing, and when we got in the car my dad drove home silently, like we were kids he didn't particularly care to know. And at home my mom said, not for the first or last time, *you are never, never, ever walking to that store again.*

"You know what I can't stand?" my mom was saying. "This wallpaper. Honestly, it makes me feel like an insane person." She moved to the wall, peeled back an edge to see what was underneath. The paper was thick with green teapots and the teapots had distended bellies, long noses that spouted steam, and grimacing faces meant to indicate they were whistling and boiling over. "They look like little child molesters," my mom said, and walked backwards, pulling at it until she was satisfied.

"I wish you wouldn't do that, Miriam." My dad hitched up his pants and folded his arms and stared at her. "Did you have to do that?"

"Isn't it giving *you* the creeps? I'm serious, Bob. And look, look at the vines underneath. I'd rather look at vines, wouldn't you? Come on, Luce, help me pull."

"Nobody touch anything," my dad said. "I mean it. Now I'm going to have to fix the damned thing, now I'm going to have to spend my weekend repapering. Just leave it alone, would you please?"

My mom made a show of trying to press the paper back down. "I didn't mean to make a new project for you. I was just trying to see." She went to him and circled her arms around his waist. "We need a new look in here, I think. Something new and exciting. I just can't stand coming in here every morning and seeing the same old scenery. New wallpaper would sure help, wouldn't it? A sunny pattern. Something cheery. Then I'd feel better."

Sometimes my mom took me to school with her. She drove us through the main gate of the University, over which hung a sign: ENTER TO LEARN, GO FORTH TO SERVE. "Enter to learn, go forth to serve dinner," my mom said. "Probably ninety percent of the female students are majoring in Home Ec. It's just silly." She drove too fast, slowing at the last minute for speed bumps and pointing out all the buildings where she had classes. "Notice anything weird?" my mom asked me, after we'd driven around for a while. "They're all *white*. Not a single black person in the bunch, at least not that I've seen."

"How come Dad doesn't like black people?" My dad liked Flip Wilson alright, and Sammy Davis Jr., but aside from that he made comments that caused fights between him and my mom.

"He's just plain afraid," my mom said. "Afraid of having an operation where he might end up getting some black blood inside him. You're dad's a lot older than me, he's from a different generation. But really he's just scared, is what it is. Not me. I could really swing, if you want to know the truth. I like the dark satiny look of their skin, plus black men are supposed to have bigger penises. Just between you and me and the lamppost. But it's strange, isn't it? There were plenty of black people in California. But not here. The Church doesn't like them. How do you feel about joining up? What do you think?"

"About being a Mormon?"

"Sure," my mom said.

"I don't know."

"It's not a big deal." She eased the car into a parking spot. "I've been talking to Mr. Poulson, well, John, and he's been sharing some info about the Church with me. I hope Julia knows how good she has it, set up in that big house where she doesn't even have to work, she probably just shops shops shops all day long, is what she does. And I just hope she knows, John might be a little bit stuffy but gee he's handsome, well and from the way he looks at me you know *he'd* be interested, I just hope she's keeping him happy in bed, is all I hope, that's such an important part of a marriage. She just better be careful is all I'm saying. She doesn't know how good she has it. Anyway if we do join up you don't have to really think anything different, but you would have to go to church sometimes. They have lots of crafts and stuff, for the kids. You really just have to look the part, is all it comes down to."

"Would I have to wear a uniform?"

"Oh you kill me, Lucy, you really do," my mom said. She laughed and kissed me on the cheek. "Well you'd think so, wouldn't you," she said. "But no, it's not like that. You'd just have to find out who the Mormon kids are at school, and then try to get invited to their parties and stuff. I've already been to two Relief Society meetings, frankly they're not really my thing, I've never been any good at crafts. In fact, next week, *next* week, I'm definitely planning on calling in sick. They're going to crochet reindeer doorknob covers, can you believe that? With little bell noses. I can't stand the thought, believe me, that one would really kill me. I'll tell them it's that time of the month, is what I'll do. That way nobody will ask questions. Do you want to see the cafeteria?" My mom rolled up her window. "They have these huge, pink, frosted cookies, we'll get you one. Your dad actually gave me a couple of dollars, for a change. He thinks I'm going to run, *ha*, like I could go anywhere with you girls in tow. Anyway the cookies are the best part about this whole place. So just think about it, okay?"

Finally I wrote my dad a letter:

> *Dear Dad,*
>
> *I love you so much and that's why I wanted a chance to tell you this. Before you found out and knew I didn't tell you. Well, Mom is hiding a suitcase in our basement (it's in that zip-up thingy by the Xmas box). I don't want you to be worried but she showed it to me and it made me feel really bad that I haven't told you, because we are YOU AND ME AGAINST THE WORLD!! I luv U!!*
>
> *Lucy*

p.s. I don't know if you'll ever find this, probably not, but I wanted you to know in case Mom just did something like take us, which I know she wouldn't. But even if she did I would ALWAYS CALL YOU, because I just love you so much!!!!!!!!

I rolled up the letter and hid it in my Tootsie Roll piggybank. I thought I might be able to give it to my dad the following week when he took me to the riding arena, or maybe one night when my mom was at her class. But a few days later, when I checked, the letter had disappeared.

My mom seemed to be right about the Mormon Church not liking black people; in the whole time we lived in Provo, I only saw two. Except for the hardworking Mexicans everybody else looked pretty much like us. The town was quiet and almost surreal in its stillness and cleanliness, especially on Sundays, where the only movement was that of churchgoers moving between the doors of the ward house and the parking lot and then back again. The town had wide streets designed by Brigham Young when he'd settled the town; the streets were wide, my mom explained, so that a horse and buggy could turn all the way around, instead of having to go around the block. There was a municipal swimming pool, and an art-deco movie theater painted a flat pistachio green where every Saturday my dad dropped us off to see a movie.

And then for a while our life moved forward in a deep straight groove, my dad making enough money to feed us all, and us girls making new friends. Our mom seemed happy, too; she looked like any other young, conservative mother in town, wearing every day the heavy dresses that hid her hourglass figure and bound her breasts, and she wore them with silvery-beige control-top pantyhose with a cruelly small opening at the top, no larger than the mouth of a peanut butter jar, through which she was expected to fit.

"You're supposed to give the blessing," my mom said one night at dinner. We were in the dining room because my dad had finally gotten around to rewallpapering the kitchen, a twining rose pattern that my mom said reminded her of the House on the Hill. The whole house smelled like wallpaper paste and Jen, who had allergies, kept sneezing. Her eyes were pink and pinched.

My dad tore open a roll, and smeared it thickly with margarine. "What?" he said. "I'm supposed to give the whodamacallit over the whatamacallit?"

"The blessing. Give thanks."

"I'm not the one who's been going to church," My dad split open his baked potato and dropped a slab of margarine in the center, then salted it thickly.

"You go with us," I said.

"Well I *go*, but I don't *listen*. There's a difference. You say it, Miriam. You're the convert."

"You're the *patriarch*," my mom said. "You're the one who has to say it. I'm not allowed. You have all the power here. All the cards. So just say something, would you please?"

"God bless this mess."

"You don't have to *mean* it." My mom picked at a piece of broccoli. "None of us have to really *believe* in the Church. But I mean, if we want to be accepted. If we want to be invited to things. We don't want to be the heathens on the block."

"I thought we had to believe in it," Jen said.

"Well you should *try*, but if you just *can't*, that's okay too." My mom ladled out creamed corn, which I hated. It reminded me of retarded people or people in rest homes. It was too sweet and dribbled around in my mouth like vomit. "The important thing is to look the part, not say anything that might make you look bad. That's why it's important for us to do the blessing, so that if you ever invite any of your friends over for dinner. Like Stacy. What if Lucy invited Stacy home, and saw how we all just plopped down and started eating?"

"I don't want creamed corn."

"Yes, you do," my mom said. "Just take one teeny tiny little spoonful."

"It looks like *throw up*."

"At the table," Jen said, which was our family warning: *at the table, we talk about pleasant things that are seen and done.*

"Stacy's family is Jewish," my dad said. "Haven't you ever met her dad? He's a New York Jew. He could give a damn."

"That means he's circumcised," my mom said. It was one of her favorite topics. She thought circumcision was cruel but, she said, unfortunately aesthetically necessary.

"Can we please talk about other things, at the dinner table?" my dad said. "Is this really something we have to discuss?"

"The girls should know all about the human body," my mom said. "It's natural. I want them to know these things."

"Enough," my dad said. "Smell that *paste.* I hope you're not going to want me to redo that wall anytime again in the next decade."

"Oh no, Bob, I love that new paper, I really do, it's perfect." She laid one of her starlet smiles on him, then turned it on us girls. "What a beautiful, beautiful family I have," she said. "Just remember, if the parents choose *not* to do it, the boy baby's penis ends up being shaped like a tiny banana, is the problem. But it's so sad that they do it anyway. And the boy babies just scream and scream and scream." She rolled up her potato skin and fed it to Brittle. "Anyway, I think being Mormon sounds kind of fun. We'll have more friends. We can go to parades. And finally we'll have some, oh, I don't know, some *history* to our family. Right now we could be anybody, people look at us and they don't think we *belong* anywhere, they just think, oh, there goes that family, now *what* are their names?"

We tried, too. At least for a few weeks. We went to church a couple of times and the missionaries paid us a home visit and my mom quit drinking even Sanka, and she stopped swearing and she practiced a small smile even when Jen and I raced around the yard, crashing through the shrubs and knocking over patio furniture. She held her legs tightly together when she sat down. She stopped wearing red lipstick and went with a neutral shade. Mr. Poulson was teaching our mom about the Church and she listened eagerly to everything he had to say, nodding happily even before he'd finished. In every way the transformation made her a lady, a picture perfect wife. My dad liked it, too, though he told Jen and me once in the car that he wasn't holding his breath. She was changeable, he said, and easily distracted. But in the meantime it was like we'd been admitted to a club. People I didn't even know at school started to say hi to me. I got invited to two birthday parties, both from kids I didn't think even knew I existed. One of them was Ellen Jorgansen; she had hair down to her waist and her mom curled it with electric rollers every morning. She had matching skirt-and-sweater outfits and her own horse, and when she walked up to me at recess and handed me a fragrant lavender invitation I knew it meant something, and ever since I'd been fantasizing about all the things I'd tell her at her party, all the ways I'd make her laugh. I didn't stand out in a crowd, but one-on-one, I thought, I had charisma. It was just a matter of getting people to notice me in the first place.

I didn't even mind going to church; the talks were boring, but there was always plenty of punch and cookies, afterward. And I liked the way the families looked all around me: singular shapes with the dad's head starting at the top and dropping to the mom's shoulder, where the dad's hand was placed. Then the children, blond and clean-looking, all around their legs. At home, when my mom brought up the gospel and the eventual possibility of our baptism, my dad looked amused. I don't think he cared either way. I think he was just happy to see my mom so happy.

But it was only for a couple of weeks. Just when I'd started to relax into it, and just when I'd started to wonder whether God might really exist—he'd made me popular, after all, and smoothed things out between my mom and dad—my mom stormed home. "Goddamn church," she told us in the driveway. "What a *dupe* I've been, you girls will never be Mormons and don't you forget it. You can just forget we ever went there, I don't want any of you *even so much as mentioning it ever again*, I really am, I'm a *sucker*. For a minute I thought well, okay, maybe, I shouldn't hold my whole history against the Mormon Church just because of that stupid jerk at Fullerton, I mean what kind of a generalization is that to make right? Do you girls know if your dad has any cigarettes?"

"Sometimes he hides them in his workboots." Jen went to the garage, searched one boot and came up triumphant. My mom lit the cigarette and blew smoke lavishly out toward the street. "I hope everyone sees me," she said. "That bastard, that's all I can say. Mr. Two-Face himself, now he feels all *guilty*, I'll bet, he probably thinks I led him on, and now he has to *repent* or some damn thing. Damn him."

"Who?" Jen said.

"You know who. You know perfectly well who. And guess what, you know what Mormons think about women and blacks?"

"Women can't have jobs?" Jen guessed. I'd French-braided her hair earlier and now she kept her head as still as she could, afraid of it coming loose.

"Women and black people *can't even hold the priesthood,*" she said. "Only the big, important men like him can do that. Well and I'll be goddamned if I'll belong to some group that says only the *men*, the *white* ones, can give orders, especially when some of them act the way they do, making promises and saying 'I'll do this, I'll do that', yeah sure you will, Mr. Have-Your-Cake-and-Eat-It-Too, what an *idiot* I was. To believe him."

"What's the priesthood?" I tightened the rubber band in Jen's braid and felt her wince. Next she was going to braid mine.

"That's where the men hold all the big, important positions in the Church," my mom said. "The ones with all the power. And I'll be damned if I'll let you girls grow up thinking you're second-class citizens. Do you know what he called me, do you know what he called me? A *Jezebel*. Ohh, I just feel so stupid."

"Can I still go to Ellen Jorgansen's party?" It was Saturday, and we'd already bought her present: purple, fizzy bath beads and a purple velvet teddy bear.

"She didn't invite you because you're really *friends*, Honey. She invited you because she's been seeing you at church, that's why. What kind of a friend is that?"

"But they're going to have pizza from Pizza Hut."

"Well, big deal. If it means that much to you, we'll get pizza delivered. I don't know why you'd still want to go, considering everything. You can just keep the present, how's that. But I can't let you go, not really, not in any good conscience."

I'd heard all kinds of stuff about Ellen's house. How she had her own beanbag chair and her own bathroom with makeup mirrors, and how we might be able to ride her horse. "I could just go for an hour."

"Why do you even *want* to go, Luce. No, I really can't, it would be hypocritical. You love that little bear, just keep the stuff. I don't know how they justify it, I don't know how everyone can walk around looking like things are so peachy keen." She stubbed out her cigarette. "Whew! That tasted good, I must confess. I don't even care who sees. You girls need to grow up knowing you're *someone*. Why don't we go get a vanilla Coke. Do you want vanilla Cokes? We haven't had *those* in a while, have we?"

Y ou'll *like* Arizona," my mom said. "The least you can do is give it a chance." It was the middle of the night and my mom was a silhouette beside my bed.

"I like *Provo*," I said. "We live here now. I have Liddy and I'm going to start soccer."

"Well, but you haven't even started soccer yet, have you?" My mom sat on my bed, trying to be my buddy. "Anyway you had something to do with this, I found your little love letter to your dad, Luce, thanks a lot, I tell you something in confidence and you go and blab it all over."

"I don't want to go." I folded my arms and when she touched my leg I yanked it away. It was easy for her to leave, because she didn't have any friends. *She* wasn't starting soccer, she wasn't leaving somewhere where she'd have to start all over with a fresh locker and kids who didn't know her name and stared at her like she was an alien. She just wanted new scenery, I thought; new scenery and new neighbors she could blab our history to.

"I don't want to go either, Mom," Jen said. "Why can't we just stay here? What time is it?"

"Don't make *me* the bad guy," my mom lowered her voice. "I'm doing this for you girls. I'm doing this so you don't feel it, too. The *ostracism*. And really mainly it's your dad's idea to go, he and Julia had some big talk and now he's *suspicious*, like always, I mean he agrees that we can't stay here. We'll never really fit in, not really, not without being members of the *Church*. And you know how I feel about *that*."

"Dad likes it here. I know he does," I said.

"Look, you girls are really going to like Phoenix. I would've waited till morning to tell you but it's such exciting news, I just wanted you to know the minute we'd decided. There are swimming pools everywhere, just everywhere, I mean, gee, I'd be surprised if we got a house that *didn't* have one, how many of *those* can there be?"

"What about Brittle?" I said. Brittle was about to have her puppies. The only time she got out of her box was to lap water from the toilet, and her stomach looked like a piece of wax fruit. I couldn't seem to put things together. The room looked fuzzy and dim and my mom was in the middle, her face keen and wide awake, planning. "Why couldn't you just tell us tomorrow?"

"Well, Brittle's family, she'll come too, she might really want to see Arizona. How many dogs do you know that get to travel?"

"I was supposed to start dance company," Jen sat up and found her Caramel Apple Lip Smacker. She smeared some onto the calluses on her feet. "We were going to do the Twenties Revue."

"I'm sure they'll have a dance company at the new school." My mom stood up. "Anyway, we can't argue with your dad. His mind's made up. And you really need to help out, you really need to pitch in and not just complain complain complain. I've already started collecting boxes. You girls are old enough to do your own packing."

IN BED,

was where we often found her kindest, most loving. In the afternoons when the migraines came she'd cry and cling to her forehead with one hand, like an actress. She'd say *oh god oh god oh god* and cling to other things: bedposts and our dad and wet washrags and cups of tea. We'd file past the bedside, bearing gifts, my mother's hand weak and papery, reaching always for us.

And all the lights in the house would get dimmed, in case she wanted or needed to wander. The television would get turned off and the draperies drawn. We were two little girls and one dad waiting for the mother to get over her headache. She was in the dark in the next room and other things came with the pain: flashing lights off to the side; and her hands got numb, and her face got numb; she'd see spirals and zigzags and flashes all in silver and then she'd barf. It was a kind of a catalyst, I guess, a crisis leading to her salvation. She had visions. I mean, people came to her and she'd try to talk but couldn't, her language got all messed up and she'd answer us kids in garbled phrases and then shake her head, ashamed that it was the best she could do at this point. Even when she wrote notes, the shapes of the letters were wrong and then what could we do? Nothing but feel sorry, feel sorry and sometimes fall asleep on the couch, my sister and me head to toe, where if our mother began to wander she could find us, wake us, and in the middle of the night would be a mother hot and suffering, speaking in tongues, her brain flashing silvery pictures. She would come this distance to tell her children how she loved them. And once, tongue-tied, she had to spell it in Jen's palm, like Helen Keller; we knew it was a joke, a sad one, since first she spelled out *water,* which was the first word Helen learned when Helen and her teacher were at the water pump. In mud on her knees Teacher knelt and felt Helen's fingers move fervently. In mud on her knees she'd looked into Helen's blank face, and saw it change when Helen realized for the first time ever there were words for things.

Years after, when I slept with a woman for the first time, I had the worst migraine of all, my mother there with me, our heads splitting, neither of us reaching for words. I knew that she'd paid me a visit partly out of sympathy and partly to spy. My mom watched, her eyes glittering and hungry. *Lezzie,* she hissed.

During one of my mother's headaches, my dad came to visit. I mean not really, because by then everything had changed. But he came to us, calling us Angelpusses like he would have, and my mom wept and held her arms out. She had her eyes shut, just pretending and sort of swaying. It's like a parade, she was saying, and waving like she was in a beauty pageant, riding on a float. *Hello everyone and all admirers,* she said. She said to him, *have we moved to Arizona? That's what made it such hard times. We were happy before that, weren't we? And then we went and moved and all hell broke loose. We didn't stand a chance, our marriage didn't. But we were happy before that.*

At this my dad's eyes went into the pained squint I always saw when the two of them fought. My mom was a scrapper and a liar who'd say anything to win a fight and my dad, though furious, always lost because he'd try to stay decent. He tried to defend himself this time, tried to make sense of her and everything that had happened, because what else could you do when it came to your own history? Except try to keep things straight.

You dragged us all over the goddamned map, Miriam, is what did it, he said. (My mom reached for her wet rag, protesting: *no no, not now, I'm in such terrible pain—.) I would've done anything to make you happy. Anything. I was a stupid goddamned fool, is what I was. And you wanted to go to Arizona, remember? Arizona had nothing to do with it.*

Arizona had everything to do, everything to do—. She was messing around on her nightstand, looking for codeine, cold water. *I hated Arizona. Hated it. You dragged us there is when the family fell apart, it was your fault, Bob, your fault. Don't put it off on me, don't come to me like this, where are my girls, my girls—.* She was reaching for us now, and we went to her.

And then again our house was empty and we were in the car. We were always in the car. My parents had never been religious: even my mom's interest in the Mormon Church had been half-hearted. *It's so bland,* she'd said, *not an exotic church at all. Give me incense and chanting, any day.* My parents' faith was in *stuff*: in things like our car, a clear symbol of hope and mobility, one that took us through neighborhoods where other people stood still, settling for things.

"I'm thinking about a T-shirt shop," my dad said. "What do you think? I know a little bit about screen printing, I wouldn't need a whole lot of capital to get started."

"T-shirts," my mom said. Brittle tried to climb across the front seat to get in my mom's lap, and she shoved her back. "Go on, barefoot and pregnant and in the kitchen. Dumb dog. I guess T-shirts would be *okay*."

"I knew you'd say that. But I have to do something. Anyway, it's not lawns. You won't have to worry anymore about me tracking grass in the house or smelling like fertilizer." My dad had sold All American to a father-son team in Provo. They'd come to the house to buy the mowers and my dad had gone over everything with them, showing them his account book and how the mowers worked, which one was hard to start when the weather started to turn and which one was best for sloped lawns, because of its weight. Both the dad and the son looked cautious, gun-shy. It was their chance for a new future, too, and they were holding it delicately between them, already afraid of making a mistake.

"Maybe something in an office," my mom said. 'You could leave for work every morning and I could stand at the door and hand you your sack lunch and thermos. I can see myself doing that."

"Well, *I* can't," my dad said. "You'd go out of your birdcage seeing me off to work every morning."

"I just hope the *house* is nicer this time." After what happened with the house in Provo, my mom made my dad get a picture of the new house; it looked alright, though the picture had been taken from far away and it was hard to see much: narrow high windows, a brown front door. "I'm not going to miss Provo, I'm really not, and especially not some dumb split level that made me feel like I was some dumb suburban housewife."

"What do you girls think about T-shirts?" my dad said. "You could use your cash register skills to help me. We could choose all different designs and then do specialty items. Like if a bowling team wanted shirts or some kind of car club."

"Bowling team," my mom said. "Car club. Welcome to my future."

When finally we pulled into the driveway my mom shook her head, incredulous.

"Cinderblock," she said. "You didn't tell me it was *cinderblock*."

"Miriam, this is what we can afford. And I did, too, tell you. We can't just keep moving and moving, it's costing us. Real estate is more expensive down here, you know that. Look, we couldn't stay there. So here we are."

"I should've come down with you before," she said. "I just plain should have, I made this mistake once already. We've always had different taste in houses. I could've found us a little adobe."

"In a million years, I wouldn't buy an adobe house." My dad got out of the car and started to untie the bikes from the back. "A mud house? Is that what you want? So it can wash away with the first rain?"

My mom smirked. "Well, you sure do know a lot about adobe. Gee. I had no idea you were such an expert."

"You kids go ride your bikes," my dad said. "Go explore."

"We haven't even seen the house." A box of Chicken-in-a-Bisket crackers had spilled open on my lap and I got out and shook off. The air was so hot that it made me want to pant, and the air above the sidewalks shivered with heat lines. Brittle dropped out and paddled over to a square of shade and collapsed.

In the house my mom walked from room to room, saying blankly and over and over *it's so ugly, so ugly, I can't believe it's come to this*. My dad shook his head, disgusted, and went out to the garage to smoke. Jen and I squabbled over bedrooms for a few minutes, then started to unpack. When we were living in the House on the Hill I'd cut a bunch of feet out of construction paper, twenty at least in red and blue, and my personal signature on a new bedroom was to start at the light switch and then scotch-tape the feet all over the walls, have them boogie a circle on the ceiling and end near my bed. By the time we got to Phoenix there were pale blotches where the tape had stuck them together. Still, I put them up. And my dad unpacked his tools, made his workshop in the garage. We were ready to start again.

I remember Phoenix now as a playground that shimmered in the heat and a German Shepherd across the street that humped me when I got down on all fours to play dog, his toenails digging lines into my stomach, his nose so glossy and black it looked plastic. I remember a restaurant called Betty Crocker's, dimly lit and way too cold, the way all public buildings in Phoenix seemed to be, and mechanical chirping parrots that swung over each table in elaborate wrought-iron cages, and the sounds of the jungle piped in, and cold, red Jell-O that came to us in the shapes of exotic animals. I remember gravel, and bulbous cacti that sprouted unlikely, delicate flowers.

Our mom painted our bedrooms the exact color we wanted, a bright coral for me and purple for Jen. She was ready to try again, too. But after a month in our new house we were on the road again, this time back to

California so we could live closer to our Grandma Jane. There was a little Danish town, my mom said, one with the most wonderful pastries and red paper flags fluttering over the door of every shop, and the people who lived there were all from the Old Country, *authentic*, she said, not like the people you met everywhere else, who had no sense of themselves or their family history. My mom had hated Arizona, she said, hated everything about it. When Jen wanted to know what she hated so much, my mom stared at her a minute and then hissed it: *the heat,* she said. *That terrible, terrible, terrible, terrible heat.*

"I don't know how you kids stood it as long as you did, I really don't," my mom was saying. "I worried about you, even when you walked to school. You could've passed out from sunstroke." We passed a sign: SOLVANG, 2 MILES, and Jen put her fingers in her teeth and whistled shrilly.

"This really is the last time," my dad said. "If you don't like Solvang, well, tough. You wanted to go to Provo, we went to Provo. You wanted to try Arizona, so we tried it. But this is it, Miriam. I mean it."

"Why did we have to leave Brittle?"

"Oh, Honey, the new people will take care of her. They will."

"Well, when are they moving in?" I'd filled Brittle's bowls and left the door between the garage and the yard ajar so that Brittle could get in and out, but still it had been awful to leave her. When we all got in the car Brittle stood up fast in her basket and two of her nursing puppies plopped off, mewling. They were blind and lovely.

"I'm sure they'll be there soon," my mom soon. "Brittle needs to rest, anyway. And just for the record I don't like moving all over the map anymore than the rest of you." My mom had made my dad pull over so she could pick a branch off a eucalyptus tree, and now she kept putting it to her nose and inhaling theatrically. She put it to my dad's nose, who swatted it away.

"I know what it smells like," he said. "I just hope I can find a job in this place. I might be able to do screen printing, but Phoenix seemed like a better market for that sort of thing."

"Oh, you'll find something. You can do practically anything, can't he, girls?"

"Will you build us bunk beds?" Jen said.

"You probably won't even need them," my mom said. "You might not even need to share a bedroom. It all depends on what kind of a house we can get. Honestly, I'll bet real estate's not all that expensive here."

"We're about out of money," my dad said. "You know that."

"Oh, I know, I know. I meant a rental. We won't be broke for long, you'll find something. And then we can buy ourselves a house like the House on the Hill, something big and rambling. Maybe a Tudor, I'll bet Solvang is packed with Tudors. I'll bet that's practically the only architecture a little town like that will have."

"I'm a real loser, aren't I," my dad said, provoked. "I can't do anything right. I never should've sold that goddamned house, I'll never hear the end of it."

"I didn't say that."

"I don't hate the idea of Solvang. But I'll tell you one thing, once we're unpacked we're never moving again, job or no job. I'm sick of it, the girls are sick of it. We need to stay put."

"You don't have to tell me." My mom brightened, looked back at us. "I can work in a shop. I can work in one of those windmills. Would you like that, your mother working in a windmill? Our family has Danish blood, did you know that?"

"Danish Shmanish," our dad said.

"We do, we're part Danish. On my side. My maternal grandmother," my mom said. "And if we find a house in town, I could walk to work."

"I thought our family was part Indian," I said.

"I thought we were part *Mexican*," Jen said, and my dad said, *take your pick.*

"That, too," she said. "That, too." And then we were in the town, slowing down to find a gas station. "Oh, look!" my mom said. "Look! Look at the Tudors! Oh, look at the wonderful little paper flags! I feel like I'm home already!"

• • •

116

On Sundays in Solvang, my dad and I bicycled to the bakery for unglazed donuts, hanging warm and brown in the white bakery bag tied to the handlebars. Then we stopped to feed dimes into a newspaper machine so he could have the funnies along with his donut. He loved Blondie and Hagar the Horrible, but his favorite was Andy Capp, a comic strip where you knew Andy Capp was drunk by the tiny lines drawn in crisscross over his pink nose and cheeks. My dad hooted as he read, then passed it to my mom, who laughed politely. He was planning small things for the day: organizing his toolbox, fixing the hinge on the bathroom door, raking leaves. It all needed to be done and my dad was the man to do it. But the smallness of these things seemed to depress my mom. Some days, she kept up. On these days the laundry wound up in folded warm rectangles delivered in stacks to our bedrooms, and by dinnertime there'd be a paper towel folded in half next to each plate, and glasses of Tang. But then there were other days when she'd disappear for long hours and come home still sad, not saying much, snapping at my dad if he asked questions.

The house we'd found was a two-bedroom and I slept in a trundle pulled out each night from under Jen's bed. The rent was two hundred dollars a month, way more than we could afford, but my dad had an idea for a new job: he was building a small-scale windmill in our backyard, and the windmill included a mural where, like at a carnival, people could step behind it and place their heads in the cutouts to have their picture taken. The windmill itself was nine or ten feet tall and my dad worked at it excitedly. He let Jen and me help paint the murals. He thought we should do several, so people would have a choice. One showed a couple standing side by side in Danish garb; the next depicted a mermaid mooning up at a sailor who scanned the sea like he hadn't figured out that there was a buxom, fishtailed blonde at his feet, and the third mural was of a stork, bearing a cloth bundle in its beak.

The day he finally finished my mom came outside to stare. She'd been hoping my dad would get a real job, maybe something in an office, one where we could count on health insurance and paid vacations.

"So *where* are you planning to put this? Are you sure it's legal?"

"On the corner of Fourth," my dad said. "Right near that little clog shop with the parrot in the window and of course I checked, I just need to pay for the license."

"How come the women are so *busty*?" my mom asked. Jen and I snickered. We'd noticed it, too. The mermaid especially.

"It's just for a good time," my dad said. He was going at it with a can of spray shellac. He stood and spun the arm of the windmill above the mural. It moved lazily, solidly. "Just so people have a photo souvenir from Solvang. What *can't* your old dad do, that's what I want to know. I should get another can." He shook the can, and the ball rattled. "That'll seal it for a few months, but a stitch in time saves nine, doesn't it, girls?" My dad loved clichés, their easy access and the way they helped order a life. "Let's take a drive, go down to the corner and get the lay of the land."

"How much are you going to charge for a picture?"

"I was thinking three or four bucks," my dad said. "That's pretty good. Don't you think that's about right?"

"I just don't know how we'll make a *living*," my mom said. "You'd have to have tons of customers, at least ten a day, don't you think, I mean, Bob, I'm not saying you haven't done a nice job, I'm just wondering. If maybe this shouldn't be a part-time thing, or a summer thing. Maybe I could run it while you did something else."

"Ye of little faith," my dad said. "This is going to pay our rent and then some. It's the only thing like it around here. Everything else is restaurants and hotels. Let's go look, come on. And we can stop somewhere afterwards, pick up a bite to eat."

As it turned out, the windmill photo kiosk did make money; my dad opened every morning at nine A.M. and by the time Jen and I got off school, taking a shortcut through Hans Christian Andersen park and over a footbridge and through a parking lot, my dad was always whistling and jingling the coins in his apron pockets. For months it went on like this; then the off-season hit and the skies stayed gray and damp and only a few tourists wandered the streets, and my dad set up a pegboard stand next to the windmill from which he sold gum and cigarettes and maps and hair combs. The kiosk, at least in summer, had been such a sure thing that we'd run up debts; my parents had a new king-sized bed with a scrolled headboard, and Jen and I had new ten-speed bikes, and my dad had invested in a new car. All we had to do was hold out, my dad kept telling my mom, just make it through to spring and we could get on our feet again.

"We need P.E. uniforms," Jen told my dad one day after school. "They're seven dollars each and we have to have it by tomorrow." My dad sat in a folding chair next to the kiosk. Every now and again he'd get up and fiddle with things, moving rolls of film higher up the pegboard, adding more eyeglass repair kits to the basket near the cash register.

"Ask your mom," he said. "Seven bucks. Really? That seems like an awful lot of money for P.E. uniforms. Go see what your mom says."

Jen and I raced each other home. She was in fifth grade, and I was in fourth, but I ran faster. Jen was knock-kneed but if I mentioned it she held me down and pulled real handfuls of hair from my skull, tufts she then dangled in front me chanting, *shrunken head, shrunken head.*

My mom was in the kitchen rolling out dough. Her new blue clogs made a soft clop-clopping sound. Living in Solvang made her want to learn to bake, and after school Jen and I liked to wander the town and collect walnuts, loading the tarry pods into scoops we made with the front of our T-shirts. Then we hauled them home and my mom shelled them, digging at the soft flesh with an ice pick. But it was disastrous, watching her cook. She hated the detailed recipes, and got frustrated and spilled sugar on the floor or said *crap* and *shit* and then lit a cigarette.

"We don't have that kind of money, we can't possibly afford that," my mom said now, and ashed her cigarette in the sink. "There's no way. Don't they have some sort of a fund?"

"Fund?" Jen had sidled over to the canister of brown sugar and was picking through it, looking for chunks.

"Yes, fund. Because we can't possibly afford that. Who's your P.E. teacher? I'll call her, maybe we can work something out."

"There's the three-dollar ones," Jen said. "But they're ugly and have snaps."

"Three dollar ones? What do you mean?"

"There are two kinds." I said. I didn't like my mom's interest. We'd always been popular at school, always had enough of the right things. "The seven-dollar ones are stripy and zip up the front."

"And what about the other ones? Is it okay if you wear those?"

"No," Jen said. "I wouldn't be caught dead in one. That's what the poor kids wear."

"Oh, is that so," my mom said. "Well, guess what, you're a poor kid now. Your dad's having a hell of a time finding work and maybe, *maybe* we can afford the ones that are three dollars, but seven dollars, no way. It won't kill you to wear them. It will be a learning experience."

"I'm not going, if we have to wear them," I said. It made me desperate listening to her. The uniforms blazed small pictures in my brain, the striped polyester suit on the left and the plain blue snap-up on the right. At school it was the pretty girls, the popular ones, who wore the polyester uniforms. They stretched the suits clear to their knees and then shifted glossy ponytails to the top of their heads and swung their arms and grunted, pretending to be cave women. Whereas the poor girls, the ones with lank hair and crabby faces, wore the solid cotton suits and stood off to the side, waiting to get picked for teams. Now I was going to be one of them and I couldn't figure out how it had happened. In Provo we'd had *everything*. Now we were poor. The two ideas kept hopping back and forth.

"Oh, come on, Luce, it's not that big a deal," my mom said. "It's just a P.E. suit, it's not like you're going to remember it in five years."

"I might just sign up for gymnastics, instead," Jen said. She made a little face to show she was sorry but I could see I was in it on my own now, because gymnastics didn't start until fifth grade. "I could wear my purple leotard."

"Well, that settles it," my mom said. "It'll be fine, Luce. It's no biggie. School's only in session for another few months. And then maybe next year, maybe next year we can get you the stripy one."

"We were poor," my dad said later. "Flat-ass broke by the time we left but your mom loved that goddamned town, she really did. I just plain couldn't make a living there. Do you remember when we left? It was the middle of the night, we had to leave in the middle of the night because we were so behind on the rent. That was a sad time. Do you remember?"

The town fell away behind us in the rearview mirror. My mom was sniffling and our dad stared straight ahead. On the way out of town we passed the public library; I still had books checked out: *The Good Earth*, and *Are You There, God? It's Me, Margaret.* I hadn't meant to renege, I really hadn't. I wanted to be like other kids, whose library book due dates got jotted on a calendar. My best friend that year was Susie Raleigh, whose family lived on the edge of town and had ponies. The week before, Mrs. Raleigh had taught a bunch of us girls how to make cinnamon rolls; it was raining outside and she popped open a cylinder of dough, showed us how to brush melted butter over the gooey yellow triangles and sprinkle them thickly with cinnamon sugar. I stood at the window of the oven waiting for the rolls to bake and wanting all of it, a house with butter in the refrigerator, a place where making cinnamon rolls in the middle of an afternoon could be enough. That was the kind of thing that would drive my mom crazy. She used Bisquick for everything, which I held against her. She rinsed dirty silverware under the tap instead of washing with soap and hot water, and then used the wet utensils like we were in some big fat hurry to get it over with. None of her Danish pastries had ever turned out and I could see clearly that it was because she couldn't stand to take the time to do things, so that the dough never had time to rise before she started twisting and wringing it, not even wanting to do it in the first place but just trying to prove through some whole elaborate display that she was *Danish*.

"I'm sick of moving," I said. "Why can't we stay in the same house for at least a year? Other kids don't move around this much."

"Somebody ask the Magic Eight Ball a question," Jen said.

"I'm sorry, girls. I really am. This one's my fault. I just couldn't eke out a living in Solvang, I just couldn't. It's all the tourist industry and when that dries up, well."

"Couldn't you have opened your T-shirt shop?" I'd spilled French fries on the floor of the car earlier and now I tried to kick them under my dad's seat, one after another, doing something pointless with my time since it didn't matter what I did, anyway. We'd just move again.

"Well, I would've needed money for that, Hon. And rents in Solvang are really high. I couldn't break in, there was too much competition."

"I don't know why you think *Salt Lake* will be any better," my mom said. Her voice was low and furious. "I hate the idea of going back, I hate it more than I can even tell you. If I didn't have these kids. And a *rental*. How can we live in a rental?"

"The money's *gone*, Miriam. It just is. We had to live on something. I just couldn't make it."

Jen spit her gum over the top of the seat. It whacked off the dashboard and for a minute my mom and dad were both too surprised to say anything. "What the hell was that all about, Young Lady?" my dad plucked up the gum and threw it out the window.

"I hate everybody," Jen said. She threw the Magic Eight Ball, and it hit the windshield and bounced off. Then the windshield had a big spider web and my dad screeched to a stop on the side of the road and stomped off into the bushes. Jen had thrown a blanket over herself and I could hear little wet noises coming from underneath. I touched her where I thought her shoulder would be and one skinny hand shot out from underneath the blanket and smacked me. "Leave me alone! Everybody just leave me alone!"

"I'm sad, too, Honey. It's okay for you to cry. I know how you liked Solvang, we all did. But your dad, well he's smart but he doesn't have a whole lot of training in things, no college education, and it makes it hard on us. That's all." My mom got in the backseat with Jen and tried to lift off the blanket and Jen smacked her arm away.

It was years before I figured out that Solvang was a *fake* Danish town. How could this have been lost on my mom, who was smart enough to wind up with a Master's degree? There were a few real Danes, like Gunther, with one eye that didn't open and the other leaking all the time, saying *yah* to all my mom's questions. But how could she have thought that any of the rest of it was *real?*—the windmills, the shops stuffed with clogs and aprons and pewter souvenir spoons and tablecloths, the refrigerator magnets with the Danish girl, blonde braids wagging, frozen in some stupid hop that meant she was *clogging*; the windmill-shaped cookies, the deep-fried doughballs called *abelskievers*, served in every restaurant in town with powdered sugar and lots of jam—the whole stupefying mess meant to signify yet again, lest there were doubts, that *this town was Danish.*

And because we were leaving it, I'd never get to return my library books. Because of it, we were stopped somewhere out on the highway, Jen practically having a nervous breakdown and my dad off in the woods somewhere.

I took the flashlight from the glove box and went after my dad. The flashlight made a weak gray beam on the ground and then I found him, sitting on the ground between two boulders. He had his glasses off and his face was wet. He kept his fingers pinched against his eyes. "I'm so sorry, Lucy," he said. "I'm so, so sorry. No one expects things. We just keep moving and moving and trying to get everything better and instead it's just worse and worse. I never, never, never should've moved us to Provo. That was my big mistake. I kept trying to make things better for us and the money just went. I don't know how things got to this point."

I sat on the ground next to him, found a tiny twig and drew in the dirt. It occurred to me that even here, in the middle of the night in the woods, I was unafraid, because my dad was here with me. He was like a giant warm flesh wall between myself and the world. But with my mom, more and more it seemed, even safe places could feel scary: like my bedside that night when she'd come to tell us we were moving to Arizona, or the desert before that with its snakes and dented trailer and everything *wrong wrong wrong*. "You and me against the world," I said. It was a line from our favorite song, our song. I took his hand, and my dad broke open. He sobbed between gasps and a string of mucus hung from one nostril. I wiped his nose with my sleeve and my dad said *oh ick, no*. By then I was crying, too.

"I'm sorry, I'm sorry for everything," my dad said. "Arizona didn't help. I should've just told your mom *no*. You don't expect things."

"Dad, stop. Please stop. It'll be okay. We just need to get there and get in our new house."

"You. I'm the dad. I should be holding it together." He put his glasses back on and I thought how old he looked, with lines running across his forehead and collected in his neck. He looked a little bit like a turtle.

We sat there a while, looking at a fire ring and a bunch of beer cans some kids had left. Then he stood up and dusted off his pants and hauled me up with one hand. We walked slowly, picking our way. Back at the car my dad opened the back door and my mom slid out so that he could sit next to Jen. Even when things were terribly wrong, my parents worked like a team. My mom handed him the Eight Ball and he knocked politely at Jen's blanket. "Come on, you wanted us to ask a question," he said. "Magic Eight Ball, is Jen going to love Salt Lake? Is she going to have oodles of friends and make captain of the swim team? Is she going to drive a fast car and have lots of boyfriends and waist-length hair?" My dad shook the cube and turned on the dome light. We waited for the triangle to bob to the surface: *not likely*, it said. My dad shook it again. *"You can count on it,"* he read.

The fifth house we lived in, this one in Salt Lake, was an honest brick rectangle of a house that looked exactly like every other house on the block. Even the plants were the same, quaking aspens grouped in clumps, and fitzers along the walkways and foundations. Beneath the aspen was cedar bark, each piece the size of a hotel soap, damp fragrant chunks that were expensive and dumped in a deep layer from countless bags hauled home from the nursery. Our yard had a red Japanese maple tree, also expensive and exotic. It had rose bushes, pine trees. The houses on the block, including ours, all looked like they were from the pages of *Sunset* magazine, like houses you could walk through with a camera at any time of day. Houses without secrets.

In the evenings when we went for walks my dad noted the land-scaping techniques wistfully, pointing out which plants might've worked better considering the shade, or wondering aloud why someone had planted finca along the foundation instead of something more appropriate like boxwood. But he never brought it up with the neighbors, even the ones we were friendly with. We were losing our hold; however nice the neighborhood was, still my parents suffered the knowledge that we were provisional, tenants, one step closer to losing everything. Whatever money we'd made from selling the house in Provo was long gone. My dad was fixing cars now in a garage across town and sometimes I went with him. It was windowless and oily, and

I always dumped over the large coffee cans filled with nuts and bolts and screws and then lifted my fingers through them, feeling their coldness and weight. "I make a pretty good grease monkey," he told me once. Then he scratched his armpits and made his best monkey noise, going *oooh oooh oooh*, chomping on an invisible banana and tossing the peel over his shoulder.

My mom thought the neighborhood was too Mormon, but my dad had had it with her opinions. Every time she complained he got up and went to putter in the garage. I put the construction paper feet up again, though by now most of the toes had been torn off. I started fifth grade, and Jen started her period.

Each morning in the house in Salt Lake, my mom stood at the huge front window, watching my dad back out the driveway. She wanted to go back to college again but she was too late for fall semester at the University of Utah and now she brooded, lurking behind the olive-green drapery, which was practically impossible to close. You had to pull at a taut set of strings even to draw the sheers, which hissed along slowly and reluctantly, and to draw the olive-green drapes I threw myself into it like a sailor in a storm, dragging and heaving while the drapes limped and hitched at their clips, finally coming to rest with a good three inches still gaping open, which meant pinching and pinning *just to get a little privacy in this goddamn Mormon neighborhood,* my mom said, *everybody wanting to know every goddamn little thing about us.* She roamed the rooms, adjusting the clip in her long, black hair.

What bothered her? What was she looking for? Staying in one place, even in one house, I thought, *wasn't all that hard.* People did it *all the time.* All we had to do was stay put. All we had to do was lug our crap in and dump it in various rooms, and of course it would be nicer still if our mom would keep all the stuff clean, and if our dad would keep it fixed—but if not, even still that was fine—and all us girls had to do was go to school every morning, and go to bed at a reasonable hour and not talk back too much and not hit each other. And if we did things like this—my dad going off to work, my mom staying home to do whatever it was mothers did—it seemed reasonable to hope there could be other bonuses, bowls of ice cream in the evenings, for example, in front of the TV set. My mom liked mocha almond fudge and Carol Burnett. And my dad was a chocolate man, who shared his side of the bed so we could all watch the Ice Capades.

"Are you happy here?" my mom asked once.

I was at the kitchen table, writing a report about parakeets: *Best known member of the parrot family. Range/Habitat: Entire inland areas of Australia.* I nodded.

"You don't think it's boring? The neighborhood? Day in, day out?"

"I don't like P.E.," I said. "I hate volleyball. Serving hurts my arm and I never get picked."

"I mean overall," my mom said. "How can you stand it, just every day going to the same school, eating the same foods, doing all the same things?"

"I don't know," I said.

"Well, you're more like your dad." My mom sipped her ice tea, thoughtfully pushing the lemon slice down beneath the ice cubes and then watching it bob back up. "You don't like change."

I cut out another picture of a bird and glued it onto a blank page. *Parakeet Budgerie,* I wrote underneath. *Black lines on head recede as bird grows older.* It was true, I did like things to stay the same. I wanted to belong, to stay somewhere long enough to become one of the popular kids.

"Your dad's always been that way," my mom said. "Sort of a stick-in-the-mud, but you can count on him. He's not one for surprises, that's for sure. That's why people always like him better than me, too, why he has an easier time making friends. He walks into a party and people are just all over him, they trust him, but me, well, people think I'm flaky. Just because I like to shake things up. Anyway, I wish I had more friends. You're like your dad that way, too, people feel at ease around you. Like you get invited to parties. I never did. I never even went to any school dances. No one asked me." My mom ran her finger along the rim of her glass, around and around. It gave me the creeps whenever she did it. Her mouth fell open a little, and she looked like she wanted someone to caress her just the same way. "Not one single boy."

"I don't get invited to that many parties," I said. I hoped she wouldn't bring up sleep-over parties, because I hadn't made it through a single one. I always called home in the middle of the night and made my dad come get me. It scared me to be in someone else's house at night, with all the lights off and the TV off and no one keeping watch.

"You get invited to plenty. Isn't there one this Saturday? A birthday?"

"Sarah Reilly's."

"'Reilly.' Are they Irish?"

"I don't know. We get to jump on the trampoline."

"I'll bet they are." My mom scooped more ice tea powder in her glass, then filled it under the tap. "I could've married someone Irish, but I never liked redheads. That was the only thing. What time?"

"What?"

"What time's the party?"

"I don't know. I think maybe at three. Can I use the sharp scissors?"

"Sure." She got them for me. "You say 'scissor,' even though it sounds funny, doesn't it? 'Can I use the sharp scissor,' like that. Do you think it would be okay if I came with you?"

"To Sarah's party?" I went at another page of parakeet photos, trying to cut carefully along the edge of the tailfeather, around the claws. My parakeet, Richie Rich, stood sometimes on my finger and peered in at me, his pupils dilating and contracting like I'd insulted him. His feet felt like twist ties and whenever my mom held him on her finger she said, *Richie Rich needs some hand lotion.*

"Why not?" my mom said. "Aren't other parents going? I could use a good time, I get so sick of just sitting around this place, I don't even remember the last time *I* got invited to a party. I could wear my yellow dress."

"You can come if you want."

"Well, don't sound so excited." My mom wandered over to the mantel and lit her patchouli-scented candle. She wasn't allowed to light it when my dad was around. He thought it was too much of a hippie thing. I liked candles, but I agreed with my dad that the patchouli smelled awful, like a man's dirty socks.

"I want you to."

"Maybe you could wear a yellow dress, too. We could be twins, wouldn't that be fun? I have to work to make friends, Luce, I really do. You don't know what that's like, really neither of you kids do, you're both social butterflies, just like your dad, but I have to work and work to get people to like me. And a party sounds fun, doesn't it? We could get up really early together and curl our hair, I have some orange juice cans I could wash out that we could use, you could even wear some of my lipstick. How would that be?"

"Just for a while," I said. "Then I think the other parents are leaving."

"What, you don't want me to come with? If you don't want me to come with you, just say so. I can handle that. I just thought a party sounded fun, is all. Gee." She started sniffling, and I put down the scissors and tried to hug her. She moved to another chair. "Don't try to make up with me, not if you don't mean it. I mean gosh, all I wanted was to come along, to have a little bit of fun, and I'm not even welcome at *Sarah Reilly's* party."

"I want you to come, Mom." I wanted my dad to come home, or at least Jen. They knew what to do when she got like this but it seemed like I always did just the opposite of what my mom needed, and ended up making her feel worse. "I mean it. Really."

"You do not, you don't, not really. Do you think things are easy for me, Luce? Do you? Because they're not. Not at all. Everything's easy for your dad, oh sure, and you're his favorite, but it's not like that for me."

When I tried again, she let me hug her. Then I stood next to her chair, feeling bad.

She was right: everything about my dad was easy. It was unfair, because it meant he got all the credit, came out looking like the hero. When my mom made scenes, my dad kept his head. Being polite in public was at the top of his list, and this was where she seemed to get the most upset, in restaurants with everybody watching from their tables, their faces still over full glasses of water and untouched hamburgers and yellow wedges of French-fried potatoes, all the food and everybody waiting to see what would happen next.

You hit me all the time, Bob, you do, deny it now but I'm sick of how it's a deep dark secret, she'd said once, and then the waiter hurried over, my dad trying fast to pay the bill, instructing us to get our coats on and zip up while my mom, weeping, shook her head, telling the waiter she was fine, really, she was coming home with us, it was all fine, she came scurrying and wrapping herself against the sharp air, one of us dropping behind to cling to her arm.

We always chose sides, and I never took hers. My dad was calm and smelled good and could be trusted. He had a man's worn wallet, and *it* smelled trustworthy, like buttery cowhide, and when we went to get ice cream he always had cash, not change but paper money, whereas our mom liked to scrounge loose change from between the seats, waving us ahead to peruse the menu at Baskin-Robbins, which we did without faith. But she liked how it felt: the sticky pennies and nickels and occasional quarter, how it made a lint, logged pile on the counter, *it's like we're getting ice cream for free,* she crowed, except that we didn't want it free, we didn't want the painful slow counting out, the way one of us had to shoot back outside to check under the floormats because we were six cents short, one of us arranging the pennies in stacks of ten or popping napkins from the dispenser like we had some *right,* meanwhile the cones were dripping and the cashier was looking more aggravated by the minute, right along with the other dozen customers who were waiting to give their order: Baseball Butter Brickle, Peanut Butter Crunch Creme. In case my mom hadn't *noticed,* we were all Americans, here, and Americans were *supposed* to have money, were supposed to walk in like my dad and not care how long the lady had to wait, since he *had* money, organized in his wallet from small bills to large; and when we were with my dad we could order whatever we wanted and hop from one tiny pink school desk with its pink swiveling stool to the next, and bap straws saucily from the dispenser and slurp from the water fountain, loudly, not caring if we made noise, organizing ourselves into a line only when he threatened, which he did playfully, like Mr. Brady.

Then we fell in, waited for our ice cream and said thank you. My mom never had that kind of authority, and anyway this approach bored her. She wanted to scrape for change, make it seem like there was something at stake. It seemed to refresh her, like the scenes in restaurants.

"I'm okay, Honey," my mom said, and looked absently at my parakeet book. "It's not you, really it's not, it's just everything. You shouldn't have to deal with this, you really shouldn't. How's your report coming? Are you about finished? It's looking so nice. Really professional. Come on, go sit down so you can finish it."

"I want us to go to the party together. I mean it, Mom."

"Well, we'll see."

"Are you okay?"

"Of course, Sweetheart. I'm just fine. I need to run an errand, maybe you can finish your report and go with me. I have to go to Sears, they've been pretty good about things but we really do need to at least make a small payment. Will you go with me?"

"Sure." I went back to work, cutting out another picture and pasting it in: *Bird length: 7 inches. Parakeet Budgeries can be trained to "talk" with patience, and perform amusing antics. Life span: 10–15 years.*

Our landlord had been emphatic about the No Pets policy but my dad, to shut me up, brought them home anyway, a brother and a sister because they were the last two in the cardboard box outside the grocery store. We named them Barney and Becca, and within a month both dogs had been mowed over by a car in the street in front of our house. This turn of events distanced us further from the gentle neighbors, who kept their dogs leashed and took them to the veterinarian every year for shots; some of the families on our block had dogs or cats that were eleven and twelve years old. My dad carried Becca, bloody and dangling, into the backyard and all the neighborhood kids turned out to watch. I read an excerpt from, *Where the Red Fern Grows,* a book that slayed me.

Later, my dad would have to dig Becca up; we had planted her too close to the boundary line, a fact that the next door neighbor lady pointed out shrilly, the sleeves of her housecoat flapping crazily. This time Becca went straight into the trash.

Once, during this time, I found a list my mom had made. It was stuck in the toe of her high boot, and folded into a tiny square:

Ten things I can't do, as Bob's wife:
1) dance naked in a rainstorm, or even just take long walks in the rain
2) swear
3) get rid of the television
4) go to Native-American things like powwows; go to black symposiums, lectures, etc., or anything Bob considers "weird"
5) have homosexual friends or parties where I invite homosexual people
6) take trips to places like Canada and Mexico
7) date other men
8) fill the house with candles, incense, and posters
9) go to rock concerts
10) smoke marijuana

I folded the list and put it back. We'd been doing pretty well in Salt Lake; my mom was enrolled at the U. for spring semester, and during the day when my dad was at work my mom took us to the mall, where we wandered looking at shoes and eating corn dogs. Then we stopped at Sears to say hi to Ellery, who worked in the credit department and had been in one of my mom's psychology classes. "Can you *imagine,* a man wearing *clogs*?" my mom would say. "Some big size twelve flopping around, whack whack. That's what all the guys in the psychology department look like, like a bunch of softies. Like they wouldn't be able to hold down a job." When my dad got wind of Ellery, my mom just laughed. "Oh *please*," she said. *"Please.* He has a *ponytail,* if you can imagine. Just the thought of it, that skinny hair rippling down his back." She shuddered. But it scared me to see her list, to read all the secret things she wanted. The only way my dad seemed to know how to handle her was by keeping her in line, shame her into acting like a good wife and mother, and I thought that overall his technique was a good one, because my mom needed limits. Without them she went crazy, like a little kid who had too much to choose from. She kept secrets from him and made lists like this one.

I took the list back and stuck it in my pocket.

y mom met Sky outside Peace a Pizza, where Sky was wading through a dumpster. Sky wasn't being shy about it. She picked along with her batik dress knotted against her knees like she was in a field looking for tiny purple flowers, and she was humming. When she saw my mom she smiled like they'd been friends forever and offered my mom a slice of pizza, which she'd peeled from the lid of a half-crushed cardboard box. My mom smiled back and took a bite and by that night Sky was staying in the guest room, her batik dress washed and dripping pink dye in the bathtub.

My dad couldn't believe it. He was beyond understanding, beyond comprehension. He'd heard the dumpster story from my mom and then again from both of us kids, and each time he heard it he got more depressed. When my dad was unhappy he cleaned his fingernails carefully with the tip of a steak knife, and tonight he'd done it so many times that finally he peeled off his thin, dark-blue socks, first one and then the other, and started on his toenails. When he was through with that he cleaned both ears with Q-tips, squinting and digging in a way that looked painful. He and my mom argued while he plucked the stray hairs from his ears, then his nose. I held the mirror for him, trying to be loyal, but I could hear Jen at the back of the house with Sky. At one point Jen showed up to borrow my mom's hairbrush and when she returned it her hair was complexly braided, with rainbow-colored strings and translucent blue beads woven in.

"Now," our dad said. "Take it out. Now."

"Oh, Bob," my mom said. "That's what I mean. Why does she threaten you so much, is all I want to know. It's just for a couple of nights until she can find her own pad."

"Pad," my dad said. "*Pad.*"

"I don't want to take it out," Jen said. "She's cool. She knows how to play the guitar and she's going to teach me."

"Go to bed," my dad said. "And take that crap out of your hair, first. I'm not kidding."

From the back of the house I could hear strumming, and Sky singing softly. My favorite movie that year was *Billy Jack.* I liked Billy Jack's middle-aged girlfriend, with her reedy voice and stringy blonde hair and strident appeals to the townspeople. I liked the way Billy Jack kept his socks on to demonstrate his latest martial-arts move. And I was a complete sucker for the hippie chick in the movie, a blonde who wore hip-huggers and her hair parted down the middle and who sang tearful songs on her guitar to the hushed townspeople, whose silence and nodding in the audience, as she sang, gave us to understand that at last, because of her ballad, they would try to make peace with the Indians. Every time I saw the movie, the part where the mustangs galloped freely over the plains, I got chills; behind the horses stood Indians, wearing headbands and mournful faces. I didn't want my mom to know that I liked the movie because I didn't want to encourage her, and I kept it a secret from my dad so he wouldn't think I was going against him.

"I'll be right back," I said.

Sky had unbraided Jen's hair and now she was applying tiny moons and stars to her cheek with glittery powder and a paintbrush. She'd draped her damp batik dress over the lampshade, casting the room in pink shadow, and she was burning a cone of incense in a small brass elephant. "Is there anything to eat around here?"

"I'll go get you something," Jen said, and when she came back with everything, Chips Ahoy and potato chips and beef jerk, Sky said, *Fucking A.*

"You're gonna get in trouble," I told Jen. "We're supposed to ask."

"Mellow," Sky said. "You won't get in trouble. I'll say I had the munchies and raided the fridge in the middle of the night." She laughed. "Your dad's kind of uptight, isn't he? I'm not going to stay but a couple of days, I need to get back on the road."

"He's just worried about my mom," I said. "She gets kind of weird. Where do you sleep at night?"

"Wherever the wind takes me," Sky said. "Parks, sometimes, out under the stars. Or sometimes nice folks like y'all open up your hearts. Benches. Bus depots. It's a big, wide world."

"You could get hurt," I said, though I didn't really believe it. Sky looked like she could take care of herself just fine. "You should get a job."

"Shut up, Lucy," Jen said.

"Wow, you're pretty young to be a *Republican*," Sky said, and toyed with my hair. "Let me put beads in yours."

"Dad doesn't like it," I said.

"Well, we'll take it right back out and he'll never know." She started braiding and for a minute I let myself submit. She was spicy-smelling and when she threw one leg out I noticed reddish hairs on her calves.

"How come you don't shave your legs?"

"Why should I? That's where the hair grows naturally. What's weird is that women *do* shave their legs." She lifted her arms and showed me the orangish nests of her armpits. "Au naturel."

"That's so cool," Jen said. "I'm not going to shave either."

"Listen, is there any more food? This all looks great but I was thinking maybe more like dinner food."

"You should be grateful for that much," I said. "There are kids starving in Africa." I didn't want to like Sky. She would be a bad influence on my mom and cause fights. But now she reeled me in for a hug and said *Silly Lucy,* and I stayed in her lap.

Jen came back with a whole plate this time, loaded with leftover beef stroganoff, dinner rolls, a carrot, and the jar of maraschino cherries. "Don't rat on me, either," Jen said.

"I won't."

• • •

My dad noticed all the missing food the next day. "Did she eat all that? Did she?"

"Jen gave it to her," I said.

"Little brat," Jen punched me on the arm.

"Girls, please don't fight." My mom had Sky's finger cymbals on and she was tapping them. She stood up and started to sway.

Sky was taking a shower and my dad said, "She'd better not leave goddamn water all over the floor."

"It's just for a day or two." My mom started to dance. I could never stand to watch. She was pretty but when she danced her hips twitched weirdly, out of rhythm, and she always touched her tongue to her upper lip. My dad couldn't stand it either. We were the killjoys and I was glad when he took the cymbals away from her and got things back to normal.

"One more day," he said. "That's it. That's nice enough."

"Why does she scare you?" my mom said.

"She doesn't scare me, she *irritates* me. She's a freeloader and she probably has rich parents somewhere and I want her out of my house."

"Because of what she represents, that's why," my mom said. "Free love."

"Oh, please."

"You know it's true. And I like her. I want her to stay. I think she could be good for us. Teach us some new things."

"Like what? How to weave beads in her armpit hair?"

"See, now why is that so threatening? Why should women have to shave their armpits, just because society says? She's a free spirit."

"Free*loading* spirit," my dad said. Then we heard the shower go off and my mom said, *New subject.*

Sky came out wearing a towel and wringing her hair. She held it sideways out from her body and ran a comb through it in slow strokes. "Morning all."

In the bathroom, my dad hucked me a towel so I could wipe the water from the floor. "What'd I tell ya?" he said. "Sure she's a hippie, sure she is. Bratty runaway teenager is more like it." He inspected the bathroom closely, peering into the shower and shaking the water from the shower curtain. There were a few pubic hairs near the drain and my dad plucked a Kleenex from the box and swabbed them up. "Oh well, now that's very nice," he said. The bathroom was foggy and smelled like Sky, the same furry spiciness. Her dress was hanging from the hook and my dad smelled it, nervous and quick at first. "What scent is that?" he said, and pushed it to my face.

"I'm not sure. It kind of smells like a tree."

My dad smelled it again, leaving his face in longer this time. He looked nervous and unhappy and then he went quickly back to the kitchen. "This isn't a nudist colony," he said, and wadded the dress and threw it at Sky. She caught it easily, unruffled, a piece of red licorice dangling from the side of her mouth.

My dad kicked Sky out the next day when he found a roach clip in her room. "Out, out, out," he said, and waited while she got her few things together. She flashed us the peace sign.

My mom stood off to the side. "I can't believe you're doing this, I can't believe you'd actually kick her out. If you really kick her out I swear I'll go too, I swear I will."

My dad had given Sky ten bucks for a room at the YWCA, and now he got out his wallet and peeled off two more fives and offered them to my mom. "Here you go. Have fun. Don't spend it all in one place. Oh wait. *Keys.*" He tossed them her direction.

"Oooh, I hate you, I really and truly hate you," my mom said. She snatched up the money and keys and looked at us all for a minute, uncertain. "I swear, if you make her go."

"Come on, people. Cool it," Sky said. "You've been a big help to me and I appreciate your hospitality."

"You can stay," my mom begged. She looked frantic. I thought she might try to hold Sky's arm or stand in front of the door. We shuffled along near Sky as she moved to the front door, a clot of family with eight legs.

"Nice knowing y'all," Sky said.

"I'll go too, I *will*," my mom said. Jen said *mom, please don't*. I knew my dad was bluffing her and that once Sky was gone we'd settle back into our same uneasy shape, my mom crying in the bedroom probably and my dad getting something together for dinner. But this time my mom checked her purse and looked hard at Jen and me. "I can't take this anymore," she said. "I really just can't. Your dad can look after you."

"Please don't leave, Mom," I said. "Sky will be okay."

"You probably should stay," Sky said. "Don't come on my account." She was at the front door and looked both ways, trying to choose a direction. It occurred to me that she probably didn't want my mom coming with her, car or no car. She wet her finger and lifted it to the air. "East it is, then," she said, and headed off.

"She'll be fine," my dad said. "There's always the YWCA. She's got the ten."

"You're a bastard," my mom said. "Good-bye, kids. You know I love you and I'll call, I promise." I kept waiting for her to fold but instead she went to the car and backed it carefully down the driveway. Halfway down the block we saw her stop for Sky. Then the car got small.

Jen started to cry and my dad put a solid hand on each of our shoulders. "She'll be back within the hour, I promise you that," he said. "In the meantime, I'll make us all BLTs."

en and I were on the couch in front of the living room window, watching for our mom. It was day two and she still hadn't called and the point was to not do anything permanent, anything that would mean we'd accepted this new turn of events. The point was to stay on-duty and so we just sat there, watching cars, the TV on but with the sound off.

The house felt unfamiliar, too still. At this time of night my mom would've been cooking dinner and Jen and I would've been out in the street with the neighbor kids, playing Kick the Can. I wondered if the neighbors had seen my mom and Sky leave.

"She'll be back," my dad said. "You know how mad she gets when I don't give her her way."

"Couldn't you have just let Sky stay here?" Jen found a loose thread in one of the sofa cushions and pulled. It left a sudden light line on the cushion, one that would have gotten her in trouble if our mom was around.

"No, I couldn't have," my dad said. "We're a family."

"Not if mom's not here." Jen yanked at another thread and this time it made a little ripping noise. But my dad didn't notice. He was stacking the magazines on the coffee table all in a tower, not fanning them out like they were supposed to be displayed.

"Do you kids need to take baths?"

"Every other night," Jen said. "We took them last night."

"Well, why don't you go brush your teeth or something." My dad sat on the sofa, acting casual with a magazine, though he positioned himself so he could see the street. "Go get ready for bed."

"What if she never comes back?" Jen held the sofa cushion hard against her chest. The phone rang once and I ran for it. But the person on the other end had hung up and I dawdled in the kitchen, swinging the coiled cord like a jump rope.

"She'll come back," my dad said. "Don't be silly. She just needed a break from things. You hungry? What'll it be? Fried postholes, or stewed rabbit tracks?"

My dad said *pillah* for pillow, and sometimes at breakfast he popped up popcorn and ate it with milk and sugar, like it was cereal. And he ate wedges of chocolate cake in bowls with lukewarm coffee poured over the cake, and when he was sick he liked bread soaked in warm milk. The stewed rabbit tracks and fried postholes always stopped me. They seemed like something you ought to be able to eat, the toe edges crisping, the soft indentations of rabbit foot like dough or sponge cake. I pictured the tracks in a blue line, in snow.

"A break from you, you mean," Jen hurled the cushion and it bounced off the front of the TV. "Why can't you let her have hippie friends if she wants? What's the big deal?"

"You don't know anything about it, young lady. Go to bed."

"I'm *not* going to bed, Not until mom comes home. Are you going to try to raise us without a mother? Because you can't. You don't know certain things."

"Be quiet, Jen," I said. Jen kicked me in the back of the leg. Once she put her mind to some sort of violence it always hurt like hell. "Are you and Mom going to get a divorce?"

"Of *course* not," my dad said. "Gee whiz, I'm living with a bunch of drama queens. *No*, we're not going to get divorced. We've been together fifteen years, people don't get divorced after that much time even if they *want* to. I'd never divorce your mom, not ever. I couldn't stand to be without you kids, not for a million years. Come on now, stop all this. Why don't we watch some TV?" He moved to the TV and switched it on and stopped halfway back to the couch, looking out onto the driveway. The relief seemed to drop over him. "Well, well, well," he said. "Look what the cat dragged in."

My mom started at the U. spring semester. Her teachers loved her, especially the instructor of her Native-American lit class, who read her papers and wrote encouraging comments all over them, which she brought home to show off. In between classes she took advantage of the University's genealogy library to look into our own family history. Eventually she decided she was part Native American Indian, one thirty-secondth at least, maybe more.

It wasn't hard to believe. My mom had a dark, chiseled-looking face, and her hair was coarse and black. She pointed out that this made Jen and me one sixty-fourth Indian, maybe even enough for us to get financial aid when it came time for us to go to college.

At first it was just talk. She kept taking college classes and my dad kept plugging away at the garage and after school Jen and I rode the bus home and played Kick the Can and Barbies with the kids on our block. But after a while my mom started to change in ways that scared all of us. She bought a pair of knee-high beaded moccasins and wore them around with her dresses like it looked normal; she grew her hair out and when it was just barely long enough, gave herself two stubby braids.

The day my mom started using a different voice, one low and solemn and meant to evoke the great suffering of Her People, my dad pulled the classifieds section from the stack of newspaper next to the fireplace and sat hunched over it with a black Magic Marker. He looked at apartments and duplexes, studios and furnished and unfurnished houses; when he was done with all that he moved onto jobs, circling a few, his gestures small and miserable.

"Want to go for a ride?" he said finally, and tucked the newspaper into one armpit. He was trying to figure out a way to fix things again. They'd had an especially big fight earlier, when my mom moved through the house with a stick of burning sage. When my dad had yelled at her my mom's eyes filled up. *You can never understand the great sorrow of my people,* she'd said. My dad said, *Horseshit.*

In the car I used the marker to circle a few things of my own: ads for free puppies, free kittens, for boarding horses. When I was through with all that I moved onto furniture, and circled an ad for a canopy bed.

My dad drove until he found a pay phone, and I sat in the car watching his mouth move into the receiver. My parents were always fighting, because my mom was miserable. If he had a good job, she pointed out, things might get better; if his job was *white collar,* instead of *blue collar,* well then, maybe things would start to look up. But he had to be a car mechanic, didn't he, walking around in his soiled white T-shirt, not even changing in time for dinner. Her friends had been to *college,* she said. *College.* And so now my dad stood at the phone, trying to change his life.

He came back, and slid in without looking at me. Then he just sat there. I loved being in the car with him, fiddling with the radio, checking the glove compartment for gum and Life Savers.

"Maybe a phone job," he said. "That would make your mother happy I'll bet. And there's an ad to be a book salesman, maybe I'll apply for that one. I have experience in sales."

"Did you talk to anybody?" I said. I was thinking about the free puppies, part German shepherd, the ad said, and part collie.

"Well, I'm not going to get a hold of anybody today," my dad said. "I know that. I just don't know what to do for her, Honey. Some days I really don't. I don't know what would make her happy."

"Did you find any new houses?" I opened the glove compartment and used my dad's Chapstick. It came in a black tube and had a weird, medicinal smell, like something that would get used in a funeral home. But it was also clean and sharp, unlike my mom's, which usually had lint stuck to the tip and was crushed along one side.

"Oh, I don't know," my dad said. He started the car. "We could look at a few, I guess, she hates our new house so much. I know she wants something older, ever since we left the House on the Hill. I never should've left that house, I really shouldn't have. She loved that goddamned place."

"I saw some free kittens and puppies," I said.

"You know Jen's allergies willl act up. And your mom would flip her lid over another dog," my dad said. But he took the newspaper from me and looked over the ads. He started the car, and drove us around town for awhile. We checked out a few houses and one duplex. They all looked smaller than the house we were living in. But there was one my mom would go crazy for, and my dad was so sure of this that he parked the car in front of the house and got out and creaked open the wrought-iron gate. It was a small white house with a porch swing and lilac bushes. While my dad moved around the house I picked as many lilacs as I could carry and hauled them back to the car.

"This would be her dream house," my dad said. "I'm not even gonna tell her about it. Look at that foundation. All those cracks. I wouldn't touch this place with a ten-foot pole." Sometimes he said things like this: *I wouldn't touch it with a ten-foot pole.* And later: *She didn't leave me so much as a pot to piss in.* "But she'd love it, I guarantee it. Do you think we've been gone long enough? Think she's cooled off?"

"Maybe," I said. "We could just go and look at the puppies. We wouldn't have to bring one home."

"Just so you know," my dad said. "Your mom never was, never has, and never will be Indian. She has some big romance going about it because that's how your mother is. And now she thinks she's part Native American because it's a cool, hippie thing, but our family is from Britain. It's important for you to know that, I'm not saying your mom's lying, just that she has an active imagination. Okay?"

"Okay."

My dad turned the car toward home. "We can play along," he said. "Humor her if it makes her happy. But don't mention that little house, whatever you do. We'll just tell her we went for a drive, stopped for a burger. I don't know why she gets these things in her head, I really don't. It's like she wants to be someone else," he said. "Like she's not happy just being herself."

"It'll blow over," I said. "It always does." I tried to think of something else to say. When he confided in me like this, I wanted fiercely to say something deep or wise or beyond my years. I wanted him to need me and keep me close always. But it embarrassed me, too, because sometimes when we listened to love songs together in the car he felt like a lover, his smell essential, his warm hairy hand covering mine on the seat between us. The car had a great stereo and with the windows rolled up it was our whole world, with no room or air for anyone else.

My dad looked over at me. "You're wise, you know that?" he said. "Pretty smart, for being eleven. Little Wise Owl, that's what I ought to call you. Little Running Bear Smart Kid." My dad sighed. "And now she wants us to call her something else. Running something, or Flying something. I don't know where she gets these ideas. She wasn't like that, when we first got married. I think she just maybe gets bored or something. But she hasn't always been like this, wanting to change all the time. Just since we left California." He put a hand on my leg. In a few years he'd stop doing this, the way he'd also stop letting me kiss him on the mouth, turning at the last minute so that I ended up with the stubbly skin of his cheek. But for now we were best friends. "I just hope she's not planning anything crazy," my dad said. "You know, like a scalping. That would be just my luck, wouldn't it?"

Sometimes my dad played a game with Jen and me, approaching us with a slow, grave step and his index finger out. *Pull*, he'd say, which sent us rushing through the house, screeching and laughing. But he could hold it. He followed us calmly, cornered us again: *pull*. There was no way out of it, and our hysteria grew until finally we gave in, both trapped on the couch pleading *no, Dad, no, no, no*. Then one of us pulled and my dad would fart, his face still calm, taking his time. We shrieked more, pinched our noses, our laughter high and maniacal until Jen, with her allergies, would start to sputter and cough and both my dad and I would have to slap her between her wings.

My mom stayed Native American Indian, and she and my dad fought all the time about it, and then about other things: money and Utah and her going to college, and my dad's new job as a textbook salesman, which my mom said was *cheap*, since it meant he had to work on commission. Sometimes the fights were so bad that they leaked out onto the driveway where my mom threw things at my dad, his electric razor and his pajamas and his toothbrush. But eventually she was awarded a two-thousand-dollar scholarship based on her need as a person of color, and now she kept her hair combed out straight and long and used her Indian voice more than ever, her sentences like heavy shards of pottery, thick and without humor.

As a Native American Indian, my mom suffered greatly: she read and reread *Bury My Heart at Wounded Knee*, and sported a bracelet with a flattened hunk of turquoise the size of a vanilla wafer. She was passionate and insistent, a browbeater to the end. My mom had learned somewhere along the way that a story was the same thing as a memory, and that the person who could tell the best story was the one the world would finally end up believing. For her it seemed a matter of truth, and one that was pointless to dispute. Us kids, of course, were foolish and tried to argue. But we were not yet orators: we had none of my mother's finesse, and when we did try to argue or disagree, she made mincemeat of us. My mother had long, beautiful arms and a voice that projected mightily. *Gee, you should be on the stage*, my dad would tell her. *The next one leaves town in five minutes.* But he adored her, was floored by her. And when my parents quarreled my dad would listen to everything my mom had to say, his mouth moving like he was lip-syncing or following along.

What was the difference, finally? Between what was said and what was remembered. But my dad, like us kids, turned into a fanatical bookkeeper. He filed receipts, letters, memo notes, index cards. When she'd gone too far he'd produce some bit of evidence to show that he was in the right. Then my mom would look at him with pity and humor. *How do I know you didn't just forget that?* she'd say. *How do I know that's really the right receipt?* This maddened my dad, who trusted all things tangible and linear. He was a carpenter: he could build a house from the ground up, could lay brickwork and pipe and find his way through a rat's nest of wiring, if necessary. But my mother was dreamy and circuitous and dishonest.

"You're the one that dragged me here," she was saying now. "I never, never, never would've left my House on the Hill. My home. And now that I've found out my heritage, now that I have the truth, you turn against me."

"Would you please cut the crap?" my dad said. "Honestly, I swear to God, I can't stand another single minute of this. You're from *Iowa*, Miriam. You're not some goddamned squaw. I've about had it with all this. I've tried to be patient, I really have. I tried to support you, even when you wanted to join the goddamned Church."

"I was misled," my mom said. "Told lies."

"*Stop using that voice,*" my dad said. "I really mean it, Miriam. I don't know what you're getting out of it, but if you want to know the truth there's something really *off* about what you're doing, it's scaring me, it's scaring the girls. So just stop."

"This is who I am," my mom said. "I'm sorry, if it is a person you do not like. This is me."

"I said *stop using that voice.*" My dad pushed her against the wall. "And take off that fucking head band." He turned to me. "Go to your room."

"They've stolen our land!" she said. The grief in her voice was real, and that scared me more than anything she'd done so far. I wanted my real mother back. "They're killing our eagles, if you even care. You can't stand it, can you, the thought that you might be married to a person of color. Because you're a bigot, is why it bothers you."

"That has nothing to do with it," my dad said.

"That has everything. Because you're afraid. Well, this is me, Charlie Brown. Get used to it."

My dad hit her, once and hard across the face. My mom reached behind herself, got the broom, and swatted at him; I saw her laugh a little. Then Jen was behind me and we watched my dad wrestle the broom from our mom and poke her in the eye. He yanked off her headband and threw it on the floor. Jen ran at my dad, who shoved her off. "You kids go to your room."

My mom was crying, curled on the floor now. "I hate this place," my mom said. "I hate Utah, I hate that you made me sell the House on the Hill, I hate you. You're a nothing, a big fat loser nothing who can barely even support us. If I didn't have these kids. If I didn't have these kids. I swear to God, then I'd divorce you so fast you wouldn't even know what hit you."

"Go for it," my dad said. "Be my guest." He was backing out, reaching for his coat and keys. We heard the car screech out of the driveway, and then my mom's quiet weeping.

After a while she stood up. I didn't know what we were supposed to do now, what would be the right move. I wanted to watch TV but that seemed wrong so I stayed where I was. "He's never coming back," she said. "Do you kids know that? Do you know what misfortune has befallen you? He hates me, he hates all of us. I don't know how we'll eat. I don't know what we'll do."

"I can make us some chicken noodle soup," Jen said. "He'll come back, Mom."

"He won't. He *won't*, I know him. He's never coming back. And there's no food, no food at all. I just don't know what we'll do, girls. Who can we call at a time like this? We don't have any friends here, not any. And I have to feed us, somebody has to provide, I can't just let you kids starve."

"We have mac-n-cheese," Jen said. "It's okay, Mom."

"It's not okay. It's not okay. You have no idea." My mom's eyes glittered and she kept pulling nervously at her fingers. Her eyes jumped around the kitchen. "You have no idea. No clue at all. We're in a terrible, terrible predicament."

"He'll come back soon," I said. He had to, because I was his favorite. I knew that my dad would never leave me. A few days before, I'd packed my blue vinyl suitcase to run away. Then I'd stood in the side yard on a flat rock overlooking the valley. It was getting dark outside and the sky was striped pink and gray. I was already learning about Big Dramas, and how interesting they could make a given day. Just before I stepped off the rock my dad came up from behind and swooped me off my feet, catching me in his arms like a bride and then the world was a friendly size again, me against his chest while the sun dropped. He would never leave me, not ever. But my mom was shaking her head, no no no.

"He won't, he won't. We need a game plan, we need to figure out how to make our food last." She got a saucepan from the drawer under the stove and went outside.

"Is Dad coming back?" I looked at Jen. She had a tray of ice cubes and was twisting it slowly, letting the cubes pop out on the kitchen table.

She shrugged without looking at me. "How should I know?" She'd cut her bangs earlier, and they fell in a crooked line over her forehead.

"Nice hair," I said. Jen threw the ice cubes at me, and ran out of the room. She slammed her door, hard, which we weren't allowed to do. But there weren't any parents now, so she could do whatever she wanted.

My mom came back. She turned on a burner, set the saucepan full of snow over the flame. When the snow had melted she got the ketchup bottle and turned it upside down, whacking at it with the heel of her hand. She was making little frustrated sounds, trying to get the ketchup out.

"I can do it, Mom," Jen reappeared and slipped in beside her. She got a knife and slid it into the jar until the ketchup blopped out. "How much do you want?"

"I don't know, I don't know," my mom said. "It'll be okay, it's not the worst dinner we could have. We just have to make sure, to save up all our food just in case. Just put some in, it'll taste okay."

"What are you making?" I wanted my dad to come home. I had school the next day, and needed help with my math homework. My mom was crappy at math but good at writing papers. I thought about how I also needed clean socks for the next day, ones that matched, but I didn't want to bring it up. If I couldn't find my own matching socks I'd have to wear some of my dad's athletic socks, which bunched above my loafers and made my ankles look elephantine and my feet look like pinheads, so that I knew I was a geek.

"Ketchup soup," my mom said. "We have to be resourceful, we have to conserve. This is what you get, because your dad has left the family. He's never coming back. So we'll stretch our food out as best we can, and if and when he decides to come back, maybe in a few weeks, well, by then who knows what will have happened. Set the table, Luce. We all have to eat." She was talking fast and running her sentences together. My mom had always had a temper but it was the first time I'd seen her like this, her face far away, her hands jumping. I felt my lips start to shake. We were a family. My dad was the safest place, gentle and steady. But now my mom was folding paper napkins in a stack, way more than we needed, and scooping the ketchup soup into bowls.

"Help me," she said, folding. "Help me, help me, why won't anyone ever help me?"

The next day my mom told my dad: *that's right, last night your children supped on ketchup soup, how does that make you feel now? Feel good now?* He looked at her, not saying anything. *Supped on.* The words made us sound like hungry children in a fairy tale, whose woodcutter father had vanished into a dark forest. Sometimes my mom used language this way, as though she were a character in a novel. And later, when I got older and learned to fight with her—both of us scratching and pulling hair, my mom winning because she was bigger—sometimes afterward she'd comfort me, making it seem small with words like *golly* and *gee whiz*. *Golly, Honey,* she'd say, *you didn't have to be so vicious. Gee whiz, there's only one of your old mother. Go easy.* It shamed me, made our fights seem unnecessary and uncivilized, all my fault. She'd check her wounds, display them, and I fell for it, felt bad, though moments before she'd had me down on the ground, her teeth clenched, her face emptied out. I never knew where she went at these times. It was someplace private, and one where she didn't recognize me. It was only afterward that she became my mother again. *Jeepers,* she'd say. *You kids can really be ugly.*

After my dad came back, things went on for a few weeks in the old way. My mom and dad didn't fight; in fact they were more solicitous with one another than ever, speaking gently, laughing carefully at familiar jokes. But one day they called Jen and me into the living room, where they sat upright like visitors in the center of the sofa. My dad clung to a handkerchief, using it now and again to wipe the sweat from his forehead and upper lip. His hands trembled. They had something horrible to say. I took the bronze horse-head bookends from the mantel and faced the wild, nostrilly heads in opposite directions. When I played with them like this one of the horse heads would whinny, tip to fix the other with an evil eye. Then they charged, swerving at the last minute to avoid a collision that would mean I couldn't play with them anymore.

"Put those away, Honey. This is important," my dad said. "Your mom and I have something to tell you kids."

"We'd better not be moving again," Jen said.

"Kids," my mom's hands were twined in her lap, her legs crossed at the ankles. She looked nervous but in control, all business. She paused. "Your dad and I are getting a divorce."

For a minute the air hung open, like someone onstage had forgotten their lines. Jen slid her arms around herself and slipped quietly from the sofa to the floor, then edged over to the armchair and stood up quickly to yank off the light. "It's not your fault," my mom was saying. "It has nothing to do with you kids, that's the really important thing for you to know. Your dad and I just can't get along anymore. We've tried, we've really tried." They waited, watching us. I galloped one of the horses across the floor, and then the other whirled and charged. For the first time ever the bookends collided, hard, and rang in my hands. Still my parents waited. They sat side by side and when I glanced over my dad's head hung down but my mom's mouth had a weird twist, like she was trying to keep from smiling. One finger made a nervous circle on her pantleg. Jen lay on her side and pushed her hands under the fringe along the bottom of the armchair, all the way up to her elbows.

"It's not you kids," my dad said. His voice shook. "Your mom and I will still be friends. We just can't live together, God knows how much we've tried, you kids have seen that."

"If you love each other how come you're getting a divorce?" Jen spoke into the fringe. Her red hair crept out over the carpet. She looked like she'd been hit by a car. My mom got on her knees and crawled over to stroke Jen's hair but Jen's arm shot backward and she sat up and scurried into a corner. "Keep your fucking hands off me." She glared at all of us.

"Everything will be the same," my dad said. "It's just that we won't be living together under the same roof, that's all." He broke and started to weep flatly, not caring what kind of noises he made. *Now are you happy, now are you happy?* he was saying to my mom.

I touched one of the horse heads to my tongue. But the roof was exactly the point, wasn't it? Staying under the same one, all together, like a family. Then my dad said, *well Miriam, you got what you wanted. I hope you're happy.* There was a sound from the curtain. Jen had stretched her arms up and was pulling, and then the aluminum rod snapped loudly and the curtains came down on one side. "Now stop that, just stop," my dad said. With the curtains down, I could see outside to the real world. Across the street Mrs. Jackson had pulled a bag of oranges from the trunk of her car. She slammed the trunk and moved up the driveway toward her house as if it were any day, one she could trust. She sat the oranges heavily on the ground, glanced absently over at our exposed house. There was no one to ask, and no way to explain. There were the phone calls from Ellery, I knew that much. There was my dad's problem of managing money and my mom's loneliness every day, the house too neat, the neighborhood too quiet; the weekdays like dead things, falling.

Then there was nothing left in one piece. Slowly the furniture was divided, slowly the boxes gone through and sorted until you could have drawn a line right through the center of our house. Now we were two half-families, dangling in the rooms, amputated.

And somewhere in the middle of all this Mrs. Jackson's daughter, Deidre—thirteen, her body loose and white—opened the oven and lifted out an apple pie. The rack tilted, and the scalding pie went face down in Deidre's lap. She was in the hospital a few days and when she came back she showed a few of us girls in the neighborhood, stretched on her pink canopy bed and peeling back the gauze. The burn had left perfect half circles high on either thigh, the shape unmistakably that of a *pie*, benign, *apple*. The flesh still bubbled and blistered, gooey, *cooking*. Then it seemed that we were all unsafe, then it seemed as though something had begun to move us inexorably forward, bearing our car mechanically toward canvas flaps that would explode onto different scenery and air and deposit us all outside, the ride over.

Pictures of my parents, before either of us came along, standing in the living room of the House on the Hill. Their faces are smug with hope: they planned, maybe, to repaint the walls, rebuild the staircase. In one picture, they hold hands. In another, they pose in front of the fireplace. They look eager and capable. They look like they have been promised something.

Two

The Fisherman's Wife

M y dad thought Ellery got exactly what he deserved, with my mother. Ellery had stolen her away from my dad and now, our dad said, he wouldn't take her back on a silver platter. *He can have her,* he said. *I wish him luck. I wouldn't take her back, not if you threw her at me.*

Ellery was fleshy and had eczema. But he was much younger than my dad, and was going to college to get his psychology degree. He drove a black VW bug and had a thin, high voice. He had pale, pink patches on his neck that disappeared beneath the front of his shirt, and reappeared where his wrists stuck out, and he was constantly checking his waistband, bringing his hands in sharply and quickly to either side of his belt in a twitchy, effeminate gesture that made me pity him. He was crazy about my mom, and made points with her by letting her do most of the talking and make some of the decisions. When Ellery himself talked, he never got to the point, and after a while it drove her crazy. *What,* she'd say. *What? Why don't you just come out with it?*

He tried to win us kids over, mostly by taking us to fast-food restaurants and handing over his penny collection, which he stored in small, paper milk cartons. Altogether he had filled twenty-seven cartons. Jen and I would dump the pennies on the floor and make stacks of fifty to stuff into paper rolls, leaving sour-smelling flakes in the carpet. I didn't care. I could already tell that Ellery was temporary, the first in a long line of bearded guys, with a gut and meaty thumbs and glasses that slid down so far that they pinched his nostrils into little pink flares. All the guys my mom went for looked alike, like this, and the thing with the glasses meant that they were also mouth breathers, and also usually psychology majors, emotionally unstable themselves, large, lonely men with at least one tweed jacket. They always started out okay: expansive and generous and self-effacing, using words like *codependent, dysfunctional.* And they looked, especially in the tweed jacket, like men you could trust, even men with a future. But they were damaged goods. One after another they drank too much and wept openly and pitied themselves; and one after another, like with Ellery, the mouth breathing seemed to get worse the longer we were with them. Jen had a theory that it was because they were getting fatter, learning to lean on my mom and wanting to be babied by her, which was the biggest mistake of all. Anyway it was clear that for my mom, Ellery was a pit stop. We gave him a year, tops.

After Ellery and my mom had been dating for a few months we moved with him to Southern California, where Ellery was doing an internship at Camarillo State Mental Hospital. We lived in Ventura, in a rented house with dusty linoleum floors. We were on food stamps and my mom and Ellery fought all the time.

"If you could fix anything," she was in the hallway, holding a toilet plunger. The bathroom floor was slippery and smelly, and there was a ring of sodden towels around the base of the toilet. "Bob could fix anything, that's what I miss. We never had to worry about that, did we, girls."

"We better call somebody," Ellery had his hands on his hips, as though he were going to accomplish something, and my mom shook her head and went again at the toilet. The water was low and brown in the bowl.

"What have you girls been flushing," my mom plunged furiously. "It better not have been a Kotex." She glared pointedly at Jen and flushed the toilet. We watched as the water rose in the bowl and settled just beneath the rim.

"I'm calling a plumber," Ellery said.

"We don't have money for a plumber. We only have fourteen bucks between now and payday." My mom held out the plunger. "You try." Ellery slipped going into the bathroom, and my mom smirked. We watched nervously. Ellery had a short fuse, and was given to tantrums. He jabbed awkwardly and flushed again. This time the water rushed up over the rim and poured onto the floor. "Goddamnit, goddamnit," Ellery said, and hopped backwards out of the bathroom. He yanked the door shut and went to the kitchen.

"I don't know what we're going to do," my mom said. "We just plain don't have the money."

"It's a clogged toilet, Miriam. What else are we supposed to do? We'll get reimbursed."

"You don't know that."

"I'm sure that Lewis will reimburse us. He's a landlord."

"Well, he didn't pay for the paint that time."

Ellery was looking up plumbers in the Yellow Pages. He started to dial, and my mom jerked the phone away and slammed it back on the hook. "Bob would know what to do. Your dad would know, wouldn't he, girls? He could fix anything. Anything."

"Well, you're not married to Bob anymore, are you?"

"I guess we'll have to. Call someone. But I don't know how we'll pay for it." My mom looked sadly at us, like we were orphans. "Your dad was sure a real handyman, I'll give him that. If you knew how to fix anything."

Ellery tried to dial again. This time she pulled so hard that the cord got him in the neck. He swatted himself free, and my mom laughed. "Let go, Miriam. I'm calling."

"How? How are we going to pay? You went and got yourself fired, and I don't make enough. You look ridiculous."

"I got laid off, not fired." Ellery was breathing hard and fast, the way he always did when she got to him. He tried to dial and she yanked the phone from the wall. She laughed again and for a minute they fought over the receiver. "You look big and ridiculous," she said.

"What do you get out of it? Is this something you want the kids to see?"

"I followed you here, that was my big mistake. I should've stayed in Salt Lake. At least I had a job there."

" 'I should've stayed in Salt Lake. I should've stayed in Salt Lake.' I don't know why you just didn't."

"And we're poor. We're poor. The kids don't have clothes, none of us have clothes, because you can't provide. You can't do anything."

"Mom, stop," Jen said. Our mom turned to her. Her eyes were full of appeal, but we never knew how to help. "He can't, Honey. He can't do anything, he's useless."

Ellery was trembling, breathing hard. "Shut up."

"Big Man."

"Mom, please stop."

"Here. Call." My mom wagged the receiver at him. "Here. Useless."

Ellery snatched the receiver, and used it to whack himself in the forehead. It was a terrible sight, and one we'd seen before. Sometimes he used a saucepan; other times, a hairbrush. The only good thing about it was that it kept him from hitting our mom. "There, does that make you feel better?" Ellery said, and smacked himself again. "There. There." He pounded himself twice more, hard, and my mom laughed.

"You're a big loser," she said. "A big stupid masochistic dork."

"You wanna see? You wanna see?" He pounded himself. "Is that better? Is it?" His forehead was bleeding. "There," he said. "There. Are you getting what you want? Are you?" He tried to throw the receiver but it boomeranged into his shin, and he did a little dance trying to get it loose.

"Maybe you should just leave. You're scaring the kids." My mom opened her arms but I backed away, feeling tricked. Our life was like this too much, the fights and then a big forgiving drama afterward, when my mom was sorry for everything. She needed to get to this point, I knew that much, before things could get back to normal: that was the part I didn't understand. Jen went to her and my mom looked at me reproachfully, keeping her arm open a minute in case I changed my mind.

"Why do you always do this?" I said.

"Me. *Me*, always do this. You saw, he can't do anything. Why won't anyone help me, help me?"

"What's he supposed to help with?" I said. "He doesn't know how to fix it so why don't you just call somebody?"

"You're a traitor, Lucy," my mom said. "A betrayer. You've never been loyal, not to anyone but your goddamned dad who's so great." She cried harder, opened her arm again. "Please come here, Luce. I'm so upset. So terribly, terribly upset. Please don't make me say these things, I don't know how to get us out of this mess. Maybe we should've moved to Santa Barbara instead. Maybe that was my mistake."

That night I called my dad.

"How are things?" he said. "Are you okay?"

"I guess," I said. "I miss you." It was as much as I could ever get out before I started crying. "Can I come live with you?"

"You know you can't, Sweetheart. I'm sorry. I miss you too. I wish like hell none of this had happened."

"Why can't I just come to Salt Lake?"

"I'd give anything for that, Honey. You know how much I miss you girls. But your mom has custody. There isn't a damned thing I can do about that."

"But I *want* to live with you. It's you and me against the world."

"I know." His voice cracked. "You just can't right now. Now let's talk about something else, or you're gonna have to listen to your old dad blubbering. You wouldn't want that, would you? Too undignified."

"Okay." I clutched the phone, trying to think of something to talk about. But what I wanted to do most was just cry for a long time, loud, keeping the phone pressed hard to my ear so that I wouldn't lose him. "I hate her so much."

"Luce, don't talk like that. She's your mom. She loves you."

161

"When are you going to come visit?"

"Your mom doesn't think that's such a great idea, right now."

"Why?"

"Well, Hon, your mom wants her new life. And she's calling all the shots. You know I miss you. You know I miss you. But I have to see you and your sister when she lets me. And right now, she doesn't think it's a good time."

"*Why*?" I was getting snot all over the phone.

"I don't really know, Honey." There was a pause while my dad blew his nose, and when he came back on the line his voice was hoarse. "I can tell you one thing that's really important, and that's that you keep the peace. You can't talk against her. If she even knew I was talking to you like this, she'd be furious."

"Will you call me tomorrow?"

"Sure."

"Promise?"

"Of course, Sweetie. Just make sure you pick up, okay? Sometimes I think your mom forgets to give you your messages."

"Okay. I love you."

"I love you too, Sweetie. Hang in there."

We had one summer with Ellery. Then he dumped my mom, and moved in with some woman named Anita who'd worked the coffee-and-donut cart at Camarillo. Now, my mom said, it was time to decide some things. Did we like Ventura? Did we want to stay? Was there someplace we'd rather be? Really, we could go anywhere, she said. The dork was out of the picture, the world was our oyster.

"Where's Dad? Maybe we could live close to him."

"Your dad and I are divorced now, Luce. We're not going to get back together."

"I just said maybe we could live by him." It scared me, listening to her. "Anyway I thought you said Ventura was home now."

"Home," my mom said. "Home. This place? It's a *rental*." She pointed out the linoleum floors, the hollow core doors. "You could huff and puff and blow this shit-shack down."

"I'm sick of moving," I said. "Plus school's going to start."

"Well, I know you're sick of moving, me too, Honey. Gosh, that's for sure. But we can't stay here."

"I thought we were going to buy a house in Ojai," Jen said. We'd done hours of research this summer with our mom and Ellery, cruising streets and looking for our dream house. We'd finally settled on a green one with lots of tulips in the front yard and an apple tree on the side of the house. But then something had happened with our finances, and they stopped talking about it. Anyway, for me, the only interesting thing about Ojai was Tally Ho Equestrian Academy. I knew I'd never go there but we drove past it every time on our way into Ojai and I hung my head out the window as we passed, my eyes slitted to the wind. The school grounds rolled open and green on either side of the road and were enclosed by a split-rail white fence. On one side of the fence was me and my family, in our Mercury Cougar with the cracked white vinyl upholstery and candy wrappers under the seats; on the other side of the fence were the students of Tally Ho, trotting their horses in the bored, restrained manner of kids who got to ride horseback every day. They wore the school uniforms—dark-blue blazers over dark jodhpurs, black velvet riding helmets—and rode alongside the rail fence without looking at us.

"Maybe we could stay and I could just go to Tally Ho," I said.

"Well, I don't know about that. What do you think, Jen?"

Jen had a mirror, and was tweezing her eyebrows. She answered my mom in the mirror. "I like it here, too."

"I know Jen at least thinks we ought to go back to Utah. And I don't know, it's so pretty there, this time of year. I kind of miss it too. Tally Ho, huh? You'd really want to go there? Hobnob with the rich kids?"

"They get to horseback ride every single day," I said. My heart was going. She wasn't saying yes but she wasn't saying no, either. In our old life, before the divorce, I knew my parents could've at least considered it, letting me go there; and even though I knew we were poor now, we were hanging on. We still had all the furniture from when they were married, and all the dishes, and even things like down parkas and skis. We weren't that bad off. Maybe my dad could even help pay for tuition.

After that I couldn't shut up about it. I already had my own riding helmet, which I thought was a start. I also had a saddle and three curry combs and a large canister of mane and tail grease. The saddle was a coup, western and intricately tooled with lots of fringe, and a neighbor had given it to me free and clear when we lived in Salt Lake. I didn't know whether I'd need my own tack but it couldn't hurt, I thought, just to have it. And I'd ridden plenty. I'd taken lessons on Liddy and I knew how to bridle a horse and how to ride bareback. From what I could see, the only thing that stood between me and Tally Ho was the cost of tuition, as well as transportation to and from the school every day.

My mom agreed that we'd had a shitty summer, what with Ellery leaving us. *Not that I wanted him to stay,* my mom said. *The loser.* But you could tell it got to her, that she hadn't dumped him, first. The summer had been too hot, and the fleas were in every carpet in the house; I had scabs up and down my calves, from where I'd scratched at the bites and made them infected. After Ellery left, my mom had started working two part-time jobs, both of which paid minimum wage without benefits. Even so, she'd always been resourceful, known how to work the system. I badgered her about Tally Ho Equestrian Academy for weeks, right up until the week before school started. I knew how to ride, I argued, and I could take the bus. I secured bus schedules, mapped out my route and crayoned it in to show her. I walked around the house in my riding helmet, buffed the saddle until it glowed. Finally, my mom said yes.

"This isn't going to work," I said. We were in the parking lot at JC Penney. It was a Sunday, the day before I was supposed to start school. "They're not going to have jodhpurs, here."

"They might." My mom was in a festive mood. She liked malls.

"They won't. We're gonna have to go somewhere else, only you waited until the last minute, so where will we go? And now what am I supposed to do? All the other kids will be wearing them and then there's me."

"What are 'jodhpurs,' anyway?"

"See? You don't even know, do you?"

"Oh Lucy I know what they look like, of course I do, I just think it's a funny word. I was just asking, is all. I was wondering about the etymology." My mom looked over at the entrance. The store had just opened, and shoppers straggled across the parking lot. "Do you want to look, or not?"

"I have to be ready by tomorrow. Why did we have to wait until the last minute?" I toyed with the door handle. I didn't know what to do, or where other kids shopped.

"Come on. You're making me feel bad." My mom got out of the car and stood with her arms folded, waiting. After a minute I got out. "I can barely afford the tuition, as it is," she said. "And even that's going to be creative, let me tell you." She trailed me to the store, talking. "It doesn't matter what you wear. Other kids are perfectly happy going to public school and you should be too, Luce. Don't ignore me. I'm your mother."

"I just don't think they're going to sell them. And how am I even getting to school tomorrow, anyway? Nothing's planned."

"You know and public school isn't such a bad idea. I went to public schools my whole life and I turned out just fine. And Viewmont's a good school, and your sister will be there. You could be together."

I stopped walking to look at her. "You said I could go to Tally Ho."

"Honey, and you can go there if that's what you really want. I'm just saying, it's an option. Gee whiz, what do you think we're doing here, anyway? You'll be ready. And we can work out the bus thing. I just hope the finances will work out, is all."

"Have you paid my tuition yet?"

"You don't need to worry about that kind of thing. Your old mother

has ways. And I know you need to be dressed a certain way. Look like
the other kids. But they're going to be rich kids, Luce, kids with silver
spoons in their mouths. And they'll be from rich families, which might
make you uncomfortable. To not have as much as they do."

"I don't care." We were in the store, and I moved uncertainly in the
direction of the Junior Miss department.

"Well, that's good. Because I never liked rich people." My mom
paused at the cosmetics counter. She squirted hand lotion from a tester
bottle onto her hands, then uncorked a small pot of bronze powder and
smeared some up either cheekbone. Next she went for a tester tube of
mascara. "Well we certainly can't afford *this* sort of thing right now, can
we?" she said. "Not with that rich-kid-school tuition." She gave me a
small smile, full of patience, and we moved off.

In the Junior Miss department, the saleslady looked baffled. "Jodhpurs," I said, feeling stupid. "Like English riding pants."

"The kind that pooch out in the thighs," my mom said. "My
daughter's starting at horseback riding school tomorrow, I'm so proud
of her, but she's supposed to have these doggoned jodhpurs. Dark blue."

"We have some dark-blue pants," the saleslady said.

"Not just dark blue. *Jodhpurs.*"

"Well, Honey, if they don't have them."

"Mom, let's go somewhere else. They have to sell them somewhere.
I can call the school."

"It's a Sunday, Luce. They won't be open." The saleslady moved
toward a rack on the back wall, and my mom went along.

"My girls have to have all the right clothes, too," the saleslady said.
"When I was a girl it didn't matter what I wore to school, but nowadays."

"Oh, I know," my mom looked at me disapprovingly. "I have two,
and they both have to have exactly the right things to fit in, shoes and
bras and money for tuition and then sports equipment alone, that puts
us in the poorhouse. You know how it is."

"Oh, I do," the saleslady nodded and clucked along. "My girls, I have three, we had to send them to fat farms this summer, and it about killed us."

"Kids," my mom shook her head. "So do you, have anything in dark blue?"

"Mom."

"We might be able to find something, Luce. We'll get you some English riding pants later in the week. But maybe just for tomorrow you could wear these. Just for one day."

"But I'll be the only one."

"Listen, Luce," my mom turned threatening. "If you want to go to Tally Ho you're going to have to be flexible. I'm doing all I can, just to get you there. Now if you want some new pants, here they are. Here. What about these," she pulled some dark-blue corduroy pants from the rack. The saleslady silently offered up a matching blazer.

"It looks westernwear," my mom said. "That's the look you're going for anyway, isn't it, with your saddle?"

"Except that 'Tally Ho' does sound English," the saleslady ventured.

"Exactly," I said. I could see Tally Ho receding, the kids on horseback turning to tiny shapes on the horizon. "*Exactly.*"

"You could do western. There's no law saying horseback riding belongs to the upper crust. There were Indians galloping the plains long before Tally Ho appeared on the scene, let me tell you. Come on, just try this on." My mom held out the jacket. It was boxy, elaborately topstitched.

"It's not going to work."

"Do you want it or not, Luce. Because I'm not going to shop all day, I'm sure some of the other kids will be dressed western, it's not a big deal. Now I'm bending over backwards just to cover the tuition, frankly I don't know how I'm even going to pull it off." She shoved the pants and jacket back onto the rack. "Why don't we just forget it. Our whole family is on food stamps and all you care about is going to private school."

"Fine, I'll try it on."

"You're making me feel just awful, Honey," my mom started to cry. "I can't help it if we don't have enough money. Your dad won't send us a goddamned penny."

"I'm sorry."

"Not sorry enough."

I never knew what to say to that. I wanted to go to Tally Ho and I wanted to be dressed like the other kids and I even wanted other things, a quirt and knee-high, black glossy riding boots. I wanted wavy dark hair that I could tuck up under my helmet, and a mansion with marble floors I could click across after a hard day of riding, and a pink telephone and a beanbag chair and a stereo. I wanted my dad. I wanted us not to have to use food stamps. I wanted a boyfriend. I wanted an Irish Setter. And right now I wanted jodhpurs. She was right; I wasn't sorry enough.

I hugged her, and she cried for a few minutes while the saleslady watched. Then she blew her nose, and I tried on the suit. The corduroy was stiff and made a *skritching* sound when I walked, but I liked how I looked in the mirror. I looked ready to ride. It wasn't until later that night that I noticed the tiny Winnie-the-Pooh profile engraved into each one of the buttons, but by then it didn't matter. My mom had started crying again on the way home from the mall, saying things like *you hate me, don't you? I can't do anything right, you kids hate me, I should just kill myself, then you'd be happy, wouldn't you? Then you could go live with your dad, that's what you want anyway.*

Later that night, she told me to forget about Tally Ho. We were moving back to Utah. She had a new plan, she said, one I'd like. Boarding school. There was a private school in town, St. Anne's, and it had a boarding department and Jen and I could give that a try. In the meantime she'd stay on in Ventura. It was only temporary, she said. Only until she got things ironed out with Ellery. Tally Ho would still be there at Christmas. Maybe she could sign me up then. I mean gee I had the suit, after all, didn't I? It was something. It was a start.

In Books of Food Stamps, Green and Orange,

which we yanked, bill by bill and with much awkwardness, from a small and tightly bound book. I kept my back to the next person in line, felt the heat in my cheeks. If there was change coming back we got it in what looked like tiddlywinks, pale blue for dimes, yellow for quarters, announcing all over the place that our family was POOR, POOR, POOR, in case everyone in line wanted to know, our PARENTS WERE DIVORCED, THANK YOU VERY MUCH, our mom was ACTUALLY EVEN SINGLE, IN CASE ANYONE WAS INTERESTED, while I waited in line, nervous, ready to snap out those bills, hurrying, and always it took too long, always my hands shook and the cashier's face incriminated me, her sorrowful middle-aged hanging face, and I knew I had weak character, no character, because even here: in line, paying for twenty-five-cent boxes of corn muffin mix and mac-n-cheese, and buying packets of almond windmill cookies (my mom's favorite, hearkening to those sun-drenched days in Solvang, Solvang, rocking in her heart, beloved Solvang where the paper flags fluttered and the abelskivers were gooey babies under their blankies of powdered sugar and jam, Solvang which we never would've left if only my dad had been able to find a job, which he hadn't, Solvang in the rearview mirror), even here in line I was completely on my dad's side, wherever he was, and I knew that it was just a tragic mistake of paperwork and all my mom's fault that I wasn't with him. It confused me that my mom and I both liked the windmill cookies and that, in weak moments, I could also be conned into weeping over Solvang. It confused me that I looked so much like her, and that I wanted in my secret heart to be a hippie chick with a headband and creaky sandals. Once, I got ready to go to the grocery store by dressing as much like a hippie as I knew how—a batik dress, my hair in a braid. I was thirteen, and knew something of what my mom knew, that if you made yourself look enough like the person you wanted to be there as at least a chance. I got to the store and stood in front of the refrigerated case, trying to think what a hippie would eat. My mom took me seriously, came and stood with her arms folded, and I was near tears because I couldn't think what hippies ate—besides wheat bread, besides vitamins—and then my mom reached for something, a bottle of strawberry kefir, and handed it to me without saying anything, without making fun. You could count on her, in situations like this. My dad was calm water but when it came to crises, to moments like this one, I wanted *her*. And then, God bless her, she paid for it with the food stamps, sparing me that one, shooing me off to go read the *Thrifty Nickels*. Then she sat cross-legged with me on the lawn outside while I sipped at the kefir, pretending to like it. My mom could be this way. She took us seriously, even when we were small. Listened to our opinions with gravity, nodding and considering our logic and using adult words: *deliberate, injunction, proliferate.*

My room at St. Anne's was up under the eaves, with a small radiator that ticked and hissed as it warmed. I had a clock radio and a pink-and-green flowered bedspread and my own desk and notebook. The nuns woke us at six, when we would wander down to the warm, good smells and bright lights of the cafeteria, the sound of chairs scraping, the lady with her hairnet who waited to offer us bacon, gluey oatmeal, single-serving boxes of Rice Krispies and Corn Flakes.

For the first few weeks I was lonely, made sad by the wide, cold floorboards and somber song that drifted up from the chapel. I could barely tell the nuns apart and had to fake my way through all the hymns. There were rumors of ghosts, and a line of twelve sinks in the bathroom, which made me feel hopeless, like it didn't much matter whether I brushed my teeth or washed my face, one of so many girls. But slowly the warmth and routine worked on me. I did my homework at my desk every night like a regular kid, and I had books and a dark-green enamel pencil sharpener which made a crunching sound as it worked over the pencils. The nuns spoke in gentle voices, and I had Jen. I learned that the cafeteria lady's name was Rose, and she learned that bacon gave me migraine headaches, and so never offered. My room had a window, and it hit me suddenly one night when I was at my desk that I was happy; lonely, but okay. "Cat's Cradle" was playing on the radio and I sat at my desk, watching the snow come down. I knew my dad would love the song and that every time he heard it, wherever he was, he was for sure singing along. The radiator ticked; voices outside drifted; I snapped off the lamp and crawled under the covers. In the morning there would be the same stainless-steel tray of pancakes in front of Rose, and the fluorescent cafeteria lights would blast against my pupils as I rounded the landing, searing its image of girls in blue at tables, Jen among them. I was ready to stay in one place for a while.

After a few weeks, though, my mom came back. *Can you believe I even did that?* our mom said. *Tried to go back? What was I thinking? Next time, next time, just tie me down if you have to,* she said. *Tie me to a tree, I don't care. I'll bet Anita's already seen him doing that saucepan routine. I'll bet they fight all the time. He was completely unstable, wasn't that the biggest joke, him getting his degree in Psychology?*

We moved into an apartment a few miles from the boarding school, and I started school again at the public school across the street. The apartment was a single, long room with '50s pink carpeting and my mom hung up sheets to make separate rooms for each of us. When you stepped in from outside it looked crazy, flowered sheets at weird angles everywhere, and I always retreated behind my sheet to sulk for a while, missing St. Anne's, missing my dad. He was working as a textbook salesman, going from college to college in the western United States, and my mom told us that right now he was in California. Why couldn't he at least call? But at night our tents were luminous and beautiful things, drooping and strangely shadowed, and they made us whisper. Our mom would light candles and we would go to bed early. If our dad looked here he'd find us like children in a sick ward, and I knew it would make him unhappy. *What's all this, Miriam?* he'd say. *What's all this?*

I made the girls tents. Like we were in Africa. The place so small. What choice did I have?

Africa?

• • •

After Ellery was gone, there were always men. It was the bearded ones that I couldn't stand, the ones who pretended to be progressive and care about Women's Lib but who really just wanted dinner every night on the table at six and to get in my mom's pants. When my mom went off to Food King, where she worked in the evenings as a checker, the boyfriends spent time sitting on the floor with us, reading our horoscopes and moving closer and sometimes asking for a neck massage or a back rub. They were so many of them: Jerry, who showed my mom how to make tortillas from scratch, and Dave, who liked to suck my earlobe and tell me how beautiful I was, already, even though I was only twelve; there was Pete, who wanted to move to the mountains and live on a farm and raise llamas; and Giles, who asked Jen to marry him after it was clear that he and my mom weren't working out. At night, the bed from my mom's room squeaked so much that I learned to sleep with a pillow over my head. When my mom was having sex everybody had to hear it, and if we called her on it she'd look innocent: *Oh,* she'd say. *Was I being too loud, was I? Darn it, I just get so excited. Your dad never liked it when I made noise. He'd always try to put a pillow over my face.*

One morning after brushing my teeth, I wiped my face on the towel and saw a white globule that had hardened and browned around the edges, like an enormous milky booger. Jen saw, and laughed. "Arn came on that," she said. I wanted to find my dad and show him, let him know what our mom was acting like these days. But there was no way to find him. He was somewhere in Idaho, my mom said, or maybe Montana. Sometimes Jen and I took the bus to the downtown library to look through out-of-state phone books. I knew that if I found his number, I could call collect and then he'd pick up the phone and send for me. It was just finding him that was the hard part.

There's too much, my mom said. *Too much, too much of everything.*

I looked around at the duplex we were living in, which was a few blocks from our old apartment with the pink carpeting. It looked empty, to me anyway, but to my mom it was a cluttered place, packed with memories and dark corners and fraught with things to stub toes on or trip over, crammed to the brim, it seemed, with papers and books and unpaid bills and newspapers, maybe that's what she was talking about, all our school stuff and hairbrushes and shoes and gum wrappers, our half-finished school projects on the floor, the abandoned sandwich or apple. But even when the house was picked up—the way it got picked up nervously and quickly by us girls, when we could see one of my mom's moods coming on, everything dumped in our rooms, the ottoman pushed to the foot of the chair and the papers stacked out of sight—even then my mom sat hunched and unhappy, looking from one object to another and saying *there's just so much, so much—*

But so much of what? Did she see things we didn't? Her eyes jumped from one thing to another and she kept shaking her head, *it's too much for me, it all just really is, kids, I'm not sure how much more of this I can take.* She moved to the kitchen to brew herself the umpteenth cup of weak and tepid tea, a beverage to cry over, which she did, sipping and weeping. Everything was wrong, we understood, and in the old days my dad would've fixed it, only now he was gone so it was up to us kids, who could never quite figure out what needed to be fixed, exactly, so instead we just waited quietly near her while her mood grew and deepened, extending to everything, not just the messy house but the Cougar, the transmission was going and it was a mess, a *mess*, junk everywhere, and the door didn't shut right, did it, other people had cars with doors that shut tight but not us, one of us could fly out at any minute, right out onto the wet road in the dark and then where would we be, no insurance, no money, no man around to fix things. Now and again one of us would try to soothe her: *it's okay, Mom. Things will be okay—*, which made her shake her head hard, *no no no, things are not okay, they're not okay, why does there have to be so much of everything, I can't keep track of everything, everything such a mess and no one to help us. Not anyone.*

I tried to draw her back by waving my arm out across the living room, the floor newly vacuumed, the coffee table dusted. "But it is clean," I said. "There's not even anything there." What did she mean, why did she keep saying it?

Behind the scenes, she explained.

Then we all just looked out the window, together as a family. Across the street a dad was mowing the lawn, and his son toddled behind him with a small orange plastic mower. That family, we could see, was still at the start of everything, still making all the right turns, still paying their bills on time and eating vegetables every day. We were somewhere else; not at the end exactly, since our mom could still meet a man who would save us and put us back on track financially, but at a place where it was essential that we find him and impress him, with how good we were and how charismatic our mom was (which she *was*) and how clean we could keep a house, even a modest duplex, because if the guy saw all of our clutter, well, good-bye to that future.

My mom moved to the sink, rinsed her teacup. Her shoulders curved into herself. She stood thinking, still in some place in her head where it was just *stuff stuff stuff*, chairs stacked on tables, cabinets with broken hinges and exploding open, the papers sliding out, a rug with frayed edges that you could trip on, and a phone ringing endlessly, and a piece of shit car whose doors you had to loop shut with chicken wire, and piles and piles of unwashed laundry.

"We could move," Jen said. "I saw a house for rent on Eleventh Avenue that maybe we could afford."

My mom chewed a hangnail, listened. "How much?"

"I'm not sure but it's where Sarah Brady and her mom used to live, so it couldn't cost that much."

"Oh yeah, what happened to Sarah Brady's mom?" Our mom asked, but in a mean voice, because she knew. Sarah Brady's mom had fallen in love with Mr. Kendricks, the Social Studies teacher, and Sarah and her mom were moving into his house all together as a family. "Have you ever seen his house?"

"Whose?"

"You know whose, Mr. Kendricks."

"I don't know," I said.

"Well, does it have big windows? Looking out on the street? Does it have big trees?"

"It ain't nothing special."

" '*Isn't.*' Well what's the style, at least? Is it a Tudor or a Victorian or a bungalow or what?"

"It's new, I think."

"And does he have other kids?" My mom toyed with her wedding ring from my dad. She wore it now on her right hand.

"He has a teenaged son," Jen said, "and he is hot, hot, hot."

"Too young for me," my mom said. "But maybe one of you. What do you think Sarah will call Mr. Kendricks? Do you think she'll call him *Dad*?"

"You might like this house, Mom." Jen brought us all graham crackers, chocolate frosted and frozen. Jen made these a lot, and she also made Bean Dreams, an oily, claylike, orange mess of pork and beans, cheddar cheese, and bacon. "Maybe we should at least go look."

"Are they going to get married in a church?"

"I'm not sure," Jen said. "Probably, though."

"Well are they going to have a *registry*?" My mom picked miserably at a graham cracker. "You know they will, you know there are going to be a million gifts, you know they won't even appreciate everything."

"Can we stop talking about Mr. Kendricks?" Jen said. "I mean it's not like he's cute or anything. You wouldn't have him on a silver platter."

"You don't have to be smart with me. Gee whiz. I'm just asking is all." She toyed with her ring some more, sighed, touched the tip of her tongue to it. "And probably some big honeymoon. That guy's probably loaded. And I would so have taken him, I would so. Well," my mom said, "so, Eleventh Avenue. So find out. Maybe that would be nice. A whole house. Is it old? Does it have charm? I hate new houses, I hate how they don't have any memories. Your dad was real big on new houses, that's one thing we fought about so much, he was really into that wall-to-wall carpeting look. Where is it, exactly? We'd never be able to afford it."

"If it had a yard maybe I could get a dog," I said.

"And anyway we could never afford a deposit. Plus landlords want so much, first and last month's rent usually on top of everything. But it would be nice. Nice if you girls could both have your own rooms, how many bedrooms does it have?"

"I think three." Jen washed out the teapot and dried it, returned it to the stove. That's how she was, my mom's right-hand man.

"Because I'm not exactly going to catch a man with us living all crammed in a *duplex,* am I. Us on top of each other, like crackers in a can. What color is it?"

"White," Jen said. " White with blue trim."

"Well, we could drive past I guess. What do you girls think? Anyone want to go for a ride?"

First we had to drive past Mr. Kendricks' house. It was new, constructed of salmon-colored, raked-face brick, but it was the front porch that really got my mom; instead of a rectangle, it was a half-circle plonked on the front of the house, enclosed in smoked-glass windows from top to bottom and punctuated every few feet with an enormous white pillar. "*No,*" my mom said. "You've got to be *kidding.*" She started to laugh. "It looks just like a mausoleum, doesn't it? I don't care how destitute I am, I would never. *Never.* Can you imagine? Oh my God, it looks just exactly like a funeral home, whose idea *was* that, none of you girls better *ever* try to get me in a house like that." My mom drove on, shaking her head and laughing. "Oh," she said. "I have to say, I feel so much better now. That's what's called a high price. It would be different, wouldn't it, if Mr. Kendricks *were* sexy. But you know what, girls, don't ever let yourselves settle for anything less than *total passion.* Because *nothing else works*, everything else goes away." She laughed again and we laughed with her, trying to imagine the inside of Mr. Kendricks' house. We were poor, but our mom was classy, and someday we'd live in a classy house, a Tudor with a huge, blue spruce out front that we could string with lights, every Christmas. "Oh the light," she said. "That *light*. I'll bet everything looks gray the minute you step inside, I'll bet everything looks *dead*, no, *seriously*, girls, I'm sorry, I know he's your teacher. Anyway. So what's the cross street on Eleventh Avenue, does anybody know?"

My mom liked the house on Eleventh Avenue so much that we drove straight from seeing it to a pay phone, so she could call the landlord. She came back smiling. "Well, that's pretty much a done deal," she said. "I just have to figure out a way to come up with a little more money, I can scheme something, I'm not worried. And guess what, it's a *four*-bedroom. He says the rooms are small with no closets, but there are *four*." She got behind the wheel and cranked the radio. It was one of her favorite songs that year, "Seasons in the Sun." "Well, I don't want to listen to that depressing thing again," she said, and turned it off. "I was thinking I need a new name, I mean Miriam's okay but it doesn't really do anything for me, if you know what I mean. And I mean gee, with a new house and everything we might as well make a fresh start. Miriam really sounds a little too much like a waitress, or even just a housewife, I can just hear some big pot-gut guy yelling it across the yard, *Miriam, Miriam, come get me another beer, caw caw,* like a parrot. That's not going to do me any good, is it? I left all that stuff *behind*. But I was thinking, just waiting at the phone, I was thinking 'Mona.' It has such a nice, classic sound. What do you girls think?"

"Mona," Jen moaned it. "Mo-naaaaah."

"See, and that's exactly what I was afraid of," our mom said. "It could make me sound cheap. But then, you know, well, 'Miriam.' That kind of makes me sound a little too prissy. I was just thinking Mona sounds nicer. What do you girls think?"

"You have to tell Dad if you list it new in the phone book, in case he looks for us," I said. "But Mona sounds pretty."

Jen kept moaning it, until my mom told her to pipe down.

"How come you keep changing?" Jen said. She had one foot up on the dashboard and was trying to paint her toenails.

"You should try it," our mom said. "It's really kind of fun, as long as your last name stays the same, which of course it *has*, Lucy, it's not like your dad couldn't come see us, if he wanted to. Anyway Mona's pretty close to Miriam. It's not a big deal. I just thought it might be a nice change. Just for today," my mom said. "Everybody call me Mona, and I'll call you whatever name you decide you each really like, okay?"

Jen was Andreanna. That day I was Heather, Heather Susanna, and our mom said our names in public, in stores and parking lots and when we went to meet with the landlord. By nightfall I felt lonely and creeped out. But my mom was Mona for a few more months at least. She could do that, just change herself into someone else without minding, like putting on a different jacket. But I missed the way my dad had said her name in the old days, *Miriam,* like he knew exactly who he was talking to.

IN HER FACE:

When she was hateful was when she looked most lost.
When she was yelling or taunting whatever boyfriend. Her
voice went flat, too, then, flat and mean, and we knew the
boyfriend didn't stand a chance. There'd be lots of smacking
and screaming. When the boyfriends lost their tempers, I
think, is when my mom felt best; finally someone was giving
her what she thought she deserved, finally some guy had her
to the wall by the hair and was smacking her head against the
wall to punctuate that he was sick. and. tired. of her fucking.
bullshit. During these times my mom's face opened back up.
It almost looked like love. She'd wait for him to finish, take her
licking, because then he'd have so much to pay for later. The
quiet and ministrations afterward almost felt like church, a
sort of sympathy in the air for what had, by the narrowest
thread of fate, been saved. No one was dead. There was plenty
after all to celebrate.

ON THE OTHER END OF THE PHONE,

where she listened in, almost always, and we fell for this

trick again and again. We were kids and seemed to forget, from one phone conversation to the next, that she could and would invariably pick up the other extension, breaking in when our whispered conversations with our dad were the most strenuous and desperate. *She lies,* I would be saying, *her boyfriends are freaks and one of them keeps licking my ear, she talks on the phone and sits in the hallway and touches herself with no pants on so everyone can see, I hate it here, Dad, please let me come live with you, please—,* and she would interrupt, furious, *I do not! I do not!* and me saying, *Mom, get off the phone! Get off! Get off!* and my dad breaking in, *Miriam get off the phone, we'll have a chance to talk after.* I could never believe she'd listened in, my mother saying, *she's lying to you, Bob, she's the one that lies, I'm a psychology major, a psychology major wouldn't do these things. Do you think a psychology major would do those things?* and afterwards the dread of the house, of going downstairs to face her. *What boyfriend licks your ear,* she'd want to know. *You should be flattered. He's a pilot, do you know he's a pilot? Do you know how much money he makes? Your dad hasn't sent us anything all year, not a goddamned penny, Lucy, if he loves you so much how come he doesn't invite you to come live with him. If he loves you so much. Just ask him that the next time he calls, why don't you?*

Frieda had long blonde hair, a motorcycle, and a searing crush on my mom. One Sunday morning she sped up and down the street in front of our house, revving the engine. Then she popped a wheelie, parked her Harley on the lawn and came inside. She took off her helmet and shook out her hair. She looked like Farrah Fawcett, except that her hair and skin both looked healthier. Frieda modeled socks on TV to pay her rent, and when she sat down Jen and I asked to see her feet first thing.

"Not again," Frieda groaned. "That's all you people care about, why doesn't somebody ask me about my *art*, for a change." But she slid off her peds and let us look. She had exactly the kind of feet I wanted, with small, tan toes and high arches, like she'd been playing volleyball on the beach her whole life. Certain parts of my own body—my toes and ears, for example, and what was between my legs—would always look primitive and ugly to me, like uncivilized leftovers from the baboons. I kept my toenails trimmed and painted but still, flat on the floor, the toes were spraddled and knuckly and my arch was nonexistent. Frieda's feet were beautiful, and now she put them in third position to show how she had to stand for the sock advertisements. Then she looked around for my mom. "Your mother is sensational," she said. "You have no idea."

My mom came out of the bathroom and looked shyly at us. She'd taken off her bra, I noticed, and smudged some bronze powder on her cheekbones and lips. Now she looked feverish and full of anticipation. "I hope you *like* abelskivers," she told Frieda. "They're not everybody's thing."

"I hope you know she's a lezzie," I told Jen when they were out of earshot. "Isn't *that* just wonderful. I swear I'm gonna call Dad. We don't have to put up with this. He'd get custody like *that*," I snapped my fingers. "Her ass would be grass."

"I don't care. I like her." Jen was painting her toenails. Frieda said you could make your toes look smaller by using a darker shade of fingernail polish on the sides of the nail, and it was true. Jen kept painting, a snake of cotton woven between her toes. "What do you care? It's not like any of the *men* she dates are so great."

"Do you know what lesbians do? They kiss each other's *twats*. It's disgusting."

"Shut up," Jen said. "I don't want to think about Mom's *twat*, if that's what you want to call it."

"Dad would have her thrown in jail. You know he would. Her ass would be grass," I couldn't stop saying it.

"Yeah okay, let me know the minute you track down his phone number," Jen said. "Just update me the minute you get a hold of him. I'm sure he's out there somewhere, and when you find him you can tell him *all* about it."

I could hear Frieda and my mom in the kitchen, laughing and banging pots and pans around. I went to the backyard and pulled a lawn chair close to the window so I could look in and hear what they were saying. I thought they might be kissing, but instead Frieda was reading ingredients aloud from a cookbook. She saw me and waved for me to come in.

"What *are* these abelskiever things, anyway?" she wanted to know. "Your mom keeps saying they're just like pancakes but they seem awfully complicated, if you ask me."

"She learned about them in Solvang, " I said. "They're authentic Danish food."

"Really? Well." Frieda looked me over. "So what do you like to do?"

"Me?" I stared at the pink pompom on her ped, making a mental note to hit my mom up for a pair. "I don't know."

"Do you like dogs? Because I have two Irish setters. Lulu and Peach."

"We can't have dogs." My mom was stirring at the stove, and she kept shooting me looks. "It's in the lease but I'm sure Lucy would love to meet them, wouldn't you Luce?"

"They're lovers and not fighters," Frieda said. "They're my big, sloppy babies." She kept pushing her hair behind one ear, using it as a hook the way that I would've like to with my own hair, except that it was too short and had too many split ends.

I slid off the chair and went into the hallway and called Directory Assistance in Spokane again, trying to track down my dad. There were seven Robert Laribee Taylors listed. I'd already been through them all, and none of them was my dad.

After that, Frieda was around all the time. I couldn't figure out the logic of it, who would kiss who and what kinds of things they would do to each other, and after awhile I didn't care. She took us swimming at the YMCA, and brought over boxes of Brownie mix and watched the Billy Jack movies with us. She brought Lulu and Peach over so we could take them for walks, and took me to swim meets to watch Jen compete. My mom seemed to like her, but it was hard to tell. One night after Frieda went home, she came and squeezed in between Jen and me. We were watching *All in the Family*. In the old days it was easy to relate to, because my dad was Archie Bunker and my mom was Edith, *shrill and dumb*, my dad would say, *as a nickel bag of door-knobs*. But now, it was my mom and Frieda. I didn't know who would boss who.

"So what do you girls think of Frieda?"

"She's cool," Jen said. "Get it while the getting's good. Do you like her?"

"I like her," my mom said. "She's nice enough. What do you think, Lucy Loo?"

"She's a lesbo," I said. "If Dad ever found out."

"Well your dad isn't *going* to find out, is he? Frieda and I don't have any big plans for the future, or anything. But I mean, she's really sweet, and she's crazy about you kids. I don't know, I mean I think I'm probably straight, when it comes right down to it. But she's so *sweet.*"

"Have you guys had sex?" I wanted to ask her everything: how Frieda smelled, and how she kissed, and if her hair got in the way.

"That's none of your business," my mom said. "You're only *thirteen.*"

"I think we're entitled to know, since you have custody of us," I said. "Dad would freak out. Girls don't have sex with girls. You're supposed to find a new *husband*, in case you haven't noticed. That's what real mothers do."

"Is that so?" my mom said. "Well, Frieda's coming over again tonight, and I want you to be polite. She really likes you kids, you know."

"Is she bringing Lulu and Peach?"

"She's bringing the dogs. She's bringing a pepperoni pizza. She wants to watch a *Planet of the Apes* movie later, so she and I might go out. What's *Planet of the Apes*?"

Jen and I looked at each other. *Planet of the Apes* was our favorite. "It's what it sounds like," Jen said. "Apes take over."

"I was kind of hoping we could go see *The Way We Were*, my mom said. "Your dad and I really used to love Barbra Streisand."

"Do you have dad's phone number?" It was a risky question, and my mom always got upset when she was asked.

"I have no idea where your dad is," my mom said. "You know I'd tell you." And then Frieda was at the door. She'd brought pizza and Crazy Bread *and* her dogs, and she kissed me on the cheek when I answered the door. The dogs ran circles and pushed their drooling faces against my leg, and I thought about how if Frieda and my mom got together, we could walk Lulu and Peach in the park every day. "Come on in," my mom called, and kissed Frieda on the lips. It was the first time I'd seen it and what was weird was how right it seemed, how Frieda was starting to feel like one of the family. She held my mom close and I felt my heart crimp up.

Frieda pushed her face into my mom's neck. "Heaven," she said.

What I liked best about Frieda was how she put things in place. It had been a long time since our lives felt organized: we were always on the move, so there was never time. But Frieda took care of things. One day she showed up when I was trying to make the yard look nice; having her around had inspired me, and I'd wheeled the rusty rotary mower from the garage, maneuvering around old woodstain cans to push the mower out into hard sunlight, where I could see it for what it was, a piece of shit. But the lawn was knee-high in weeds and it looked horrible when you drove past, like we were white trash or hillbillies holed up watching *Wheel of Fortune* inside. We had to start somewhere, though, and Frieda gave me hope. My mom had never had the patience to learn to do things; yard work bored her, and practically any other domestic chore frustrated her so much that she had giggle fits and quit. It was either mirth or despair, feast or famine, when it came to my mom. But Frieda made me think there was such a thing as a life under control. She put little Pyrex trays in every drawer so that each item had its place, and took stuff to the Salvation Army and brought over a sharp potato peeler and nail-polish remover. She took phone messages on a single pink pad designated for phone messages, WHILE YOU WERE OUT, it said, with little boxes for checking things off.

I got the mower to the edge of the grass and pushed. It chuffed forward a few inches, making a dry scraping sound; I pulled it back and this time rammed forward, then backed up, paused, rammed, and when Frieda showed up I'd done maybe a three-foot square and the wooden handle was already wearing blisters in the grooves of my fingers while the blades chewed onward and forward, like geriatrics. I couldn't help but remember the lawn in Provo, so deep and plush you could lose pennies in it. I kept trying to mow and as I worked I got madder and madder. Everything was wrong with my mom. Everything. Now we didn't even have a decent lawn mower and it was because of her, because of Ellery the Fat Ass who'd lasted a whole six months and that's what had broken our family up, sixteen years with my dad pissed down the drain for: *Ellery*. When Frieda walked up, I ignored her. I kept ramming, backing off, ramming. Then I quit. I sat on the grass and let myself cry like the big fat baby I was.

"A rotary," Frieda said. "Cool. Think of the aerobic potential."

"Fuck you," I said. A blister had burst in my palm and I chewed away the skin, watched the water seep out. It was sort of a relief, I thought, to be the one who got to have the tantrum. Usually it was my mom. Then Jen and I would turn into wallflowers while our mom wept and wailed and hammered her chest in front of whatever boyfriend. People practically fucking *applauded*, when she was done.

"Do you want some help?" Frieda pushed. She moved a whole lot faster than I had, the tall grass toppling away on either side. "Where's your mom?"

"I could give a rat's ass."

Frieda stopped mowing. "What's your problem?"

"I hate her," I said. "I really do. I know kids aren't supposed to hate their moms but I *mean* it. I'd kill her if I could. I really would." It excited me to talk this way. *Kids aren't supposed to hate their mothers.* And I was the exception, the demon seed. Because I did.

"It's alright to hate her." Frieda started pushing again. "You're still hurt about losing your dad. You might even hate her for a long time. Nobody asked *you* if you wanted a divorce, right?" I could see that Frieda was playing the therapist but I didn't care, because something in my chest felt bubbly and hot, spitting at the surface every time she said something understanding.

"Right," I said. "And she's a fat fucking bitch and I hope she gets hit in a crosswalk walking home today. And if my dad ever finds out about you."

"Well, *I* don't hate her." Frieda moved to the tiny square of lawn on the other side of the walkway and started up again. "I for one am crazy about her. And I think her kids are pretty great, too."

I wanted to tell her to cut the shit, but I couldn't. I felt like the Grinch, my heart growing three sizes until whang, it burst the magnifying glass. "I like you, too," I said. "Thanks for helping with the lawn."

"Sure."

"When I say I hate my mom I hope you know it's nothing personal."

"It's cool," Frieda said. "You're going through a lot of stuff." She finished mowing and lifted her hair from her neck, fanned the front of her T-shirt. It embarrassed me, how much I noticed her body. I couldn't stop looking, couldn't stop trying to get her smell. Then I knew I was evil because I was thirteen and Frieda was at least thirty. But her hair was an impossible color, caramel in some places and almost white in others. I wanted to brush it down her back and then push my face into the lemony-smelling curtain and never come up for air.

"I'm beat," Frieda said. "What say we hoof it to Food King for popsicles?"

My mom was drunk. I could hear her in Jen's bed, where she always went to talk when she was sad or scared. "It's okay, Mom," Jen was saying. "It's okay."

"I *should* love her," my mom was saying. "It just figures, doesn't it, that the right person would come along and she'd be a girl. It's not that I don't like her, I *do*. I just think I like men better. I don't know how to tell her. She's *so* sweet, and she's just crazy about you two, that's what makes it so hard. She has money and she's *nice* to me."

And then one day my dad really did show up. I came home from school and his brown sedan was parked out in front of our house. He was listening to Frank Sinatra and had his English gents cap pulled low to his eyes, like he didn't want to be recognized. He gave me a bear hug and I started to cry, hard and right away, because my dad's bear hugs always felt like home and now here he was to take me away, back to wherever it was he lived. Back where I belonged. When I got into the front seat of the car everything snapped back into place and I was his girl again.

"I miss you kids. I miss you kids," my dad said. "Sometimes I swear to God, I hate your mom for breaking up our family, I really do. I know I shouldn't say that but it's true. She'll kill me, too, when she finds out I'm here. Have you eaten?" I shook my head. "Where's Jen? Should we wait on her?"

"She has dance company rehearsal till six. She gets home usually right after mom." I was thinking about Frieda, who was supposed to pick me up after school so we could go buy new tennis shoes. But there was Frieda and there was my dad. Then I heard her motorcycle. She parked behind my dad and beeped and waved. I could see the extra helmet on the back, just like she'd promised. We were planning to go to the mall.

"Who is that?" my dad said.

"Frieda," I said, but my old life was rushing back at me, all the times my dad and I had conspired to make my mom act like a Real Mother and not some crazy hippie with no responsibilities. I was ashamed at how much I'd let Frieda in, ashamed at how I'd been right on the brink of changing my life, rearranging it to include Frieda the twat-licker and her stupid dogs. "I hate her," I said. "She has the hots for mom."

"*What?*" my dad said, as he started the car. Frieda was still standing beside her motorcycle. *What's up?* she mouthed, and I gave her the finger, off out to the side so my dad couldn't see. "God, I missed you," he said.

My dad took me to International House of Pancakes. "So what's this Frieda all about?"

"She loves Mom. She's okay."

"She *loves* your mom, what does that mean?"

"I mean love love. Like a boyfriend."

"I'm not all that surprised." My dad sawed at his stack of cherry pancakes. They were huge, almost orange, and the little flecks of cherry made them look diseased. International House of Pancakes was from the old days, when our family was still together, and it made me sad to be there, though I knew my dad intended it to have the opposite effect. "I think your mom has always had leanings. I just didn't know she'd ever act on it."

"It makes me sick. They kiss."

"In front of you girls?"

"Of course in front of us. They *make out* in front of us." My dad didn't seem worried or disgusted enough. "They stick their tongues in each other's mouths."

"Well I can't say I blame your mom for not wanting to be with men. If I were a girl that's what I'd do. I remember when I first married your mom I thought, if I were a girl I'd never let a guy stick that thing inside me. I probably shouldn't tell you that, Hon, but it's the truth. I just want to come clean, I'm not saying I approve of your mom's choice."

"Can I come live with you?"

"You know you can't, Sweetheart. Your mom has custody."

"Even if the judge found out about Frieda?" I puddled more syrup over my chocolate-chip pancakes. I liked Frieda, but between her and my dad there was no contest. "Couldn't you get custody back?"

"Maybe," my dad used the tip of his knife to finish off the whipped butter in the crock. "Your mom's a scrapper, Luce. She's one hell of a fighter, she'd make it ugly. And I'm not even sure I'd know how to take care of you girls. I would dearly love to have you, I'm not saying that I don't want you. You know I'd give anything. I just don't know if there's really any way to prove this thing about your mom. Are you about finished? Should we hit the road? Listen, we'll go get your sister, we can call your mom so she doesn't freak out and then maybe you kids can use the swimming pool at the motel. How's that sound?"

My dad was staying at the Travelodge downtown. After all the times I'd looked for him it was strange to finally have him there, solid and safe and making dumb jokes, just my dad. Jen and I spent two days hanging out at the motel swimming pool and our dad gave us money to walk to 7-Eleven for drinks and hot dogs and Heath bars, sunscreen and new flip-flops and magazines. Anything we wanted, he bought us. Then we'd go lay by the pool again, slathered in coconut oil, our tongues stained from lime Slurpees. Our mom and dad talked a few times on the phone, and it was on the second day that my dad told her what I'd said about Frieda. Then my mom came flying over in the Mercury Cougar, her thongs whapping furiously across the parking lot. "Get in the car," she said, and made my towel into a ball and threw it at me. Jen slipped out of the pool, wrung her hair out, and gave my dad a long hug before she headed toward the car. Then my mom lost patience. She yanked at my arm and shoved me. *I don't know what you told him, I don't know what you told him,* she kept saying.

"You know it's true," I said.

"What's true? What's true?" My mom had had her sunglasses propped on her head but they'd slipped sideways and were hanging above one ear. She didn't even notice. "That Frieda loves me? That I've finally found somebody decent?"

"She was just telling me the truth, don't chew her ass out," my dad said. "Be mad at me. I'm the one who's gonna tell the judge."

"You're not telling the judge a goddamned thing," my mom shoved me in the car and got behind the wheel. I let myself out and she went berserk, shrieking and racing around to shove me back in. "You stay there! You stay there or I'll kill you!"

"Just go for now, Hon. It'll be okay." My dad kissed me through the window and blew Jen a kiss. "I love you kids. You know I love ya."

Frieda was waiting at home. My mom had driven fast and my wet hair had flown all over and now it was frizzed around my face, not parted, and I'd left my barrette by the side of the pool. I needed face lotion and Chapstick and a hairbrush and to put my clothes on and now I was going to have to deal with Frieda, who was squatting next to the car, her face a sad puzzle.

"Why did you do that?" she asked me.

"Do what?" Everyone was making me the bad guy. I got out and kicked the door shut and stomped to the house.

"You know what, Luce. I thought maybe we were all going to be together. I'm good for your mom. You know I am. And I thought you liked me."

I turned on her. "You're a *girl*, in case you hadn't noticed. You make me sick. I want my dad." I was dropping stuff and Frieda helped me pick it up. I just wanted to get to my room.

"I'm calling him right now," my mom said. "And Frieda, keep an eye on her. God only knows what she'll do next, to hurt me."

"Your mom has custody of you kids, Luce," Frieda said. "Come on, can we please sit down? Can we please talk for a minute?" It struck me how reasonable she was being, like a Real Parent, and I thought *that's not the way things are done around here.* Our family was supposed to have big screaming matches that were punctuated with big endings, a door slam or something breaking or someone driving away. But Frieda had some different idea about *working things out.* I felt a sudden knife of sympathy for her. She really wouldn't fit into our family. She was too normal.

"I want to go to my room."

"Come on Luce. Please, just for a sec." She followed me, and when I slammed the door she talked to me through it. "Is that what this is about? You wanting to live with your dad?"

"What do you think!" I was facedown on my bed, my hair wet underneath but flyaway on top. I felt like the girl in *The Exorcist.* "Go away!"

"Lucy, your dad's a good person. And I know it's hard for you to hear this and I know you're going to want to tell me to go to hell, but I'm saying this as a friend. I really am, Lucy, and I know you're not going to believe it. But your dad just isn't up to it. Your mom can be hell on wheels, and she's your *mother.* This is *Utah.* Even if he did want to fight for you. That doesn't make him a bad person. He just doesn't have it in him."

"You don't know shit about it. You don't know shit. You're just a lesbian."

"And cut the lesbian stuff. That's not what this is about and you know it."

"My dad does too want us back. You don't know shit."

"Oh come on. Think about it. Your dad sends checks every month, he knows where to find you." Frieda could've come in, but she didn't. She stayed right there, yelling through the crack.

"He doesn't send money," I said. "He can't afford it."

"Of course he sends money."

"That's not what my mom says."

Frieda was quiet for a minute. Then she said, "Well, I'll probably get in trouble for telling you. I'm sure she has her reasons. But I know she gets checks. You should know that. I don't have any reason to lie to you, if I wanted to lie I'd tell you just the opposite because what I'm getting at is that he loves you like crazy, but honestly, Sweetie, I don't think he's ready to be a single dad."

"Thank you o' lesbian mind reader."

"Oh, please. Would you please stop it?"

I opened the door. "And anyway she's just going to chew you up and spit you out, too. That's what she does to people, even when she likes them. She can't even help it." I wanted Frieda to hug me but I didn't know how to ask. I was bad. My dad was going to take my mom to court and it was all my fault, and even if we got to live with him at the end, in the meantime they all hated me. I could hear my mom on the phone at the other end of the house, giving my dad hell.

I was all set to fight it out with my mom, ready to say whatever it took to make her give in and let me live with my dad. But I didn't need to. My dad stayed in town a few more days and he and my mom kept going to restaurants, and at the end of it all she said I could go live with him if that's what I wanted so goddamned much, if I was going to ruin her life over it, if I was so goddamned loyal to him. She wasn't relinquishing custody but I didn't care. I'd take whatever I could get. Jen would stay with my mom in Salt Lake, and then my suitcases were in the trunk of my dad's car and we were really going. I said my good-byes and Frieda lingered in the kitchen, waving from the window. I missed her already, and thought how maybe, if my dad hadn't shown up when he did, we might really have turned into a family.

But Frieda didn't last. Jen told me about it later, how one night my mom flew off the handle and threw a bookend at Frieda's head and then started dating some guy named Dave without telling her. By then I was in my new life in California, beyond the reach of my mom, and I didn't much care. Already Frieda seemed faint and unlikely, and once, years later when I asked my mom about her, she looked at me with clear, hard eyes: *I never,* she said. *I never.* And then Frieda really was gone.

My mom met Frank through an ad she'd placed in *Mother Earth News*, which, my dad said, *figured*. Every time my parents got on the phone she reminded him about how she still officially had custody, that she was just letting me stay with him for a few months out of the goodness of her heart: if he tried anything fishy, she said, his ass was grass. Things hadn't been going too well for her, in Salt Lake: the job at Food King gave her big blue veins in her legs, she hated wintertime, and she called on Christmas day to say that she and Jen had shared a packet of raw hot dogs for their Christmas dinner. My dad wrote her out a check for two hundred dollars and sent it Overnight Express.

"*Mother Earth News*," my mom was saying now. "But I need help with editing, you're such a good writer, it has to be perfect. And don't tell your dad, he'll just think it's flaky. But I really do need your help. I'll send you a draft, the ad can't be more than fifty words. You can just call and tell me what you think, okay? Please?"

Wanted, she'd written. *Outdoorsy, well-educated man for girl of the mountains, divorced okay, for camping, sailing, skiing. I have two children, am well-educated, vivacious. Seeking companion (financially secure please) for candlelight dinners, bubble baths, long walks at twilight, world travel, and other adventures.*

As far as I knew my mom had never been sailing or skiing, but I thought it sounded good. She mailed me a rough draft and I helped her with revisions, cutting the word "children" and replacing it with "daughters." Also, I thought she should be more pointed than to request a companion; on the rough draft, I crossed out this word and scrawled in, "husband." But my mom thought this sounded pushy, desperate even. We settled on "male friend," and my mom said she'd let me know the minute she heard from anyone.

Frank answered the ad the first week it ran. They wrote back and forth, then spent a weekend together in a cabin in Montana. By the end of the weekend, Frank had asked my mom to marry him. My mom said yes, then called and asked me to come home for a visit.

"One summer," she said. "Not even the whole summer. Six weeks. Big deal. You can stand me for that long. I haven't seen you since *November*, Luce. You've had six whole months with your dad. I miss you."

"I have to be back in time for school. I'm going to Evergreen."

"That won't be any problem."

"August twenty-sixth, is when we have seventh-grade orientation."

"You'll be back by the end of August. Don't you want to meet Frank? See what a success our ad was? I couldn't have done it without you, Sweetie, I really couldn't have. Anyway, I know your dad would miss you terribly but gee, it's just summer vacation."

"You have to promise. I live here now, remember."

"I promise. Now put your dad back on."

"Will you send me a ticket that's round-trip?" I was in the kitchen, eating thick curved stacks of Pringles potato chips. It was one of the luxuries of living with my dad. I could eat as much as I wanted of anything I wanted, and then we'd just go to the store and buy more.

"Gee whiz, Honey. You're giving me a complex. Don't you want to see your sister?"

"Miriam?" my dad picked up the other extension. I made a production of hanging up the phone, then lifted it again, trying to be stealthy.

"I wouldn't do that to her, Bob," my mom was saying. "You know I wouldn't."

"I know," my dad said. "I think she's just a little bit scared, is all."

"I told her I'd send her back. You know I will."

"I know. I think she's a little anxious, is all. She's really doing good in school."

"How are you? How's bachelorhood?"

I hung up the phone again, and went upstairs to my dad's room. He was scribbling on the back of a magazine and nodding into the phone. "Lucy wants to talk to you again," he said. "Take care."

"Honey?" my mom said. "I think it's hard for him, to hear about Frank. Is it hard for him, do you think?"

"I don't know."

"Are you going to be okay about this, Honey?"

"I want the ticket to be round-trip. I want you to send it, first."

"Honey, I wouldn't do that to you. California is your home. I'm not going to keep you here against your will."

"Are you going to send it?" My dad sat on the edge of the bed, listening, his head tilted and his mouth open a little.

"I promise. I said I would. I'll talk to you again soon."

After we'd hung up my dad said, "You don't have to go you know, if you don't want to."

"I know."

"She'd have to take me to court first. She doesn't have that kind of money. It sounds like this Frank character might have money, though. Do you think he's planning to move to Salt Lake?"

"I don't know."

"If he's such a good catch why'd he have to use an ad? That's my only question."

"She better send me back."

"She promised," my dad said. "I think she's starting to figure things out. She wouldn't break your trust like that."

"She scares me. Her creepy boyfriends."

"Well it sounds like that'll be settled now, with Frank. Your mom's always liked the attention she got from guys." My dad rummaged in his nightstand drawer and peeled open a pack of Rolaids. "You know, even if I do have a lady friend over, I'm too old for that sort of stuff. You don't have to worry about anything. I hope you know that, Hon."

"I know." He was dating a woman named Marina, and always buying her gold jewelry in the shapes of insects and birds. But I thought I knew what he was getting at; that even if Marina did ever sleep over, the house would stay quiet. My dad slept with his bedroom door open, and the only sounds I ever heard from his room were the TV or the crinkling of a cellophane potato-chip bag, or sometimes the clink of spoon when he polished off a bowl of butter pecan. I could hear crickets and, if he stayed up late, Johnny Carson. He slept in a king-sized bed under a burgundy-and-green pinstriped bedspread, the bedspread masculine and impersonal and the bed always made up, sharp-cornered, the coverlet so lightweight that even a shifting knee would have been detected, suspect. If my dad was doing anything he was doing it the same way I was learning to, in the bathroom with the fan on and the lights off. And when I stayed home sick, propped up in his bed and watching daytime TV, I occupied his bed politely, using a Kleenex to blow my nose instead of wiping my boogers on the edge of the box spring; and kept my hair in a barrette and my legs straight out and together, like I was under surveillance at a bank. If someone came to the door, even sick, I would be in good enough shape to answer it, because that was another thing about my dad, you always answered the door and you always answered the telephone, unlike my mom, who would sometimes let the phone ring and ring, just sitting next to it, browsing a magazine, paying no attention.

"Anyway, she promised she'd send you back," my dad said. "That's one thing we can count on. She promised me."

"Sometimes she lies, though."

"I don't think you have to worry, Hon." My dad took my hand. His was reddish-brown, a soft bear paw. Everything about him seemed trustworthy: the *TV Guide* on the nightstand and his decanter of aftershave on the bureau, shaped like a bag of golf clubs. Our house had security lights, sprinklers that hissed at dawn. There was lunchmeat and cheddar cheese in the fridge, and plenty of 7-Up. When I'd lived with my mom and Jen we'd all squabbled over everything, snacks and nail polish and postage stamps, and we held the empty shampoo bottle under the shower tap, then shook it up to use the froth as shampoo. There was never enough of anything, and with my dad there was more than plenty, all the time. Sometimes when I told my mom things on the phone—*we had barbecued chicken for dinner, Dad and I just got back from Baskin-Robbins*—my mom made little moaning sounds and said things: *I don't remember the last time your sister and I had ice cream.* And *chicken! What a luxury! Your sister, your sister and I had mac-n-cheese, again!* All the same, I missed her. She was the only one who understood when I got a migraine headache, and her hair always smelled faintly oily and pepperminty, and she knew who Three Dog Night was and always let my sister and me listen to the radio, loud. She drove fast and didn't care how late we stayed up.

"Anyway, I don't think we need to worry," my dad said. He let go of my hand and stood up. "Your mom's made a lot of mistakes, but I think she's coming around."

My mom picked me up from the airport in a U-Haul truck, and by night-fall we were halfway to Wyoming, where Frank had his veterinary practice. I had a bad feeling about things. I missed my dad, and kept feeling for the round-trip plane ticket, zipped in the inside pocket of my jacket.

"You didn't tell me you were moving," I said.

"I didn't think it was important." My mom said. "I didn't think you'd care."

"I don't care." I said. "But you could've at least told Dad."

"It's none of his business." She glanced at me in the rearview mirror. "I think you'll be happy there," she told me. "Horses. Dogs."

"I hope you're planning to drive me back down here in forty-one days," I said. My ticket's for the Salt Lake airport, remember."

"You don't have to use that tone of voice with me. I'm still your mother." She watched me in the mirror. "Look at us. We could be sisters."

"I think I look like Dad."

"No. You look a tiny bit like him around the mouth, but that's it." She laughed a little. "What's the matter, you don't want to look like me?"

"I don't know."

"At least you don't have my teeth. Your dad used to tell me to keep my mouth shut when I smiled, he said I looked prettier that way. And I smiled that way for sixteen years. Can you believe that? No more," my mom said. "I am a free woman."

"I'm calling Dad as soon as we get there."

"You can call him anytime you want. You're a free agent. I love your new *haircut*, by the way. Très chic."

"It's supposed to look like Dorothy Hamill's," I said. "Dad likes it, too."

"Well of course *he* would," my mom said. "He all prophylactic, all Mr. Safety and security lights. He doesn't like it when women have long hair, because then they look *slutty*."

"I need to get it trimmed pretty soon or I'll have split ends," I said. Everything my mom did scared me. My dad thought I was going to be spending my summer in Salt Lake, and now we were halfway to Frank's, wherever that was. Somewhere in Wyoming. I could feel my old life slipping away, the safety and neatness and predictability. "Can I for sure call Dad?"

"I already said you could. What do you think Wyoming will be like, anyway?"

"Is Frank a cowboy?"

"He's a real outdoorsman, that's what I think is so sexy," my mom said. "He takes his horses on pack trips, leading them through the wilderness. And when we went camping, we sat around a campfire and then stayed up for hours after that, just gazing up at the stars."

I liked the idea of someone who might take us camping, and I especially liked that Frank had been researched and then chosen from all the guys who'd answered my mom's ad, of which, my mom said, there were *a lot*. After Ellery my mom had changed direction and started dating men that were obviously useful, TV repairmen or carpenters or carpet layers, men we owed favors or money to. They all seemed to have poor hygiene and bad toupees, men who were down on their luck and thought nothing of moving in with us, sleeping in my mom's bed and issuing orders to us kids and using up our food stamps. They needed dental work, and had bad grammar. My mom's last boyfriend, Jerry, had taken Jen on long car rides, offering her tequila, finally pulling the car to the side of the road and doing things to her. It was as if we were up for grabs; as if, fatherless, we were somehow freebies.

"I'll bet we're going to love it there. I'll be the veterinarian's wife, you know, finally I'll have some status, for a change. Are you okay, Jen? Jennie?" My mom adjusted the mirror so she could see Jen, who'd been crying in the backseat. Now she sat slumped against the window and when she saw our mom in the mirror, she gave her the finger. "There'll be other boyfriends," my mom told her. "Other fish in the sea. You're only sixteen, Honey, gee whiz, I mean you can help make a sacrifice for our future. Rick can always come visit, not like we're moving to Florida. It's only Wyoming. A whole seven hours away."

"Fuck off," Jen said.

My mom delicately readjusted the mirror. "I'm making a sacrifice. We're all making sacrifices. Do you think it's going to be easy for me? I don't know a soul in Riverton, not a soul, and Frank's probably got tons of classy socialite friends that I'll have to win over, which won't be all that easy, gee whiz I've been single so long I'm not even sure how to do it again. Be a wife."

"You haven't been single one single millimeter minute of your entire life since you and dad got divorced," Jen said. "You've always had some stupid ass boyfriend."

"I most certainly haven't. I most certainly have not. Like who? What boyfriends?"

"Ellery," Jen was holding up her fingers, striking off the boyfriends savagely. " Jerry. Dave. *Frieda,* don't forget. Plus the other Dave. Pete."

"What other Dave?"

"That one, that creepy psychiatrist. Scott, that Ted guy, Mike. And then the other Mike. You've never been single."

"How do you think I've managed to pay the rent all these years? They don't count as boyfriends. None of those count, as actual romantic relationships. I'm just using my natural resources."

"I'm not even going to say the word I'm thinking right now," Jen said. "At least Rick and I love each other, and what's in Wyoming? Nothing. Dirt and horse shit, that's what."

"Money," my mom said. She was taking the off-ramp, steering the car toward a gigantic lit-up penguin whose wing flashed, LITTLE AMERICA TRUCK STOP AND CAFE. "I don't want us to have to be on food stamps anymore, I don't want to have to worry about you anymore, with me working two jobs. And I don't want you to keep having to do without. When's the last time you got new clothes? When's the last time we didn't have to worry about every single thin dime?"

That shut Jen up. You could see she was thinking about it, especially the new clothes part. "Luce hasn't had to worry," my mom said. "Your dad always manages to live real nice, doesn't he? I could see right when you stepped off that plane, you've filled out, plus your new haircut. Well and both you girls deserve that kind of treatment. We all do. And his house is big enough so you can both have your own room, it's been a while since that's happened, it's just crazy, I didn't bring you into this world so you could be white trash. You'll both get to have your own room."

"I don't need it anyway," I said. "I'm only going to be here a couple of weeks."

My mom looked over at me. "That's right, that's absolutely right. Let's go get some lunch. You know what I am? You know what I am right now? I'm the happiest girl in the whole U.S.A."

Just outside of Rock Springs, a cop pulled us over.

"Goddamn him," my mom said. "He's going to get me for speeding, damnit, and we're not even there yet. I don't have any money. He's gonna want money. Damn him."

I wasn't worried; I'd seen her crying act plenty of times. She was masterful. In all the times we'd been pulled over she'd only once gotten a ticket, and that was when the cop was a woman, with whom our mother chatted reasonably, agreeing that she'd exceeded the speed limit, acknowledging the problem of our broken headlight. That time my mom took the ticket without complaint and said, later, well, she was nice enough. But male cops always let her off the hook. They seemed to eat it up: our battered car with us and all of our crap piled inside, and my mother's pretty face, her ingratiating demeanor. Still, I hated the performance. I was afraid of cops, and wanted them to like me.

The cop tapped on the window. "Any idea how fast you were going?"

"Was I going too fast? Oh my. We're trying to get to Wyoming before nightfall. Was I, was I speeding?"

"Can I see your license?"

"Sure." We could feel her trying to gauge his mood. She had a number of options. Crying seemed to work best but it depended on the cop, and what kind of a day he was having. If he looked lonely or middle-aged she took a different route, toying with her hair and asking questions about his personal life. This cop was somewhere in between, and we could see her wavering nervously between the options. He was middle-aged, with a huge belly that slung out over a large belt buckle, but his demeanor was indifferent, bored. Most men fell for her right off the bat, we'd noticed, or not at all.

She decided to flirt. "Was I going fast? Darn it, that always happens in this car. It just loves the open road. It just goes and goes and I can't hardly even tell. People tell me it's a collectible. A V-8, whatever that means. Anyway, it's got loads of power."

The cop tugged his sunglasses from his face and squatted next to the window. He chewed a toothpick, taking her in: her thick, dark hair, her smile. "Can I see your registration please, Ma'am?"

"Are you going to write me a ticket?"

"I clocked you at seventy-two. You were going pretty fast, for a fifty-five-mile-an-hour zone."

"I do that," my mom laughed again. "I get all excited about where I'm going I guess." While she talked, Jen dug the registration from the glove compartment. A pink lipstick rolled onto the floor and my mother snatched it up, taking a split second in the mirror to apply a coat.

"Where are you going?"

She perked up. "Wyoming. Riverton, do you know where that is, have you ever been there? We're moving there. Trying something new, just for an adventure." We noticed she left off mentioning Frank.

"Adventure's good. Pretty lady like you though, has to be careful and watch out for creeps."

"True!" she said, and wiggled a little in her seat. "So are you going to give me a ticket?"

"Do you know your registration's expired?"

"We're on food stamps," Jen offered.

"That's true, Sweetheart, we are on food stamps. My registration is expired, isn't it, I guess it is." Her smile wavered, and she pushed a piece of hair unhappily behind one ear. Her fingers traveled down her throat and rested at her neck. "I've been meaning to take care of that but darn it, things are so hard with two girls. Just making sure everybody has warm boots and coats for winter. Do you have children? You must know what it's like. Or maybe your wife sews their coats."

I snickered, and my mom shot me a dangerous look. The cop was staring off down the road, the toothpick moving loosely. "Nope," he said curtly, and started to write.

"Are you? Going to give us a ticket?" She was panicking now, trying to figure out her next move.

"I'm afraid so," he scribbled away, through playing. "Seventy-two miles per hour."

"But we're going to Wyoming. We haven't got any money. My husband left us, we haven't got anything, I'll never be able to pay it."

"Sorry, Lady." He tore off the ticket and pushed it through the window. "Have a good one."

"But we haven't got any money!" My mom rolled the window down all the way, her head tilted up at him. She started to cry. "You could let us go just this once! I don't have any money! Please!"

"Sorry, Ma'am. Drive safe." He headed back to the patrol car.

Jen watched him in the rearview mirror. "Dick," she said. "Pencil dickless wonder. Pig."

"Goddamn him." My mom crumpled up the ticket, shoved it in the glove compartment. "He could've let us off. He was trying to decide, did you see how he was trying to decide? I look too much like a hippie for his taste, is the thing. I could tell right when he came to the window. I look loose to him. They all love that look when you're going to have sex with them but right now, no, he was carrying a grudge. Against his wife or somebody, could you tell? Damn him." She pulled back onto the road, watching the speedometer. Her tears were gone, and she looked betrayed. "I've only gotten one ticket in my whole entire life, and that time she was just doing her job," she said. "That's what I hate about cops, how they just toy with you. Did you see? He was looking all over at me." She drove on, and we stayed quiet, embarrassed for her. "Anyway, Frank will pay for it, but that's not the point. I had a perfect record until now, did you know that? A perfect record."

Frank made plenty of money, though as it turned out, he didn't like to spend it. He lived in a double-wide house trailer sheathed in white aluminum siding, and the trailer was almost completely without furniture. What was there, when we moved in, was brown: two brown sofas and a matching recliner, dark-brown paneling, brown shag carpet, and tweedy mud-colored and orange-flecked curtains that hit the floor over every window, though the windows were small and high. By way of decoration, Frank had maybe a dozen prints depicting water spaniels in various and noble poses: they pointed, or held birds in their jaws, or did both of these at once, or languished before fireplaces, all with the same faraway gaze in their eyes. He also had an extensive gun collection and an assortment of preserved snakes. His veterinary office was another trailer a few hundred yards from the house, and the two buildings were connected by a white gravel path, which was lined on either side with chain swags connected to lampposts. The weathervane, mailbox, and lampposts all sported the same metal cutout, a silhouette of an English country gent astride a prancing horse. It was a complicated effect, one Frank had designed himself.

Even though he was a vet, Frank was unsentimental about pets; he thought animals were there to work, like the six sled dogs chained up behind the house. They were beautiful and vicious, each chained with a short length to its own doghouse. Though we never saw him race the dogs, now and again Frank went on a sort of patrol from one dog to another, issuing commands. From the window in my new bedroom, we watched him order the dogs around. He'd make each of them sit, stay, lay down. He'd have them hop up onto their doghouses, then hop back down. The dogs were afraid of him, but they loved him, and their tails flapped low and fast at the sight of him.

I hid my plane ticket under a broken square of linoleum in the closet. I knew my mom would send me back, but I didn't want to take any chances. In the meantime I glutted myself on horseback riding and went with Frank on his veterinary rounds and played with the sad animals caged in the clinic. I called my dad at the end of the first week and told him how happy my mom was, and how much I couldn't wait to come home.

Sometimes Frank took me with him on veterinary rounds, explaining distorted bowel syndrome or anemia like I was his assistant, and he let Jen and me watch surgeries in the clinic behind his office. This was also where he operated on the horses, strapping them first to a huge, vertical metal table. He'd inject the horse and wait a few minutes before pulling a lever that slowly tipped the table to a horizontal position, and the horse went over with a fantastic and horrible crashing sound, which made us applaud. We watched him anesthetize cats and dogs and then tie them to the table in humiliating positions, on their backs with their arms and legs outstretched, and then shave the belly and swab on a thick, acrid layer of betadine before making the incision. The animals slept, heads thrown back like those of drunk or dead or snoring men. They looked anonymous and twisted, like roadkill, and Frank worked on them without tenderness. Later we watched them come to in their cages, blinking and tottering toward the water bowl.

At the end of the third week, homesick, I tried to call my dad. This time the number was disconnected, but I didn't worry too much; I had my plane ticket. It seemed, finally, like things were working out for us as a family. I would start Evergreen Junior High in the fall, in California, and spend summers in Wyoming. And my mom, who'd always liked to see new places, finally seemed to be settling down. She was crazy about Frank, unlike practically all the other men in her life, who fell for her and then got stomped on. She'd never been able to stand men who fawned over her, and in this situation Frank had the upper hand. He had a thin, craggy face and icy blue eyes and was quiet every night at dinner, though my mom hauled out recipe books and cooked like it was the old days, when she'd made our family meat loaf and beef stroganoff and turkey casserole. She even tried her hand at pie crusts again. Frank ate every meal with his face held low to the plate, shoving the food in, his fork held in a menacing, fisted way. After dinner he'd return to his office to smoke while my mom cleaned up and us kids snooped through the trailer, looking for evidence of his previous life, which included three teenagers and a wife in a wheelchair. She'd had a stroke, my mom explained, as a result of a broken heart when Frank divorced her. Later she told us the stroke had been Frank's fault, from when he'd smashed his ex-wife against a cupboard. Either version of the story seemed possible.

Mornings, we could hear the huskies out in the pasture, barking and howling to be fed. Sometimes Jen and I went out to look at them, stopping just short of their ring of dirt. When they heard us they rose slowly and terribly on stiff legs, and the air seemed to quiver in a single menacing growl, and we always retreated with much stamping down of grass and shrieking and laughing, though each time we meant to free them.

"Frank says you're quite the horsewoman." My mom was cooking again, trying to impress Frank. "Are you having a good time here?"

"Alley Oop went all the way to the trees this morning. I didn't even have to kick her. I just made a kissing sound, and she walked."

"You're pretty good. I've seen you." She clipped a candy thermometer to the side of the saucepan and stood with her hands on her hips, looking out at the gravel paths. "You know, that's really an ugly effect. Tacky."

"What is?"

"Oh, that horse-and-buggy crap. I really hate it. You'd think he had taste, with all his money, but no." She moved to the table and plunked down. "Money doesn't matter, what matters is having an education. Sometimes I wonder if I did the right thing by bringing us all here. I only needed one more class and then I would've had my degree. Come sit on my lap," she said, and patted her knee. "I miss you, my Lucy Loo. You and Frank are together all the time, Jen goes off, where does that leave me?" She settled for pushing my hair behind my ears, her fingers oily and hot. "My sweetest. You're growing up so fast, you kids, you've both grown up so fast."

"When are we leaving to drive back to Salt Lake? I need to be there by two weeks from today. My plane leaves the fourteenth."

"You don't like living here? I thought you loved it. You love Frank. And you have a horse, how many kids your age can say that?"

"I like it here. It's just that I live in Southern California now. I'm supposed to start school. August twenty-sixth."

"Are you sure your dad wants you back?"

"What's that supposed to mean?"

"I'm just asking, Honey. I mean he's a bachelor, maybe he'd like to be able to go out on dates at night."

"He can go out on dates. I'm old enough to stay home by myself."

"Have you ever asked him? Because maybe he'd like to bring home a lady friend, but he worries about the impression it might make on you."

"Just tell her," Jen called from the living room.

"Tell me what?"

"That you're not going back." Jen was in the doorway now, looking at me sympathetically. "Mom thinks it's better if we all live here."

"But I have my plane ticket. I'm starting at Evergreen."

"They have schools here, too, you know." My mom was stirring fast, not looking at me. "You and Frank do practically everything together. I thought you wanted to stay."

"I'm here on vacation. This was only supposed to be for *six weeks*."

"You can try it, Honey. If you don't like it, if you hate living here, you can always go back. I just want you to try it, so we can be a family again."

"You said you'd send me back. You promised."

"Honey, it's not my decision. Your dad moved, he just doesn't have room for you anymore, I'm sorry but you just have to face facts. You live here now."

"You *swore*. You *promised*." I started to cry. I should've known she'd do this. My mom had always been a liar, and she always got her way. I should've known.

"He knows you're here now, that we're a family. He's not even living in the same place, you know that. You've tried to call."

"He does too want me back. I know he does, no matter what you say."

"He doesn't, Honey, just try to call him if you're so convinced. Go ahead." She held out the phone.

"You bitch."

"What did I do? What did I do?" my mom was wide-eyed, innocent. "If you're going to get mad at anybody, get mad at your dad for once, why don't you? He moved without even telling you."

"You're a lying bitch." I slammed into the bedroom, hauled out my backpack and stuffed a few things inside. Maybe Frank could drive me back to Salt Lake, or maybe I could hitchhike. I had a roll of dimes and

I put these in the backpack, then went to the closet for my plane ticket. The broken piece of linoleum had been peeled back and the ticket was gone. *I should've known.* There was never any place free from her, never any way to change things once my mom had made up her mind about what our Perfect Life should be. I sat on the floor of the closet until it got dark outside, listening to the clink of chains against pie pans as the huskies wolfed down their nightly scoop of kibble. At one point Jen brought me a grilled cheese and I thought about how, if I ate it, it would mean that things were a done deal, and that my new life had started. There was California and my dad was somewhere in it, in our old life where he made banana waffles every Sunday morning or drove us to International House of Pancakes. His car was air-conditioned and freshly vacuumed, with a scented, cardboard pine tree dangling from the mirror. Every day with my dad had been the same, a safe waking to familiar jokes and then a leisurely stroll through it all, school or TV or lawn mowing, then homework and an early dinner of bland components, corn and chicken or hamburgers and broccoli. Then dessert, ice cream or packaged cookies, and an early bedtime. Every day was like that. Our house in Ventura had had white tile surfaces that were easy to clean, and a bathroom fan that drowned out embarrassing noises. It had sliding glass doors and a patio with hanging plants and my dad always bought stuff like cream rinse, *always*, and I didn't know why his phone was disconnected, where he'd gone, or why he wasn't looking for me.

I cried some more, then plucked at the sandwich. My bedroom in Ventura would be empty and I couldn't imagine my dad anywhere in the house. In the living room there would be no furniture, just curtains billowing open over freshly shampooed carpet. There would be dead flies on the windowsill, a vacant driveway. And outside there would be kids playing, looping their bikes in bored circles. Outside in Ventura it was still summer.

Then my mom was in the doorway; and that was the moment, I thought, when my new life did start: the moment of her waiting for me to go to her, which I did because I lived then the way any kid did, in the present, hungry and needing to pee, and sad, and because she was my mom. We seemed to have a marginal future, all of us as a family with Frank, a skinny chance at happiness. When she held out the sandwich, I didn't object. We ate quietly, both grieving, watching the huskies from the window. They were beautiful animals with blue circles for eyes, and like us they were waiting for something to happen: something better, some crazy move that would bring them love, or a person walking toward them to release them, finally, and shoo them off into the darkness. *Go*, the person might say. *Beat it. Scram.* Then the dogs would dissolve, gray smears in the dusk, and wouldn't come back no matter how you called and called, the grass and crickets all around, the smell of cows and cat tails all around, and the dogs startled into joy, an ecstasy of paws and tongues and leaping. We were all on the lam, all making soft sounds in the dirt as we landed.

TIED TO A TREE ON A DESERT ISLAND:

the kind you see in comic strips, just big enough for two
people. My mom would be tied to a tree and I would be saying
everything I'd ever wanted to, and asking all kinds of questions, and no matter how much she yelled and screamed and
flailed it wouldn't help because finally she was going to have
to listen. Not hang up the phone, not tell lies or drive away.
This way she'd be plenty goddamned stuck, a sitting fucking
duck. Just the two of us.

In Riverton I thought maybe finally we were going to land, finally we were going to stop and be a family again. For the first time since our parents' divorce, my sister and I were friends with the popular kids. For the first time in years we had new clothes, and there was soda pop in the fridge to offer our friends when they came over. We had horses to ride, and two TVs, and a strobe light. We did homework every day after school, and got into the habit of making our beds every morning. For a while it seemed like things were going to work.

Sometimes, remembering my round-trip plane ticket, I'd threaten to run away, back to my dad in California. *Go ahead,* my mom told me. *Good luck, he doesn't even live in the same house anymore.* When I got homesick enough I tried to call him, but his phone was still disconnected, with no forwarding number.

My mom tried to settle in. She was madly in love with Frank but she hated Riverton, a tiny town with one movie theatre, five bars, six gas stations, and one mental hospital. She hated the trailer, its wee stainless-steel sink and miniature cupboards. When we left for school each morning my mom leaned in the doorway, wearing a pink chenille bathrobe and looking exhausted and hateful. She hated the dirt, she hated all the sky and quiet.

I couldn't help myself: I loved Riverton, the way my best friend Susie and I could walk from one end of town to the other in less than an hour, and I loved that there were pastures and horses everywhere and that you could hear crickets in the evening. I loved the way the trailer made our life feel manageable, safe and contained, and the way the windows could be cranked open, and that my bed could be folded up into a sofa. And I loved Frank, who looked like Paul Newman and smoked cherry-flavored tobacco in a pipe. He wore thin, plaid, polyester pants and cowboy boots with manure packed up under the heels, and he let me sit on his lap, though this irked my mom, who thought he was trying to cop a feel. *At least sit on your own chair*, she said. *He's a grown man with desires, I can't satisfy all of them.*

But it wasn't like that with Frank. We were friends. He was gentle with me, and worked hard and shuffled around the veterinary clinic with his toes turned out. He made dumb jokes and waited for me to laugh. Frank gave me a horse and in the evenings we rode together out onto the road, where the horses left hoofprints in the warm tar. After dinner at night we sat in his office where Frank smoked his pipe and read veterinary journals. My mom would wander in, looking sad, trying to make conversation. She had headaches all the time that year; I did, too, though I hated having that in common with her. Frank didn't believe in being sick. He said illness was psychosomatic, and that a little hard work would take care of even the worst headache, the worst ache or pain. My mom told him that was a bunch of bullshit, and what did he know about it? Had he ever suffered migraines, had he?

Migraines. That year, in Riverton, was when they were worst of all. The first time was when I was nine, in the car on the way to Park City, and suddenly I was seeing half-faces, and half-barns and cows out the window, and the other half was silvery and wildly zigzagged. My hands looked huge and white and blurry, like hands underwater, and I could only see half the fingers. I crawled into the front seat and put my head in my mom's lap. *I think she's getting one, Bob*, my mom said. *I think she's getting a migraine.* And that was the only one until Riverton. Then they came all the time, so that my year in seventh grade was divided between the dreamy grief of the trailer, my mom and Frank at each other constantly, and the cot in the nurse's office, where I lay shivering and puking and blinded by the lights and silvery zigzags that pulsed, peripherally, behind my eyes. Every fifty minutes a bell would ring, jangling my brain the way it got jangled when Mr. Murray, the history teacher, slammed a yardstick into the side of his metal garbage can to make us all shut up. He liked doing it; anybody could see that. He waited at the front of the classroom, letting us get loud; I was one of the good kids and waited nervously with the other good kids, like victims or rabbits, until Mr. Murray brought the yardstick in with a long reverberating, *thwwooonng,* the look on his face sexual and self-satisfied. Some of us kids were friends with the hip art teacher, Ms. Mallory, who had a bowl-shaped haircut and small wire-framed spectacles. Once, in the faculty lunch room, Mr. Murray had tried to kiss her and touch her breast and later Ms. Mallory told us about it, the whole class. She didn't come back to teach the next year but in the meantime we were slavishly devoted and in love with her, and anyway, anybody could tell that Mr. Murray was a pig. The school nurse tended to me patiently and without affection, and at fifty-minute intervals the doors would slam open and then the other kids would stream by in a bright blur, and then it would get quiet again.

It wasn't long before my mom started to get on Frank's nerves. Secretly I knew he'd disliked her from the first, her voice and embroidered Mexican dresses, her yellowed teeth and nerves. At night we heard their headboard bumping the wall like it had since we'd moved there, but in the daytime he ignored her. In the meantime I loved him completely, guiltily, because even at thirteen I knew that she was the new wife who deserved the attentions and affection he seemed to save up for me. I felt bad, but not bad enough to leave the two of them alone, marriage or no marriage: she'd dragged me to Wyoming, when all I'd wanted was to live with my dad. And now what was I supposed to do about it? At first she'd wanted me to love him, wanted me to think of him as our new dad, and then when things started to go bad she wanted it to be the exact other way. *We're a Package Deal, Pal.* She said that all the time, usually when we were fighting, so that it came out hissed between her teeth. I was Pal.

• • •

My mom had picked me up from school, and we were driving. She loved being in the car, loved road trips and all the fresh towns and people we were about to meet, people we didn't have histories with. And she liked leaving early, having the windows down and the music loud, and truckers always fell for her, yanking at their horns and trying to make her pull over, though my mom would wave and speed up and shake her head, laughing. Driving this way made us feel like we were on an adventure, as though any life could start with us in it. But when we did stop moving was when all the trouble would start, and in the same way that mornings in the car were happy, twilight in the car always made us sad. That was when we drove through towns and saw people unloading groceries from cars and dads on the lawn coiling up the garden hoses like dads in slow motion. The kids were taking baths and checking their school supplies, pushing pencils into handheld sharpeners that squeaked and made pink fragrant wood peelings, each pencil coming out too sharp and ready for action, the lead silvery and warm-smelling, and probably there were sneakers tumbling in the dryer, whacking loudly and smelling of burnt rubber; and everything about the domesticity in all those houses in all those towns behind us made me want to cry and hang on to something, I didn't know what, the White Pages that might have my dad's phone number listed somewhere, the photo album with pictures of my mom and dad before us kids were even born, my mom's calves bowing sweetly from yellow pedal pushers. She looked like she bowled a lot in those days. And my dad beside her, plain-looking though the big secret was that he was one hell of a lover, my mom told us, though looking at the picture you'd never think about it. About how they must have been together at night and then the next day, in a photo, innocent and pleased, not hurting anyone. All this before us kids were born, my parents posing in front of a fence.

Since we'd been living in Riverton the only driving my mom did was to the grocery store or the school. We never went fast enough for the wind to blow her hair, and the town had too many speed bumps and stop signs, anyway. She eased over the bumps in a pained way, making fun of Riverton's street names: Rodeo Way, Buckskin Circle.

This day, a Tuesday, I'd found her parked out front, waiting for me like all the other moms, something she almost never did. Even when they were married it was my dad who picked us up from school. But today, she said, she'd just been driving around, thinking about things. Did I like Riverton? Did I love Riverton? Did I really want to stay, the whole rest of the school year? Was there someplace else I'd rather live, somewhere I'd never seen, like maybe even Hawaii or Mexico? My mom said, *in case you can't tell, Frank pretty much hates me. He loves you, and I can understand because you're my beautiful baby girl and I love you too, but I think he's pretty sorry he ever answered my ad. I even tried to write a new one today*, she said. *I sat at the kitchen table but I just couldn't think what to say. What would you do*, she said, *if you were in my position? How can I make Frank love me again? He loves you, so you should have some advice.*

We parked outside the high school, waiting for Jen. I hated when she talked to me like this, like I was the adult.

"I don't know," I said.

"Well you do too know, since he's completely nuts about you. Isn't he."

"You're the grown-up," I said. "You're the wife. How should I know?" I felt like this every time. One minute my life was taking shape in an orderly way, like it was now, and the teachers at Riverton Junior High liked me and I was getting good grades, and the Christmas dance was coming up. I was trying to figure out a way to save up for the dress I wanted, and tomorrow I was going to try out for the school play. A normal life *wasn't that hard.* And then there were times like this, with my mom circling Riverton in her hippie car, thinking of what she could do next.

"Well isn't he crazy about you?" my mom said. "I'm supposed to be the wife, but no. I mean I understand, you're my sweetest baby. But still it's hard on me, that he's picked you, darn it. It doesn't seem quite fair, does it?"

"Why don't you just send me back?" I watched some of the eighth graders practicing a cheer on the lawn. Their breasts were developed and they had long hair. They were strutting, sticking their hips out and bouncing imaginary pom-poms. But already they were falling like flies, especially the pretty ones. Janet Silver and Leslie Gee had both gotten knocked up just before Christmas, and had fast weddings and now lived in parallel trailers at Mountain Acres. They dropped out of school along with their new husbands and by the time we left Riverton Leslie was pregnant again, and when I saw her in the store her face looked marshmallowy, her mouth a gluey pink line like it had been done in frosting.

"Send you back where?"

"To Dad. If you hadn't taken my plane ticket. You could just get rid of me."

"We're a Package Deal, Lucy, if you could just understand that. I don't know what your deal is, I don't know why you think we're separate, because guess what, Lucy, we're a family. And families don't split up. What plane ticket? What, just because your dad promised?"

"The one you stole. The one you cashed in." I didn't want to be fighting. I never knew how it got like this.

"What are you talking about, Honey?" My mom shook her head, looking puzzled, and held her palms up in the air. Acting 101. "You sound like a crazy person. I would never do such a thing, I'm a psychology major."

"Stop denying it." The side doors from the gymnasium opened, and kids spilled out. I wanted Jen.

"There was never any ticket. I don't know why you have to make up this kind of stuff, just because you think your dad is so great."

"The one you stole!" I started to cry, and yanked my baseball cap down so the eighth graders wouldn't see me blubbering. There were no tiny hidden tape recorders, never any way to prove my mom was lying. I turned the radio on, loud, and looked off out the window. *Sheesh*, I heard my mom say under her breath. *Plane* ticket.

"Please don't be mad at me, Luce. Just because we remember things differently, is that such a crime? We're both right, in our own way."

Jen got in the car, scooting forward to push in the lighter. My mom pulled away from the curb, then hit the brakes hard and started to cry. "I always thought I'd marry a Greek fisherman who sang a lot," she said. "Do you girls know that? I really did. I always did."

"Want to help me with a postmortem?" Frank put his hand on my shoulder, and we went out to the corrals where a cow lay bloated and frozen on the gravel. I touched the cow's snout, then smelled my hand.

"We need jackets," Frank said. "Now you know what Wyoming's like; we might as well get out the skis." He filled his pipe with cherry tobacco and held it between his teeth while he cut along the edge of the animal's neck and peeled back a little of the skin. "Jesus," he said. "Too bad for us it wasn't just a beagle."

"What are we doing?"

"Peeling a cow," Frank smiled at me and handed me a scalpel. I squatted and moved along behind him, cutting, then peeling. Under the skin, the cow looked like raw bacon. Frank tested me like this sometimes, giving me jobs to see if I'd hold up. Another time he took us out into the desert, both us girls and two of the sled dogs in the back of the pickup. He let the dogs out behind the truck and then sped along, the dogs going a few miles before their mouths started to drip white globs, their legs churning furiously, and then gradually they turned to small gray dots and by then we were screaming *stop, stop*. Only then did Frank turn the car around, his face hard. When we got back both the dogs were retching in the sand, bowed over like big croquet hoops, and Frank had to lift them into the truck.

The screen door slammed, and my mom came to watch. She kissed my head and rubbed her arms.

"I'm lonely in there," she said. "I need some company. All day long Jen just watches TV and you two run all over the place, not telling me where you're going." She smiled blankly, looked at the cow. "She watches Lawrence Welk."

"Postmortem," Frank said. "Marty said she just keeled over."

"It's the cold," Miriam said. "Probably she wasn't ready for it."

"Cold wouldn't kill a cow," Frank said, and made another incision.

"It would kill a wife, though, wouldn't it? I don't even know what you dragged me out here for. Make your dinners, bring you my sweetest daughters, is that what you want, my sweetest daughters?"

"We're working," Frank said. "Can't you see that? Nobody's trying to keep anything from you. We're just trying to do a postmortem. We'll be in as soon as it's finished." And though my mom shook her head and went into the house, stooped and pink, I understood that something had happened that would change things all over again; that once my mom appeared in this way, menacing and small and pleading, it meant the end of that piece of our life and the beginning of a new one from the green Cougar, the car heavy with what we owned and my mom keeping one hand out the window, letting the wind flutter her fingers as she said: *Keep your eyes peeled for a rest stop, would you?*

I walked Frank to the car. "I'm not gonna be gone that long," he said. "Three days. You'll be okay for three days."

"*Please?*"

"I can't let you come, Luce. It's a convention; what'll you do around a hundred and fifty-three veterinarians? What if they call on you to explain some procedure?" Frank filled his pipe and leaned against the truck.

"I'll stay in the hotel. I can watch TV. Please. Please, Frank."

"You'll be okay. " Frank got in, and I stood next to the window. "Tell me good-bye."

I kissed his cheek, than hugged him as hard as I could through the car window and Frank laughed and said, *You're breaking my neck*. He kissed me, started the engine. I stood in the driveway, waving at the blue rectangle until it disappeared. Then my mom was outside, slamming me into the lamppost with a single open-palmed smack saying, *I'm his wife, not you!* She had me by the hair, and I got her wrist between my teeth; fighting like this, I could smell her sweet sticky breath. My mom smacked and smacked me, her voice warbled with rage.

"He is my husband!"

"Mom, stop it!" Jen pulled at her, and my mom started to cry.

"Mine!" She hit me again on the side of the head, and Jen got a hold of her arms. My mom looked disheveled, scarecrowed, all angles and malice. "Mine!"

"You're fucking crazy," I said. My mom got me by the hair then, swinging me out and then yanking me into herself in a way that seemed to please her.

"Oh yeah?" she said. "Oh yeah?"

"Lucy, stop it!" Jen was crying now, too. "Just shut up!"

"Me, stop!"

"That should've been me out there," my mom said. "It should've been me, waving him off."

"If you hate me so much why don't you just send me back to Dad right now!"

"He doesn't want you, either."

"I hate you," I said.

My mom clapped me again on the side of the head. "Why do you kids always do this to me?" she said. Her face looked pink and creased and old. She backed away from us. "Why do you always do this to me?"

"I'm calling Dad. I can look him up in Directory Assistance."

"Go ahead then. Go ahead." She spit into her palm and showed it to me. "Look at that. Blood, you little bitch. Do you think you're the wife? Do you?"

"Mom, she doesn't think that," Jen said. "She's only thirteen."

"That's old enough to know about things. That's old enough. I promise you that. She knows exactly what she's doing. She's doing it on purpose, aren't you."

"Fuck you," I said. "You're a fucking, completely insane lunatic. I'm glad Frank doesn't love you."

"What did you say? What did you say?" My mom went down on one knee, then sat flat on the ground. She cried, shaking her head. Her fingers moved through the gravel, pushing it into little heaps. "You are bad," she said. "Bad, bad, bad. And if Frank knew what you were like, if he could see this, he'd rethink his opinion of you, oh I guarantee it. You are bad, Lucy. Evil. Help me," she said. "Why doesn't anyone ever help me, help me?"

Later that night, she took us to A&W to discuss our options.

"Things just aren't working out with Frank," she said. "I've tried, you know I've tried. And I need some help."

We were crammed into an orange booth, eating corn dogs and sipping from junior root beer floats. Since Frank, we didn't have to worry as much about money, but tonight some of the old worry had come back; my mom hadn't ordered anything, and when I left my corn dog sitting too long she swabbed it through a puddle of ketchup and greedily finished it off.

"I was still eating that."

"You were? I'm sorry. I'm sorry. I can't do anything right. I'm just hungry, is all, like you kids, and Frank didn't leave us very much money, for this weekend. But when he comes back things will be better, I promise they will, but I need some help from you girls. I need to know what I can do, you girls are young and pretty and have all sorts of resources. So I thought you could tell me what to do."

"Oh yeah, today you're beating me up, tonight I'm pretty and I have resources."

"No more fighting," Jen said. "Listen to Mom."

"I did not beat you up. I most certainly would not beat up one of my daughters, Frank's the violent one, Frank and your dad both. I sure know how to choose them, don't I? Anyway, we need a plan," my mom said. We were both waiting for Jen to come up with something.

"Maybe a new outfit," Jen said.

"Just act like a normal person," I said. "That's why you bug him so much." It was true. Around Frank my mom was chatty, all nerves, throwing herself up against him when he leaned against counters, or in doorways. She wanted him too badly, and he could see.

"You don't want me to get him back, do you? Just so *you* can have him. Well there are things you can't do, things that only a wife can provide for a husband, you don't know about it and you don't need to, but you can't compete. And if you know what's good for you, for all of us, you'll help me out."

"I'm not competing. I'm only thirteen. And I know what you're talking about. He thinks you're so good in bed, that's what you always say."

"Be quiet, Luce. Mom needs our help."

"Well, he does." My mom stared off into space, running one finger around the rim of my root beer mug.

"I hate when you do that. It looks perverted."

"And we need to think what attracts him. Because he won't even sleep in our bed anymore, I'm losing him. But all that's going to change and if it doesn't, if it doesn't, we're out on the street again. That means you too, Luce. No more horses. No more dogs. So you'd better think of a way to help me out."

"Maybe you could look like a cowgirl," Jen suggested.

"That's an idea. That's a good idea, in fact that's a *very* good idea. I could get a hat."

"And a belt buckle and jeans," Jen said. "Do we have any money?"

"We have enough," my mom said. "Enough for this. What do you think, Lucy Loo? Do you think that would work?"

"I don't know."

"I don't know why I didn't think of it sooner, I really don't. Frank wants a wife who can do things like ride horses, doesn't he? And I haven't really been dressing the part. I mean I have my embroidered Mexican dress, and my Indian blood, so that's good for when I want to ride bareback. But western wear would look better, wouldn't it? More appropriate." She sucked at my root beer until there was just froth and ice cubes in the bottom. She opened her purse and stuffed it quickly with the extra napkins and packets of ketchup, then tossed in the brown ceramic ashtray for good measure, snapped her purse shut, and slid out of the booth. Her voice was bright. "Let's get started."

First we went to the western-wear shop in downtown Riverton. My mom tried on tight jeans and a belt with a turquoise-inset belt buckle, as well as a plaid shirt and a large, pink, cowboy hat. The pink hat was on sale, and because the owner of the shop knew Frank, he let her take the rest on credit. In between trying on clothes my mom asked if she could use the bathroom, holding me in front of her like I was the one who really needed to go. It was a favorite trick, and one I hated. "Kids," she told the owner, rolling her eyes. "They have to go all the time, are you a dad, don't they just constantly have to go? Daughters are the worst, the *worst*." He showed us to the bathroom; my mom winked at him, then locked the door behind us. She dropped her pants and sat on the toilet and opened her purse, all in one swift gesture, then took inventory of the small bathroom, which functioned partly as a storage closet. This was exactly what she'd betted on.

"Mom, don't. Frank can give us money when he gets back."

"You think?" my mom laughed. "Maybe, if my plan works, we won't need to go anywhere. But if it doesn't, we have to be prepared." She was clearing one shelf, dropping cleaning solutions and an industrial-sized bag of steel wool pads in her purse. When she finished peeing she flushed and stood up and went for the medicine cabinet, taking a large, unopened bottle of aspirin and a crusty roll of underarm deodorant.

"Mom, stop it. He's gonna hear."

"Lower your voice, lower your voice." She was hurrying, excited. "I can't wait for Frank to see me. I think that hat is perfect, so perfect." She opened a cabinet, where a number of tooled leather belts were spooled in a basket. "Flush, if you don't need to go."

"What?"

"I said *flush*, hurry, before he gets suspicious." My mom lunged past me and flushed the toilet, then dumped the tooled belts in her handbag.

She thought for a minute, then retrieved a few and returned them to the basket. "I don't want it to look too suspicious," she whispered. "But these are valuable, these are something I can sell if we need to. Oh my God, look at those, Luce. Look at those. I can't afford boots, no way. But look." On the bottom shelf of the storage cabinet were a pair of electric blue cowboy boots; my mom looked at them a minute, then flushed the toilet again and ran the faucet, giving herself time to haul out the boots and cram one on her foot.

"Mom, no. You'll get caught." I felt the water come up in my eyes. "Why don't you just send me back to live with Dad."

"They fit." She clambered onto the toilet seat and looked at herself in the mirror. "I'm not going to take them, even if it would complete my look. They're so perfect."

Jen rattled the doorknob. "Mom?"

"We'll be right out, Sweetie." My mom put the boots back, then looked at me. "I wouldn't take them. I don't steal. Is that what you're thinking? Well Frank is important to me, but I'm not that desperate, I'm not a thief, am I. Is that what you think? Why are you crying?"

"I want to go live with Dad."

"Don't you like our new life? You love Frank. I thought you liked living here." She stroked my hair. "And what would I do without you? You're my Special Lucy. Come on. We'll go to Ben Franklin next, do you want to go to Ben Franklin? We can look at the parakeets." She dropped her voice again. "Gee whiz, Honey, you know I wouldn't steal. I just wanted to try them on, the blue is so nice." She flushed the toilet one last time, then pulled out a compact.

The owner of the shop watched us come out of the bathroom and when he saw my mom powdering her nose, peering into the tiny mirror, he smiled. "Frank's a lucky duck," he said.

When Frank saw my mom dolled up like a cowgirl, he shook his head and laughed, in a mean way, like she was just too much. "Where'd you get those boots?" he wanted to know. She had on the blue boots and when she saw me look at them, she smiled and shrugged. But even with these, even with the pink hat and Levi's, we could tell Frank still hated her. That evening my mom insisted on horseback riding, but she'd never learned to ride, and her horse seemed to know; she made it as far as the mailbox before her horse started turning circles, first one direction, then the other, while Frank yelled commands. Finally her horse meandered back to the corral, and after that night, my mom put her cowgirl outfit away.

UNDER FRANK:

Under his knee, I mean. He had her pinned. It was Christmas day. Holidays were the hardest, especially for my mom. You could tell she never even suspected: she shopped for weeks, exchanged things, wrapped and then rewrapped gifts in different wrapping paper until she had it perfect. And she would cook, and lay beautiful tables with centerpieces and mismatched silver forks she'd bought at the Salvation Army, which she polished until they glowed. But none of it added up. We were the wrong family in the wrong house, and her face was pinched to prove it. Then there'd have to be an explosion, so we could see what was left when the debris had settled. And what we saw was always the same: each other. Our own sad familiar faces, only now we looked relieved because at least *that* scene was over with, and, my mom reasoned, if you didn't know what you stood to lose each and every second of your life, well then what was the point in having it?

So Frank was kneeling on her chest.

I hid behind the couch and now it was just the three of them in front of the Christmas tree, Jen standing off to the side and screaming in a single, high note, Frank's hands on my mom's throat. My mom struggled a little, turning her head from side to side. She looked like she was trying to remember something. Her face was bright red and her mouth moved, trying to remember a word. Frank was saying, *is this what you want, is it?* Jen dragged at Frank's arm, *stop it, just stop.* He pushed her, shook her off like she was a squirrel. Then he kicked and pushed my mom until she was out the front door, crying and crawling over the threshold. *There, she's gone,* Frank said, *she's gone, she's gone, stop that yelling, she's gone, come here now, it's okay, stop—.* He tried to reach for Jen—*it's okay*—tried to hold her, but when he touched her she clamped both hands over her ears and started up again. The tree winked; we'd just gotten through all the presents, and now there was a bow stuck to Frank's boot, flattened partway under the heel.

Then there were police. We were in the backseat of the squad car and a bright stain was spreading across the front of my jacket. A pen had broken open in my pocket and I held my butt insensibly off the upholstery to keep it from staining, held the stain higher still, watched it spread red. The upholstery was gray-blue, freshly vacuumed. *Just sit,* the cop said finally, *don't worry about that.* But I imagined I'd been shot and I kept staring at it, the red seeping wider, gobbling up individual fibers and finally only stopping when it hit a seam, near the zipper. Riverton was hushed and decorated and other cars passed us, also with families inside, snow spitting from the tires. We were already starting to erase the old life. We were in a tiny capsule spinning up over the town. There was Riverton but we weren't stopping. It whooshed away, silent. Already the town was forgetting us and my mom said then, from high up and to no one in particular, her voice still tight with nearly having been strangled, on Christmas day, in 1976: *good riddance.*

It seemed to burn my mom that Frank was well-liked, or at least well-respected, in Riverton. She wanted everyone to know what went on behind closed doors, what he was like In Private. She meant to expose him for What He Really Was, a wife beater and a child abuser and a penny-pincher and an all-around sonofabitch who'd hauled her to Riverton for nothing, *nothing,* and now wanted her to leave, for the price of one hundred dollars. My mom had no intention, *no intention of leaving whatsoever,* until she was good and ready. Out of the goodness of his heart, and also because he had the hots for my mother, Riverton's police chief had offered to let us stay in the guest house, a yellow cinderblock building in his backyard; it was one room but it had a bathroom and a kitchen and Ralph took us there the night that Frank beat my mom up. After that my mom talked about Frank to anybody who'd listen, Ralph especially, who was fat and oily-looking and who wept real tears when my mom told him everything that had happened. Ralph was married, and when he stepped out to the guest house to visit us his wife puttered in the backyard, staring down the guest house and pulling weeds or repotting plants until he came back out.

First, though, we went to the police station, where my mom filed a domestic abuse report and I leafed through a huge spiral-bound book filled with photos of Missing Persons and ate Strawberry Twizzlers from the candy machine. My mom answered questions about Frank, and filled in plenty of other details, during any break in the conversation. I was stuck on a page in the spiral notebook, on a photo of a dead guy who'd been shot to death and dumped out in the desert. I got the picture up as close to my face as I could. I'd never seen a dead person and I was trying to figure out whether they'd taken the picture with him just lying there in the dirt or whether they'd propped his head up or what.

"You never know," my mom was saying. "You just never really know, do you, what people are going to be like behind closed doors, I mean he seemed like a nice person, just like my husband Bob was at first, but you just never know what's going to happen. When someone's provoked."

"Were there ever incidents before this?" The clerk was typing, getting it all down. "Any indication of violence, before tonight?"

"Well, he'd always seemed like a walking time bomb. I think it's because of his last wife, she's in a wheelchair you know, everyone says she had a stroke but I think it could've been from something else, I really do, I'm not saying what but he's got an awful awful temper. He was driving me out into deep snow, I mean he kicked me and was shouting and shouting, even with the girls right there he just kept kicking and shouting. For me to get out." My mom shook her head. "Not like we have anywhere to go. Not anywhere. I don't have any money. Where would we go?" She looked at Jen, who moved closer and took her hand. "At least I have my girls, that's one good thing, isn't it. I wish I were in Santa Barbara right now, is what I wish. Smelling the eucalyptus trees and putting all this behind us, like a bad memory. I never should've married him to begin with."

"You hit him first," I said, though I knew better. I hated her then, the way she'd kept after Frank even when we could see that he was being pushed too far, the way he'd started to move in a jerky way, his sentences broken and strange, his head twitching around to look at all of us while he and my mom screamed things at each other. He looked like her; that's what had scared me the most. Before Frank we counted on men like my dad, who argued loudly but stupidly, and folded the minute my mom started to cry. But with Frank it was different. After arguing a while they started to move in a small evil circle around the kitchen table, menacing each other by shoving at the chairs and circling, and the blankness in my mom's face, the terrible faraway look of damage and drowning, was in Frank's face, too. That's what scared me most of all. My mom didn't seem to want things to stop, she seemed to want to go forward into it, stepping into Frank's mouth so that he could crunch her small bones. Because my mom *was* small, and her flesh was white and soft on her arms, on her calves and bottom, and Frank was going to hurt her terribly, any of us could see. And still she said things, still she taunted him, *Big Man, Big Man,* she said, *you think you're so tough but you're nothing, nothing, you're a big fat loser is what you are, just a divorced cowpunching loser, loser, loser.*

"*Whose side are you on?*" my mom said. "That is a *lie*, Lucy. You just keep your big mouth shut."

"Well," I said. It was true, she had hit him first, with the telephone receiver; but even hating her I could see that it didn't matter, that she was the one now with the bruises, the one who'd fallen, weeping and with a bloody nose through snowdrifts, trying to get to our car. And that Frank had pushed her with the tip of his boot, when my mom was on all fours. And still I wanted to be with him, and I knew that because of this there was something wrong with me, something wrong with my emotions.

Our mom decided, considering all that had happened, that we needed a vacation. She wanted to go to California, she said, and smell eucalyptus trees and drive with the wind in her hair and Be Free. School had just ended for the summer and Frank wasn't showing any signs of coughing up the three hundred dollars my mom thought we deserved, so we left Riverton one morning in the Cougar. Ralph watched us drive away, standing unhappily on his big legs, his complexion shiny though it was still early.

"He's in *love* with you, Mom," Jen said. "Look at that, you're killing him. You're breaking his big, flabby heart."

"I know he looks unattractive to you," my mom said. "But that's the amazing thing about getting older. Even those kind start to look good. You wait until you get older, even the bald ones start to look sexy. Just you wait."

"Doubt it," Jen said. My mom had promised to stop in Salt Lake on the way to California so Jen could see her old boyfriend Rick. That morning Jen had used a curling iron to flip her bangs away from her face and now she kept tipping forward and then flinging her head back to make her hair stay feathered. I was trying to give her a wide berth, since every time she did it her head flew up and back with freakish velocity. After she flipped she pulled a flared comb from the back pocket of her jeans, combing from the part until her hair was frizzy and manelike. Then she'd wait a few minutes and do the whole thing over again.

"Your hair looks cool like that," my mom said. "Sexy." When she wanted to my mom could act like one of us, offering her lipstick and saying *shit* and *goddamn* and wanting to hear our stories about the popular kids at school. Sometimes she even bought Jen menthol cigarettes, though she made her throw them out once the mood had passed. The one thing she couldn't do right was sing along to the pop songs on the radio. When "Proud Mary" came on, Jen and I sang "toinin', boinin'," which drove her up the wall. "Why can't he *enunciate*," she said, and sang it primly, rounding out the consonants. "Big wheel keep on turning, Proud Mary keep on burning," she sang happily, reaching for her sunglasses.

It was morning, and I woke up on the floor of an empty housetrailer. Jen stood over me holding out a chocolate donut on a Kleenex. We were in Baker, California, which was as far as the Cougar made it before overheating for good, and my mom had gone looking for a mechanic. I worked at the donut while Jen poured us both fruit juice in tiny paper cups.

"Where are we?"

"Somebody let us sleep here because it was vacant," Jen said.

"Are we still going to California?"

"We're *in* California."

"But are we still going to the beach?"

"I guess."

We explored the trailer. There wasn't much to see—a broken toilet seat, an empty room with a psychedelic poster taped to the closet door—so we wandered outside. The town seemed abandoned, with cracked sidewalks in places and no sidewalks in others, and closed stores with homemade items in the windows, dolls with crocheted skirts that were meant to sit atop Kleenex boxes, and knitted Santa Claus heads that slipped over doorknobs, and flowers cut out of wood and stuck on dowels and then painted. The town's main attraction was the Original Bun Boy restaurant, and atop the restaurant was the huge cutout figure of the Bun Boy, chubby, with a pompadour, holding aloft a two-ton cheeseburger. He had the same creepy expression as the Bob's Big Boy kid, and the same flared shoes and shiny pink cheeks and mouth. But there was something menacing about him; he was the Big Boy gone bad, like our whole life.

We made our way over to the Bun Boy to check out the gift shop. I thought I might send Frank a postcard, let him know where we were and that we were definitely planning to come back so he wouldn't worry. Halfway across the parking lot we ran into my mom, wearing a white waitress's uniform and a small white hat.

"Did you girls get breakfast? How'd you sleep? I hardly slept at all, I mean you should've seen it, the car just made this awful sound and then steam started shooting out and we're just lucky we were close to a town, is all. But I'm exhausted. Well, what do you think of Baker? It's a sweet little town, isn't it?"

"What's with the getup?" I said.

"Well we need to make some money, don't we? To pay for the car. I like this place, don't you think it's cute? So I thought we'd just stay here for a while, find a cheap place to crash, I think we can stay a few more weeks in the trailer and then get something better and in the meantime, if you can believe it, I've already found a job. Never let it be said that I don't take care of you girls, I'd walk across fiery coals if that's what it took. You're my top top priority. And Frank, *Frank* can go to hell. We're starting a new life. I don't need a man."

"I thought we were going to California," I said. I didn't want her to walk across fiery coals. I just wanted her to be like other moms, planning a birthday party for me and driving me to a gymnastics meet, if there's where I needed to go. I wanted her to dress like a mom instead of like someone's hippie girlfriend. I wanted her to stop bringing home her Happy Hooker paperbacks, which I read privately, excitedly, and I wanted her to stop leaving them out where everybody could see.

"We're *in* California." My mom pulled a name tag out of her purse and stopped walking long enough to pin it to the pocket of her uniform.

"How come it says, 'Summer'?" I said.

"Well," my mom winked at us. "No sense in giving away family secrets, I don't see why I shouldn't be able to call myself whatever I want, do you? 'Summer Anna,' is what I was thinking, for the whole name." She pronounced it, *Ahna*.

"That sounds completely stupid," I said. "And I'm not living here. I hate this place. We're supposed to go to San Diego, I thought you said." We'd reached the trailer, and Jen came out carrying a donut for my mom.

"That's just like you, Luce, to not support me. You don't have any money. Do you have any money? How am I supposed to get us the rest of the way, if I can't even pay for gas?"

"You should have thought of that before we left Riverton."

"Why are you always so hard on me? All you care about is *men*. First your dad and now Frank. That's all you care about, and let me tell you it's pretty unhealthy. You should want to be an independent woman, instead of chasing some guy all over the map. I didn't raise you girls to want some *man* in your life, all the time. Thanks, Jen. Thank you for helping me." She took the donut and worked at it, looking sorry for herself.

"Are you going to work at the Bun Boy?" Jen said.

"I don't only care about men."

"Well then how about being more supportive? Think of this as an adventure. I like the idea of being a waitress, and I've always been a good cook, or maybe I'll meet some cowboy who can help us out of this jam. Not for romance, but just someone who can help us get the car going."

"I don't want to live here either, Mom," Jen said. "You'd hate being a waitress. I know you would."

"I look *good* in this uniform. In fact I look *great*."

Behind us, as if on cue, some guy whistled. He crossed the street toward us, a wiry, shirtless guy who looked like everyone else I'd seen so far in Baker, his skin leathery and too tan, like the heat was cooking him to fruit leather. It was Joe, the mechanic who'd fixed the car, and now we owed him.

We were in the bed next to my mom and Joe's. I could see my mom in the light from the window; she was straddling Joe, bouncing away, and then Jen's hands went over my eyes and one ear. Jen was whispering at me to be quiet, to just wait and then it would be over. I turned my other ear into the pillow. Couldn't she tell we weren't asleep? She was the *mother*. She was being loud, theatrical, and when I woke up later Joe was carrying me to the car. He smelled like old car oil and bubblegum and I twisted in his arms until he set me down. It was dawn, and they were fighting in a whisper about the motel bill. "You said you'd *pay*," my mom said. "Not *abscond*." My mom left her Bun Boy uniform draped over the shower rod in the motel room, and by breakfast we were halfway back to Riverton.

Joe looked like a Hayseed, with greasy flattened hair and filthy hands, and dark, streaky stains down the thighs of his Levi's. His teeth were yellow and snaggled, and when he laughed it made a hissing sound out the side of his mouth. After a few days with him we realized that this was his personal way of appearing snide, or superior, to comments he didn't understand. Joe wasn't smart but he was at the helm, racing the Cougar along the highway with expert, blackened hands. My mom seemed to like him; she laughed at all his stupid attempted jokes, and let him monopolize the tape player with the single possession he'd brought along, an 8-track cassette recording of a song called "Dream Weaver." My mom was peevish about hearing songs played over and over, and the fact that she was letting him get away with it was a bad sign.

Still, by the time we finally made it to Wyoming, you could tell he was getting to her. The car had broken down twice more between Baker and Laramie; it had taken us two days to go two hundred miles. Joe was as broke as we were, so we slept in the car. He called it the Sugar Shack. He and my mom took the front seat, and us girls took the back. In the mornings he took his leak right next to the car, his stance authoritative and pleased. We could see that he thought he'd scored. My mom had gone to college, and when she needed things repeated she said, "Pardon me?" which made her sound British and upper crust. She was down on her luck but clearly, even hauling around us girls, a catch.

We stopped in Evanston for breakfast. Our mom looked road-weary, and when Joe slapped her on the butt, as was his way, she didn't laugh. Restaurants seemed to make her sad, the fake plants and cheer. In restaurants she drank too much coffee, brooded and spilled sugar packets on the table, asked us if we missed our dad.

We slid into the booth, and Joe ordered like we had money: a sausage omelet, extra hash browns, OJ on the side. My mom ordered only coffee, but insisted us kids get something. When Joe went to buy cigarettes Jen said, "When are you going to lose the loser?"

"Well, Honey. We're not exactly home yet."

"Close enough. He's totally gross. He never brushes his teeth."

"Beggars can't be choosers," my mom said.

"Is he going to live with us?"

"I don't know yet. I don't think he's that awful, and he knows cars. That's for sure." She turned to me. "What's your opinion?"

"He's okay," I said. I didn't much care either way. I just wanted to get back to Riverton. I thought there might still be a chance, with us so poor, that my mom would let me go live with Frank.

Jen folded open the map and scrutinized it. "Riverton's only two hundred and forty more miles," she said. "What are the chances that we'd break down again, before then?"

"You never know." Joe came back, and my mom gave him her dazzling smile, the one she reserved for men. But she was looking at him carefully, taking in his marijuana-leaf belt buckle, his Harley Davidson T-shirt. I thought of my dad, whose body was wide and safe and smelled like Old Spice aftershave. And Frank. My mom had to be measuring Joe against Frank. Every time Joan Baez's "Diamonds and Rust" came on the radio she started to cry, wondering aloud how it was that he could just suddenly stop loving her, how it was that he could suddenly just dump us all, just like that, like the whole year together had meant nothing. She cried right up until the line about eyes being bluer than robin's eggs, when she would burst into a phlegmy warble, and afterwards ask us all again what we thought she could do, specifically, to get Frank back. She said whatever it was it couldn't cost too much money. And it couldn't be obvious, since Frank didn't like it when people had motives.

I knew what Frank wanted. He wanted me. My mom was out of the running. But our stuff was still in Riverton and Joe was the only one, right now, who could help us.

"I'm tired. I'm so tired. I didn't sleep last night, did any of you sleep, damn it, that car isn't exactly designed for that sort of thing."

"The Love Shack," Joe said, and grinned.

"I wish you wouldn't call it that. Not in front of the girls."

"It rocks," Joe said. "Up and down, back and forth, humpa humpa."

"Do you have to embarrass me, right here?" my mom said. "This is a family restaurant, if we could just behave like a family."

"We're not a family anymore," I said. "Not without Frank."

"That's all you care about anymore, isn't it, your precious Frank," my mom said. "Well, surprise, Young Lady, but if Frank won't have me than he can't have any of us. We're a Package Deal."

"I could just live with him for one more school year," I said.

"What about the rest of us? That's how you are, Luce, is just plain selfish. Because what are the rest of us supposed to do, live in the guest house? Wait for you to graduate, or go to your junior high prom, or whatever it is you care about? Is that it? Listen," my mom leaned close, "you're not his wife. *I'm* his wife. Me."

"I don't want to be his wife. I just want to stay in Riverton, for the rest of junior high. You dragged me out there. I have friends there, now."

"Want, want, want," my mom said.

"What's the guest house?" Joe was shoveling in his pancakes.

"That's where we're all living, Buddy," my mom said. "The sheriff in Riverton was kind enough to offer so now we're staying in his backyard, thank you very much. In a teeny little cinderblock shack. There's barely room for us but at least it's somewhere, at least it's a roof over our heads. It's something."

"Why do we have to go to Riverton? The peaches are in season, or we could go to Oregon for the cherries. They pay real good up there." Joe lowered his face to his water glass and pretended it was a bong, holding his finger over the carb and then releasing it to inhale sharply. He leered at all of us and held it out to my mom. "That's some good shit."

My mom laughed a little, but she looked distracted and miserable. She'd wanted to be a lot of things in her life, but we could see by the look on her face that a migrant worker wasn't one of them. We could see that of all the men she'd been with Joe was probably the lowest of the low, with his concave chest and the way he walked on the balls of his feet, his arms held a little out from his body like he was a tough guy, instead of some puny, unemployed pothead. I rolled my eyes at my mom to show her what I thought of him and then she laughed for real, in appreciation, so that my heart opened up. "Grapes of Wrath," she said. All we ever did was fight and I loved her and I missed her, and I knew that she used to love me and that maybe she still did. Because once she had taken my baby photos and pasted them in a book. Once she'd had a nickname for me, Lucy Goose. Once she had taken me with her to the campus of BYU, and walked holding my hand. The sky was a hot and vivid blue and the fountain sprouted white lines of water and I was with my mom, at college, and then she took off both our shoes and we waded in the water and I was so happy. And once, when a neighbor's high-strung spaniel snapped at me, my mom went at the dog with a board, swinging it in an arc to make a wide circle of safety with us and no one else inside.

And in Bed Again, Where She Called Us into Say Good-bye:

A mother could do this. She could wait until we got home from school. She'd dressed up for the occasion, in a pale peach, rayon bed jacket. We recognized it as the one Frank had given her at Christmas, and her hair was back in a clip, and she looked as lovely as I'd ever seen her, like someone famous and tragic, which she was.

Joe stole the food stamps, Jen said. She was on the bed with my mom, clutching her hand. They were both crying.

I didn't know he was planning anything, my mom said. *I had no idea, I went to the post office to get stamps, I didn't even have my purse with me, I had no idea he would do such a thing. How could he do such a thing?* My mom kept scratching her forearm, her fingernails scraping back and forth, back and forth, like a crazy person. Finally Jen stilled that hand, too. *Please don't do it,* Jen said. Her mouth let out little gulps of air as she cried. *Please, Mom.* She turned on me, ferocious. *Mom's going to kill herself and it's all because of fucking Frank. Please, no, no,* she said.

How much money did he steal? I sat on the bed. I was shaking, and when a car went slowly down the alleyway outside the window I wanted to rush out and flag it down, to get help. There were things we could do, policemen to call. Everything outside the window looked sturdy, the telephone pole, the tree trunk of the sugar maple in Ralph's backyard. Through the chain-link fence, and beyond to the street, I could see a guy walking two basset hounds. His feet came down heavily and he wore a hat with the flaps over the ears. There were ways of protecting us but I couldn't think what they were, and now there didn't seem to be any time.

I just can't live anymore. I can't, I'm sorry. I'm so sorry. And I wanted a chance to tell you kids good-bye, you won't have such a bad life without me. Why would he do this? He took all our food stamps, right down to the last dollar. We have nothing. At least if I kill myself, you can live with your dad, Lucy you can go live with Frank, if that's what you want. It'll just be easier this way. And I wanted to say good-bye, is all, you kids will have good lives. It will be okay.

You can't kill yourself. I was crying now, trying to figure out what I could do.

How can I save you, my babies, my babies? my mom said. *This will be better, it will be better this way, I promise it will. Me out of the way. I just don't want to be alive anymore. Can you girls please just understand that? I don't want to live without Frank. I don't want to be alive. And it just keeps happening this way. Every day and every day, I just can't stand it. We used to be a family, we used to. And can you see? Can you girls see where we're living now?* Her eyes jumped over the room. *This is their storage, girls. This is where they keep stuff they don't need anymore. I was going to be a girl of the mountains, only Frank doesn't want me. I just can't stand it. That's all.* Jen moaned, and lay her whole body across my mom, right across her middle. Our mom smiled and shook her head a little, and put her hand on Jen's back. *It'll be better this way,* she said.

Jen shot up, talking right into my mom's face. *What are we supposed to do, go live with your precious Frank? Is that what we're supposed to do?* She had hold of my mom's shoulders, digging. Then she collapsed again, sobbing into my mom's armpit.

You can't do this, I said. *There are police.* I went to the bathroom, opened the medicine cabinet and cleared the shelf, flushing everything, aspirin and Band-Aids, Pepto Bismol tablets. She couldn't do this. There were *police,* we were in a policeman's *backyard.* I wanted to run across the yard to get Ralph but I was afraid my mom might try something. I went back to the bedroom, trying to stop shaking. *Go ahead,* I said. *Go ahead and try something. I flushed all the medicine down the toilet.*

My mom looked at me, smiling a little. *Honey,* she said, reaching. *Baby.*

We can't live without you, I said. *You're not supposed to do this. There are police. We need you.*

Jen shot up again. *If you kill yourself I'll kill myself, too, I swear to God. I swear to God. I'll kill all of us. Mark my words.*

Shut up, I said. *There are police.*

Everybody shut up! Jen said. She flipped over, laying face up on my mom's lap, and shot one leg far out sideways to kick me. *There aren't any police!*

Stop, my mom said. *Everybody just stop, okay? I want us all to just be able to sit here for now. Please? Okay? Like a family.* My mom wiped her nose on the edge of the blanket, and I got a wad of toilet paper. Jen took it, held it to my mom's nose. *Blow,* she said. We waited until it was dark outside, waited until my mom blew her own nose, apologized, and shuffled to the tiny kitchen to make us all pancakes.

After Frank, we went back to Salt Lake. It was always the town we returned to, for all my mom's talk of California, her dreams of orange and lemon trees *right there just in people's front yards,* and avocados year-round and the sound of the ocean, and patios of orange baked tile. California was expensive, our mom pointed out, plus it was hard to get around, too many freeways and too much concrete.

Also, though my mom didn't bring it up, our dad still lived in southern California. He had a new girlfriend, and a good job and plenty of lemon trees, probably, and visitation rights, which made my mom nervous.

In Salt Lake our mom worked two jobs, as a secretary during the week and then taking care of an old dying lady, Mrs. Black, on the weekends. She finished up her bachelor's degree and was accepted into the graduate program in psychology at the U. of U., and we could hear her at the typewriter almost every night, long after we'd gone to bed. Jen and I spent most of our time that summer on the roof of the garage, slathered with Banana Boat tanning oil, the radio blaring. We turned and turned, browning and then reddening like oily hot dogs, and drenched our hair with Sun-In so that by the end of summer we looked pretty much the same, our hair streaked and frizzy, with single curling-iron curls on either side of the face that could then be combed through to feather. We both wore Hash jeans, black leather chokers, wooden Dr. Scholls sandals that smacked and flipped on the sidewalk, and sometimes slid off the foot midstep, ramming the wooden edge cruelly into the heel, which hurt like hell. We walked to the store a lot, and I shoplifted everything I could get my hands on, cigarettes and Long-n-Silky shampoo and Yucca Dew conditioner, and frosted lipsticks and Lipsmacker lip gloss and sugarless gum. Jen would have her boyfriends over, and the first summer after Frank went pretty much this way, us girls loose in the world, Nairing our legs and calling in to request songs on the radio and going roller skating whenever we could afford it. Jen had a radio she'd ordered from the Avon catalog; it looked like a Magic Eight Ball, and hung from a short silver chain, and she carried it everywhere.

When school started it seemed possible that I would be popular again, especially since we were back in Salt Lake. Some of the popular kids from elementary school still thought of me as one of them, it seemed; like Emery Peters, who called me one night not long after school started to ask what the geography homework was. But now something separated me from Emery; I hadn't been to that class in days, I had no idea. In the old days I would've known the homework and maybe even be doing it myself at that time of night. Before my parents got divorced I'd lived on the same block as him, and our parents would stand in the driveway talking to each other, and we both got called in for dinner at the same time every night. But now everything was different. Emery and I had had whole states between us, and all over our house were raunchy paperback books, *The Boston Strangler* and Xaviera Hollander novels, and our mom worked almost 'round the clock to support us. Emery had been Student Body President the previous year and though it was only the second week of school, I could already see that I was going the wrong direction. *Goody Two-Shoes*, I said to the empty kitchen, after I'd hung up.

Now I almost never did my homework, unless it was for my English class. Now in the evenings Jen and I hung out at the mall. I wanted to be one of the good kids, and I was a sucker for any teacher who'd pay attention to me. But our family was poor, and it marked me, and anyway I didn't want to dress anymore like one of the popular girls, with loafers and socks and button-down denim Oxfords over white T-shirts. The popular girls wore headbands, and Clinique makeup, and Danskin leotards in P.E. class. I wanted to be one of the sexy ones, in a tight black concert T-shirt, with a flared comb in my hip pocket, but I was uncool and flat-chested. My locker was stuffed with books. I had a weakness for Shaun Cassidy. I'd tattle on anybody for anything. And if a teacher wanted me to button my lip I buttoned it, unlike one of the tough girls who smoked outside the 7-Eleven and who would get suspended for giving a teacher the birdie.

One weekend my mom took me to Mrs. Black's, just so I could see what it was like. We sat in the kitchen and ate slice after slice of Pepperidge Farm bread slathered in real butter and thick raspberry jam. Just before bedtime my mom said she needed something from home. I could handle it, couldn't I? If Mrs. Black beeped all I had to do was go and stand politely at the door and ask her if she needed anything. She wasn't going to bite me. She was a sick old lady. *If she beeps just go to the door and stand there and call in, try to sound friendly and professional, ask her what can I get you and I'll be right back anyway, I'm taking a taxi and I'll take a taxi right back. Okay, Honey? Think you can handle it?*

After my mom left I prowled the living room. Mrs. Black had been a ballerina and she had a whole collection, little porcelain figurines on point, and lamp shades painted with ballerinas and framed photographs and playbills of herself in her heyday. Off to the left of the living room, I could hear the ventilator going. I went back to the kitchen and gorged myself on Pepperidge Farm Goldfish and frozen pound cake that I ate still frozen, in grainy slabs.

I went to bed with the TV on, waiting up for my mom. Mrs. Black gave me the creeps and I didn't want her to die on me. It would figure if she did. It would figure, if she went into cardiac arrest right when my mom was gone so that I'd have to deal with it. It got later and later, and I started to worry. Our house was only a few miles away; my mom should've been back by now.

I fell asleep and woke to light coming in the window, the buzzer going like crazy. My mom's bed was still empty and I stayed in mine, listening to the pauses between the buzzing, which got shorter and shorter, while the buzzes themselves got longer and longer. I was in her house. We were poor, and she was rich. Her house smelled like old men's suits, and the heat was up way too high, and even her kitchen full of fatty expensive food wasn't going to save her. She was in there dying by the second and I wanted my mom as badly as I'd ever wanted her, the way she was when she got home from work every day, her cheeks chapped from the cold. My mom wore a dark-blue peacoat and it always smelled like her hair when I hugged her. It wasn't like her not to call, and I was afraid that if I went into the kitchen to use the phone, Mrs. Black would hear. I could see her in there, gripping the buzzer with her fossilized monkey hand that was probably dripping with jewels. I wanted Jen; she would know what to do.

"*Shit*," my mom said. She was in the doorway, trying to get her coat off and get her apron on at the same time. "Can't you hear that? Has she been beeping long? I fell asleep, Hon, I'm sorry, I just put my head down for one minute and I was out like a light. Has she? Has she been?"

"How could you have fallen asleep with me here?"

"I just *did*, Luce, look I'm sorry."

"You could've at least called me."

My mom wouldn't meet my eyes. It was true, I knew how tired she was all the time. She went off, still trying to get her apron tied. The buzzing stopped but I still felt sick and mad. How could she have just fallen asleep? My dad would never have left me like that, I thought, not ever. I'd been my dad's favorite, but so what? Because now Jen was my mom's favorite. They had telepathy. When my mom slipped on the ice and broke her arm, Jen felt it at school and ran all the way home. When my mom talked about starting a wallpaper business, Jen was going to do it with her.

I watched it get lighter outside, listening to Mrs. Black call for my mom to bring her the bed pan. My mom liked it when we cooked and cleaned, not her. She dressed like Stevie Nicks most days, and drove her car too fast and never brought home groceries, which was also us kids' job. She let us stay up as late as we wanted and never even cared if we did our homework. *It's your problem*, she'd say. *Do it or don't, it's your future.* It was like I had to keep reminding her that she was the mother, and even that didn't work. She just laughed. *You kids are old enough*, she said. *You can make your own decisions. I've mothered you for fourteen years, Luce. That's long enough.*

I listened to my mom murmur, heard her go to the kitchen to get Mrs. Black's morning cup of Earl Grey, which she drank with real cream and cubed sugar. I knew I should've gone to Mrs. Black, calling from the doorway into a bedroom that had probably looked the same for twenty years, the same dried flowers and glossy salmon-colored bedspread. People had lives like that. All they had to do was stay put. The flowers were dusty, probably. There were probably light-colored rectangles on the wallpaper, behind Mrs. Black's portraits of herself dancing the part of Giselle. That was the kind of life I wanted, and the kind my mom was running away from. She had to go away from people so she could miss them, leave places like California behind so she could cry over them later. That was why we were always fighting. And no matter what, I was only fourteen, and had at least four more years with her before I could make any of my own decisions. We were a Package Deal.

Sometimes my mom talked like there was a cartoon balloon over her head. *Sniff sniff*, she'd say, if you didn't offer her a bite of whatever you were eating. *Cry cry.*

Kiss kiss, she said, leaving for work.

Woof woof, Sadie, she told our dog. *Barkity bark bark.*

Or talked like everything was too big for her, too much for just one tiny woman to handle: *help me, help me, please,* she said often, during fights. She'd look around, like someone other than us actually was going to show up. *Please, why won't anyone ever help me?*

• • •

And then for a few years, we did stay in one place. My mom finished her master's and got a job as a therapist, and I went to high school, and Jen got a job at Pretzel Maker. I hung out with my best friend, Kiri, and we'd go to the mall and shoplift, leaving the hangers in the dressing room, which was how we finally got caught. It was Christmas Eve, and between us we'd tried to steal over three-hundred-dollars worth of stuff, lingerie and scarves and yolk-colored angora sweaters. Two security guards led us to a small room and called our houses. I had a hundred dollars in my pocket, which I showed to the guards. I had the money to pay for stuff; I just liked to steal, liked to see how much I could get for free. Because it was Christmas Eve they took us home instead of to juvenile detention, and Jen was waiting in the doorway, shaking her head and saying *Lucy, why?* I could see how bad she felt. Worse than I did, even. She had a conscience, when all I wanted was to get to my room and be left alone. I knew my mom would tell my dad and that then the image he had of me as his perfect little girl would be destroyed.

My mom was behind Jen, waiting. When Jen let go, my mom let me have it, smacking and smacking. "On Christmas Eve!" she cried. "So all the neighbors could see! A police car out in front, what do you think they think of us now, thanks a lot, goddamn it, Lucy! On Christmas Eve! Christmas Eve!" She couldn't stop hitting, and when her cheek came down close I bit it, letting my teeth go deep. She screamed and reared off, then stood crying. "What do you think the neighbors are saying, huh? What do you think they're thinking right now, in their houses, looking out to see a police car!"

"Just please don't tell Dad," I said. "Please. You can do anything but don't tell Dad."

"I will too tell your dad, too, I guarantee it. I guarantee it."

"Please don't tell. Do whatever you want to me but please don't tell."

"That's all you care about. All you ever care about! You haven't even seen him in years! He'll hear, believe me."

"It's your fault," I said. "You're the one who taught me to steal."

"My fault! My fault! Me! A thief! I've never stolen, Lucy, not ever, I don't do that kind of thing! Don't you dare put it off on me."

"Just let her go upstairs, Mom," Jen said. "Lucy, it is not Mom's fault. You did it to yourself so just shut up and go upstairs, okay?" Jen was crying, too. That was our household, women crying everywhere you looked. That's what the neighbors would see if they looked in.

She called everybody by their first names. Making it a point to squint at a waitress's name tag so that she could say, *thank you, Marie, Marie could I get some more coffee? Is there a pay phone? Could I maybe just use the one behind the counter, Marie? Oh thank you, Marie, I really appreciate it, their dad's living somewhere in California and not even sending us a nickel of child support, do you have kids, Marie?*

Why do you have to do that? I said. *Keep using her name. It sounds so fake.*

People like it, Luce. I know, I took psychology classes. It makes them feel important.

Sometimes waitresses called our mom by a name we'd never heard before: *take care, Julia*, one would say. *Susan? You left your coat in the booth.*

"Run in and get me some." My mom was parked in the red zone in front of Safeway. She was waiting, holding out a five.

"I'm not gonna buy them."

"Honey, I can't, I'm bleeding."

"You should have thought of that before." I was sick of my mom, sick of how every day there was some new drama. "Just park. I'll wait in the car."

"I need them, Honey. Please." She turned off the engine.

"Why can't you plan ahead? Other moms don't put their kids through this kind of shit. Why can't you stock up?" I thought of the kinds of things other families had in their houses: vanilla extract, fabric softener, postage stamps, cream rinse, extra toilet tissue, soda pop. Our family was always making do. We bought postage stamps one at a time, and tore up paper napkins to use for toilet paper. We were poor, but mostly just disorganized, plus my mom didn't like to spend money on things that seemed frivolous. She used vinegar on her own hair in the place of cream rinse, and when she did laundry she frequently skipped using laundry detergent, altogether. *Plain old water works just as well,* she'd say. *That's what the pioneers used to use.*

"Oh Honey, don't be so hard on me. You'll know, once you start menstruating, any day now. You just go through those pads like crazy. Come on, help me out. I can feel it, I'm leaking all over the place."

"I don't want to hear it!"

"Don't yell at me, Sweetheart. Jeepers. I'm just asking you to do this one little thing."

"You go in."

"I can't go in, Luce. I'm flowing. Just go in, go to the express line, just get me the cheapest pads they have. The smallest box. Come on. Hurry."

"What if I see somebody I know? What if I see one of my teachers?"

"Honey, it's not like they're going to ask. If they notice, people are polite, they're not going to bring it up."

"You know, other mothers are normal. Other mothers would not ask their kids to do this." I stared out at the people moving across the parking lot. "I don't see anybody out there having a big drama. Nobody else is *leaking*."

"Now you're just being mean."

"And we need dog food. We always run out of everything."

"Honey, please. It's coming through my panties."

"Shut up!"

"Fine. Fine. I do so much for you kids, you know, and you're just a brat." She got out, slamming the door, and limped to the entrance. I could tell she'd started to cry, but I didn't care.

I rolled down the window. "Get some dog food!" I yelled, though I knew she wouldn't. Also, we were out of eggs. For nearly a week now

our dog Sadie had been living on raw eggs mixed with cooked macaroni, with powdered milk sprinkled on top. Sometimes I threw in half
a cube of margarine, or grated in some cheddar cheese. We were out of
cheddar cheese, too.

I listened to the radio, feeling sorry for myself. Queen's "Bohemian
Rhapsody" came onto the radio, and I tried to sing along. "I see a little
silhouetta of a man, gottamooch, gottamooch, will you do the ban-
dango." The coolest kids in school knew all the words, but that was
because they had the record at home, with the lyrics printed on the back,
whereas that was another weird thing about our family. We didn't even
own a stereo. When the song ended I turned off the radio, making a case
against my mother. For starters: for starters, our car was a piece of shit,
an old gas-guzzling wine-colored Buick that my mom insisted was vin-
tage, and not just huge and ugly and one that made us look like white
trash, or pimps. We'd always had old cars, and not only because we were
too poor to afford better. It was my mom's little match girl routine, I
thought, her way of demonstrating to the world how much help we
needed, how this car was the very best we could ever possibly possibly
afford. For another thing, she was a lousy cook. She danced too often
around the house, twitching her hips; she flirted with our boyfriends.
She listened in on our phone calls. She'd moved us all over the place
during our school years so that we never hung around long enough to
get yearbooks; sometimes our pictures got taken but then we were off
again, our pictures appearing in yearbooks we never even got to see. And
any minute, I thought, just like me, she would get busted for
shoplifting. Like daughter like mother. She pilfered incorrigibly, just like
she had in the years right after my dad had left, and we'd been on food
stamps. In those days she kifed industrial-sized rolls of toilet paper from
public rest rooms; she stole motel towels, and collected the tiny soaps by
the dozen. At fast-food joints she copped packets of ketchup and mus-
tard and relish, tiny nondairy creamers and packets of sugar and Sweet-
n-Low, napkins and plastic ware and stacks of coarse brown paper
towels from the rest rooms. At home we refused to use them, at least until

we ran out of toilet paper; then she'd produce them, triumphant, torn into small squares to keep them from clogging up the plumbing. And she stole cleaning supplies. Chain restaurants were less promising, because they had whole locked rooms set aside for cleaning stuff; but in the bathrooms of smaller restaurants she almost always scored, jamming huge containers of Ajax or Windex or pink petroleum-distillate cleaners in squirt bottles, into her purse. At home she used the stuff just like it was ours, offering guests the sugar packets, the creamers.

After a while I saw my mom come out of the store. She was carrying an enormous package of generic brand Kotex tucked under one arm. That was another thing, she always had to make some big public display of not being ashamed of her natural bodily functions.

When she got to the car she said, "You happy? There, I'm stocking up, just like other mothers, if you're so unhappy with the one you have. I bought a jumbo box. And I got dog food, just like other mothers do, but when I got to the line I ran out of money. I had to put the dog food back. In the meantime I'm bleeding, young lady. I was standing there in line because you refused to go in and I could feel it, my panties are soaking wet, I'm surprised it didn't leak straight through. But no, you wouldn't even do me one small favor. Not one."

"You could've at least asked for a bag," I said. My mom shot me an evil look in the rearview mirror, like she couldn't believe I was her daughter.

It was Halloween, and that year I was going as a hooker. Like most of the other girls in ninth grade I'd chosen my costume for its sex appeal, which meant my options were kitty cat, cheerleader, and prostitute. I had a bit part in the school production of *Death of a Salesman*; I played Letta, a floozy who wore a fur stole and giggled and smoked, and because I already had the costume I dolled myself up as Letta but shortened the skirt and added a black garter and stiletto heels. I knew I looked good in it, and anyway I had to compete, somehow: my body was still angular and boyish, and I hated myself every time I looked in the mirror. I had zits on my forehead. My nose was too big. I had nipples that itched and burned and made little pointy marks in the front of my T-shirts.

As Letta, I got to wear lots of dark eyeliner, and the dress was black, close fitting and strapless, and the first time I got into costume, for rehearsal, I looked in the mirror and thought, *finally*. Finally I looked sexy, not mature, maybe, but at least game. Finally I saw that even without breasts, with enough lipstick and leg showing, I stood a chance, and the first time Benny saw me he said, *wow*. That night I went to his house where we made out on his sister's waterbed for hours, him humping slow and dry against my pubic bone. When he tried to touch my chest I panicked at what he'd find, and moved his hand instead to my crotch, which made him moan. His eyes rolled back, and he humped harder and then he said it again, *wow, wow*, and then his whole body shivered. Suddenly I could see at least a little of what was in it for my mom with all her boyfriends, the way the guy was so sweet and grateful, the way just by laying underneath him I had all the power in the world. It was like Benny loved me, like he was a teensy glass frog I could hold in my mouth.

When I stepped into the kitchen, my mom took one look and started laughing. "Oh my God, oh my God," she said. "What are you supposed to be?" She gripped the counter, laughing, using one hand to shade her eyes but peeping out at me, and every glance sent her into a new spasm. "You look ridiculous," she said, when she could finally talk. "You look absolutely ridiculous, do you know that? What are you, exactly? What are you supposed to be dressed as?"

"I'm going as a floozy," I said. "And I'm supposed to look ridiculous. It's Halloween."

"I'll say. I'll say." She went off again, then plopped down at the table to wipe her eyes. "So ridiculous. So ridiculous! Do you have any idea how awful you look? How silly?"

"You're jealous," I said. I went into the front room and stood at the window, watching for my ride. I could feel the anger like a scooped-out place in my chest.

My mom followed me. "You look stupid, is what it is. Seriously, Lucy. You're my daughter, so I can speak frankly, but do yourself a favor and don't leave the house looking like that." She started to laugh again, hiccupy and hysterical. "My God, if you could just see yourself."

"You know you're jealous. Admit it." I was afraid to step outside, afraid she was right. Upstairs in my bedroom mirror I thought I'd at least had potential, but now I wasn't sure. It was hard to tell. Besides Benny, the boys at school weren't noticing me much, but I did get looks from older men, men my mom's age who let their eyes wander like hungry beetles over my legs and butt. I let them look as much as they wanted. Looking was free. I wore cutoffs that climbed up my crack, and shoplifted Nair, which stung and rinsed off in a gray, petroleum-smelling froth.

"Jealous!" my mom kept laughing, sliding me a look now and again. "Jealous, of what!"

"Because you secretly know I look good." I stayed at the window, not looking at her. I was right, I knew I was. She wouldn't admit it but she'd always treated me like a rival, first with my dad, then with Frank. She made us competitors. I didn't want to go to the party anymore. I didn't want to look stupid. I wanted breasts like hers, huge and hanging and white, breasts that looked like they were filled with Jell-O. I should've followed my first impulse and gone as a cheerleader.

"That's a good one! Jealous! Jealous, of my fifteen-year-old daughter! You've got to be kidding me!"

My friend Kiri had pulled her dad's brown sedan to the curb. She honked, holding up a bottle in a brown bag. *Party!* she mouthed, and honked again. Getting to the front door, my foot twisted in the high heel, which my mom found funniest of all. "Oh God you kill me, jealous, you really do," she said. "Oh seriously, Luce, I don't know when I've ever laughed so hard. Well have fun Sweetie, please do. And don't stay out too late, okay?"

My mom's first office was in an L-shaped cinderblock building on State Street. She had a job counseling developmentally disabled adults, helping them get on food stamps or find a job or an apartment. Her office was sandwiched between a Chinese restaurant and a craft store, and sometimes we met there before going to lunch. I was impressed by anyone with an office, my mom not excluded. She answered the phone from a gray swiveling office chair and mouthed things while she was on hold. I'd sit in the air-conditioned waiting room with my feet up, reading *People* magazine and working through a bag of salted sunflower seeds, leaving the soggy shells in a small pile on another magazine to prove I had jurisdiction. My mom's clients were mostly fat, either that or they had Down's Syndrome. They'd shuffle in and out, thanking her in large, flat, retarded-people voices while I spat seeds. My mom counseled efficiently, an egg timer set to twenty minutes while she *uh-huhed* and nodded sympathetically, pretending to listen to her clients while on hold with this or that employee or landlord.

"How can you understand them?" I said once, after the client had left. "I can't even tell what he's saying."

"Well Hon, it's really just the intention." My mom straightened the magazines. "You know you just nod along, plus you can think of generic things, like sometimes I just might say 'Wow!' or 'No kidding!' because I mean they just want to be listened to. I'm starving. Let's get over there, try to beat the lunch rush."

"Dave gives me the creeps," I said. Dave had cerebral palsy, and saw my mom three times a week.

"Oh now, what have you got against Dave. How can you even talk like that. Gosh I mean he's in a wheelchair, it's not like he's all there, how fair is that, to pick on him? Have a heart. I always wondered, I mean I'd never say this to anyone else, but I always wondered how it would be to have sex with a guy in a wheelchair, not like I'm interested in Dave, I mean, it just makes me curious, is all."

"Mom, that's sick."

"What's so sick about it? People in wheelchairs have desires, just like the rest of us." We were at the restaurant, and my mom peered in, then turned to me. "Lars said he'd meet us here. I told him how much trouble we've been having financially, he offered to buy, and so *please just keep your little mouth shut.* When it comes up."

"What financial trouble?"

"Don't give me any of your lip, Luce."

"I'm just asking."

"And stop smirking."

"I'm *not* smirking." I'd learned it from her, I thought, but it was pointless to blame her because now it had become my signature expression, one I couldn't shake even when I tried. I'd pass before store windows and see it, the wry twist to my mouth. *Me smart ass, me know everything.* "I just didn't know you were hurting for money."

"You know for someone so smart, you sure don't know much about men. They like it, Luce. They *like* when you let them pay for things, it makes them feel needed." Lars waved us over and my mom slid in next to him. Lars was fifteen years younger than my mom, and worked as a freelance photographer. And there was something about him. I'd never told anyone, not even Kiri, but I'd had dreams about Lars, dreams where he'd held me and worked down my body. I was still a virgin but if I ever did it with anybody, I thought, it would be with someone like Lars, with his soft voice and small ears. Which was totally creepy, us having that in common, like we were slutty sisters instead of mother and daughter.

"I ordered you egg-drop soup," Lars told me.

"What about *me*?" my mom said.

"And you, my beauty, for you I have ordered not *only* a Heineken, but also Kung Pao chicken. *Without* the MSG. How's work?"

"Oh, you know. Everything is someone else's fault. You know, I mean I know they have a lot on their plates but still, they sure do *whine* a lot, not like the rest of us have it so easy. Dave's a great example of someone with negative thinking patterns. He's depressed depressed depressed but do you know his family has *money*, he grew up on *Coronado Island*, I mean gee I'll bet that house is worth half a mil at least. His folks bought it in nineteen sixty, that thing's probably paid off by now but he's all depressed because he wants to be in the work force, even though I'm having a hell of a time. Landing him a job."

"I'm so sure you're talking about Dave that way," I said.

"Listen, I love my clients. I *help* my clients. I'm the therapist, here. It's just that he's so *whiney*, even with all his money. And I mean damn it, with us struggling, well sometimes it's just hard to take." My mom shook her head, doing Exasperation, which I knew would be followed by Wry Laugh. We were exactly alike. After that would come Rueful Apology.

"I shouldn't talk like this," she said. "I'm not being very nice, am I? Gee, I can sure be heartless."

"That's what I like about you," Lars said. He went in for a kiss, and I looked away. Being attracted to Lars was the most disturbing thing that had happened to me all year. He was too *normal*. He was *cute*, and he played the guitar.

"Have you gotten that invitation yet?" Lars asked me.

"No."

"What invitation?" my mom laughed a little. "Someone fill me in."

"To Junior Prom," Lars said. "She's a-waitin'. She's a-hopin'."

"Quiet," I said. The prom was in two weeks, and Kiri and everyone else I knew had already been asked. Benny was a possibility, but I'd set my hopes on Jonathan Briggs, who sat in front of me in algebra class and was on the swim team. During algebra I'd inspect the three freckles at his hairline, which, if you connected the dots, would make a frowny face.

"They'd better hurry," Lars said.

"I never went to my prom," my mom said sadly. "Not to a single one. We just kept moving and moving, plus with my bum hip I probably didn't look like much of a catch. Plus my dad, you know, he was diagnosed manic-depressive and had a terrible terrible temper, some real anger management issues I guess you could say, now that I've finally studied it and gotten some insight. You know when you're a kid you don't think of it that way, you just think gee, isn't everyone's dad like this? I'll bet the boys were too intimidated to even come around. So I just stayed home that night, I remember, all the couples would walk past on the sidewalk in front of our house with the girls wearing their corsages and the air smelled so good. I remember I just sat on the porch swing and cried."

"You did so go to prom. You showed me that picture, the one where you went with Eric Hernandez," I said. It was true. My mom had even written on the back. She'd worn a blue satin gown and her lipstick was too dark, and her hair was in a beehive.

"*Eric Hernanadez*, who is that, are you kidding me?" My mom picked the peanuts from her Kung Pao chicken. "I sure as hell did not show you some picture, my dad would've run some Mexican right out of town if he'd showed up to court me, I kid you not about that one. My dad was a real racist. A real bigot."

"Oh, okay. That must've been my other mother," I said, and Lars snickered.

"Very funny. You don't know what it's like, you girls are lucky, you never had toxic parents, ones who would just poison poison poison you because they were all about me, me, me. I *listen* to you and your sister, that's why you're so lucky. Because I really *care*. I have *empathy*."

"You have so much empathy, you're bitching about Dave the gimp." I couldn't help myself, not ever. She'd say things and all of a sudden I'd be saying something even uglier, making things worse.

"Hey: be a mirror, not a microscope," my mom told me.

• • •

Lars did Glamour Shots. For twenty bucks an hour he helped girls like me to look good, taught us that in spite of our chest size we could still do things like fluff out our hair and arch our backs in photographs, and this much I was sure of: If I could get Jonathan interested in me, even if it was just long enough to get him to invite me to junior prom, it would be worth it. I had a vague plan, some idea of taping up one of the pictures in my locker so Jonathan could see.

Lars met me up Millcreek Canyon, and asked me to wear something *mature*. I chose a frilly, white-lace blouse and paired it with tight jeans and high-heeled cowboy boots. Lars encouraged me to part my lips and tousle my hair, and he photographed me standing in the crook of a tree. My mom didn't know; I didn't know how to tell her. She'd get jealous, and want Lars to take pictures of *her*, and anyway after prom, it wouldn't matter.

"Sweet," Lars said, as we were finishing. "Sweet. Too bad you're not ten years older." He moved toward me and snapped at the elastic of my top. My boob was three inches away from his hand. We were so different, my mom and me. Our bodies. And Lars would notice. She was *Playboy*, I was *National Geographic*.

"Don't."

"Your mom's weird," Lars said.

"News flash."

He kissed me then. I hated it, knowing that his mouth had been on my mom's. Knowing it had probably been *everywhere*. But it felt good. And there were futures, right? And I had one, so I kissed him back.

"My mom's probably, like, frantically calling your apartment," I said when we came up for air. "We should probably get going."

"Just come over here for one sec." Lars got up and went over into the privacy of some trees, where he spread his jacket on the ground and crooked his finger at me, as in, *come hither*. He reclined. "You sweet thing, you sweet, sweet creature," he called, and crooked his finger again, thinking it looked sexy.

"*What?*"

"Just come here, Luce. I knew the minute I saw you."

"My mom and Jen are going to be totally frantic." I went to him, not knowing what else to do. "And anyway, you're supposed to be dating my mom."

"Hey, there's plenty to go around." He kissed me again and got on top, sliding his hands up my shirt.

"Slow down, okay?"

"Why?"

"We're just *kissing*." I said. Lars had his hands all over me. It was hard to believe he was the same Lars, the same one from my dreams. I was shivering, trying to think of what I could say to make him stop.

"Oh, we're doing more than that, Baby."

"So when will the pictures be ready?" He kept groping my chest. It wasn't doing anything for me, but I could tell he thought I was shivering with excitement or ecstasy or whatever, and that really got him going, *sweet creature, sweet creature,* he kept murmuring, like I was something with tentacles, or like it was some line he'd heard in a movie. He sat up suddenly and pulled out a rubber.

"Lars, we can't."

"*We can't, we can't,*" he mimicked, and laughed nastily.

"I mean it. I'm supposed to be back by three o'clock. You're kind of scaring me." I got up and went to stand by the car. "I'm still a virgin."

"Oh, you tease, you tease, you *tease*," Lars stayed on the ground, pinching his own nipples with one hand and pulling his penis out with the other. He yanked at himself feverishly for a few seconds. "Come here, beautiful creature, come here, come here," he said, and then his eyes rolled back in his head and he squirted everywhere, twitching on the ground. I thought about hitchhiking down the canyon.

After a while he opened his eyes and looked over. "The pictures will take about a week," he said.

I kept shoplifting, kept getting myself into trouble. I wanted new stuff all the time, clothes and bras and lipstick and peel-off face masks. I babysat as often as I could so that I could wheel the stroller into the store and then pull back the cloth flap behind the stroller seat, which offered a cubbyhole that I could shove all kinds of stuff into, eyelash curlers and

Tabu perfume and one-pound candy bars and tube socks. I kept getting caught, too, and finally wound up in juvenile hall, where my mom had already taken me a few times for being incorrigible. I wanted to change my life, I just didn't know how to do it. Every time I stole something my eyelid ticked and my hands shook. Sometimes I didn't even want the stuff, sometimes I didn't even know why I was doing it. I wanted people to like me, and I especially wanted people like cops and social workers to like me, but every time I came into contact with one of them they were seeing someone else, not the kid I knew I could be but a law-breaking juvenile delinquent who used the "F word" and talked back to her mother. It was like the real me was living in some parallel universe, trying out for cheerleading, getting straight A's, getting invited to prom. The real me looked like Natalie Wood and drove a red sports car and wore her hair in a French braid. She had tight, angora, turtleneck sweaters, a stereo and a horse and a British accent. The real me was someone else.

Once, when my mom took me to juvenile detention, the social worker wanted to talk to me alone. Usually it was the three of us locked in some office, with my mom enumerating her complaints and me trying to look disinterested. I was always terrified to be there, afraid my mom would leave me for good with the other kids, who had bad grammar and were wickedly good at foos ball. She could do this, she pointed out. Just leave me, so that I'd have to go to a foster home, if I didn't shape up.

"Why don't you wait in the hall," the social worker said. "Just let Lucy and I talk one-on-one, okay?"

"What difference does it make if *I'm* here," my mom said. "I'm a *trained professional*, don't you know I'm a trained professional? I have my *degree.*"

"Just for a minute." The social worker was waiting, fiddling with a jar of pens on her desk.

"She'll just lie to you. She'll tell you things that aren't true about me."

"Could your daughter and I just talk privately?" The social worker, Elsie, was staring my mom down. "It won't take long."

My mom shifted. "I don't see why I should have to."

Elsie stood up, opened the door, and waited. Finally my mom shuffled out, giving me the evil eye as she went, mouthing *don't you tell her anything*. It was the first time I'd ever seen something like this, someone who had authority over my mom and could actually make her do something she didn't want to do. And when Elsie shut the door behind my mom she turned and rolled her eyes at me, like she had some idea of what my mom could be like. I was still in trouble, still the one who kept stealing. But finally someone outside the family seemed to be getting a feel for our family, for how messed up everything was and how it wasn't just me being bad, me being the criminal. That day the world opened up for me. I even went looking for Elsie years later, to tell her thanks, but she'd left the job a few years back, and no one knew where she'd gone.

Kiri helped by escorting Jonathan to my locker, where I had the algebra homework done three days before it was due. "You can just copy the answers. I don't care," I said. "And next time you can do it and we'll trade." Then I made a big production of not being able to find it, my locker door wide open.

"Is that *you?*" Jonathan said.

"Oh. Yeah."

"You look really good there," Jonathan said. He kept staring.

"My mom's boyfriend took it. He's a professional photographer."

"A sweet creature," Kiri said. Sometimes it was *disgusting creature,* and sometimes it was *slimy ejaculating-from-his-tentacles creature.*

"Shut up." I handed Jonathan the homework, scanned my locker carefully one last time, and slammed it shut.

"You're on your own with this one," Jen said. She was sitting on the front porch, jangling her car keys. "I waited but now it's your turn."

"What's wrong?"

"Some guy made a mess in your room. He and your little friend Kiri were here, and now she's freaking out."

"What?"

"I'm outta here," Jen said. "Go in peace. Good luck. I was supposed to be at work at three."

"What happened?"

"I told you, some guy who wants you to go to prom was here. With Kiri. I think he put rice and newspaper in your room."

"Benny?"

"Eww, not that little geek. Some other guy. John. He's cute. So anyway congratulations, I'm glad you got asked, but now mom's all freaking out, and I'm *late*. Break a leg."

I could hear my mom's sobs before I got to the top of the stairs. There was wadded up newspaper all over my bedroom floor, and a dozen red balloons with a torn-open envelope dangling from a curled red ribbon, and there was rice scattered across the carpet and in the middle of it all sat my mom, weeping, a piece of paper in her fist.

"How am I supposed to clean this. How am I supposed to clean this," she hurled the piece of paper at me.

"What are you doing in my room?"

"What am I doing in your room, what am I doing in your room, look at this, look at this, they come busting in here like they have some right, not even thinking about *me*, not even thinking about this *nice new carpeting*, there's going to be ink all over the floor, just all over, and I'll tell you what Lucy *you are going to pay for it*, you're going to have these carpets cleaned with your *own money*. Just look at this mess. Just look at it." She moved around the room, snatching up pieces of newspaper and throwing them back down.

"Who was here?"

"Oh, whoever your little friends are. Some *guy*. They tromped right on up here, they barely said two words to me. And now look at this mess."

I tore open the envelope. It was a note from Jonathan, inviting me to prom.

"You just get everything, don't you," my mom said savagely. "You think you're so big. I never went to one single school dance, not *one*. *Not one*. Look at this, ink all over. And there's rice down the heater vents I'll bet, not like that would concern you, not one bit would it. I'll probably have to buy a new furnace."

"Mom, just get out. I'll clean it up."

"That's right you will. This is gonna cost money, I don't have any money, these carpets are practically brand-new and then some *guy* just comes busting in here, acting like he owns the place. Who does he think he is?" She fixed me with a stare.

"Just get out, Mom! It's just newspaper! I'll clean it up!"

"Well, don't think you're going. Not after he pulls that kind of stunt."

"I am so going."

"Oh no you're not. Think again, Wise Guy."

"You're jealous, that's why. You're not even happy for me. I'm your *daughter*. I got invited to *prom*. You're supposed to be *glad*." I started to cry, scooping up newspaper so she wouldn't see. "You're the biggest bitch. I hate you. You're a fucking bitch. You ruin everything."

"Why is this all my fault?" she widened her eyes. "Did I come barging up here and ruin your carpet, did I?"

"Just get out of here! You're a fucking freak!"

"I'll take you to juvey hall again, don't think I won't." She liked to say it like that: *juvey hall*, like she was in *West Side Story* or something. "I'll load you right up in that car and then no more boyfriends, no more prom night, you can go live with some foster family."

"I wish I could."

My mom slapped me. I clawed her neck and down her chest, drawing blood. We lurched around for a minute, clumsy. When I bit her shoulder she reared backwards, then slapped me again across the stomach.

"Oh, what was that, was that supposed to be a punch?" I said, half-laughing, half-crying. I could feel blood where she'd scratched my ear.

"You are not going to that dance, you are not going to that dance," she said. "We're a Package Deal, get it, Luce? *A Package Deal.*"

My mom called my dad the next morning. I could tell she was talking to him from the way she kept giggling and exclaiming, and also from the way she'd dragged the phone into her bedroom closet and locked the door. I picked up the extension in my bedroom. "She's just gotten in with a bad crowd," my mom was saying. "I don't know, first it was the shoplifting, now she's hanging out with these *hoods*, they just traipse all over like they own the place."

"You can send her here," my dad said. "It's always been an open invitation."

"Well, gee, I mean she has all her friends here and everything," my mom said. "I just don't know. I'd hate to do *that* to her."

"Well, if it didn't work out, she could come back. We could just make it a temporary thing."

"I don't know. I just don't know. Who would've thought, all those years ago, that someday we'd be divorced and talking like this?"

"Well, water under the bridge," my dad said. "But think it over."

"I mean you were my first real love, Bob. I just never thought we'd get *divorced*. Sometimes I still can't believe it."

I hung up and sat on the floor of my room for a minute, trying to think of what to do. My eyes burned from hearing my dad's voice; I wanted to snatch the phone back up and tell him what was really going on, the thing with the prom and Lars and how much my mom seemed to hate me, and how much I hated *her*, and how really this was all about my *prom*, and about how I liked Jonathan, who I knew my dad would also like, because he was clean-cut and always used a respectful voice when he was talking to the teacher. I wanted to explain things to my dad, like how more than anything else on the planet my mom seemed intent on wrecking my whole entire life.

I went to my closet and threw a few things in my backpack. The prom was only ten days away. If I could just hide out for that long, I figured, at least I could go, and then my mom could do whatever she wanted with me. She could send me to the North Pole after that, for all I cared. I snuck out the back door and took off running. I had forty bucks. I had plenty of friends. I'd figure something out.

• • •

"Well, you can't stay here," Kiri's dad told me. "We really like you, Lucy. You know that. But you know what it's called, if we let you stay here? It's called harboring a runaway."

"It's just for ten days," Kiri said. We were in her basement, in the family rec room.

Kiri's dad was leaning against the pool table and he had his arms folded. "Bad, bad idea," he said. "*Horrible* idea. No way. I'm sorry, Lucy. I really am. We can't let you stay. This would be the first place she'd look."

"What am I supposed to do?" I was trying not to cry. I unzipped my backpack and got out my peach lip gloss just to have something to fiddle with. "I just want to go to the *prom*. That's *it*. If I had a normal mom we'd be out shopping for my *dress* right now."

"Can't you just talk to her?" Kiri's mom said. Her name was Ruth and she was the smallest woman I'd ever seen. She was sitting on the edge of the pool table and her legs dangled clear above the floor. Kiri had told me that her mom's shoe size was a size two. "Couldn't you just let her know how important this is?"

"Yeah. Right," I said. "You don't know my mom."

"Isn't she a therapist?"

"Good one, huh?"

"Come on, Luce," Kiri's dad said. "That kind of an attitude isn't helping things. What are your options?"

"I don't *have* any," I said. "All I know is I'm not going to California. No fucking way."

"Please watch your mouth, okay?" Ruth said. "Let's go over this. What are your choices?"

"Staying here," I said. "Running away."

"You can't run away." Kiri's dad rolled a pool ball absently back and forth. "She'd find you in a minute, and then what?"

"Then you'd go to juvey hall," Kiri said. "That's what she calls it."

"Well, she could do that," Ruth said. "Maybe you two just need a break. Do you think she'd just let you stay here, until after the prom was over?" It killed me, that they were being so nice. They were so *clueless*. They were talking about her like she was *reasonable*.

"No," I said. "The whole point is for me to *miss* the prom."

"That can't be true," Ruth said. "Why don't you let me give her a call?" It was getting dark outside. I'd been there a couple of hours already, and I knew that by now my mom was probably out looking, driving around in her big boat car and calling all over the place.

"Whatever," I said.

"Look," Kiri's dad said. "I'm just going to make us some popcorn. Then one of us will call your mom and see if there's anything we can work out, okay?"

Ruth drove me home. "I'm sorry, Lucy," she said. "We would've loved to have you for a couple of days. But your mom just really doesn't think that's the best idea."

"I know," I got out. "Thanks for trying, anyway."

My mom was waiting with her arms open, her face full of appeal. "Thanks, Ruth," I heard my mom say. "Gee, teenagers can be so hard. I'm sorry she dragged you into this."

I went straight to my room and locked the door. "Come on, Luce," my mom said a few minutes later. She rattled the knob. "Let's talk about this." I ignored her. I moved around my room, trying to collect the important things: my journal, my Love's Baby Soft perfume, my favorite red sweatshirt. My plan was to stay locked in my room and give her the silent treatment until she left the house. Then I'd take off for good. "Open up. This is silly. This isn't getting us anywhere." She lurked in the hallway for a while, and after that I heard her talking on the phone.

Once I'd finished packing, I sat on the bed, trying to make a plan. I couldn't go to any more friends' houses, that was for sure. I thought about all-night diners, bus stations, anyplace where I might be able to catch a couple hours sleep without looking suspect. In the middle of it all I started crying again, sick of things, sick of using my energy to figure out problems like this one. Because there *wasn't* a problem: that, as far as I could see, was the whole point. There were real dramas and there were fake dramas. There were real problems, and unless I was missing something, this wasn't one of them. My shoplifting: now *that* was a problem. But that wasn't even why my mom wanted to get rid of me. I zipped and unzipped my backpack, trying to make sense of it. I was about to run away, about to sleep in a bus station like some sort of white trash chick even though I had school tomorrow, even though tomorrow I was supposed to get to see Jonathan in algebra class. And I didn't *want* to run away, not really. I wasn't like my mom; I *hated* leaving places, I hated seeing new things. I wanted to go to the prom: that was it. I wanted to slow dance with Jonathan, and I wanted to French kiss him afterwards. That was about all I had planned.

But there were ten whole days between me and all that. And there was my mom looming in between, saying *over my dead body*, saying, *if I don't get to go, no one goes.* Ten whole days where I'd have to wipe that smirk off my face. And for what? Even if she did let me go to the dance, I thought, after that there would just be something else. Some giant fake problem that I didn't have any control over. Some pseudo-drama that I'd have to take seriously. I wanted a *normal life*: was that so weird? And I knew I could do it. I knew I could toe the line. I wasn't perfect, but I had potential.

The next morning, after my mom left for work, I ransacked her room. It took awhile, but finally I found what I was looking for: a single sheet of lined yellow paper, folded into a remodeling book, and on it were a bunch of phone numbers, scribbled in her tiny nervous uphill scrawl. Next to my dad's she'd used just his initials: R. T.

I took a chance, and my dad picked up.

"You'd like San Clemente," he told me. "And God knows I'd love to have you. You can even have your own bathroom. You can get your-self a job, maybe somewhere in the mall. You can even use my car if you want."

His voice was warm and calm. I felt my heart lift a little, imagining my new life in sunshine, no mother in sight. I could see myself speeding away in a sports car, my mom screaming *stop!* and *come back!* I could see her flailing like a crazy insect on the horizon, sorry for everything.

I thought about it for a few more days. It would mean missing the prom, but she'd managed to ruin that already, anyway. She couldn't help herself. And in exchange, I'd at least get to get away from *her,* once and for all. I'd get to have a new life, one where she wasn't ruining things all the time for no reason.

I called my dad back, and told him yes.

It was just easier somehow, living with my dad. All the days in his house were the same, and I could count on things. Eventually I broke down and called my mom, and after that we talked on the phone every week. There was no more craziness. I couldn't believe how easy it was, to just be someone else. All you had to do was move into the right kind of house, one like my dad's, which was new and on a cul-de-sac. All you had to do was have nice clothes and the right things in the cupboard, name brands and canned foods with staid, trustworthy fonts: *New England–style clam chowder, diced carrots and peas, Manwich.*

I was popular all of a sudden. I got invited to parties. I started getting good grades in school. And I fell in love for the first time. Ben was small, with a dark, wiry pad of hair on top and flat white feet that reminded me of friendly fish. His skin was clean and odorless, the way my dad's house was odorless, not yet decaying, not yet historical. When I lived with my mom everything was meaningful, laden. The houses we lived in had layers of smells, other people's dramas played out and absorbed into the plaster, cigarette smoke and diapers and cooked food. Our clothes smelled from too few washings, and we all smelled from too few showers. My mom's approach to personal hygiene was, she said, *French*, which meant that she sprayed her hair with a shampoo called Psst! and then brushed it through in place of shampooing it, or rinsed just the tips of her fingers after using the toilet, or stood over the sink just to wash the back of her neck and her armpits. She called this method a *whore's bath*, though for the longest time I thought she was saying *horse bath*. We girls did the same thing, and when I did go to live with my dad, at first I was amazed at all the washing that went on, the wiping of counters, the hosing down of driveways, the sweeping of porches and the vacuuming out of cars and the way I was expected to shower every morning before school. My new life, like Ben, didn't seem to smell like anything, which suited me fine. It meant that he and I had a future, instead of a history. It meant that maybe, someday, I could have a life like his own, uneventful and redolent of nothing. In his house nothing smelled, either. Meals were microwaved and dispensed with quickly and all the kitchen surfaces got wiped down before his family retired to watch TV. His life was safe and settled, with a basketball hoop in the driveway and a dog that had lived to old age (though the *dog* smelled—this I remember—of dampness and decay and feces and dog shampoo, and the smell drove my boyfriend's mother to a sort of mania: she hurried the dog with her foot, coaxing it from garage to laundry room, scowling after it, watching the dog's butt for leaks. She held a rag soaked with disinfectant, and spritzed the dog bed with Lysol, and asked me: could I smell it? Could I smell anything?) and a bedroom so permanent that I wanted to lay on his wagon-wheel boy's bed and never leave, surrounded by golf trophies and clean, folded, white T-shirts. I knew I couldn't keep him, the way my mom must've known with Frank. I loved him too much. Even when we were together, parked on some side street and fogging up the windows of his car, I yearned for him; and no matter how close our bodies were always he receded, a cruel trick, though still I could open my eyes and see his beautiful face. During those times in the car I would start to cry, though I tried not to. I didn't want to be the crazy one, the melodramatic one, the girlfriend he would leave. I wanted to be the one he would choose, the popular one with a shiny blonde ponytail who'd had braces and all the same evenings he had, evenings in a safe house, and who kept a box in the attic with all of her childhood drawings and hair clippings and baby teeth and report cards. Once, in the car, I sat on top of him and lifted back the waistband of his cotton underwear and inside was a web of clear fluid, the lines spun and translucent. I reached through the sticky web to touch him and the smell was like moldy leaves and then it was as if we really had had a lifetime together, a long one that we were looking back at, with children and houses and pets that had grown old and died. At this moment he seemed crazily fragrant, like some dazzling tropical flower that was finally too potent for me, too full of joy.

Anyway, I knew that eventually he'd see through my little normal-high-school-girl act. I might be living on a cul-de-sac now, but the year before I'd been a juvenile delinquent, white trash, and I suspected his parents knew. In their house I felt like a thief, an interloper. Everything was in its place, and they had extra rolls of toilet tissue in the bathroom cupboards and a Kleenex box on every nightstand, and a refrigerator in the garage for labeled, frozen meals, and a pegboard for spare keys. I could play along for a while, pretend it was the same kind of world I was used to, but eventually his parents would see right through me. Back in Salt Lake I'd been the shoplifting queen, and called my mom a fucking bitch at least once a week. Now, in southern California with my dad, I was trying to be someone else, and meanwhile their son and I were having sex in his car every weekend night in elementary school parking lots, and I knew it was just a matter of time before I was found out.

In the meantime, I thought it was best to just play along. I hardly ever talked about my mom, and in front of friends I tried to represent my life with my dad as a sort of sitcom, full of pathos and single-dad jokes. I stopped swearing and stealing. I had dreams about my mom, a lot, but even those burned off quickly, until the past few years started to feel unreal even to me and dreadful and hilariously funny. When I looked, once, and couldn't even find Riverton on the map, I wasn't surprised. Even Frank felt made-up. Maybe this was how things felt for my mom, the people in her life like shapes on a felt board that you could just keep moving around. Like in migraines when she'd say, *pretend it's not happening, pretend you're somewhere else. Where would you like to be?*

Pretend you're in a meadow, with the buzz of bees, pretend it's a beautiful blue, blue day and the sun's coming down. Pretend you have a striped umbrella. And then I was there, carried on her voice and dropped, a kerchiefed bundle from a cartoon stork, into reeking sweet grass.

People change: that's how she was always explaining it. And I guess my mom was right. Living with my dad healed me. After two years in the house on the cul-de-sac I had a pretty good idea of how peaceful things could be, water dripping from potted geraniums on the back patio and how my dad and I could sit together, like tonight, pushing away our plates and wiping barbecue sauce from our fingers with paper napkins. I remember the crisscrossing plastic of the chair on my back and under my legs, and my dad's voice going up and down as it got darker. *How do you think your mom and sis are doing?* The feeling seemed to hit my stomach before it hit my brain, making a tight hot spot in my center and then winnowing up my spine with its message. My throat got tight and water rose in my eyes. I still had my sunglasses on, which helped, and my dad talked on while I tried to beat back the message, tried to replace it with the other feelings, the ones I usually had and that always ended with the words, *hate her*. The geraniums were like wadded pink balls of Kleenex and I stared at one, they looked so fake, they were old people flowers. I remember crossing my arms, my legs, holding everything in. But then it was over me in a rush and I really was crying and I had to go inside, telling my dad, *be right back.*

    I missed her; I did. I knew that it made me pathetic and still my throat felt hard, like I'd swallowed a ball of sandpaper, and the tears kept coming in waves. I cried quietly, though I wanted to make noise. But noises were histrionics. Noises were fake. Noises were about something other than the feelings, I knew that much from living with my mom, and I wanted whatever tears I wept to be pure and hot and scant. I sat on the counter, knocking my dad's green speckled soap-on-a-rope into the sink. I hated my feelings. But we were a family. We *were*. We were a family, I thought, that had never actually had a chance to *happen*, not because there was anything wrong with us but because of other things, money and jobs and moving around always trying to find something better. It was true, I thought, that my mom was nervous and unhappy, but maybe that was because of how much she'd lost. She could never choose right: which things to keep, which ones to give away.

I blew my nose and went back outside. My dad looked closely at me. "You okay, Hon?"

"Yeah. I guess I just kind of miss Mom," I said. "I even miss Jen. A lot." The words came out all over the place, filled with water. "Sometimes I wish we could just go back."

"I kind of miss your mom, too," my dad said. "Isn't that crazy? And Jen, I'd give anything to have her, I know she's your mom's right-hand man but still. But your mom and I had a lot of good years." He rocked back on his chair. "I even thought maybe we should ask them to come out here, isn't that crazy?"

"Do you think you and Mom would get back together?"

My dad laughed a little. "Oh, I don't know about *that*." It hadn't occurred to me until now; my mom always had some other boyfriend, and my dad had dated Marina until last year, when she'd run off with some guy she met on the golf course. I tried to get my mind around the idea of us all together again as a family, picking up where we'd left off years before.

"Do you think your mom's still the same?"

"I think she's doing better," I said. "At least before I left, she wasn't as nervous as she used to be. Plus she's stayed in that house for three years. That says something, doesn't it?"

"How does she look?" my dad said. At first I didn't know what he meant; she looked like she'd always looked. Her hair was dyed flat black and she had bangs. Her toes still went in when she walked, and her eyes were forever roaming all over the place, even when you were having a serious discussion. She was looking for things like crumbs or loose change. But I saw that my dad was asking me now as a friend, the way one of my male friends might ask about a girl I knew, whether she had a boyfriend and whether she might want to go out with him. My dad hung around the house every night; he hadn't met any other women and he still hadn't bought any living room furniture besides a second-hand plaid couch. He was a bachelor, I saw suddenly: a lonely one, nearly bald and pushing fifty.

"She looks really good. Mom's pretty."

"Don't say that," my dad said. "That's all I need." We were quiet for a while. "Do you think they'd come, if I paid their tickets?" he said finally.

"Probably," I said.

Then it was like getting ready for a party. My dad and I cleaned the house, vacuuming dust balls out of all the corners and wiping out shelves in the pantry. We bought a futon mattress for Jen to sleep on in my room, and new sheets and an extra pillow. I didn't have the nerve to ask where my mom would sleep. The more my dad and I got ready, the more it seemed like the right thing to do; as if simply by turning our hopeful faces we could start all over, the Taylors, and try again. My mom was excited, too. She kept calling and calling.

"What do you think I should wear?" she asked. "Does your dad still like pink? I cut my hair, you should see, oh he'll just love it I'll bet, it's feminine and I'm even thinking about painting my *fingernails*, Jen said she'd help me, and tomorrow we're going to the mall to buy shoes. Do you really think I have a chance, Luce?"

"I think you and Dad still love each other," I said. I never knew if I was saying the right things. Sometimes I'd be blabbing to my dad, or sometimes my mom, and then I'd think, *how should I know? You're the parent.* But they seemed to need my advice so I gave it.

"I'm just so thrilled that your dad wants to try again. I mean I know we're pretty different people, but people *change*. And not like any of the men I've met have been so great. *Frank.* Are you sure this is something your dad really wants to try? Tell me the truth, Luce."

"I know he wants to see you," I said. "We both miss you." My mom and I were so *alike:* we both got one little twig in our hands and then built a whole birdhouse. The first time we'd talked, a week before, all I'd said was he wanted to see her again. Now she was off and running. Or maybe she'd heard something in my voice that first time, maybe I'd said too much. "I mean I think you guys should just get to know each other again. Who knows what will happen?"

"Well, I'm not going to traipse all the way out there just for a *who knows,*" she said irritably. "Aren't you getting any vibes?"

"Do you want to talk to Dad?"

"No, no," my mom said. "I just wanted to ask you about pink, tell you about my hair. Jen's really excited too. She's bringing her swimsuit. You guys have a pool, right?"

"We don't. But there's one in the recreation complex. It's about three blocks away."

"I thought you said you had a *pool* last time. Well, tell your dad I can't wait. Do you *really* think I have a chance?"

My dad and I picked them up at the airport. All the way home my mom hopped around in her seat, exclaiming over everything: look at all the wonderful stucco *houses,* she said, I just love California architecture, even the new houses, I just love how they look so fresh and clean and new, what do people do for *work* around here, it's just flowers flowers flowers and new cars new cars new cars. My dad and my mom had kissed on the lips at the airport. He seemed excited but on his guard, driving with one hand and keeping the other tucked safely under his butt. Our car had bucket seats so my mom had no choice but to stay on her side, strapped in. But she kept touching my dad's leg. Jen was showing me stuff from her suitcase, a windup music box and her swimming medals and some beaded bracelets. She let me pick one out and tied it on my arm.

"Anybody getting hungry? I was thinking of hitting the Jolly Roger," my dad said. He had on a new kind of aftershave. It smelled warm and male and reminded me, in a good way, of a man's underarm. "They have a pretty nice French onion soup. They put cheese over the top and then zap it and it is de-lish."

"Oh, it's been so long since I've eaten in a restaurant. We can't afford it at home, we plain can't. It's been *ages* since I've eaten at a restaurant." We pulled into Jolly Roger and Jen and I walked ahead of them.

"I have a boyfriend," Jen said. "Mom doesn't know. His name is Rudy and he has a car."

"Me too," I said. "Have a boyfriend, I mean."

"Have you guys done it?"

"Yeah. Have you guys?"

"It was cool," Jen said. "I didn't think I'd like it but I did."

"Do you think Mom and Dad will get back together?" I asked.

"I don't know. It feels kind of weird. Anyway, even if she did move here, I'd stay in Salt Lake. I can't leave Rudy. Plus I have a job now. I do press-on nails." She fanned her pink fingers to show me. I hadn't thought about that part of it; if they got back together, I wanted it to be all of us. But Jen was almost eighteen, and could do whatever she wanted.

In the booth we were symmetrical. That was something I'd missed: all four of us and one at each corner, the way people were supposed to look in a restaurant booth. Sometimes it was three people—me and my dad, say, and Marina—and then we were shaped like a tricycle, or a family with one leg missing.

My dad draped his arm across the back of the booth, and my mom took a chance and slid closer. "Get whatever you want," he said. I wanted fish-n-chips and Jen was getting the Ranchburger. Once we decided we closed the menus and just sat there a minute, getting used to being all four of us again.

"What'll it be?" The waitress collected our menus and started with Jen. My mom was doing some weird little nervous thing with the paper from her straw and she kept glancing down at the table, then looking up at the waitress appealingly. "Just water for me, please," she said. "And a side salad. A *small* one. No dressing."

"Are you dieting?"

"Oh no," my mom said. "I just don't want to impose."

"Mom, he's offering." I saw with dread that she was doing her orphan act; she used it all the time on men, and they always ate it up. But now they both had good jobs, plus my dad sent money for Jen, and I knew because I'd watched him write out the checks. She didn't *need* to do it now, but she didn't seem to be able to help herself.

"Just eat," my dad said. "Don't only get a salad. Get something else. Spaghetti."

"Oh no no no." My mom was fluttering all over: her napkin, the straw paper, her eyelashes and hands. "No please no really just a side salad, it's only a dollar, that'll be perfect."

"Why don't you order something?" Jen was playing with the syrup caddy, flicking the sticky lid open and shut. "Are you just not hungry or what, Mom?"

"Oh no, I am, actually I'm starving, I just don't want to be any trouble."

The waitress said, "I'll come back." Then we all seemed to be moving at once. *Get something*, I was saying, my dad saying *bring her the Spaghetti Plate, the Spaghetti Plate,* my mom saying *no no really oh okay, alright, if it'll make you happy*—and Jen going *thwock thwock,* with the syrup lid, absent and mooning over Rudy, from the looks of it.

"Why are you doing that?" I said. "Putting on that act?"

"Honey, please don't start criticizing me. Gee whiz. I haven't even been here an hour."

"It's okay, Lucy," my dad said. "It's not important."

"It's *fake*," I said.

"Lay off," my dad patted my mom's shoulder. "It's no biggie, she's getting the Spaghetti Plate. Okay? We're all happy?" My mom was still over there acting helpless, tucking herself into my dad. Our eyes met and my mom scowled, mouthed *don't ruin it.* Then the waitress plonked a basket of rolls in front of us, and Jen and my dad dug in.

• • •

"I thought you *wanted* us all together again." My mom was sitting on the edge of the bed.

"I do."

"Well then don't jeopardize things. Your dad and I have a certain way of interacting. We always have, it's just the way we are."

"You acting pathetic, you mean?"

"You can call it whatever you want," my mom smoothed my hair and flicked off the bedside lamp.

Jen was in bed with her fingers splayed out across the blanket; she was drying her nails. Every now and again she lifted one hand lazily and blew at them. "Everybody pretends sometimes, Luce," Jen said. "Don't you ever do it with Ben?"

"No." I thought about how I always faked an orgasm when he got close, out of sympathy for his spasticness as much as anything. "At least not like that."

"You have to help me, Luce. You do. You're closest to your dad and he'll sense it if you don't want me around. Don't you want to try again, too? It's so wrong, us all being split up. We're a family. We should be together."

"What's Dad doing?"

"As a matter of fact, your dad is waiting for me. If you get my drift. We'll try not to be too loud."

My dad lasted two days. Then he cornered me in the back bathroom while Jen and my mom were watching *Cagney and Lacey*. "I can't take it," he said. "I really can't. We're not the same people anymore. She wears me out."

"She wears everybody out. Don't feel bad."

"I thought you said she was different."

"I thought she *was*."

"How am I gonna tell her?"

"I don't know. You're the parent."

"Great," my dad said. "Now you tell me."

• • •

The next morning my mom and Jen went back to Salt Lake. My mom cried big alligator tears, saying, *what did I do? What did I do? How did I ruin it?* And grabbed my arm hard, just before she got on the plane. *What did you tell him, what did you, what did you—?* I didn't know how to answer. I missed my mom, but then as soon as I saw her again, I couldn't wait to get away. And then when I did get away I forgot all about the bad times, and started to miss her all over again. I couldn't make sense of it.

Afterwards, my dad took me to Souper Salad for lunch. "Thank goodness that's over with," he said. "Honest to God, I don't know what I was thinking. I'm sorry about all that. A part of me still loves your mom. And then I get confused."

"Me too. It's okay."

"I want to tell you something," my dad said. He had all three kinds of soup on his red plastic tray, the clam chowder and the vegetable beef and the chicken noodle, along with a huge pile of Saltine and oyster and Waverly crackers. We both did, because it was a buffet. "I've never told you this, I'm not even sure I should be telling you now. But you're old enough. I just never wanted to turn you against your mom."

"What?"

"Remember how, when we told you girls about the divorce, I had to go to Idaho for a couple of days? Do you remember that? Right after I started my job selling books?"

"Yeah."

"Well, your mom and I had decided to split you up. The plan was that you were going to live with me and Jen was going to live with her." He swigged his iced tea. "Is your salad okay? I probably shouldn't even be telling you this."

"It's okay, Dad. I'm old enough."

"Yeah. You are. And I want the record to be straight." He mopped his forehead with a paper napkin. "So anyway, we were going to divide you kids up. Which probably wasn't the best idea anyway. But that was the plan. And then, like a big dummy, I left the state. I called your mom from Idaho, I only had to be there four days, and I'll never forget what your mom said. She said, 'It's all over now, Charlie Brown.' Just like that. She charged me with desertion, and that's how I lost you girls. She told the judge I'd left Utah for good. That I'd deserted the family, and that I was never coming back. And the judge believed her."

"She *did?*"

"I swear to God, Lucy. I swear to God. I'm not making this up. I just want you to know. I just want you to know, if I thought I'd have stood a snowball's chance in hell, I would've fought for you. I would've tried to get both you girls. But there was no way. No way. 'It's all over now, Charlie Brown.' Those were her exact words. For as long as I live, I will never forget that."

"It's okay, Dad." I went over to his side of the booth. I felt—I felt sorry for parents everywhere, divorced parents especially, who fucked things up without even being able to help it. "Jen and I turned out alright."

"You *did,*" my dad said. "That you did."

"Eat your soup before it gets cold, okay? Look at all these *options.* Anyway, I'm glad she's gone."

"Oh boy. Me too." He popped a Saltine in his mouth. I loved watching him eat. I loved how much pleasure it gave him, I loved how he waggled his eyebrows and slapped on the butter without worrying about cholesterol or fat grams. I loved my *dad.*

"Can we go to Baskin-Robbins for dessert?"

"Sure," my dad said. "You can get that one flavor. That gross one, bubblegum or cotton candy or whatever the heck it is."

281

IN AIRPORTS. IN AIRPORTS,

Because I always, always went back to her.

think you and Ben just outgrew each other," my mom said. She nosed the huge car into a parking space. She drove like an old lady, hogging both lanes, slowing for green lights, everything in her own head so busy that she couldn't pay attention to much else.

"This is Handicapped."

"Well, then, it's a good thing I have a sticker, isn't it?"

"A sticker for what?"

"A *handicapped* sticker, now come on. I want to beat the lunch rush." She swam from the interior of her big car like something coming up for air, one hand still trying to figure out how to release the seat belt. She was always like this, always in a hurry, like we'd miss out on things, otherwise.

"Since when are you handicapped?"

"I got it from work, Luce. You know about my hip, that thing with the polio. Watch out for the ice, by the way, it's really bad. I don't know why I even live in Utah, every winter I wonder. I hope they still have that dressing. That peppercorn. She told me last time it was lowfat."

"Since when do you have polio?" I got out to inspect the sticker. It was such a fine line. We fought all the time but she paid every time we went to lunch, and now she and my dad were both helping me with tuition. "How did you get this?"

"Look I told you, come on now I want a booth and we're not going to get one if we dawdle, I got it from work, they keep them in a drawer and not like it's any of your business, I can't walk far without my hip hurting, damn it you just pick and pick and pick at me. Don't you. For just everything."

"I just thought handicapped parking stickers were supposed to be for handicapped people."

"Goddamn it I told you! Lucy! Why do you have to treat me like this! Now damn it, it hurts for me to just stand here! Why do you!" She limped over to a bench. She'd started to cry and now people going into the restaurant were watching me accusingly.

"Let's just go in."

"I'm not going in like this. Not if you're going to accuse me of stealing. Not if you're going to make fun of me, I don't know why you have to treat me like this, darn it, all I wanted was to have a nice lunch together, then I thought maybe we could go shopping and you have to go and ruin it, don't you?"

I sat next to her. "Alright, I'm sorry."

"You are not."

"I *am*. Let's go eat." I put my arm over her shoulder. "Come on."

"I *did* have polio, I was just a little girl so I can understand why you'd be surprised, I mean, gee, it's not like I want the whole world to know. You know and it flares up sometimes, that's why. There are certain things you girls don't know about me."

"Okay."

"I don't know why you treat me this way sometimes. I do so much for you."

"Mom, I'm sorry, okay? I'm sorry. I didn't know about your polio, I mean it's a little weird that this is the first time I've ever heard about it, even you have to admit that."

"Well, why would I? Spread it around." We moved toward the restaurant. She kept up the limp, pausing to rest, her face wincing in pain when she started up again. "I was trying to tell you, before you started all this, I think you and Ben just grew apart. I mean here you've got a whole future, you're in college, and what's Ben doing with his life?"

"The Ben topic is off-limits. What time do you have to be back?"

"Oh, I can stay gone as long as I want." My mom's job seemed to mean that she could pretty much come and go as she pleased; she took whole afternoons off for lunch, whole mornings to go to the mall. The waitress showed us to a booth and my mom slid in, picked up a menu and squinted down at it. "I knew it. I knew it. They got rid of that dressing, it was my very favorite, it was the whole reason I came here. Do you want to go somewhere else?"

"We're *here.*"

"Did you get rid of it, that great peppercorn dressing?" my mom called to the waitress, a few tables away. "Darn it, she didn't hear me. Well I just can't believe it, *now* what am I going to eat. Why can't I talk about Ben? He was a big part of your life. Anyway I just think there was probably too much commotion for you in California. That's how it was for me too. You have to drive drive drive everywhere, plus I know I'd miss winter, sure the weather's nice but I'd really miss it, the four seasons. And gee, autumn is just my favorite."

"That's nice." I was thinking of ordering a Bloody Mary, something I could easily get away with, with my mom, but that would've been absolutely not okay, in front of my dad. Probably that was part of the reason I'd come back. My dad had ideas about my future. He wanted me to make a plan and stick with it, but I didn't even know what I wanted to be when I grew up. I cared about guys, and I cared about my grades at the U, and I wanted an old Volvo, and I liked when my mom paid for my meals at restaurants. That was about as much as I'd figured out.

"He was just such a big part of your life, I think it's healthy to discuss it. And seriously, Lucy, I know you hate it when I give advice but what's he doing, last you told me he was working at *Disneyland* or *some* damned thing. You're a college girl. You don't have time for that. There are more fish in the sea."

"You weren't even *there.* Ben and I had a great relationship. And he's going to college, too. Now stop it. New subject." Every time she said his name aloud, every time anyone did, I wanted to stuff my head under the mattress and cry for about three years, because Ben had dumped me, *Ben had been too good for me*—in case she couldn't figure that much out—and now he was in San Francisco; and all of those sacred times we'd had together in his car, all the private times, me trying not to cry and always crying, and his beautiful hands and his hiccupy laugh and just his goodness, his goodness, he'd been so kind to me, messed up as I was and still he'd managed to love me, all that was gone, and what she was saying made me want to bare my teeth or shake her, just shake her.

"Oh, don't get all touchy. Your dad told me things, how you couldn't stand to be away from Ben for a single day and I just think, like I was trying to say outside, you know I understand these things, about why people do things psychologically, I just think you know there are other fish in the sea and that Ben was holding you back, is all."

"Like you know how to pick them." I'd only been back for three months and a part of me was still trying to figure it out. Because what had been wrong, with my life in California? Nothing. And yet here I was.

"What am I going to eat! What am I going to eat!" my mom pounded the table playfully. "I had my *heart set on it*, that dressing, oh it was so perfect, it had just the exact right amount of vinegar. We could go to that other place. That new place by my office. They have salads. I do so know how to pick them, sure I do, the problem is they all pretend to be one kind of guy and then turn out to be another, gee that's not my fault is it? *People change*, Lucy, is what I'm trying to say. If you could just get off the defensive for a minute. Now I have training, just listen to me for once. I'm not saying you two didn't love each other, of course you did. But sometimes it's time to move on. And I think that's what Ben's trying to do. Which is a healthy and good thing. And you both just need time to heal."

"Fine. Thanks for the free advice."

"People usually pay me, you know. I know that's hard for you to believe but I am a trained professional. You could at least hear me out."

"Fine. What." The waitress had appeared and I handed her my menu. "I'd like the chicken salad and a Diet Coke," I said. My mom gazed up at her, lost. "Who in the world decided to get rid of that great peppercorn dressing?"

"One of the managers, I guess. I think it was seasonal."

"Well what *season* is *peppercorn?*"

"Do you need more time?"

My mom leaned in to whisper. "Are you sure you don't want to go somewhere else?"

"Mom, please just order."

"Well alright. I guess. The minestrone, I guess. Just a cup. With breadsticks and crackers." The waitress moved off and my mom sighed, dipped her finger in her water and doodled on the table. "There's something I really want to talk to you about, that's part of why I wanted to come here."

"What?"

"Well I just wonder, I mean some of the guys you spend time with, I know sometimes they stay over, Honey, and that's okay, that's great, we both like having boyfriends. But I just need to put my mind at ease, make sure about something, I know you're going to tell me it's none of my business but you have to be careful, you have to look out for number one. And I know I'm your mom and that makes it hard to talk about some things but this is important, if you were one of my patients, well, I'd tell you the very same thing."

"I'm on the pill, if that's what you're trying to weasel out of me."

My mom laughed a little. "Well now I know *that*, gee, who do you think you're talking to?"

"What's your point?"

"My point is, it's important that you not just give too much of yourself away. That you stay independent. Because with Ben, you know, I really sort of think you got in over your head, sort of got into a thinking trap where you thought you couldn't survive without him, I think maybe that's what all these other guys are about. That you're just feeling rejected."

"You don't know shit about Ben. We were *friends*. We were *happy*."

I felt the sandpaper in my throat, how it always felt before I burst into tears over him. Ben was California, he was cool damp nights and the pale blue vinyl upholstery of his Toyota, him on top of me in the passenger seat, Ben with his thick dry dark hair and his voice, his voice, saying my name, keeping his mouth fastened on mine as though he might lose himself otherwise, we pulsed slowly and our bodies were amazing things, amazing.

"I'm independent." I drained my glass of water and the waitress was there again, soundless, refilling before she disappeared.

"I just want to know what you're getting out of it."

"The same thing you get out of it. And I don't feel like talking to you about my *sex life*, if you don't mind."

"This is not about your sex life, Luce. I don't want to hear those details, do you think I want to hear those details? I'm your *mother*."

"I'm not going to get any diseases, if that's what you're worried about."

"Can you just let me finish? Gee whiz, Lucy. You're just like your dad sometimes. You personalize everything, you really do, Honey, you really need to practice getting off the defensive and learn to listen with a more positive attitude. Do you know what I heard, I heard you add an hour to your life every single time you laugh. Isn't that something?" She laughed lightly, getting credit.

"I have to pee."

"Listen, I'm paying for this lunch."

"Well then just *tell* me."

"I just want to make sure you take care of yourself. That if you have guys sleep over, that they're not just going to take take take and leave you with nothing, which really in the long run could make you feel pretty shitty about yourself, Honey, could really effect your self-esteem and well just make you feel used, like that's what you're there for, like you're just some sort of freebie. I didn't raise you to be some little bee-bop slut. There's more to life than just men, men, men."

"What's a bee-bop slut?" I laughed, nervous, but I could feel the heat in my cheeks. I was just like her. We were twins. We were both loose, for one. People pleasers. If a guy wanted sex, all he had to do was *just ask*. It was true for my mom and it was true for me. I couldn't resist them, they were *starving*, they came one after another, dark-headed and eager, I made them so happy. But guess what, none of them was Ben, none of them was Frank, and that meant my mom and I being stuck together in a restaurant booth for the rest of our lives.

"I'm just saying, it's not like I could talk to you like this before now, but I think it's important. That if they want to buy you things, maybe a scarf, maybe even a nice angora sweater, you let them. And at least try to go somewhere fancy for dinner sometimes, you can always order some wine, most guys really like when you make them feel needed."

"You mean I should charge them if we're going to screw."

"I wish you wouldn't use that language. You know if I'm going to be with a guy, I let him know. That he has to treat me a certain way, wine and dine me a little, show me the town. Not just act like I'm some vagina on wheels."

Oh, that killed me. *Vagina on wheels.*

"You mean on *legs*. Well, guess what, news flash, I'm not sleeping with guys to get things out of them. I'm *dating* them, I know that sounds old-fashioned but in fact, surprise, unlike you I actually like the idea of being in a relationship." I fiddled with my straw. It was a total lie. I was sleeping around because my heart felt pulpy and rotten and I didn't know what else to do on Saturday nights. I was sleeping around because I drank too much wine.

"Well, okay, I can see I'm not getting anywhere. I tried to help. I'm speaking from experience. I know you don't see it that way but I've been married *twice*, Lucy, that's like job experience, I know what I'm talking about and you can just wipe that smirk off your face, you think you know so much, I have way way way more experience than you." My mom opened her paper napkin carefully on her lap, looking injured. "You're just like some of my patients. Stubborn, stubborn, stubborn. I'll tell you what, Luce, I know you think it's so funny now but in the long run, if you don't make sure you're not getting taking advantage of, letting some guy just have his way with you for free, you're going to regret it. I promise you that, young lady. Mark my words."

Mike and I met at a kegger. He was a surfer from Florida who worshipped Jimmy Buffett, and he was tan and leggy and smoked pot every night and was on academic probation at the U. We were at some frat house, watching people fill up their paper cups from the keg in the bathtub.

"Handy, isn't it," Mike said. "Having it in here, so when it's time to throw up. Do you want to leave? This is boring." I'd already slept with his best friend, Eddie, and Eddie's roommate, Kip, and I knew Mike knew.

"Let me just have one more beer," I said.

I slammed two more, and then we went back to Mike's apartment. I almost never remembered the sex itself, and I didn't care. For me there was lovemaking, like it had been with Ben; and then there was just sleeping together because I couldn't think of a good reason not to, like now. But after we'd made out on the couch for a while, Mike pulled back. "I think you should just sleep over," he said.

"Don't you want to screw?" I didn't care either way, not at that point, considering how I barely even knew him. Sex was just the thing between partying and bedtime. Actually, most of the time it went: partying, sex, puking, bedtime.

"Let's wait," said Mike. "I *like* you. I want us both to remember it."

"Wow. How heroic," I said, but I was touched. Mike brought me his toothbrush with a squiggle of blue toothpaste on top, and loaned me one of his pajama tops.

We went out three more times before we did finally do it. And then it felt sweet, like the old days. Not as perfect as it had been with Ben, but close.

A month later, as if my mom really had been trying to warn me, I missed my period. I waited two more weeks before I took the test but by then I knew. I called my mom crying.

"It's okay," she said. "It's okay."

"I made an appointment for Tuesday. But mom, you have to loan me the money. I can pay you back. I just don't have it up front."

"Of course I will, Sweetie. Damn it, I'm so sorry this had to happen. This really sucks."

"It *does* suck. I'm just not ready to have a kid."

"I know, Hon. You're too young. I can drive you, okay? Or Mike can. Is Mike the guy you're seeing right now?"

"Yeah."

"Well, or he can give you a ride. I love you, Honey. And I won't tell anybody. Not even Jen. She's so busy anyway, not like she has time to talk to me."

"Thanks, Mom."

"Well of *course*."

My mom called the next morning. Mike had slept over, and he answered the phone, than handed it to me.

"I won't let you do it, Luce. I can't."

"Mom, what?"

"The priest, Luce. I talked to the priest. It's a *sin*, is what it is."

"Priest, what priest? Since when are you religious?"

"I've always been religious," my mom said, but that was too much for her, and I heard a tiny giggle escape. "Now look, I'll stand by you regardless, but I can't in any good conscience loan you the money, I just can't. Put Mike back on the phone."

I hung up on her.

The clinic was set back from the street, like liquor stores were in Utah, and advertised itself in small letters. All the same there were picketers out front, shoving pamphlets and pleading with me. I sat in the waiting room listening for my name to be called. There was one girl placidly watching a *Gilligan's Island* rerun with her Latino boyfriend, laughing politely along with the laugh track. A few others leafed through magazines, pretending they weren't there. When finally they took me back, two hours after my scheduled appointment, the nurse explained that they'd have to do a few extra tests.

"Your mom called," she said. She kept her back to me, doing something with a tray of vials. "I know you're eighteen but she mentioned your hemophilia, and just to be on the safe side, I want to check your blood for clotting."

"My what?"

"Are you a hemophiliac?"

"*No.*"

"Well, she's worried. She's called half a dozen times at least. We have to check."

"I've never had hemophilia."

"I know." The nurse finally met my gaze. She pricked my finger, swabbed blood onto a slide. "So your mom's *really* a therapist?"

"Get out of the way," I said. My mom and Jen were waiting by my car. My mom held out a box of See's candy and shrugged, then started to cry. *Why did you? I'm sorry, I'm sorry,* Jen was saying.

"It was my grandchild," my mom said. "My grandbaby."

"Move, mom. I have to sit down."

"Please get out of the way." Mike said, and unlocked the car door.

"*You.*" My mom turned on him. "*You.* What kind of a man are you, huh?" Huh?" She jabbed at him with a puny fist, and Mike laughed. "You're a *monster*, that's what you are. A *murderer.*"

"Whatever," Mike said. He'd reclined the passenger seat for me and was clearing it, throwing cassette tapes onto the floor of the car. The huge Kotex I was wearing was already soaked with blood, I could feel, and the pain kept shooting across my lower belly. I leaned against the car, waiting for the pain to pass. No way was I wearing a seat belt.

"The priest made me do it, Luce. The priest. You know that. I wanted to help. I wanted to. I could've taken that baby, I could've raised it, I could've raised it, how could you do it, how could you have *killed* it—"

"Shut the fuck up. And go away. My stomach hurts."

"Why couldn't you? Why couldn't you have just given it to me? I don't understand. I don't understand."

"I would *chloroform* a baby before I would give it to you, do you know that? You told them I was a *hemophiliac*, since when have I ever been a hemophiliac, I would chloroform it—!" I said, and my mom put a hand over her mouth, backing away from the car, doing Shock. Jen let out a cry then; it was hardest on her, I thought, because she really believed it. That it had been a baby. *Luce, stop,* she said.

"How could you say that? How could you say that? How could you possibly ever say such a thing?" my mom was yelling.

"Because I mean it. You're insane. I hate you. Couldn't you for once in your life act like a real mother?" Suddenly things were spinning, and I threw up.

"Goddamnit, Lucy, that's exactly what I'm *doing*. *Real* mothers don't let their daughters have abortions!"

"Jesus, mom, shut up," Jen said. Mike had found a napkin in the glove box, and Jen stroked my hair, waiting for me to finish. She was my real mother, I thought. *Ooh child*, she'd sing to me sometimes, right after our parents got divorced. *Things are gonna get easier—*.

"I *confided* in you. This was *my decision*." I wiped my mouth and got in, trying to escape before I had to throw up again. "A *hemophiliac*. I can't believe you'd try to stop it."

"It was *alive*, Lucy!" my mom cried. "It was alive! This morning it was a *real baby* and you killed it, you killed it—!" she flew at Mike and slugged him again. "Ooh, you loser, you big fat *loser*, can't even take care of your own *family*—"

"If you hit me once more, I'm hitting you back." Mike said.

"You just try it, Charlie Brown. You just try it." My mom shook her fist at him. Then we were pulling away, past the dumpsters where probably it was now, the size of a fingernail clipping, bagged tragically with all the others.

"Are you okay?" Mike said. He waved to the picketers as we passed, and one guy flipped us off. "*He* should've been an abortion," Mike said.

"Shut up!"

"Sorry." He took my hand. "That was horrible. I'm sorry." We drove home without saying anything else, and Mike carried me inside. He set the fan up right in front of the bed and carried the small TV set in from the back room. "Can I get you anything?"

"Maybe just lay down with me."

"Sure." He lay carefully on the edge of the bed, and we stayed there most of the afternoon. At one point Mike got up to unplug the phone, which had been ringing on and off for hours. He brought me peanut-butter-and-cracker sandwiches and a heating pad for my stomach.

"I don't feel guilty. It's weird, I feel like I should."

"Me neither."

"Thanks again for borrowing the money."

"Of course. It's fine. I just wish it hadn't happened."

"I *know*. I meant, 'Come inside.' Not, '*Come* inside.' "

"Luce, it wasn't my fault. It was an accident. I'm sorry."

" 'Come inside,' as in, 'Enter but leave nothing behind.' "

"I know! Quit telling me. I just misunderstood, okay? I'm sorry. I'm sorry. I will forever after use a rubber. I *promise.*"

My mom met Roy right before Thanksgiving. He'd been in Salt Lake for some mental health convention, but he was from Alaska, and he was *rich,* my mom told me excitedly over the phone, rich *and* divorced, and he had a house on the water, and he'd offered to pay her way if she'd consider going up there for Thanksgiving.

"Would that be okay with you?" my mom asked. "I know you two were planning on it, my doing a big meal and everything, but really I hate all that cooking, I always have, it's just expected of the woman. Anyway maybe you could even go up with me, Roy said that would be fine, maybe you could even bring Mike. But I mean it, Honey. I think Roy might really be the one."

"That's okay. Mike and I can just go eat out somewhere. It's no biggie." We were at Mike's apartment and I wrote him a note and held it up: *Thanksgiving is off!* Mike gave me the thumbs up.

"Well, I don't want you to feel abandoned. I mean golly, I am your mother. I *should* cook a turkey."

"Honestly, Mom. I don't care. So what do you like about this guy?"

"Well, Hon, I told you. He's *rich*. And he says his house is just *huge*, you guys could come visit anytime, he has tons of bedrooms I'll bet."

"Yeah, but what do you *like* about him? Is he funny? Is he smart?" I picked on her all the time, I noticed, just to prove that we were nothing alike. But sometimes it seemed to backfire, and instead I just heard myself nagging, being a spoilsport.

"Of course he's *smart*. I'm not just some *gold-digger*. I have a job, I don't just need some *guy* to come along and give me *money*. Gee, but I was thinking, this is the kind of thing *you* should be doing, isn't it? Having some kind of crazy Alaskan adventure."

"I like my life. And I do so have adventures."

"Like what?"

"We go camping. It's not like I can just blow off school."

"Oh, don't get defensive. I'm not *criticizing*, Hon. I'm not saying there's anything wrong with your life. I'm glad you're in college. You were always smart that way, just like me. I wouldn't be surprised if you went into the mental health field, yourself. You're such a good listener."

"I want to do art."

"Oh, I know, I know, I'm glad you're doing the painting thing, I'm just saying. If you ever wanted to switch career tracks. Anyway, thanks for letting me go. I'll call you as soon as I get back, okay? I think Roy could really be *it*."

My mom and Roy got married eight months later, in Hope, Alaska. I didn't go to the wedding, and anyway within a month they were divorced, and in court the judge laughed at my mom, called her a *gold-digger* when she claimed *rape*, and my mom cried and ran from the courtroom. *I should've gotten something,* she told me later on the phone. *That bastard, here I go and leave everything, my job, my home, everything. I should've gotten half of that damned house at least, for all my trouble*—but it was hard to listen, hard to care. She was so far away. There were whole tundras, whole bodies of water between us.

She came back once, for a week, to put her stuff in storage, and after that Mike and I moved in together. And she'd changed her name, Jen told me not long after. She was going by Kachina, not Kachina Taylor but just plain Kachina, like Madonna or Cher. She was living in Hope and learning to carve Tlingit Indian masks, and it would be a year before we saw each other again. It was all or nothing with her, I was finally figuring out. I was either drowning in her or I was ashore. There was no in between.

y mom was living in a youth hostel in Hope, Alaska. It was just until she could decide, she'd told me, just until she knew for sure whether Alaska was really *home*. But she'd been at the hostel over a year already, ever since Roy had kicked her out.

Mike parked the car and I took my time getting out. Then we went in, past the cork bulletin board and saggy couches and vending machines. My mom was in room six. We found her on her bed, pulling stuff out of a backpack. She ran—she *ran*—to throw her arms around me, then Mike. She looked suspiciously ethnic again, her hair parted in the middle and drooping over each cheek. Plus she was wearing some sort of animal skin vest, and right away she hauled out a carved wooden bird.

"It's from my people," she said. "I've been saving this for you. Just for you!"

"Who are 'your people'?"

"Oh now, don't start, don't you start making fun of me. We've got Tlingit blood, you know that. Honey, you look great, just great, you really do! I've been sitting by the window all morning and when you got out I thought well now *that* can't be her, can it? That beauty? And then it was *you*."

"Thanks, Mom. I really like it."

"It's a *totem*. From the *spirit world*. It's to *protect* you."

"Well, thanks. Nice digs." There was a guitar in one corner, and a curtain of beads in front of one window. There was a portable stereo, a bookcase, and a striped Pendleton blanket on the neatly made bed. "I can't believe you *live* here, though. Why don't you just get an apartment?" I climbed onto her bed to check out the photos she had taped to the wall. There were pictures of my mom in a bar, holding a pool cue and wearing a cowboy hat. And pictures—lots of pictures—of what must've been people passing through the hostel, taken with a Polaroid, the people all posed on the same sofa I'd seen in the lobby. There was a photo of Jen and me taken years before, and a few Alaskan landscape postcards.

"Well, you know, after that goddamned Roy, I just didn't have a penny left to my name. He really cleaned me out, I sure couldn't come up with some crazy down payment *and* first and last month's rent. And anyway I *love* this place. I mean people bitch about them, oh sure they're not four star hotels, but really you have everything you need, and there are all kinds of people to talk to. People from all over. I like to sit in the lounge at night, there's always someone, we just swap life stories and sometimes somebody brings a guitar and I just, well, I just get up and dance! And nobody cares. Nobody makes fun. We're all just on the same path." She snapped her fingers and swayed a minute. "That's what I love." She was doing her, *When I Am an Old Lady, I Shall Wear Purple* act, and I didn't even care. Maybe it was because I hadn't seen her in so long. But did I care, did I? I had my own life. My mom looked hard at me. Then she clutched me again. "I have loved you very much," she said.

"I know. How's everything?" I wanted to keep it light. At the same time, I felt like ransacking her backpack, smelling her clothes, searching her wallet. *Anything.* I missed her.

"I'm *so* glad you two could make it up here finally. We can day trip to Juneau, bum around and then go get coffee, I have all sorts of plans, there's just tons and tons of stuff to do up here. I've told *all* my friends about you. And tonight there's a concert, I was hoping you might want to go, this local guy who sings all about Alaska, he's kind of like a John Denver–type and he's playing at the local coffeehouse."

"We'll have to see," I said. "We're kind of tired from the trip."

"Well, gee, I mean I did pay your way *up* here," she laughed a little, and fiddled nervously with her hands. "I mean, I guess if you're too tired. I was just really excited, this guy's so terrific, his name is Jamie Pherson McKnight, maybe you've already heard his stuff being played in Salt Lake. I wouldn't be surprised."

"We should probably go," Mike said. "I don't know if I'm legally parked."

"Oh, okay. Sure." My mom paused at the front desk. "This is my *daughter*," she said. "And this is her lover, Mike."

"Boyfriend," I said.

"Well you know, 'boyfriend,' 'lover,' whatever. 'Lover' just sounds more gender-neutral, is why I say it. That's why, like if I'm introducing my gay friends, I can say it without feeling like I'm being heterosexist."

"Nice to meet you," the guy at the counter said. "Listen, do you need clean towels?"

"Oh, sure. That would be great."

"And have you signed up for kitchen duty yet, this week?" he pulled out a chart and looked it over.

"I haven't, actually," my mom said. She scribbled her name in quickly. "Listen, my daughter and I are gonna go bum around a little. Could you hold all my messages?"

"We hold everybody's messages," the guy said. His beard looked like it had been rubbed through, in places. "So of course we will."

"I don't like that guy's attitude," my mom said, once we were out of earshot. "You know, I *live* here. I mean it's people like me who keep this place in business, I'm the reason people like him stay *employed*. And then he wants me to do K.P. or whatever he wants to call it, like I'm some sort of *washerwoman*. Who does he think he is?"

"I thought that was part of living in a hostel," I said. "Isn't it supposed to be communal?" Hope was so *green*—did all of Alaska look like this? The houses were small, placed far apart on large lots, and you could see the ocean from pretty much anywhere.

"Well, yeah, sure I mean unless you're *paying* for it, like me, for long periods of time." She leaned over the seat and slid in a CD. "You've just got to hear this guy," my mom said. "He's the voice of Alaska. He really speaks for the people."

"So is he from here?" Mike said. "Is he Tlingit, too?"

"Nobody's really *from* Alaska," my mom said. "That's what I really like about it. And the *men*. There are just tons of lonely guys up here, not that I'm looking, but I mean these rich oil guys are just a dime a dozen. And people don't question, you know, not like in Salt Lake, where everybody has to know everyone else's business. People up here don't have *suspicions*. They come from all over, and they're just free, free, free, no one has to pretend to be anything they're not."

Mike lit a joint and passed it to me. "In the *car*?" my mom said. "So how is Salt Lake, anyway? What do you guys do for fun?"

"We go to work," Mike said. "We come home. We make out. We eat. We go to bed." He giggled.

"You kids. You're so *middle-aged*, already. I'm just glad, I mean I know I'm no spring chicken but I'm just glad I finally *found* myself. In Alaska. And I don't miss Salt Lake, not one teeny tiny bit. I have a great life here. A *great* life. Are you *listening* to this?" As Jamie sang, my mom repeated the lines aloud, nodding, *um humh, yeah,* like someone at a church revival meeting. "The ocean *does* look seal-gray at twilight," she said. "It *is* 'the town of broken promises,' are you listening? Are you listening? This is *important*." She cranked the volume, tuned us out as we sped toward the ferry landing. "There *are* 'lanterns across the water,' " my mom said, sighing, as he got to the end of a song. "You kids wouldn't know. Why would you? You're from *Utah*. But this is all about Alaska. Alaska. My homeland. Oh, I can't wait to actually see him *in person*, he's practically *my idol*."

We spent the day in Juneau, and then Mike and I went back to the hotel to shower before the concert. "Please, kill me now," Mike said. "Don't make me go to this thing. Let me just stay here. Just me and my trusty minibar."

"You *have* to go. You're my emotional support."

"She just *talks* so fast. Seriously, Luce, I'm worn out. If you ever, I don't know, turn into her or something, I might have to kill myself."

"She's not as bad as she used to be," I said. "At least she seems *happy.*"

"I guess. If cruising rich widowed men in wheelchairs and living in a youth hostel for the rest of your life is your idea of a good time."

"Shut up," I said. "She's my mom."

"She's never been a mother to you."

"Shut *up,*" I said. "I mean it. Don't make me defend her." I threw him his shoes. "We have to go. We're a team."

Mike looked at me a minute, then sighed and put his shoes on.

The parking lot was packed. There were pickup trucks, old Volvos, old Subarus with ski racks. We elbowed our way inside, and found my mom looking raptly at Jamie Pherson McKnight as he sang. He had a beard, naturally, and wore leather shoes that looked homemade. He looked movingly into the eyes of his fans, and at one point between songs he said softly into the mike, "I love you people."

"Oh brother," Mike said, and went off to get us decaf lattes.

"Isn't this *great?*" my mom said. A table opened up, and we snagged it. When Jamie started singing again, a hush fell over the crowd. I studied the rapt faces around me. None of them looked like I thought people from Alaska would really look; in fact most of the people in the audience looked like my mom, middle-aged and lost, wearing clothing that looked like it had been bought in the Juneau airport. There were Native-American vests everywhere, and Patagonia jackets, and most of the women wore heavy silver earrings and pendants in the shape of bears, eagles.

I glanced at my mom. She was watching Jamie with the same ecstatic expression as everyone else, and she clapped enthusiastically after every song. I could see that she was happy, and that was the part I didn't get: how this was her *life* up here, it really was, the one she'd chosen for herself. It was the life she *wanted*. I wished suddenly that we could be alone together someplace quiet, my mom calm in a way she almost never was, and that then we could tell each other things. I didn't want to talk about the old days. I didn't want to get all weepy with her about how much we both missed my dad. I didn't want to fight. I wanted to be friends with her, in the present. I wanted her to ask questions. I wanted her to care about books I'd read, or ask me what classes I was taking at the U. I wanted her to act like a mother. But my mom didn't *want* to be reminded of things. She didn't want to be her age, and she didn't want to have gray hairs, and probably she didn't want to have adult daughters who *wanted*, who *kept expecting her*, to act like a mother. And so she clapped and swayed, chattering pointlessly with strangers. Her face was bright and vacant. Only the smell of her hair was familiar, only the smell of her hair made me lonely.

OTHER PLACES TO LOOK FOR A MOTHER:

It is from her, maybe, that I've learned the irresistible sweetness of loss. My mom has always wanted things, and it was better if they were things she'd given up or given away, or—sweetest of all—plain couldn't have: hopelessly expensive houses, someone else's children, someone else's husband.

I think of her, always, as weeping: weeping and nostalgic for something, someone other than who she was. Weeping because she never just *cried*: my mom was *theatrical*, she was beautiful, a regular Sarah Heartburn, my dad used to say. She could break hearts, baby hearts especially, with her histrionics. We didn't know any better, especially as children, than to wail along with her. We wanted to help. We loved her. We thought they were real tragedies. Once, during a fight, I wound up chasing her across a parking lot. We were at the airport and she was running and sobbing and yelling things: *Go away! Just go away! You don't love me!* and most of me was thinking *I can't believe I'm actually fucking going after her like this* but the other part of me was still small, galloping to catch her because parents could, after all, hate their children, and she could, after all, leave us. And I felt sort of elated—I remember I was chasing her, and *smiling*—because I was high on it too, the potent emotion of this melodrama, this way of making everything a tragedy, grand and phony. She was moving in a crooked run between cars and it was Thanksgiving, one of the times when she got the most unhappy. I went and sat in the car, waiting for her to come back, because this was the way it always happened. A short time later she'd be smiling, refreshed, ordering pumpkin pie in some coffee shop.

I found her in sick headaches that made it impossible for her to speak. And in the trunk of her car, filled with items she planned to return to stores; and on menus, where what was offered was never what she wanted. And in all the *stuff* of our childhood that we'd once felt entitled to and that disappeared, after the divorce: the turquoise tweed couches, the crappy Parisian street scene my parents purchased on their honeymoon; the camping equipment, the bedroom sets, the rock tumbler, the Twister game and Barbies and bicycles, the guinea pigs and skis and sets of dishes, stuff we assumed would be passed onto us girls when finally we left the house, one by one, to occupy our own intact kitchens. Where did it all go? For that matter, what became of our rabbit, Peanut, with us two years and then—the papers signed, the stuff divided, us kids divided—suddenly gone? What happened to the photo albums, our birth certificates?

I could find my mother here, in objects that I longed for, begged for, into adulthood. She was too sentimental to have let go of it all—unlike our dad, whose bitterness drove him to give the stuff away, get rid of it so he wouldn't have to be reminded—and she would tip us off now and again, tempt us. *I think I've seen them,* she'd say. *I know your school pictures are somewhere, I can't think where, but I know I've come across them*—. In her house were locked closets, locked drawers, areas that meant long, fruitless searches, when we were teenagers, for keys she insisted didn't exist. We knew she had the stuff. My dad's baby plate, engraved with the year he was born, had been missing ever since the divorce and I looked for it each time I ransacked, though my mom vigorously denied having it *(why would I want some goddamn baby plate of his, why would I even give a damn—)*. Finally, at fifteen, I pried open a drawer and found the plate wrapped in a sheet; I remember holding it, unable to steal it back; and calling my dad to tell him I'd seen it, returned it to the drawer. Most of this was cowardice. But also it was sadness, a great sadness for my mom, who had only their things to cling to, when people left her.

Sometimes, after particularly bitter quarrels, she gifted us with these things: Jen's wisp of blonde baby hair, or a photograph of one of our great-grandparents. They arrived in the mail, never with any note, as though the wisp had been snipped just yesterday. The wisp like a string my mom had kept around her finger all these years, to remind herself that she had children. Opening the envelopes made me feel homeless, destitute.

A baby tooth. One of Jen's swimming medals.

My Baby Book, which arrived in the mail after years of estrangement, wrapped in grayish-silver reused paper, funereal. We'd fought about the book for years, *I don't have it,* she'd say, *ask your dad, go through those boxes in the attic, check the garage. I don't know where it is.* She was tearful, insistent, unconvincing. And was it mine to have? Mine, or hers? With the congratulations-on-your-new-arrival cards from friends who'd played gin rummy with my parents on weekends, who remained in Southern California while my parents went on to divorce, those same friends still there, still remodeling the same ranch-style houses in Whittier, the children gone now, the friends learning to be grandparents. My cards, or hers?

The day Jen got her baby hair in the mail, she called, crying. *Do you know what she used to tell me?* Jen said. *She used to say, I tried to breast-feed you, I really did, both you kids, but you just cried and cried and pounded your little fists on my chest. You were so mad, you just couldn't get any milk. But I tried and tried. That witch,* Jen said. *Why doesn't she just pick up the fucking phone and call me, instead? That would be nice. Why doesn't she call and tell us where she is instead of moving all over with her stupid boyfriends, why aren't we important to her? Do you even know what state she's in? The postmark says Alaska; is that where she's living now?*

I could hear Jen snuffling into the phone. *She's probably been keeping it in her storage unit all these years,* she said. *Just waiting for a chance to use it, just waiting for a big enough argument. She can keep my fucking baby hair,* she said, *she really can.*

Once, right after she'd left for Alaska, I let myself into her house. I was surprised at how easy it was: the key under the mat, the boxes of papers in the unlocked attic. I took my time. I went through the boxes of papers, and after an hour or two I saw how *ordinary* it all was, our whole life. It amounted to so little. There was no big mystery, no drama. There were my parents' divorce papers. There were the love letters from Frank to my mom. There were a few pictures, a few old birthday cards. *Big deal,* I felt like. *Big fucking deal.* But later, I thought how that couldn't have been everything. And now I wished I'd looked harder, instead of doing what I did when I got bored with the papers, which was stuff like smell her hairbrush and check the titles in her bookcase (*Looking out for Number One; Way of the Peaceful Warrior.* And a *Diagnostic and Statistical Manual of Mental Disorders,* where my mom's handwriting appeared in the margins of various chapters, diagnosing various boyfriends, as well as my dad. *Bob,* she'd scrawled repeatedly, next to the description of Passive-Aggressive Personality Disorder. *Frank!!!!!* she'd scribbled, in the chapter on Antisocial Personality Disorder.)

You kids, my mother was saying. We were in a restaurant. We were always in a restaurant. *You kids, why do you hate me so? Why don't you ever remember nice things?*

I remember nice things.

You don't. You always take your dad's side. You always have. Why do you believe him, and not me?

Dad hasn't ever lied to me.

I don't lie to you! My mom's hand landed hard next to her coffee cup. *Why are you always calling me a liar!*

You have lied to us. A lot, I said. And when my mom started to cry I was twelve again, listening to the bright clatter of her voice each time she got on the phone with my dad, who said, once it was my turn on the phone: *no matter what, she's your mother and she loves you.*

And I do remember nice things. I do. I remember how she would sing to us, before sleep: *Down in the valley, the valley so low. Hang your head over, hear the wind blow—.*

And how often she read to us, her mouth close to our ears as though each book, each reading, was a secret, ours alone. *This is the girl with the curl in the middle of her forehead,* went one. *And when she was good she was very very good. But when she was bad she was horrid!*

How at night, if we slipped into their room, it was she who awoke to our voices, while our dad slept on.

I remember a game called Catwash, when she moistened a handkerchief with saliva and rubbed my face clean. Her breath was gummy and sweet.

She made fabulous cocoa. Thick and sweet, like saucepan chocolate pudding. Both, as they cooled, grew skins.

Sometimes she danced for us kids, whirling a colored scarf, spinning. She loved best being admired. When our attention wandered she did inane squats, handstands.

Later, prepubescent, we picked on her. Once, when she was dancing, I told her she had a big fat butt, which made her cry. And I wished if she were going to clap, she'd at least do it in time to the music. That if she was going to sing, it would be nice if she could at least do it on key. *I want to be the pretty one,* she'd told me then. *Is that so wrong? You girls have your whole lives ahead of you. Leave me be, let me have my fun.*

Another time she said, *this is the kind of butt men like. One they can hang on to. Not yours.*

Your dad, my mom told me later. *He was so great in bed. He never should've dragged us to Salt Lake. Because we were happy before that.*

But that was my fault, my father said, when I was fifteen. *I never, never, never should've moved us there. Your mother loved that House on the Hill; she never forgave me for dragging the family to Utah. She became a whole different person.*

It wasn't your fault.

It was like living with a perfect stranger. And then that god-damned Ellery came into the picture. My dad drove in the right-hand lane, ignoring the cars that tailgated and finally blasted past him. *You want to know how I found out about it? We were in debt, we owed Sears two thousand dollars and Ellery worked there, in the credit department. And that's how they met. I never should've moved us to Arizona. Because that's when things started to fall apart. Your mother was unhappy and I was getting us further and further into debt and then, things just fell apart. And I want you to remember something,* he said, looking over at me. *It wasn't just your mother. It was me, too, I wouldn't let her do anything, wouldn't let her have any money, because I was the macho male and she was the woman. I was an asshole. A real asshole.*

A letter written from my dad to my mom, just before the divorce: *Miriam—I am sorry to be such a screwed up husband! I called grocery store—will pay them today—called Sears—spoke to someone named Ellery—terms will be arranged—will bring back money for food. I still love you. Bob*

How she could smell sickness in the cracks of our necks.

IN GIFTS,

Her face still looks taut to me, closed and dry, like a face done in charcoal. She looks sorry for everything, and maybe she is. For as long as I can remember my mom's hair has been thick, straight, and dyed a severe shade of black. She wears bangs because they hide the horizontal lines on her forehead, and refuses to wear glasses though she's terribly nearsighted; so that now, middle-aged, negotiating city sidewalks, she keeps her head averted, her gaze near the ground. I'd know the stoop and broken beetle of her walk, anywhere. She walks with small steps, her purse drawn closely to her side like she's afraid of having it snatched: if you saw her coming, you would guess that here was a woman who'd been beaten up all her life. Even standing at the sink looked like it was too much for her; she leaned against it, one elbow propped on the edge as she rinsed a dish.

My mother, leaning. You wanted to urge a chair behind her knees so that she would sprawl, looking sexy and happy like she did on sofas in department store lounges. There weren't a lot of these left but she always seemed to know where they were, rest rooms with a sitting room off to the side for nursing mothers or tired shoppers like us, who collapsed on the velvet sofas, our shopping bags rattling. Shopping made her happiest of all, and she was good at it. She never bought much for herself but the gifts she gave us, especially when we were teenagers, were lavish and sentimental. They were things we'd been pining all year for, and my mom would take mental notes and then kill us with great surprises on Christmas day. Crystal champagne glasses, so delicate they felt like a cold, curled leaf in the palm. Down comforters. Wool rugs, hardback books from our babyhood that she'd found in some secondhand store. See's candy. The presents were sumptuous and expensive, all for us as though only we deserved rich, fatty lives, while my mom went on consuming her spartan diet of cheap things for herself. Her work wardrobe, for example, consisted of acrylic sweaters and blazers and elastic-waisted pants, all in solid colors, dark blue or dark green or maroon; she wore the clothes in one limited combination after another. And she wore flats, sad-looking things like the house slippers of a sick person. The shoes were pointed so that her toes were smashed cruelly into the tips, or they buckled in a braided strap low on the foot, just in front of the toes, which made them look girlish and pointless to me. The shoes were always dark blue or black, rounded with years of wear; and they made her feet look strangely small and narrow; and this, combined with the limp, combined with her never looking up, just watching her own small, pointy feet move along, breaking backs, oh, she looked so miserable, truly, you wanted to offer her your arm or money or something, *anything,* to make her feel better.

She bought so much for us, so much that would make us, her daughters, look strong and capable and outdoorsy: wool sweaters and pricy nylon hiking boots, Gore-Tex jackets. *Oh, you look so nice,* she'd say, sounding pained and envious but also proud. Yet her own way of dressing, at least what she wore on the outside, was noncommittal, the cheap, thin fabrics suggesting priorities elsewhere. And she did have other priorities: she shopped constantly for lingerie, frilly teddies and tap pants and camisoles. Her intimate wardrobe was extensive and expensive, with a single tall bureau devoted to her acquisitions. She was still waiting for the right man to come along and let her off the hook. What did she get out of them? The men she likes now are cowboy types who wear tight pants, boots, tinted aviators, hair swept in wisps up and over the skull. Not too long ago when I saw her at the mall she was with one of them, holding his arm tightly. He held one hand on the back of her neck up under her hair, paternal and guiding her into a happier future, one he surely thought he could provide. *Help me, help me, please, why won't anyone ever help me?*

She never carried a checkbook or credit cards. Instead she paid for everything with cash, which she kept in small bills in plain white envelopes and which took, incidentally, much rifling through of her purse—small and worn and dark blue, generic and female, a purse too puny to be useful—to find. It was crammed with receipts and lipstick and wads of Kleenex and she dropped it frequently, spilling the contents as though to prove, once and for all, that she *needed help.*

IN PHOTOGRAPHS,

where she was utterly, utterly beautiful. Even during our worst times, my mother in photos looked like a million bucks. I can remember tense moments before these same pictures were taken (the quarreling, the hasty composition on the couch) and never once was she caught off guard. Never. And Thanksgivings on videotape: she looked good there, too, though the tapes don't reveal the terse editing, my mom hunched on the couch watching the first cut, and if she didn't like the looks of it we'd traipse upstairs and take-two filming until we looked, on videotape, like one big happy family. *(The coffee and dessert part at least,* my mom would argue. *I realize we can't reenact a whole entire Thanksgiving meal.)*

Well, once. Once the camera caught her. She was walking. Her head was down and she was scowling. She looked so much like herself, vulnerable and aging, so authentic, finally. Small of me, to like the photograph so. I framed it and put it on the mantel. It makes me sad that I've learned to look at my own mantel without actually seeing her picture. My eyes have learned to skid across it, as though it were an urn that held ashes and bits of pulverized bone. *Cremation doesn't get it all,* a friend told me once. *They have to crush it up, use hammers and shit.*

Would there be teeth?

He thinks about it a minute. *I don't think they'd leave teeth.*
In the photo my mom looks betrayed, as though someone
has been spreading rumors about her, revealing secrets. My
eyes skid, return to her.

IN MIGRAINES,

Always she is with me in migraines, nearby, the Real
Mother. I miss her. She takes my hand. The water on the
nightstand is tepid, dust eddying on the surface. If I open my
eyes I can see only half of her, half face and hand, half explo-
sive silver curlicues and pulsating zigzags. She smiles and
says, *pretend it's not happening, let yourself go far far away.
Want me to sing? Hush little baby, don't say a word, papa's
gonna buy you a mockingbird.*

There is no other way than her. Does that sound extrava-
gant? Or should I say there is no other place than her. My bitch
of a mother, in whom I am placed, all these years later, still.

Now it's behind us, the people small. My mom lays next to
me on the bed, helping me wait it out. She keeps the wash-
cloth pressed to my eyeballs, the cold white blocking out
everything except her voice so that I want to give her things,
though I never know where to start. Never know which day to
go back to, which net to haul up.

I'd give her Frank, for sure, if that would make her happy.
I'd give her back my dad. I'd give her a Greek fisherman who
sang whatever it is Greek fisherman sing when they cast their
nets out from small, bright boats, and all the flickering dying
fish between us. A life jacket. An oar.

IN DREAMS,

where she appears, weeping. Saying *no, no.* In one dream,
laughing, watching me jump on the trampoline. I'm four, she's

thirty. She lifts me from the trampoline, kisses me, wraps me in a yellow sweater that smells of her hair. I tug it over my face and her voice is wrapped in gauze, pleasantly distant, a murmur that rises, drops. But she's never been one to coddle and soon she sets me down: *you're a big girl now, you can walk yourself.* Eggs are *coddled,* I know already, because they come to my dad in a little pale, green, cup every morning and he punctures them with the edge of his toast. There's the yellow flood across the plate for him to mop up, and he does it so happily, he's so steady, you know he could do it forever.

Then we're in the backseat. It's long before seat belts: Jen and I ride on our knees, one at each window, hanging our heads out like dogs. We keep our mouths open, *catching flies,* my dad says, though that's not it at all. We're in it for the joy, the dry whipping away of our voices. Our mom is saying things inside the car, probably, but we hear none of it. When the engine stops we stagger out, senseless, our hair knotted like the hair of crazy children left on some desert island. There the children are in charge, there the children set fires and mete out their version of justice. There our faces burnish and we look skyward every day for airplanes, seaward for corked bottles or ships. They're dutiful gestures, ones we've seen shipwrecked kids do on TV, so we're half-assed about it: Jen scans with one hand over her eyes, like a mime, and I collect too many shells. All around us is a sort of yellowy calm, like a fever. In the car we'll have melon squares in Tupperware and iced lemonade in a plaid thermos. The air's full of us, and when we climb in we leave sand on the floormats. My dad hesitates and for a moment we're perfectly still, freeze-framed in the enormous interior, the steering wheel pulpy and white as a life preserver ring, the speedometer's numbers magnified, glowing. Beyond it our faces, pink and expectant. *We're everything:* we are. My dad looks both ways, then pulls into traffic.